TWISTED
ROOTS

Shelly Goodman Wright

TWISTED
ROOTS

A Light into the Darkness
— SECOND EDITION —

TATE PUBLISHING
AND ENTERPRISES, LLC

Published by Tate Publishing & Enterprises, LLC
127 E. Trade Center Terrace | Mustang, Oklahoma 73064 USA
1.888.361.9473 | www.tatepublishing.com

Tate Publishing is committed to excellence in the publishing industry. The company reflects the philosophy established by the founders, based on Psalm 68:11,
"The Lord gave the word and great was the company of those who published it."

Book design copyright © 2015 by Tate Publishing, LLC. All rights reserved.
Cover design by Nino Carlo Suico
Interior design by Shieldon Alcasid

Published in the United States of America

ISBN: 978-1-68164-205-5
Fiction / Christian / Suspense
Fiction / Fantasy / Romance
15.08.27

"And My people who are called by My name humble themselves, pray and seek My face, and turn from their evil ways, then I will hear from heaven, forgive their sin, and heal their land." (2 Chronicles 7:14)

Acknowledgments

Writing is a journey.

I'd like to thank everyone who continues to follow me on this journey. Thank you to all those who have volunteer to spend hours to help polish the rough edges on this second edition: Fiction Foundry Writing Group, Laura, Danette, Christina, and my special shout out to Bobbie Mesite, who went over and volunteered and beyond!

I'm blessed to have the full support of my husband, my three girls, two dogs, and five guinea pigs.

Lastly, and most important, I thank God for allowing me to serve Him wherever He leads.

Contents

Prologue

A little girl watched her father's silhouette stomp back and forth along the moonlit shore. She yawned and stretched her arms toward the starry sky. "Can I go back to bed now? We've been out here a long time."

Samuel stopped to face the fair-skinned child who nervously twisted a strand of her dishwater-blonde hair around her finger.

"Mother said I'm supposed to be well rested for tomorrow's party." Jessica let go of the strand, letting her straight hair fall against her chest.

"You hate your mother's parties," he scowled, tucking his hands into the pockets of his pants.

The seven-year-old lowered her head while she dug her feet into the cool sand. She hated her mother parties, too. They always ended up with a room full of people she didn't know with a funny smell on their breath. But that wasn't the main reason she hated her parties. She hated them because her father always managed to disappear until morning.

"But this party is for me, Daddy. This party will be different than all the others, and you won't have to hide." Jessica's green eyes watered, staring at her father.

He quickly shifted his focus to the mansion on the hill. "Different isn't the word I would use. She'll never change. She'll never love you like a normal mother would." His hands moved through his short brown hair, down to the stubble on his chin. "I can't go through with this, no matter what the consequences are."

Jessica's fists rested on her hips. "What...what choice?"

Her father continued to mumble, paying no attention to her, so she plopped down on the sand and watched the water come and go, reaching closer to her each time it spilled out. The sound of the ocean soothed her worries as her father argued with no one. Although Jessica loved the sound of crashing waves, her favorite sounds came from the notes of the black and ivory keys. When her parents would fight or she needed an escape, she'd sit at the piano and play. Her initially forced lessons had not only become the one thing her mother praised her for, but was another way to release the hurt inside for all the things she felt she hadn't done right.

"Jessie," he pulled his daughter to him. "I've been praying for a long time. I knew this day was coming. You know I don't agree with your mother on a lot of things, and if it hadn't been for you, I would have left a long time ago."

Her eyes glossed over again, and tears streamed down over her cheeks.

"No, no, don't cry. I'm not going to leave you." He wiped her tears with the edge of his shirt. "Of course I wouldn't purposely leave you. I love you more than the entire sky even more than my own life. It's been mostly you and me since the day you were born. But what your mother has planned isn't right. I won't sit aside to watch." He hugged his daughter tightly. "I want to tell you something very important. I need you to listen closely and don't forget. I'm not sure how much more time I have." He bent down to her eye level, grasping her shoulders. "What I mean to say is I might not always be—"

Samuel stopped and shook his head at the night sky as though it knew the secret he was about to reveal. He then pointed out a very vivid star high above them. "There are magical places in this world, Jess. Places the Master Architect created to balance good and evil. The time will come when you will leave this house and enter into another life that awaits you. A life you deserve and one with a greater purpose. You don't know how special you really are."

"But I don't want to leave you." The little girl's body trembled. "I'll be better around Mother. I'll be extra quiet so I don't give her headaches, and I'll play extra hard to be the best pianist ever. Then, she won't be so mad all the time. It's my fault she fights with you. It's always my fault."

The corners of Samuel's mouth fell. "It's not your fault. It's never been your fault, and I don't want you to ever think the troubles between your mother and me are because of you." He pulled his sobbing daughter into a tight embrace.

"If I go, you'll come too, right?"

"It's not that simple, Jess." He stroked her long hair for quite a while, then stopped. "Maybe it is that simple to return. I'd have to face the consequences, but she'd be safe."

Jessica pulled away from his frozen hold, stopping Samuel from rambling longer. He kneeled in front of his daughter, reaching out to stroke her fair cheek.

"Did I ever tell you about the angels who watch over us?"

She thought for a moment about the creatures in the stories her father told her about, but she couldn't remember any angels in them. She shook her head, rubbing one eye with her little fist while looking around with the other eye to see if someone else were there watching them. She shivered.

Samuel took both her hands into his. "You're not alone in this world, my sweet Jessica. There are angels who watch over us all the time. Some watch us from above, while others walk among us. They're here to help shield us from the evil living among us. In our worst times or in our best times, we are not alone. All you have to do is believe, and help will come." He stroked the inside of her palm and smiled. "Just in case something happens and I'm not around, I wanted you to know."

A large wave crashed onto the shore and splattered in their direction. The salty fish air inundated Jessica's nose while the cold, bubbly wetness covered her ankles. A chill ran up through her as the water retreated, pulling the sand out from under her small feet. She squeezed her father's hand, holding her breath, before letting it out slowly.

The next wave crashed louder and harder against the shoreline.

Samuel pulled a small piece of folded paper out of his pocket and placed it in her hand. "Put it in your pocket. Hide it somewhere safe. I pray it will help you remember what I told you."

The little girl hesitated, wanting to look at it that very moment. She marveled at the perfectly folded square resting on her palm.

"I'm sorry, Jessica," he said, looking past her.

Jessica didn't have to turn around to know who was coming. At the smell of her mother's perfume, she balled up her fist with the note inside and stuck it in her robe pocket before she turned to face her mother's bitter, cerulean eyes.

No one spoke as the three walked up the only decent path between two steep cliffs to reach the house. They entered through the back kitchen door.

The frazzled Spanish maid quickly caught Evelyn's white fur coat before it hit the marble tile as she made her way to the liquor cabinet. She drank one full glass before strumming her fingers against the granite countertop. Her eyes narrowed at her husband. "Jessica, go back to bed. You need your rest for tomorrow."

Jessica hesitated. The tension in the room made the hair on her arms reach for the ceiling. She looked over at her father. "I'll see you tomorrow morning?"

Her father's forced smile and nod was far from reassuring.

She reluctantly glanced at her mother. With one look, Jessica felt tiny shards of ice moving all through her body. "Good night, Mother." She quivered before running up the stairs to her room. She went to shut the door, only she didn't close it all the way. She wanted to hear what they were saying.

Moments later, Jessica heard her father coming up the stairs. She shut the door all the way until they both entered their bedroom, keeping her ear close to the space between the panels.

"I should have done this a long time ago," Samuel said with a nervous chuckle. "You'll never be able to find her, not ever."

"You will not take her anywhere," Evelyn fired back.

Their bedroom door slammed shut, and Jessica could no longer hear what they were saying. She slowly opened her door and crept out into the hallway in the direction of her parent's room. She could see the shadows pass in front of the light, which filtered out through the bottom of the door. She was close enough to touch it when the voices stopped. She placed her ear against the door, but it cracked opened and she could see inside.

Jessica watched her father move from the closet to the dresser, placing his clothes in a black suitcase on the bed. Her mother sat at the mirror and brushed her blonde hair in long, calming strokes. A third figure brushed past the seven-year-old's eyes, and she gasped in horror.

Both her hands covered her mouth, and she shut her eyes tightly. She couldn't breathe, and her heart thundered in her ears. A strong, pungent odor masked all of Jessica's senses and covered the tip of her tongue with the bitter taste of blood. She heard her mother's calm voice over the madness in her mind.

"I told you, dear Samuel. No one gets in my way."

The Deal

My mother hated me.

From my earliest memories, I tried very hard to make her love me. I did anything she asked without question to keep the peace between her and my father. He once told me she didn't deserve a daughter like me, but to know, no matter what, he loved me, and he would never leave.

But everything changed the night he fell into a coma.

I was seven when it happened over twelve years ago. Since that time, I no longer did things to please her. It was quite the opposite. However, it didn't stop my mother from getting what she wanted from me. She'd threatened to cut off my father's lifeline every time I resisted. Since I clung to the hope he'd wake someday, I'd cave. The requests were small at first, like letting her dress me up, having me play a recital for her friends, or pretending we had the best mother-daughter relationship of anyone else. But her last demand was the cruelest yet, and I was determined not to give in without a fight.

Looking at my clock, he was due any minute.

Seth sauntered into the room with his usual "I own you" expression. He didn't own me, not yet anyway.

Deep inside, I think my mother had something to do with the attack that night, but I couldn't remember. I think my father knew and if he'd wake, she'd be in jail, and I'd be free from Seth forever.

"Hello?" Seth stared at me, irritated I didn't acknowledge him.

My scowl and clenched jaw were all he needed to approach the edge of my bed. "Get out of bed and have breakfast with me, now."

"You could knock when you enter my room. I may not be dressed appropriately."

Seth's ice-blue eyes watched me kick off the quilt to reveal the tattered blue sweats I wore to bed. His disappointed expression gave me a chuckle.

He shook his head before walking over to the bistro table next to the window where I liked to read. "Don't start with me today." He snapped his fingers for the maid to enter the room. She brought in a breakfast tray, set it on the table, and hurried out.

"I wanted to surprise you." He tried his fake, prince charming smile on me. If I didn't know what a snake he really was, I may have found him attractive. The man was over six feet tall with broad shoulders, a tone body, and when he flashed his perfect smile in any girl's direction, they'd just about fall over themselves to get close to him. "Some girls would find this very romantic."

"Big surprise." I sneered and moved to the edge of the bed where I put on my slippers.

If I hadn't been so hungry, I would have stayed in bed. Being up very late the night before, sitting at my father's bedside and making sure to keep his head elevated so the liquid in his lungs wouldn't drown him, I couldn't remember the last time I ate.

Sitting at the table, a plain egg white omelet laughed at me. Of course, he got the plump bacon-and-cheese omelet.

So not fair.

A sigh escaped while I gazed out the window, trying to ignore the rumblings of my stomach. The promise of another day streaked across the sky with the faint light touching the tips of the ocean waves. They looked more like white shimmering clouds as they rolled onto the shore. It all looked so calm and tranquil, and I wished to be standing on the shore with my feet dug into the sand, miles away from my prison. Leaving had always been on my mind, but I never really thought of a plan to carry it out. Besides, I couldn't leave my father.

She'd kill him, that's what she would do if I left. She didn't care one bit about his life or mine. She'd sell her soul to the devil to get what she wanted.

I jumped at Seth's touch, not realizing he had moved behind my chair. His lips grazed the top of my ear as he whispered, "You know what would really make my day better?"

The lava in my stomach boiled. His last request that I refused ended up with me on the floor, sliding across the marble on my knees. Despite the gashes, at least I had gotten in one good slap across his face before he threw me.

"Agree to marry me now willingly. I really dislike using your mother's tactics of persuasion. I know I'll make you happy, and soon I'll have all my father's money and position." He licked the backside of my ear, and I could feel the lava moving up into my chest. "You know you belong to me."

I jolted up from my chair. "I belong to no one."

Seth grabbed me and spun me around to face him. Red blotches appeared on his cheeks, the blue veins in his forehead pulsed, and his breath felt hot on my face. My eyes closed, ready for whatever was coming next.

How much longer can I endure his mood swings? Forever? Until my dad is at peace, or until Seth kills me with his bare hands?

Seth loosened his grip on my arms and slid his hands down my waist. "I bet if I gave the same offer to Rose—" His hands went over my outer thigh and he squeezed me against him.

My eyes popped open, but I didn't look at him. The words that should have stayed in my head exploded like Krakatau. "Then go find the maid. Better yet, why don't you marry her? Why do you think I told Mother to hire her in the first place?" I kept my eyes on his black leather shoes. "I know you've been with her. She's told me. I was hoping she'd be pregnant by now, and then you'd have to marry her. You'd have to leave. This isn't the life I want." As the words came out, my stomach cramped, and my head spun.

Stop talking! If he puts me in the hospital, Mother will pull the life support for sure, and Father's death will be my fault.

It wouldn't matter. Seth's strong, cold hands went around my throat before I said another word. His thumbs pressed against my vocal cords as he lifted my feet off the ground. I gasped to breathe, thinking this was it, until my feet touched back down, and he released my throat.

Gasping to breathe, his hand grabbed the back of my head. "You keep in mind everything I have done for you, your mother, and especially your father. He'd be dead if it wasn't for me. I can take it all away." He released me and went to sit back in his chair as though nothing had happened.

Coughing, I rubbed my throat before sitting back at the table. My body felt numb watching Seth straighten his tie before opening the newspaper. It was amazing to me how he could change from one demeanor to another so quickly. He reached out for the cup filled with coffee and looked at me. "Rose," he called, lifting the cup to his lips.

The maid entered seconds later.

"Yes, sir?" She smiled and batted her fake lashes.

Seth winked. "Miss Jessica requires some water. She seems to be choking."

They both laughed before she sauntered out the door to fetch the water. I didn't care if I was the butt of their inside joke as long as the end result was them leaving together. Rose was young, pretty, and naïve. I put it in her head if she could land Seth as a husband, she'd be set for life. However, she wasn't the first maid to sleep with Seth. Once my mom found out, Seth would get a light lecture, and the maid would be fired. I liked it when he was busy because he'd leave me alone for a while.

I calmed down enough for my body to remind me it wanted food. Although the eggs on my plate looked undercooked, it was better than nothing. I poked at them, debating whether or not to consume.

"Here." Seth slid his plate in my direction and continued to scan over the news articles. "You're getting too skinny eating the crap your mother plans for you."

Just the smell of the sautéed mushrooms and bacon got my mouth to water, but I pushed the plate back in front of Seth. I didn't want to accept his abstract apology, no matter how hungry I was.

He flipped over to the next page.

I couldn't help but stare at his food. My brain kept telling me to take a bite.

"Ha!" Seth slammed the paper down, almost knocking the plate on the floor.

My eyes closed waiting for him to strike me or choke me again, but instead he laughed. Not a normal laugh, but one that made the short hair on the back of my neck tingled. I opened my eyes to see him still looking at the paper.

"That'll show him for getting into my affairs. Missing? The guy's not missing. I know exactly where they buried the body." Seth folded up the paper and looked into my wide eyes. "That's not the only body missing either." He flicked the paper with his index finger. "I hope no one else tries to derail my plans. I've got people all over the world willing to do as I say. No one can escape me."

I swallowed hard. "You've killed people?"

"Of course not. Soon I'll be governor, followed by president of the United States. I could never associate with people like that. Let's just say I have loyal followers who can make problems go away. I'm not responsible for their actions."

He's just trying to scare me. He's not really had anyone killed.

Of course I was scared of him, but my mouth had a mind of its own. "Your father is governor, not you. How do you know you'd even get voted in, if your father died?"

"Just a matter of time, my love." He winked with a sideways smile.

I cringed. I hated when he called me "my love."

"My father is on his fourth stroke, and he can't even add two plus two. He has one foot in the grave, and it won't be long before the state hands over the title to me for filling in these last six months." His blue eyes twinkled. "At age twenty-six, I will be the youngest governor in history."

The thought of Seth in office sent chills down my back. "But your father will recover like he has before."

"He won't. Not this time." He wadded a sheet of the newspaper into a ball and tossed it in the trash can next to my bed. "Besides, the people will elect me. Why else do you think I pushed through the recent stimulus? Not because I care about jobs, taxes, or the welfare of California. It was to secure my position. My staff assures me we are moving in the right direction. The recent polls are in my favor."

Seth's one ambition was the same as my mother's. They both wanted ultimate power. They saw the presidency as that ultimate power. My mother never had a son, so she sought out a family whose heritage dripped with political presence and with a son she could manipulate. Although she hated me, she needed me. She needed me to marry Seth so she'd have the son she always wanted. Seth becoming governor was the first step to get what they both wanted.

Would they really vote him in? Doesn't anyone see the evil he's capable of?

"This is boring. Let's go back to our first topic, shall we?" Seth glanced at his watch. "Our official engagement is less than six months away. Why your mother said she wouldn't let you marry until you were twenty-one is beyond me. A year's engagement seems odd in this day and age, but I agreed to it. Seems like ages already."

The deal was mine, not my mother's. Two years ago, the doctors urged my mother to stop the machines, but I couldn't let her do it. I said I'd agree to marry Seth as long we delayed the wedding until my twenty-first birth year. At the time, it seemed so far away. My gut feeling told me my father would wake before then, and I wouldn't have to go through with it.

I needed another plan. "Yep, well, she must have her reasons. You are six years older."

"Ha!" Seth belted. "Your mother hasn't been much of a mother. I doubt she's looking out for your well-being. She does have other qualities I admire." His tongue swept over his lips. "I'll be proposing publically, as you already know, and I don't expect to be turned down."

The usual outright defiance hadn't gotten me very far, so I thought about using another tactic.

"Seth," I purred, trying my best to sound sweet and caring. "I don't deserve someone like you. You could have any girl you wanted, probably even some Jamaican model who would adore and worship you. I'm just a plain, dull, normal person with no interest in being a governor's wife or even a president's wife. Wouldn't you rather have someone by your side who will help you achieve those things?"

Yeah, that's good. Perfect, in fact.

My little speech only made him smirk.

I sighed. "Why me?"

He leaned back in his chair just staring at me. "You don't know what I see. Your mother says things that aren't true, and you believe her. You look more like her every year as your body fills out. Your mother makes you think you're nothing like her, but it's just not true. In fact, you're more attractive because you're a younger version of her." He chuckled. "That's probably why she's so mean to you. Practically twins, except for the darker blonde hair color. Jess, you are beautiful, even if you don't see it."

Despite not wanting to listen to him, his words felt nice even if they weren't true. My mother was beautiful and sought after by many men.

However, what he thought wasn't the point. "Wouldn't you rather have someone who adores you, who wants to be your wife? Who wants the same things?"

He leaned against the table, looking out at the Palisades Verde cliffs. "You will. Even if it takes years, you'll see. It's like training a dog to be obedient." He glanced down at this watch and grabbed his driving gloves.

I fumed.

A dog—how dare he!

My fists came down on the table. "I don't love you! I've never loved you, and I never will. In fact, I hate you, and I hate my mother. I'm not going to wear fancy dresses and go to parties, and I'm not ever going to wear negligees."

Seth pushed his chair away from the table, smashing it hard against the wall behind him. "You will not disappoint or embarrass me, or you'll suffer the consequences. You will act exactly how you've been told. You'll wear what I say to wear!" He looked me up and down. "I'll be burning all the clothes I don't feel are appropriate attire for my wife, so you'll have no choice in what you wear!"

I swallowed hard, knowing what he considered appropriate clothing. "I'll never accept—"

"Oh, but you will accept." He took in a long breath while he unfolded his fists and looked at his watch again. "I'm late. You might like to know I can be generous. I'm giving away some of Father's antiques to a charity auction this morning. You'd like it. It's to help the bastard children."

I cringed. "You mean the orphans."

He fiddled with his tie. "See? You'll be great at that sort of crap. Think of all the good you could do as a First Lady. Maybe I'll make it as far as the United Nations chairman." He stopped. His stare felt hot against my face. "Anyway, the press will be there at seven sharp, so I'd better go." He walked behind my chair and kissed the top of my head as though nothing had happened. "I'll be back later to finish our discussion. I have a feeling you'll be a bit more relaxed and agreeable by then."

Seth walked out. I heard the maid giggle in the hallway, assuring me Seth had a few minutes to spare before heading out.

"Please let her get pregnant," I mumbled, before inhaling Seth's omelet.

———◈———

The low click-clack of her stilettos woke me.

Great.

My mother pushed through my bedroom door. "Sleeping late?" Her voice seared through me like a hot branding iron. "It must be nice to sleep away the morning with nothing important to do. Are you sick?"

"I was up late." I flipped to my side so I didn't have to look at her. "Enjoy your time at the spa? Or were you out shopping with money that isn't yours, putting us further into debt?"

"Yes. I know where you were last night." Her jaw clicked back and forth. "The liquid is filling up in his lungs again. The doctor is urging me to pull his feeding tube."

I flung the sheets off me and sat up. "You can't! You can't just let him starve to death."

Her smirk made my body shiver. "Well, that's completely up to you now, isn't it?"

Once again, she was dangling his life for something she wanted in exchange.

"So what do you want this time? Dinner at the club? Recital for your loser friends? My soul?" I reached for my escape, but my iPod was missing from the nightstand.

My mother's straight blonde hair hardly moved against her thin face as she tapped her foot against the floor. She struck her acrylic nails against something shinny in the palm of her hand. "We need to talk. Or should I say, you need to listen." She put my music device in the pocket of her skintight black skirt.

My eyes rolled before I fell back and covered back up with the blankets. Only I kept my eyes on her wondering if she was bluffing. If she wasn't, I'd have no choice but to agree to whatever her lame request would be.

"Jessica, why does everything have to be so dramatic with you?" She rubbed her temples with her long, bony fingers. "For once, could you just do what's being asked of you without me having to force you? You should be happy. Do you even know what this means for us?" She sauntered over to the window.

Oh no, not this, not today. That's why Seth said I'd be more receptive later.

"Mother, I—"

"You know, I didn't want you." She stared out at the sea. "When I found out you were going to be a girl, I wanted to abort you. Your father threatened to leave me with nothing if I did. He didn't mind using threats against me to get what he wanted."

I knew from an early age she had no desire to love me, but knowing she wanted to take my life and my father protected me shed a new perspective. I was fighting for his life just as he had for mine.

"Seth is the son I wanted. He'll be a powerful leader with me orchestrating his moves as long as you agree to marry him." Her hand grasped the white lace curtain. "I'll show them, I'll show everyone who treated me like trash," she whispered.

"Show who?"

"Never mind," she said. "I've groomed you for this. Seth will make a good son-in-law, and now you have the opportunity to make me proud. It's your turn to pay me back for giving you life."

"But Mother, isn't—"

Her sharp turn from the window made me stop. "You will marry him. He has gone to great lengths for this family. His father paid off our house, and he provided the very expensive equipment to keep your father alive and pays the doctors' fees. Do you even know what it costs to have around-the-clock care?"

I shook my head. "I can take care of him. Those doctors don't do anything for him. I change the bed, I read to him, I exercise his legs—"

"And how are you going to pay for the machines? Pay for food? You hardly step out of this house."

"I'll get a job."

My mother laughed. "No you won't. You'll marry Seth. I don't think you even understand his potential. To have the world at your fingertips, to have anything you ever wanted, to have the respect. No longer will anyone point their finger at me and say, 'Poor Evelyn.'"

"No one said that."

"Shut up! Just shut up!" She pulled the curtain rod right out of wall. "I'll show everyone. I'll be the most powerful ruler yet. Together, Seth and I will make the world see things my way." She came at me, throwing the curtain. The rod just missed my cheek. "You will not take this from me." My mother stood at the foot of my bed, staring at the wall behind me for the longest time.

She grinded her teeth before turning to sit at my vanity, combing my sandalwood brush through her hair in long strokes. "Seth is very handsome, just like his father used to be before all the strokes. You should be on your knees thanking me for arranging this union."

"Mother, I was seven when you met Seth's parents. You couldn't have—"

"Yes. Well, be glad I did. Forcing the two of you together like I did was brilliant. Seth fell in love with you, just like he did with any of his possessions." She kept brushing her hair. "His father helped some, too. Brainwashed his son into thinking you were the catch of the century, and he'd be stupid to let you escape. He was easy to convince you belonged to him." She laughed, catching my expression on the reflection of the mirror. "You remember how he felt about his things? His toys?"

I couldn't help but remember. He had just tried to strangle me for refusing to marry him.

"Trust me." She put on her phony smile. "I'm doing you a favor. You don't even know what it's like in the real world. You spend all your time with a dying man in a small room."

My heart dropped. "Don't say that. He's not dying."

"You need me, Jessica. You couldn't make it a day without me."

Besides the things I read in the newspapers, I had little knowledge of the outside world. When time was my own, I'd spend it with my father, either reading to him or just talking to him as though he could hear my woes.

Maybe I wouldn't make it a day, but I'd rather die than live a life of misery.

My mother set the brush down. "You won't get a better offer."

I moaned. "I don't love him. Maybe I'll never love anyone. After your example, I don't want to ever marry anyone."

"You will."

"I won't."

"Of course you will marry. Every woman wants someone to provide for them. I'm just making sure you marry the right man. Then, you'll have a son who can continue his father's legacy. Don't make me force this. I hope you know I don't want to see your father starve to death."

Oh, of course you do. You've wanted him dead for years. You have some nerve, lady!

The calm discussion was about to get ugly.

"Whether I marry or not, I will not have children. No child deserves to be brought into this world, especially if you and Seth are going to ruin it."

My mother's lips tightened. The look reminded me of the day my father came home after the attack. The veins on her forehead bulged as she struggled to push the wheelchair over the front door entrance, but she held in her anger.

"There is a paper in my other pocket. All I have to do is sign my signature, and it's all over."

"But—"

"The doctor is already in his room, I could just text." She paused, calmly watching my face turn red.

"Fine! You win!" I sucked in my bottom lip to chew.

"You'll thank me one day. Everything I've done, I've done for your best interest." She turned her back to me and put her hand on the brass doorknob. "It's a mother's love that will do whatever it takes to see their child happy, even when they don't appreciate it."

Who does she think she's talking to?

Seeing me unmoved by her words, her gloat of victory disappeared. She left the room, shutting the door behind her, only I didn't hear the sound of her heels against the floor. She was waiting to hear me break down. I kept quiet until the click-clack of her shoes faded into another part of the grand house. Even if I didn't give her the gratification of tears, she had won, nevertheless. I sat there for a long time just staring at the door before slipping on my robe and heading to my father's room. None of the doctors or nurses were in there. She might have been bluffing about his condition getting worse, but I hadn't known for sure.

"Hi, Dad." I crossed the room to the only window, opening the shades. "I'm sorry I haven't come by before now." The sun had dipped down into the kaleidoscope of colors. I felt badly for depriving him from feeling the sunlight on his face.

I turned around and leaned against the window ledge. The scenic pictures I had torn out of a calendar and tacked up around the room were missing.

How dare she throw them away, again.

"Don't worry, Dad. I'll find them. I always do." I pushed off the window ledge to walk over to the trash bin next to the bed, but they weren't there. I looked around the hospital-like room, but there was no sign of the photos.

My eyes followed the wires and tubes wrapped around the bar of the bed to the life-support machine. "Sorry, Dad. I guess this time she really did—" I gasped. Stacks of photos lay under his left hand, pressed against his chest.

The absence of the normal hum and beeping sounds of the machines sent a chill through me.

"Is he?" Seth's voice came from somewhere behind me.

"Please. Not now, Seth." I walked to the chair and sat next to my father's bed, taking his ice-cold hand into mine.

The door click shut before I spoke. "It won't be long before he brings her." I stroked the inside of his palm. "What am I going to do without you?" I cried, tasting the salty tears on my lips. "You were my only hope for escaping this place. I can't do it alone. I'm…I'm afraid if I leave, Seth will find me. I'm not strong enough to go out alone." I sobbed harder, clenching his hand in mine. "Daddy, Daddy, please don't leave me here."

I felt rotten, selfish for crying for myself. I was envious of his death and wished it were me. I brought his hand up to wipe the tears on my cheeks and tried to remember what it was like before he was hurt, specifically the stories he'd read to me about kings, queens, princes, princesses, and happily ever after.

"Tell me one last story, Daddy, like when I was little. Tell me there is a fairy-tale ending for me. Tell me you're in a better place now and you're happy. Send me a sign—any kind of sign. Tell me what to do."

The clack of my mother's shoes moved down the hall. She entered with the doctor at her side. He lingered at the doorway while my mother enjoyed her moment. "I've sent Seth home for now. There are many things to be done in the next few days, so go to your room and let the doctor attend to the body," she said and waved the doctor in.

That's all he was to her—a body.

I hate you. I hope you get what you deserve someday, and I hope I'm the one to give it to you.

I got up to leave and passed the doctor in the doorway.

"Oh, and Jessica?"

I paused, staring at the door with my hand on the doorknob.

"Remember, you gave me your word."

Although I felt numb, the little voice in my head was right.

Don't let on. They'll watch me like a hawk. They want me to be scared to keep me here. I'll act scared while I plan the escape. I have to leave. I have to take a chance or suffer in this prison for the rest of my life.

"My word," I said as an unexpected smile formed on my face.

One More Night

In my room, I fell onto the mattress. My eyes shut. My father's cold, blue face was etched inside the lids. Forever in eternal slumber, my hopes of him waking were dead, and if I didn't leave soon, I'd be dead too. My pulse quickened, and my eyes flew open. I didn't want to remember him that way. I looked around the room for another image to take its place, but everything blurred through the fresh tears. I searched for the photo of my father, in its usual place, but it was missing. The portrait of a young, happy, and carefree man with wild brown hair, reduced to a dirty outline of a frame against the wall.

I wrapped the comforter tightly around me and lay back down. Sleep soon swept over me, tossing me into a white dream. Soft music played as I reclined my head back against my arms. The peaceful world I wished would let me stay was interrupted by a black cloud. It drifted into my world. With one flicker of light, followed by a sizzle, my peace was gone, and I was back to reality.

Glancing over at the clock, it read two thirty-two in the morning. I tossed my legs over the side of the bed, stumbling to the window. The moon peeked in and out of the growing clusters of clouds. Waves crashed hard against the shoreline. The fierce wind bent over the surrounding palm trees, creating an eerie, hollow sound like air blown through an empty log. A light sparkled below on the sand. An object grew brighter in the darkness. It held my stare for several minutes, taunting me. Then the light danced along the surface of the sand like a ballerina lost in a musical recital.

Nonsense.

I laughed, rubbing my eyes.

The tide moved closer toward the object. The sea would soon take possession of it if I didn't move fast enough.

Changing clothes, I climbed out the open window, ascended down a few emergency ladders to the dirt path leading down the cliff. It wasn't long before my feet felt the sand on the beach. The object was still bright and easy to find. Picking it up, I shook off the sand, and it turned dull.

"How did you make that little light?" I said to the rectangular piece of folded-up card stock. "How very strange." The weathered postcard unfolded in my hands. On the front was a picture of a parade with families lined up along the street. Flipping it over, in big black letters across the top it read Welcome to Folkston. A metallic, oblong sticker read City of Folkston, Georgia, and along the bottom it read The Gateway to the Okefenokee Swamp.

The words my father said to me so long ago echoed in my mind.

The time will come when you will leave this house and emerge into another life that awaits you—a life you deserve, a life with a greater purpose.

I remembered something else too, something I'd forgotten so long ago, a piece of paper my father had given me on the last night of his normal life. I never read it, and I doubted I could find it after all these years.

Maybe he's telling me now. There is nothing left for her to hold over me except death. But I don't know how to be on my own. I'd never make it. And even if I did leave, he'd find me. He'd find me, and I'd be dead. He'd find me and kill anyone who helped me.

The salt of my tears burned the corners of my dry lips. I was afraid to leave, but I was even more afraid to stay. I screamed at the roaring sea. "Is this all the help I deserve? If this is Your way of proving to me You exist—" I yelled at the God my father talked about, pacing and kicking at the sand.

A thought entered into my head, one that if I walked out into the ocean and let the undertow drag me out, no one would ever find my body.

Seth should have never saved me. He should have let the current take me then.

My fear of experiencing that again wouldn't allow it.

If I stayed, my mother would continue to dictate my every move. I'd be scared every day my husband might kill me for anything he disliked. I was in a swirling pit of endless darkness, a hole of eternity, and the only future ahead for me was to leave. There was no other way.

"Death would be better than staying here." I looked at the postcard again. "She wouldn't go anywhere near a swamp." A vision of her getting her limited-edition heels stuck in the mud brought a smile through my tears.

The next morning, I grabbed the hidden key to my father's office and entered. Bookshelves lined the walls, covering them completely except for the wall behind my father's desk. A book on every subject and about every place, including every imaginary story ever written, was all contained in the room. I had read them all. There was a stack of journals my father kept in an oversized, beat-up, wooden trunk locked with an old-fashioned golden key that dangled out of the lock. Years ago, I had looked inside, but on the pages were unreadable markings and sketches.

"Hello, Chief," I said to the painting hanging on the wall, behind the desk between two wooden crosses, as I moved around to the leather chair.

The geographical book in the middle of my father's desk lay open. Because it was the last book my father touched, I had left alone. Blowing off the dust, I ran my hand across the page, making me sneeze. The pages flipped in a flurry and abruptly stopped.

Jeez, I didn't sneeze that hard. How strange.

"The Okefenokee Swamp?" I read, looking closer at the handwritten oversized bookmark on the page. "There is a time for everything and a season for every activity under heaven, a time to be born and a time to die, a time to plant and a time to uproot, a time to kill and a time to heal, a time to tear down and a time to build, a time to weep and a time to laugh, a time to mourn and a time to dance, a time to scatter stones and a time to gather them, a time to embrace and a time to refrain, a time to search and a time to give up, a time to keep and a time to throw away, a time to tear and a time to mend, a time to be silent and a time to speak, a time to love and a time to hate, a time for war and a time for peace.' Dad, are you trying to tell me something?"

I couldn't help but doubt my previous thoughts on the whole God thing. Maybe there were angels watching us.

But if they do exist, where have they been? Stick to what I know, and it's not angels. I suppose an afterlife of some sort could be possible. A soul that continues to live after the body is gone.

My father was trying to help me escape. At least I wanted to believe it.

"Well, Chief, it's time to leave this jailhouse. I might not make it out alive, but I have to try." If I didn't know better, I would have thought the chief smiled at me. "I guess I'd better find out about my new adventure." I pulled the book into my lap and began to read.

The day was just about over when I exited my father's office and peered into the kitchen, just in time to see the cook exit out the back door.

My stomach growled, and with no one else around, I raided the refrigerator. Carrots, celery, a jar of green olives, and a container full of hummus were not helpful.

"Yuck."

My mother came in through the door. "What are you doing?"

I shut the door. "Nothing."

"Where were you?"

I turned to face her. "I've been here all day."

My mother no doubt spent most of the day out of the house making funeral arrangements. She didn't care where I was.

"Oh well. Seth said he came by, and when he didn't find you, he thought you might have gone with me. I was concerned, although I knew you were here somewhere."

I rolled my eyes at her.

Yeah, that's why you locked all the doors from the outside just in case I tried to leave.

"I am surprised at you. I thought you'd want to help make the arrangements."

"I want nothing to do with the plethora of flowers, the lavish funeral home, the bronze casket, or the media spectacle you've planned. None of it is for my father. Besides, my day was better spent reading."

"Fine. Whatever." She rubbed her temples and then tossed a garment bag at me. "Go try this on. The funeral is tomorrow at noon. I can have Eleanor come over in the early morning if the dress needs to be pinned."

I held the bag, but didn't move fast enough for her.

"Now," she barked.

Instead of telling her to shove it, instead of igniting more threats, I walked past her and up the stairs to my room.

Soon I won't be here for you to kick around. Soon I'll be gone, and you'll never find me.

At least I hoped not.

Destination Nowhere

My mother barged into my room. "It's going to be a lovely day." She crossed the room to the window and threw open the new curtains. "The sun is brightly shining down on us today." She spun to face me, lacing her fingers together. "So let's not be late."

My mother noticed I was already dressed. Her reflection smiled as I put on the final additions to my face. I wanted to look nice for my father, not for her or the freak show already gathering at the front gate.

"Good girl. I want you downstairs when you are finished. Seth is here and waiting for you."

Brilliant. Seth will keep her occupied.

Anytime the three of us were in public, I became invisible. It was the perfect setup for my plan.

I finished the last touches on my hair while my mother watched me. She stared at me and waited for some sort of smart remark.

What? No argument today? No protest? I imagined the words in her head.

A low sigh moved out of her parted lips, as she exited the room. There wasn't anything for me to protest, because I was leaving and never coming back.

I grabbed a sweater and headed downstairs and into a white limousine.

The vehicle pulled up to the curb of the funeral home. Camera lights flashed against the dark, tinted windows. "Now don't forget, Seth, what we practice. We want them eating out of our hands." My mother grinned, lifting up her champagne glass to clink Seth's before swallowing the last drop of liquid.

I hoped they enjoyed their moment of triumph. It would be their last conquest over me anyway.

"We're ready, driver," my mother said as she pinched her cheeks.

"Yes, ma'am," he answered, getting out of the car to open her door.

As the door opened, the camera flashes blinded me. I pulled over the black veil attached to the hat I wore to shield my face. Until then, except for my mother's cocktail party friends, my face was not well known. I wanted to keep it that way. There would be no recent photos of me to send to every police station across the US. I dodged the media by escaping out the opposite side of the car. Questions fired at Seth the moment he stepped out. My mother stood at his side, and neither one looked for me.

"How's your father doing?" one reporter asked.

"He's strong and encouraged by all your support. I deeply appreciate the cards, love, and prayers being said for my family," Seth answered.

Like he would ever pray. He had them all fooled.

"The people know how much you've helped your father, and they really admire you for your commitment not only to him, but to the people of California," another spoke out. "But they want to know if your father takes a turn for the worse, will you consider taking his seat?"

Seth put on his best fake expression of grief. "I hope that day never comes. My father is a great man, and he will overcome his cancer like before. If God decides to take him, I will do what I can to continue his work and help others." He wiped tears from his eyes, and the crowd let out a sweet sigh.

"Fraud," I whispered, moving around the outside of the crowd to cross over to the parlor entrance.

A man standing guard at the door wasn't allowing anyone in.

I'm the daughter of the deceased. Of course he'd never let me enter without permission from my mother.

But just as I was ready to reason with the man, a woman approached with a small child dancing behind her. "Restrooms?" she asked. He turned and pointed, giving me the perfect opportunity to slide behind him, and through the red double doors to where my father's casket rested.

The parlor was lined on both sides with stained glass windows. Sunlight radiated through them, making it very warm in the room. Angels painted on the glass, watched me as I walked down the bright red carpet to the shiny coffin. My hand reached out to touch it. "I'm going to do it. I'm leaving tonight on a train, and I'm not coming back." I felt a jab into my heart, and it ached. "I hope you are in a better place. Maybe I'll see you again someday." I couldn't bear to look at the box anymore, as the tears streamed down my face. A painted angel with outstretched arms looked right at me. "I want to believe it like he did. I do, but how can I after everything we've been through? You haven't been there for me ever." The angel just stared at me. "I've always tried to do the right thing, to put my father's needs before mine. I sacrificed having friends, going to a regular school, and for what? He's dead."

Don't lose it.

I pulled a tissue out of my pocket to wipe the tears. "Show me, Dad. Make me believe."

The doors squeaked open. I darted out the back door of the building before the people began to enter. The train station was just around the corner at the end of the block. I was able to buy my ticket, and get back to my seat with a few minutes to spare.

Seth entered with the bereaved wife. My mother would have made a spectacular actress as she purposely took the time to visit with anyone in an aisle seat. At least it gave me time to calm down from my jaunt to the station and back.

Finally, my mother sat down on my right and Seth to my left. He propped his hand behind my chair and touched my shoulders.

"I delayed your mother so you could have more time to say good-bye. I hope you used the time wisely."

"Yes, I did," I said calmly. "Thank you."

The reception followed at our house and spilled out into the evening hours. I looked at my watch a million times, but it only made me more nervous. Even if the party ended at midnight, the last train boarded at one thirty. There was plenty of time. My mother oscillated around the room, downing one drink after another.

After a while, it was all I could take before I approached her. "It's almost midnight. I'm heading up to bed."

"Why don't you play something?" she slurred, spilling the contents in her glass.

"No. I don't feel like playing, Mother. I'm tired." I looked over at the piano. It would be the only thing I would miss. The only comfort I'd ever known.

"Oh, Evey." Another drunk put his arm around my mother's waist and twirled her away from me. "Let's dance."

"Don't forget to say good night to Seth," she called out as she was whisked into another room.

Seth was equally drunk and hanging all over a blonde girl with a rather large chest. I looked down at mine. I still didn't get it. Why me? I had neither the perfect figure nor large breasts. Regardless, I could safely assume neither would be looking for me tonight and possibly not until late afternoon. It gave me time to get far away before they discovered me missing.

I ran upstairs and began to get ready.

My idea was to make it look like an abduction. I tossed my possessions around the room and ripped open a feather pillow. The fluff fell on everything in the room. I knocked over a lamp, the chairs, and the table by the window. I tore my jacket using the tip of the bed post and left a piece of it to dangle down the side of the bed.

"Not bad," I said, looking around at the mess.

I shoved some clothes into a backpack along with a stash of cash I had saved, and then I noticed the music had stopped.

"Party is over." I looked at my watch. It was quarter to one.

It's now or never. But I better hurry.

I put my hand down on the window ledge to climb out, and I felt a poke. "Ouch." My finger bled. It wasn't a huge cut, but it was enough blood to give me an idea.

The blood trickled out of my finger as I squeezed it along the window ledge and onto the floor. I grabbed the bag and went out the window. Once I got down to the ground, I took one last look at the house. An excitement went off inside me, a feeling of valor and adventure, but it lasted only a moment.

I'm crazy to do this! How will I eat? Where will I live? I'll have to find a job, but who will hire someone with no experience? And don't forget, Seth will find you and kill you.

Once again, death sounded better than staying. I took one last look before heading to the train station.

For nearly twenty-five minutes, it was just me in the darkness before the glow of the lights from the station grew brighter.

"All aboard," a man hollered in the night.

I hurried in the direction of the train until the panic inside stopped me. I hid in the shadow of a building, watching a handful of people gather around the man. The same voice of doubt went over all the reasons to stay, like a CD stuck on the same song.

"Ticket please," he said to each of them, and in turn, they handed him a ticket. He punched it with a shiny tool, before the passengers stepped up onto the train.

Simple enough, and I have my ticket in my pocket. Will I live under a bridge? Steal food to eat?

"You're stalling, Jess." I rubbed my hands together, trembling like I was cold, but I wasn't. Actually, I felt hot, uncomfortably hot and faint.

No one would have been in my room yet. I could still return and forget leaving. Was it possible I could make myself love him?

"Last call," the man shouted in my direction.

Tears streamed down my face as I felt defeated once again. I couldn't do it. I was weak and helpless just like my mother said. I hoped my father wasn't watching. I hoped that I was right all along not to believe in ghosts or spirits, because if he was watching, I couldn't bear the disappointment he must be feeling.

Turning away from the train to go home, I put both hands in my pockets. The edge of the postcard poked my finger. I pulled it out, carefully unfolding it. It didn't sparkle or come to life as it had on the sandy beach. It was just a worthless piece of trash, not a message from my father's spirit. I flung it toward the trash, but the wind caught it. Up into the air it flew like a kite. I followed it until the wind stopped and it fell, allowing me to snatch it before it hit the ground.

"Ticket please."

I looked up, surprised to be standing in the front of the conductor. Reaching into my pocket, I pulled out a ticket. He took it, punched a hole it in, and handed it back.

"You'll need to keep your ticket."

I nodded and boarded the train.

Soon after the train left the station, the worry faded. I was still scared, but the overpowering paralyzing fear was gone for the time being.

Thanks, Dad.

The one good thing about a departure at one thirty in the morning was having an entire row to myself.

I can't believe I'm really doing this.

Glaring out window, the train picked up speed, making the far off lights smear into a blur. I pulled the shade halfway down, reclined my seat as far as it would go, only to glower at the seat in front of me.

It's not too late. I can still go back. I'm not really going to some hick town after the life I've lived with cooks and servants? But I was a servant, a servant to Seth and to Mother. And look at how many years I took care of Father and all the things I gave up to care for him.

All the reasons to go back, all the reasons to run, swirled around like water circling the drain of a tub. The motion of the train calmed me some, and the arguing became less. I shut my eyes. Before long, the battle stopped, and I fell asleep.

The warmth of the sun, peeking below the shade, woke me. I must have been asleep for hours and in the same position because my body did not want to move.

"Excuse me," the first voice I'd heard since the ticket man.

Stretching out of the fetal position, I sat up and yawned.

"I'm sorry to wake you. Um…well, all the seats are taken and—"The red-haired young man smiled and stuck out his hand in my direction. "My name is Mark."

"Oh. You need a place to sit." I scooted next to the window.

The man dropped his hand down to his luggage and lifted it up into the overhead compartment. He bumped his head as he sat.

"Long legs. I guess not many tall people ride on trains." He rubbed his forehead.

"I suppose not."

"I'm sorry for waking you. You looked quite peaceful, rather angelic."

"No. It's okay," I said, taking a glimpse at my watch.

It's only seven-thirty. Still a long way to go.

Opening the roller shade, the landscape had changed from dark city lights, to morning countryside. I would have enjoyed the scenery, if it hadn't been for my mind wanting to argue again.

"I'm not going back."

"Sorry. Did you say something?" My seat mate asked.

"Just talking to myself. Sorry."

"Oh. I do that sometimes too." He paused for a long moment. "So, where are you headed?"

The first thought to pop into my head was the story of Little Red Riding Hood. "My grandmother's house." I smiled, remembering how my dad read the part of the wolf with a low growl in his voice.

"I'm on my way to New Orleans. I'm a youth leader, and we're taking the kids there." He pointed to kids who sat across the aisle and those in front of us, all wearing bright yellow shirts that read TEAM GOD. "We're going to help clean up the neighborhoods after the hurricane."

Perfect!

Mark continued to talk about his mission. The more he talked about his calling to aid others, the more I felt at ease. I was in awe of the good work he was doing for others, up until he mentioned how God was working in his life. That's when I grew less interested and stared out the window. The redhead stopped talking for some time, and I felt bad for the silence. He was nice to me, but because I blamed God for my miserable life, I really didn't want to hear all the good things He was doing for others.

I wiggled in my seat at the uncomfortable silence between us. "I'm sorry. My father believed in God, but I just don't. You've been really nice to me, and I'd like to talk about something else if you don't mind."

"I'm sorry too. I've done nothing but talk at you the entire ride. So tell me about yourself. What is your favorite thing to do? What are your fears?" He laughed. "Tell me everything."

I laughed too. "I like to play the piano. I hate water unless I can drink it or if it's only a few inches deep, and I love the smell of roses."

"Why do you hate water?"

I hesitated to tell him since it involved me running from Seth. "When I was young, I went out into the ocean, and the water pulled the sand from under my feet. The current was strong that day and I was pulled out to sea. I thought I was going to die."

"Must have been scary."

We talked for the remainder of the trip. I wanted to tell him more about my life, but I stayed mostly on the surface. Seth's threats stayed in the back of my mind. The less other people knew about me, the safer they would be.

The conductor walked through the train. "Waycross, Georgia. Thirty-minute stop."

"That's where I get off. We are picking up some donations from a sister church before our final stop. Can I at least buy you a soda? Any kind you like."

"Sure." I smiled. It was my stop too, but it was better not to let on. "I could use a stretch and a decent bathroom break."

"Yeah. Not too pleasant, are they?" He stood up to grab his bags. "Where did you say you were going?"

"I know it's the next stop, but I forget the name. My grandparents are picking me up," I lied. I stood up, slinging my backpack over my right shoulder and followed Mark down the aisle off the train.

"Oh no. There's our bus to the church." He viewed his watch. "I guess they don't want to waste any time."

"I'm fine. Thank you though. You don't want to miss your bus."

The soggy, humid air hit me for the first time, and I coughed. "I'll take a rain check on the Coke."

"Thanks for keeping me company." He winked before hollering at the kids exiting the train. "Okay. Let's get a move on it," he commanded. "Well, maybe we'll run into each other someday." He shook my hand.

"That would be nice."

He took off in a sprint, counting heads entering the vehicle. I waited until the bus pulled out of the station to find the bathroom.

The train station was a long, one-level building with a gravel parking lot. The green bathroom sign caught my attention, so I headed in that direction. Sweat beaded on my skin, and I smelled stale from the trip. There was at least an hour before the bus to

Folkston would arrive, so I had time to change my clothes. That was until I smelled an awful stench of feces and urine.

"Ugh."

I pinched my nose and pushed the door open. Fecal matter covered the walls, and I let the door shut to stop the smell from escaping. "Gross." I wanted to leave, but the urge to go and having no other options prompted me to turn right back around and enter the stench with only one goal—to pee and exit without touching anything.

I was quick and flushed the toilet by lifting my foot to use the bottom of my shoe, which was dirty anyway. Thankfully, I remembered to pack hand sanitizer and slathered anywhere my skin was exposed, before heading back to wait for the bus.

A man wearing dark sunglasses and a black trench coat headed in my direction. He didn't say a word but grabbed my pack, knocking me into a steel pole.

Everything went dark.

My head hurt, throbbing against the top of my skull. For a moment, I forgot what had happened.

Oh yeah. My pack, clothes, bus ticket, cash, and everything I possessed is gone. Now what do I do?

As I opened my eyes, I realized, that was the least of my problems. I was in a jail cell. The door wasn't locked shut, but the familiar stench of scotch filled the air. Seth's favorite drink.

Seth is here to drag me back, but I won't let him. I'll fight. Then when he kills me, it won't be in vain. There will be witnesses, and they'll put him in jail.

"Hey, look. The girl's awake. Now, what's a pretty thing like you doing in here?" Across from the cell I was in, two men sat on a wooden bench, handcuffed together.

"You two, pipe down," a woman commanded.

"But she's awake now," one of them said. "Aren't you, sweetheart?"

"I bet she's a runaway," the other man slurred. "My daughter has run away ten times, but we always manage to drag her back. She puts up such a fuss." He laughed.

"Shut up. I wasn't talking to you, moron," the first man said.

But the second man paid no attention and continued. "They just need someone to break their spirit, and eventually, they give in."

They're not going to break my spirit. I'm stronger than that. I have to be.

I needed to get out of there fast. I put my palms down on the side of the cot to sit up.

"Oh no, you don't." A young woman sat on the edge of the cot, forcing me back down. "You've got a pretty good lump on your head, young lady." She handed me an ice pack, some aspirin, a bottle of water, and a half of a sub-sandwich. "Are you allergic to anything?"

I shook my head, making it throb harder, while scarfing down the food. "Thanks," I held the pack to my head, noticing the woman's pink tube socks and two different kinds of sneakers on her feet.

"You were robbed last night. Do you remember anything else? Did you see anyone?" she asked and patted at her flower sundress.

"Um, some guy took my backpack and knocked me against a pole. He wore a black coat and shades, but that's all I remember."

"How do we contact your parents?"

"I don't have any. Besides, I'm twenty, almost twenty-one," I stuttered, and I saw my fingers were trembling. I had to tell her something else so she'd believe there was no one to call and not comb through any missing persons reports. I wouldn't have put it past Seth to file one. "My father died when I was five, and my mother died shortly after. I've been in and out of orphanages most of my life. When I turned eighteen, they gave me some money and told me to leave, and I've been on my own ever since. So you see, there isn't anyone to call."

She nodded as though she believed me, so I continued. "What time is it? I've got a job lined up in Florida, and if I miss my interview—"

"You were brought here around seven last night and it's almost noon."

"Noon? I have to go."

Someone for sure knows by now I've gone. I have to get out of here and quick.

"Okay, dear." She got up. "After the doc gives you the okay, you can go."

"You don't understand. I can't stay here. You don't want to be responsible if I don't get the job," I pleaded to the odd woman.

"You just give me the phone number, honey, and I'll give them a call to explain." She laid me back down on the cot and covered me up. "See? No worries."

"I don't have the number," I said.

"Sorry, but that's the rules. You've got a serious head injury. It wouldn't be right to let you go off. What if something bad happen to you? Then it would be my fault. I could lose my job, and not many people are willing to hire someone with cerebral palsy." The woman slowly shuffled toward the two men.

I don't want to get her in trouble. But I can't stay either. If I run out of here, she wouldn't be able to catch me.

She released one of the men from the cuffs. I sat up, ready to run.

"Now go sleep it off." She pointed to a vacant cell, while I made my way to the exit. "And you…" I heard her say as I slipped out the station doors.

That was easier than I thought it would be.

"Now to hitch a ride." I looked at the sun in the sky. "East." Off I went in the opposite direction of the sun's path and down the road.

Hours passed by, and there was not one car. I began to wonder if I had missed a Road Closed sign or something, although at that point, it didn't matter if I had or not. I wasn't going back.

My stomach rumbled, wishing I had taken food with me. The night was coming, and the weather was changing rapidly. The clouds filled in around me. There was dampness in the air.

I breathed in the wet particles, watching the dry road begin to reflect the intermittent sunlight. Another hour or more went by. My feet were soaked and sloshing around inside my shoes as I entered the canopy. The green, wet moss covered the branches of the trees, weighing them down. The same fungus also covered the trunks of the trees like sap on a pine tree.

My heart beat fast in the dim and gloomy surroundings, but at least that meant I was heading in the right direction.

The chatter of birds filled my ears. Some sang with a sweet and steady melody, and some were high-pitched screeches, and together, they created a musical harmony. I liked those noises. It was the rustling noise, moving along the bushes at the edge of the road I didn't like. I tried to ignore it, watching only from the corner of my eyes until the silhouette of an animal stopped on a path between two large trees. I stopped too and muffled my breathing with my hands.

It's a wolf.

Noticing the long snout and pointed ears through the brush, his body was smaller than a wolf. It didn't growl or even look in my direction. The beast just stood there fixated on the tops of the trees.

I removed my hands from my mouth, while walking backward with tiny steps. The animal turned to face me, blinked its orange eyes in my direction, before letting out a growl. I turned and leapt into a run, running as fast as my legs would take me down the wet road. I ran for a while, but realized if it had been chasing me, it would have caught me.

I stopped to rest. The chatter of the birds grew louder, and the buzzing, hissing sounds of the cicadas hurt my ears.

What am I doing here? I'm not ready to die. I shouldn't have left. I should have made a better plan.

Covering my ears to muffle the noise, I continued my journey down the road. I tilted my face to the sky. "I need you, Dad." The dainty drizzle accumulated on my face and dripped off my chin.

"If there is an angel watching over me, I need help now. I don't know where to go from here."

The mist turned into a downpour, and the swamp became instantly silent.

That's just about the answer I would get. Jeez. Thanks.

I scurried under a large tree for cover. "Fine. I'll do it without your help. I've gotten this far, alone, haven't I?" I'm not sure who I was trying to convince, but it felt good to say it out loud.

The farther into the trees I went, the drier I stayed, which was good. Losing track of the road as it got darker, was not good. It was dark. I moved slow, knowing at any moment the small twigs bending under my feet could turn into a waist-deep bog. My hands stretched out in front catching small branches from whacking at my face. A million things went through my mind, mostly comparing death there to death by Seth later, and neither appealed to me. I was in an unknown place with bugs and animals at every turn blinking their eyes at me. I was sure to be something's dinner soon.

"Just get it over with," I called out.

A light appeared, much like the one at the beach, dancing in the distances.

The postcard.

I reached into my pocket, but it was no longer there. "I've come too far not to follow." I combed through the bushes to find a rough path lit up by the light. "Here I come," I said, feeling a little more confident I was heading in the right direction. I followed it over fallen logs, weaved in and out of trees, and jumped over bushes. My enthusiasm and energy level were wearing off. "Where are you leading me?"

The light didn't reply.

"Is it really you, Dad? Are you taking me somewhere special? Or am I just a fool?"

The light sped up, and if I wanted to keep up, I'd have to as well. The faster pace made me clumsy, and I tripped repeatedly over branches, the mud, and my own feet. I reached a large, flat rock and imagined for a moment I was looking at a plush bed. I leaned my body against it. I just needed to rest.

The light will wait for me.

"Just a few minutes," I said to the light and climbed onto the rock. "Just a moment of rest." I laid my head down and closed my eyes. "Then I'll follow."

I drifted off into a dream, away from the wetness. I floated on a cloud in a summer sky. The warm rays of the sun bounced off the white cotton fluff. But my body was too heavy for the cloud, and I began to seep through it.

Down, down, down I fell until I woke up to face new surroundings.

Five people in an unfamiliar room stared at me.

First Impressions

"Leave that child alone," a voice came from the shadows, where a rocker sat next to a fireplace. A black dog lay by her feet and barely moved as she stood up from the chair and reached for a lantern on top of the mantelpiece. I noticed a wooden cross on the wall above.

Just like the crosses in my father's office.

The round silhouette of the woman waddled to me, her tattered dress brushed against her cocoa skin. She plopped down on the corner of my bed. Her long, black, wavy hair was bound with a piece of tied cloth, dangling along the side of her face.

"Hows ya feel, honey?" She placed her hand on my cheek and smiled.

"I'm fine," I said and tried to sit up to see the other figures in the room. Moving too quickly, white static electricity flew around the room like sparks from a fire. I felt nauseous.

"Mmhmm." She pushed me back down and placed a wet cloth on my forehead. "No fever. But that's one nasty bump."

"I fell." I lied.

"Well, yous go on and get some sleep. It's nearly 2:00 a.m." She stood up and looked down on me. "Yous had a long journey. Gets some sleep, child. We's talk in the mornin'."

How does she know how far I've come?

I watched the woman walk between the many beds in the room, back to her chair. She turned down the lantern and set it back on the mantel.

"Oh, the outhouse is just outside the back door to ya right if yous need to use it before mornin'. Just make sure to light the lantern at the back to take with ya. Lots of critters roam 'round at night, and it's black as coffee." She sat down in the rocking chair.

Outhouse! Did she just say outhouse?

"Yes, ma'am," I answered.

"Miss Mabel. Everyone calls me Miss Mabel. Not sure why. Theys just always has. Now, for the rest of yous young'uns, time for bed." She yawned as the other four in the room jumped into their beds. "It's a good thing tomorrow is Saturday."

How did I end up here, and where did the light take me? Maybe she's fattening me up, for supper. Just like in Hansel and Gretel. Wait, why do I keep thinking about fairy tale stories?

Of course that was silly to think she was going to eat me. I looked up at the cross, barely able to see it by firelight.

Okay, Dad, show me.

The room went quiet, except for the occasional crackle from the fire. I wondered if the woman had called my mother, and if she was on her way to get me. How else would she have known how far I'd come? But despite my worries, the warmth of the bed embraced my body like a glove.

I yawned.

I'll leave in the morning before they all rise and before my mother has a chance to get here.

The heaviness of my eyelids finally had its way. My mouth opened wide, and my eyes watered as I stretched down into soft covers.

But I didn't wake before everyone else.

The sun burned through my eyelids. I pulled the covers over my head and rolled over to the other side of the bed. Forgetting where I was, I waited for my mother or Seth to barge into my room with some sort of obscured request.

"I think she's awake." A small child's voice rang in my ears.

Oh no. I didn't leave.

I thought about the woman's words about a long journey, thinking my mother was probably in the room to retrieve me. I swallowed hard before I opened my eyes.

The black woman left the kitchen and strolled in my direction. Whatever she was cooking smelled delicious, and my stomach rumbled. My mother would never let me eat something that smelled so good.

"Good mornin'." The woman smiled. "Sleeps well, I hope?"

"Yes, ma'am, I did. Thank you."

"Miss Mabel," she corrected.

"Yes, Miss Mabel."

"There's a bag under yous bed. It's got things a young woman might be needin', includin' clothes 'bout your size. A tub with warm water to wash up in, just over yonder." She pointed to a small room off the main room before heading back to the kitchen. "Go on now. We's don't has all day."

It was on the tip of my tongue to ask if anyone was coming for me, but glancing around the room, I didn't see a phone.

I could still sneak out the bathroom window, just in case.

A little blonde girl skipped to the bed with the black dog following her. She smiled big and opened her mouth to speak.

"May, I needs yous to set the table," Miss Mabel cut in.

The little girl huffed and changed her direction. The dog followed her out the back door.

No one else was in the room besides the three of us. All the beds were neatly made except mine. I picked out a few items from the bag including a change of clothes and headed for the small room. Inside, there were no windows to escape from.

I sighed, dipping my body into the tub. The water was more lukewarm than hot. I looked for the faucet to add more hot water, but there wasn't any plumbing over the tub.

Outhouse, remember?

I washed up the best I could before drying off and getting dressed. I found a comb, but no blow dryer. Even if they had one, there wasn't any electrical outlets in the room.

Ugh, I've stepped into a Little House on the Prairie *novel.*

However, no electricity meant no phone. No phone meant she couldn't have called anyone. A sense of relief fell over me, but there was still the matter of a fake story. My first impression told me she wouldn't be so easy to convince.

I placed my hand on the doorknob. Taking two deep breaths, I emerged from the washroom.

Miss Mabel was there, waiting for me with a young girl by her side. "This is May." Miss Mabel introduced the child with the long blonde curls.

"You're pretty." The little girl bounced to my side, taking my hand. "We're going to be great friends, even better friends than me and old Scraps."

"Scraps is the old hound dog. Just shows up one day. May feeds him our leftovers so he's no bother and he comes and goes as he pleases," Miss Mabel babbled.

I smiled at the little girl. "I'm Jessica," I noticed her blue eyes sparkled like tiny stars in the night sky.

Darn, I didn't use the fake name.

"This one is Joseph." Miss Mabel pulled the thin, fragile boy by the arm. His dark brown eyes shifted to the ground, causing his black hair to cover his face.

"Hey." Joseph's voice crackled.

Miss Mabel let go of him, and he walked out the front door, letting the screen door slam shut behind him.

A girl, who looked similar to Joseph in size and age, stepped up and took my free hand into hers. "I'm Josephine." She smiled, almost apolitically. "Excuse me please, Jessica."

I nodded.

"Joseph and Josephine are twins," Miss Mabel said, as she watched Josephine chase after him. "Just because he's fifteen, he thinks he is all grown, ready to do things on his own, but Miss Mabel knows he ain't. Sometimes that boy gets on my last nerve. It's a good thing I'm a Christian and is forgivin'." She shook her head while scanning the room.

May tugged on her dress. "Remember, he was taking the blankets to the orphanage and then over to the—"

"Oh yes. That's right. Thanks, May," Miss Mabel patted down her apron. "I suppose you'll meet him eventually. Have to forgive us old folks. We sometimes can't remember from one moment to the next." She took out piece of paper and laughed. "There's my list." She read it over, folded it up, and put it back into her pocket. "I bet yous are hungry." She led me into the small kitchen at the back of the square room.

A black, wood-burning stove sat in the corner of the kitchen with a long pipe going out through the top of the roof. The red-hot coals were visible through the glass window, and warming the small space. I sat down on a thin wire chair across from the stove and put my hands on the square table with a beige tile top. Above the table hung a picture of a white, colonial-style house surrounded by a lush garden and angel statues. A silver plaque was attached to the bottom of the frame. I read it aloud: "As for me and my household, we will serve the Lord."

"Amen," Miss Mabel said while she set a plate of food in front of me. "Now that yous said a prayer, yous may eat."

"I didn't say a prayer. I was just reading the—"

"Now I's sure yous rather eat than argue with an old woman." She smiled and slid the plate closer to me.

My father would have liked her.

The food smelled amazing, and I was starving, so I nodded and grabbed the fork. It wasn't long before I gobbled up the entire plate. My mother would have killed me for eating all of it.

Miss Mabel sat across from me, placing two tea cups on the table.

"Tea?" she asked, pouring the hot liquid, from the white tea pot already on the table, into her cup.

I quickly chewed the last piece of bacon and swallowed. "Yes, please."

"So, Jessica," she began, "how did you end up so far from the road?"

My stomach fluttered. "I'm an orphan. I've been on my own for quite some time. I heard about a job." I paused, looking up into her face. She was not buying it. "A good friend said her father's cousin, who works for the Okefenokee Swamp, is looking for help in their gift shop."

"That's not what I asked you." The old woman picked up her cup and sipped the tea.

"I was on my way there when I was robbed. A man took my money, clothes, and my bus ticket. I tried to hitch a ride, but no cars came by." I sprinkled in some truth. "It started to rain really hard, and the only way to stay somewhat dry was to take shelter under the big trees. I guess I got turned around and could no longer see the road." I was there all over again, and my heart raced, chasing after the little light. Or was the light my imagination? Was all of it my imagination?

I didn't tell her about the light.

She'll think I'm crazy and drive me to some hospital, and then they'll find me for sure.

"Interesting. And no one told you to come here?"

Yes. My father's dead spirit led me here. That would go over well. But do I really believe that's what happened? How I ended up here? No, well maybe a small part of me does.

"No, ma'am. I mean, Miss Mabel," I answered.

She took another slip of her tea before setting the cup down on the tile.

"Well, if it's work yous' lookin' for, I sure can use a couple more hands around here for plantin' and then for harvest. I can't pay you much, but I can offer you room and board, and yous can stay as long as yous like," she said. "We might not have much, but we always have plenty." She stood up to walk over to the sink.

I nodded even though what she said sounded odd. It wasn't just her broken Southern speech, that came and went, but her vagueness. I wanted to say in return, *"Thank you for hospitality, but I must be going now."* However, the only part that came out was thank you.

"No need for thanks, but it's much appreciated." She beamed and reached for my empty plate. I tried to help clean up, but May bounced in and tugged on my shirt.

"Go on, you two. I got this." Miss Mabel placed the dishes in the deep sink full of soapy water.

"Let's go outside." May tugged on my elbow, until she pulled me out the front door.

I gazed at the barren field in front of the little shack. Beyond the yellow meadow, tall, deep-green trees, with branches hanging down to the ground, horseshoed around the front. A thin gravel road disappeared into the thickest part of the wooded area. On the right side of the house, a stream, covered with purple water lilies, weaved like a snake in the grass. A slight pungent smell drifted intermittently in the air, as did the smell of the lilies.

May sat down on a long swing, hanging from the rafters, and patted the seat next to her. As soon as I sat, May began to chatter. She talked a mile a minute. I caught bits and pieces of her words as I debated in my head whether I should take Miss Mabel up on her offer to stay. The house was perfectly hidden by all the trees. My mother would never think to find me in a swamp. I would have preferred somewhere with electricity and running water, but it wasn't like I planned to stay there forever.

"Hey, there's Hunter. He's back early." May interrupted her monologue on the dangers of the swamp, to point at the road. "You'll like him. He's nice like you."

I recognized Joseph as he came around the side of the shack. He ran down the gravel road to the guy May called Hunter. They talked for a few minutes, then looked in our direction. Mortified they caught me watching, I turned my focus on the rose buses.

"Look. They're going to race. But I'm faster than both of them," May said, which prompted me to look back at them.

The two boys stood side by side, before they took off in a run. Hunter, wearing torn, tight-fitting jeans, was faster than Joseph. His long hair jetted back behind him, exposing his cheerful, carefree smile and perfectly tanned skin. As he ran, his feet firmly met the ground and gave him even more power behind his well-formed legs. His arms moved along the side of his body in consistent swings. When Hunter realized Joseph was far behind, he stopped and turned. Joseph didn't look happy about losing.

"Come on," Hunter laughed. "You're not giving me much of a challenge."

Joseph ran faster and tackled him. I cringed and looked away before seeing their bodies hit the gravel. After a moment, I searched for them, but they were gone from sight. However, I could hear them laughing around the other side of the house.

May giggled. "Did you hear anything I just said?"

Embarrassed I hadn't, I shook my head.

"It's okay," she said. "They are silly sometimes and fun to watch. It really is the only time Joseph seems happy these days. I don't think he likes being left with all the girls. Miss Mabel said he's not ready to go with Hunter."

"May." Miss Mabel called from inside.

She stood up quickly. "I'll be right back. Don't go anywhere without me," she said, entering through the screen door.

The thought to runaway had occurred to me.

If I do leave, it should be when everyone is asleep.

I stood and walked to the edge of the porch to smell the flowers. Roses lined the outside of the porch and climbed up the white lattice. Each white rose had a brilliant red outline along each of the delicate petals. I breathed in the sweet perfume, reaching over the railing to touch one of the soft petals.

"Watch your fingers. They can be sharp," someone said as I heard the screech of the screen door.

I turned around.

"Although they are beautiful to look at, they produce thorns bigger than the average rose." The tan-skinned boy blinked his thick, black eyelashes.

"Oh," I said, startled by the absence of his shirt.

I tried to keep my focus on his light blue eyes and away from his tight, firm chest, which made my skin feel hot all over. Seth worked out and had a nice build, but this felt different.

Dizzy. I can't breathe. Please don't pass out.

I held my breath so I wouldn't smell the alluring earthly musk coming from his skin and hoped the loud thunder in my ears would stop. I gripped the railing behind me and shifted my gaze to my feet.

Don't speak, it will just come out stupid. What the heck is wrong with me?

"Sorry I wasn't here this morning to greet you. Properly, I mean. I guess since I found you, technically, I met you first."

Great, his first impression of me was being covered in filth.

I looked up as he wrapped a bandana around his hand. "What were you doing out there anyway? And how did you get so far from the road?"

"I…I just got lost is all."

His questioning made me even more nervous. "I guess we'll know soon enough." He tucked the ends of the cloth under the folds. "Who would have guessed a little girl would be out in the middle of the swamp in a rain storm?" He chuckled, meeting my eyes. "It's a good thing we needed firewood last night."

Although I wanted to tell him my age since it was clear he couldn't have been much older than me, I kept my mouth shut.

He jumped over the railing, vaulting himself with one arm. He jumped clear over the roses. "I'm Hunter, by the way." He plucked one of the roses, pulled out a pocketknife, and trimmed off the thorns, before holding it out for me to take.

I took the rose, staring into his handsome face. He lifted one eyebrow, waiting for me to say something, but I stayed frozen.

Hello, he's waiting for me to say something.

I just stared into his eyes.

"Okay. Well, I've got chores to do." He shook his head with a smirk. "Have a good day, whatever your name is." He turned, whistling as he walked away.

"Jessica," I called out with my entire body leaned forward against the railing.

He turned around. "See ya later, Jess." He picked up an ax from the ground, hoisted it up onto his shoulder as if it weighed nothing, and disappeared into the trees.

The static electricity in the air was back and danced before me, just like all the times my mother or Seth had burst into my room and made me sit up fast, causing the fireflies to appear— only this was more pleasing.

What is that?

The pins and needles stabbed me all over, although I enjoyed the feeling. "I'm definitely staying."

Ghosts in the Wind

In the first few weeks, I barely had time to breathe. Miss Mabel was smart to keep me on as a laborer. There was a lot of work to do, and with Hunter gone during the daytime, the five of us worked the soil and planted seeds in the garden behind the old shack.

Two weeks became two months, but I barely noticed how fast time had moved. Soon, the harvesting would start, and she would need me for that as well. I liked feeling needed. They treated me more like a family member than the hired help—well, all except Joseph, who either bossed me around or stayed clear from me, but I tried not to let it bother me.

The thoughts of leaving had faded until the night of the storm.

My fears came in the fierce winds and paraded in the shadows outside. The wind howled through the cracks of the floor boards and doors, creating a long screeching sound. Outside, a tree branch scratched back and forth against the window. The sound reminded me of my mother's long fingernails against the top of the metal machine that kept my father alive. I shuddered, pulling the covers tight against my body. Another shadow danced in disguise in the bright flashes of light, followed by the cracking thunder. A dark silhouette, looking more like a cloaked man, appeared in the low glow of the porch light. It stood brazen, looking right at me. I quickly yanked the covers over my head, feeling the rush of blood flowing throughout my body. My mother's small but irritating voice echoed in the back of my mind. *You're being way too dramatic, Jessica.*

Slowly removing the covers from my eyes, I glanced over at Hunter asleep in his bed.

Although I only really saw him on Sundays when the preacher would come, Hunter's mere presence calmed my spirit of dread. I felt safe with him near. But something else was at work, something even he couldn't help me with and the reason I woke in the first place. I needed to go outside to brave the absolute darkness in the wind, the rain, with the creatures, and whatever else might be out there, to use the outhouse. The thought occurred to me, if I woke Hunter by accident, he'd walk me out, but then I'd wake everyone else too.

Just hold it!

I tried for as long as I could before sitting up and stepping into my boots. At the back door, a lantern burned low for just such an occasion.

Nothing is going to hurt me. I've been there and back before plenty of times alone.

My hands trembled putting on a raincoat. Then, taking the lantern, I peered into the blackness. It wasn't the fear of the dark making me tremble but what might be in the dark waiting. A vision of my mouth covered over by a hand as Seth dragged my body across the swamp, scrolled through my mind.

Seth knows how to get rid of a body.

I shook off the image and stepped into the night.

The wind continued to shriek a high-pitched, whistling sound, piercing through my ears. I held tightly on to the back porch door so it wouldn't blow off or slam shut. Once it shut, I stayed close to the house, as it protected me from the full force of the wind and slanting rain. At the edge of the house, I turned to leave the shelter of the eaves and made a run for shed. The wind blew out the lantern's flame. Nothing was visible, including the outhouse.

My hair continued to whip at my eyes as I stumbled in the dark with my hands outstretched in front of me. Seconds felt more like minutes, but finally my hand found the familiar handle on the outhouse. I pulled it, but it wouldn't open. The wind, blowing even harder, wrestled with me. "Come on!" I yelled, pulling with both hands. The door swung open. I heard a crack, but the door was still intact. Once inside, I gave it one good pull with all my might, and a lot of luck, to get it shut.

I plopped down to take care of business and closed my eyes. In my heightened state of observing everything around me, I didn't want to deal with whatever might be in there with me. Just the thought of little, hairy creatures with eight legs dangling over my head, webs in each corner of the ceiling, and the eyes of insects looking in my direction made my skin crawl. I should be grateful for the hissing and whistling of the storm. It was all I could hear and not anything scurrying about.

Bam! Bam! Bam!

A bang at the back of outhouse made me jump, and I pulled up my undergarments. Another thump rattled the structure. I placed my hand reluctantly against the wall where the sound came from. No longer afraid of the insects around me, I opened my eyes and placed my ear alongside my hand. I felt another thump against my cheek. It jolted me back. Not wanting to waste any more time, I turned around and fumbled to get the lock undone.

It took me a moment, but as soon as the door flung open, I ran as fast as my legs would go without looking back. The feeling someone was running after me make me too scared to look for sure.

Panicked and confused at where I ended up, I called out. "Where are you, shack?" I stopped running to extended my arms straight to feel my way back.

Finally, the tips of my fingers felt the porch railing, and I let out a big huff of air. I climbed under the railing to sit on the swing. No one seemed to be following me, or they would have caught me. I laughed and placed my head in my hands. The shadows chasing me were gone, if they had existed at all.

No more liquids late at night for me.

A strong gust of wind swept over the patio, chilling me down to my bones. I went inside and back into my warm bed.

"Now don't I feel silly," I said to myself, looking over at Miss Mabel sleeping in her rocker with an old, crocheted blanket draped across her shoulders.

I focused on the throw with its fall colors of brown, gold, and amber. Beautiful as it was, it was worn down with loose and broken yarn dangling from it. The old woman shifted in her seat before noticing the low embers. She bent down to add another log to the red-hot coals. The wood caught, illuminating the room. She turned to glance around the room before pushing herself up by the arms of the chair. She walked through the aisle of beds, stopping at May to tuck the covers around her, before returning to her chair. She yawned, rocked back and forth, and hummed a tune.

Soon, my eyelids felt heavy, and I drifted off to sleep.

Dreams had been scarce since my arrival in the swamp. I was thankful for that since most were not pleasant. But the ghosts of my past loomed in the familiar sounds of the winds, bringing my nightmare somewhere new.

It was a dream. I knew it. The soft, squishy ground of the swamp was under my bare feet. Everything shimmered, in the moonlight, like a reflection on the water. Stepping farther into the magical setting, something hard and prickly wrapped around my ankle. It tugged me down into the soil up to my knees. I fought to free myself, but nothing worked. I looked around for something to grab on to and saw the moss-covered vines hanging down from the trees. I reached up, but only the tips of my fingers could touch them. A hot breeze, with the stench of rotten eggs, swirled around me. I gagged, even though I managed to wiggle one leg from the muck, and then the other.

A line of dazzling light filtered in through the canopy of cypress, maple, and pine in a star-like pattern, blinding me. A silhouette of a man, in the middle of the light, appeared in front of me. Instantly, I wanted to be near the figure. I desired it more than anything else in the world, even more than a real family or being rid of Seth for good. I was drawn to it like a magnet to a refrigerator.

I tried to move faster, but the ground wasn't going to give me up so easily. No matter how much I tried to stay above ground, the further my body sank until I was waist deep in a thick, tar-like chasm. I couldn't move any further.

Something soft and smooth swirled up and down my calf. I looked down to see the ground had changed, but I still couldn't move. The muck hardened around my waist like ice forming on top of a lake and looked more like black glass. I could see a creature moving around my legs. The serpent was long and narrow. Every time it touched my skin, a pleasing shockwave moved up my body. I felt almost hypnotized by it, leaving me with a desire to join the creature below.

A strong, sour smell drew my attention above my head. A giant hand reached down through a thick, gray mist. The familiar smell brought me sorrow, followed by pain. I reached out to the hand, even though my senses told me not to. But at least I could pull myself out of the mess and out of the dream. I hoped.

The bright light waiting for me at the end of the glass, flared up. A smile broke through the silhouette, filling me with love. "Are you waiting for me?" I called out, reaching for him. "I need your help."

He didn't respond, but continued to blind me with his smile.

The serpent tied my legs together pulling me down farther. I looked around again for something to grasp before the creature could get me into its den. The giant hand extended down, only inches from my face. I strained to see the face of the person who was my only option.

I screamed.

"Jessie."

I felt Hunter's hand on my face as he gently and quietly woke me. "Bad dream?" he asked in a whisper, sweeping away the hair stuck to my cheek.

I nodded, breathing in the woody pine smell lingering on him from stacking firewood.

"Scoot over," he said, sitting on the edge of my bed with his own blankets tightly wrapped around his body. He propped his pillow against the headboard and sat up straight.

My heart sped up, which had nothing to do with the dream.

"Some night," he said. "I'll have to inspect for damage in the morning. Hope it's not too bad." He paused. "When May can't sleep, I tell her stories." He chuckled. "Puts her to sleep every time."

"I know you do, but I can never hear what you're saying to her."

"I don't want to wake anyone else in the room, so I'm especially quiet. The trick is to speak directly into the ear. So—"

His arm went around my shoulders. I leaned against him, letting one ear rest near his heart just like I saw May do and the other ear ready to listen.

Please stop shivering. Don't get the wrong idea about this. Remember, he does this with May all the time. He treats me the same as a six-year-old.

"Let's see," the air from his mouth tickled my ear.

"How do you feel about history?"

"Sure," I said, trying hard to breath slowly.

Hunter's voice was soothing, comforting, and when he spoke, his tone caressed my soul. I felt safe and serene. I longed for everything about him in a way I didn't fully understand.

But I can't stay here, not forever. Seth would find me.

"How about the Cherokee Indians who live in this very spot?" he asked.

"Lived," I corrected.

"Yeah, lived, that's what I meant, many years ago." His hand shifted from my shoulder to rest on my arm, sending my entire body into a quiver.

"Cold?" He pulled up the blanket over my exposed arm and placed his hand on top of the quilt.

Are there such things as fairy tales? My father wanted me to believe each one had some truth to it. I could relate to Cinderella the most with my mother as the wicked stepmother. Could this new life be my glass slipper? Could Hunter be my Prince Charming? Now I really am being ridiculous.

"The Cherokee Indians lived on this land for hundreds of years before the Puritans came here to settle. They were a peaceful people, living out their lives according to centuries of beliefs and customs handed down from generation to generation. The women spent their days doing domestic things like cleaning, preparing meals, sewing clothes, and making baskets out of the river cane that grew abundantly along the riverside.

"The men were the providers and protectors of the tribe. Not only did they hunt and protect, but they also trained the young boys to be men. But their lives would soon change as the white folk entered their world." Hunter paused with a big yawn as the wind continued to whistle through the cracks in the walls.

"At first, it was a good thing. The first white people wanted to help the Cherokee. They brought with them medicine and food. They taught them to read and how to govern. The Indians in return taught them about the land and how to plant crops. Eventually, the tribe embraced their friendship, and as time went on, the Puritans shared their God with them. Soon after, the tribe accepted their God as their own."

"But didn't they have their own gods? Didn't they believe god existed in all living things?" I asked, remembering a book I had read on Indian beliefs.

"They believed in one creator at one point, bits and pieces of an even older belief. So really, they transitioned back to the original belief. We were all created by the same God. We all come from the seed of Adam."

"Oh." I squirmed uncomfortably at the conversation of religion. "Go on."

"Times changed when gold was found in the swamp. The white man wanted the land for themselves. They felt the Indians had no right to it, so they began suggesting to government officials that the land was too good for the Native Americans, and that the white people deserved it more. Some didn't want to wait on the government and raided the land. Many on both sides died." Hunter yawned again. "Eventually, the Cherokee were forced off their land to the new land no one wanted. The path to the barren, dry land is known as the Trail of Tears." Hunter stroked his hand along the outside of the blanket where my arm laid underneath.

"Jessie?" he said in a faint whisper.

"Yes?"

"Shouldn't you be asleep by now?" He chuckled, softly stroking my arm, sending a minor quake through my body.

"I'm not tired." A knot rose up in my throat. "Your story isn't over. It can't be." It was so sad.

Those poor people.

"I'll stop for now and continue it another time. You really should get some sleep." He squeezed my arm, gently sending another wave of sensations throughout my body.

It's late, and who am I kidding? Why would this person want anything to do with me anyway, even if he did see me as a woman? No. I need to see him the same way he sees me, like a sibling. It's a safe and less-complicated feeling. No one would get hurt or stop my departure when the time comes.

It was easy to convince my logical mind. Not so easy to convince my illogical heart.

The haunted howls and screeches, along with the ghosts in the wind, had gone. They left the little shack quiet once more. Only the rhythm of my heartbeat echoed between my ears as I watched Hunter return to his bed.

"Good night, Jessica," he whispered in the dark.

A Lazy Saturday Morning

The bright sunshine streamed in through the open windows, allowing the humid and sticky air to linger in the room. For a moment, I wondered if the whole encounter with Hunter the night before was just another dream.

In the kitchen, Hunter and Miss Mable worked around each other like two dancers. They didn't get in each other's way but operated together in a way that looked perfectly coordinated.

Everyone else in the room still slept, so I grabbed a change of clothes. The perfect opportunity to use the washroom, before May. She liked to splash the water right out of the tub, leaving me inches of leftover water. It was gross, but I didn't complain.

My mother would have complained, but what didn't she complain about?

Once in the washroom, I wasted no time, climbing into the warm tub. I leaned my head against the side and tried to focus on something other than the return of my mother's words in my head. Her voice grated inside the walls of my skull.

Do you have any idea what you've put me through? What Seth and his father have done for us? You owe me your life.

"Shut up," I whispered, before getting out of the tub to dry off.

As I dressed, I thought about the dream. I remembered screaming but not what made me scream. The more I thought about it, the more it was like the evening fog rolling in from the ocean, covering everything in its path. Something was coming, but what?

"Jess!" a small voice pleaded at the door.

Opening the door, May was doing a little dance. "Sorry. I didn't know I was taking so long. It's all yours." I stepped out.

May rushed passed me, shaking her tiny, impatient finger at me before she closed the door behind her.

The aroma from the kitchen drew me there next. I peeked over Miss Mabel's shoulders to see what was in the cast-iron pan on the stove. A whiff of the Applewood bacon overpowered my sense of politeness, and I reached to snag a piece.

Quick as a humming bird, Miss Mabel whirled around with the spatula and tapped my hand. "No, no, yous get. Go be useful and check the mailbox. I don't remember if I'd done it in a while. I's so absentminded these days." She paused. "That's if the mailbox wasn't blown to bits." She winked and spun around to scold Hunter, whose eyes were on me. Her eyes narrowed at him. "Boy, yous gonna burn them eggs!"

Hunter snickered. "I won't." He winked at me.

I felt a flash of heat on my cheeks. "Sure. I'll go check."

May bounded out of the washroom already bathed and dressed, wrapping her wet hair up into a bun.

"Did yous scrub behind them ears?" Miss Mabel screeched, keeping her eyes on Hunter's skillet. She sighed, "Never mind, just go with her, please."

"Where are we going?"

"The mailbox," I answered, crossing over to the front of the shack to open the screen door for May. I glance back as Hunter faced Miss Mabel.

He folded his arms against his chest. "Now what did I do?"

Miss Mabel glanced in my direction, but I pretended not to be listening. She whispered back, "Last night?"

What about last night?

May pulled my hand off the door. "Race you," she said, darting off the porch, leaving me in her dust.

I stood just outside the door to hear his answer, but had no such luck.

May stopped almost halfway down the road to yell at me. "Come on!" she whined.

I ran to catch up to her. "What was that about? Was Hunter in trouble for something?"

The little girl shrugged her shoulders. "Ready, set—"

"How about we just walk?" I giggled at the hyper child, who couldn't be still for a moment.

"Fine," she said in a pout.

We walked about a mile to the mailbox. There was quite a bit of damage from the storm all around us. Branches from the trees were snapped off and lying all across the ground like matchsticks. I was grateful to be walking on top of the branches instead of wading through the oozing quicksand that would have swallowed our shoes.

We came across a wide and thick puddle. The sun reflected off it, creating a glassy, mirror-like appearance. Below the surface, a long, round object wiggled. I grabbed a broken tree limb and dipped the broken end into the pool of dirt.

Like the dream.

My pulse raced, digging the stick around until the creature looped its body around it. I pulled it up slowly, not letting it escape. It was big, long, black, and round. I couldn't believe the size of the earthworm. It was a least four times as big as an average worm, covered in a thick, tar-like mud.

"What are you doing?" May asked. "Are you listening to me?"

I let out a nervous laugh and placed the worm down, away from the puddle.

"Sorry, May. I guess I wasn't. Doesn't that worm seem a bit larger than it should be?"

"I heard Miss Mabel say everything is different here than in the real world. The worms are great for the garden. She calls them natural gardeners."

"You mean like how we plant seeds one day, and the next day the plant is an inch tall?" That was strange, but Miss Mabel had said the soil was richer there than in most parts of the country. I fathomed it could be true, especially after Hunter's story. It took at least three weeks before I saw growth in anything I planted back home.

"Oh look. We're here." May pointed to the mailbox. "You know, I think it's going to be a lovely day."

I pulled down the rusty handle to peek inside. "Nothing in here."

"It's not like we get real mail anyway," May said with a stutter and looked at the ground. Her hands twisted behind her back.

"What you do mean, no real mail?"

"I'm not supposed to tell." She squirmed.

"What, you don't get mail? I'm not surprised being way out here."

The little girl shrugged her shoulders. "Don't tell that I told you or about the other thing."

"But you didn't tell me anything, May." I placed my hand on my hip. "Okay. I won't tell," I said, thinking maybe she'd read too many fairy tales. I wondered if she had ever been away from the swamp.

Like I had hardly been away from the mansion taking care of my dad.

"Thanks." She smiled.

"Well, I guess we'd better head back. I'll race you this time."

May loved to race, but it wasn't my reason for suggesting it. I was anxious to get back to find out why Hunter was in trouble.

"Go!" May said.

I took off faster than May, but a quarter into the race, she passed me. I laughed and then began to choke. I stopped to catch my breath, watching bits of water kicking up in the air behind May's feet.

The smell of breakfast loomed in the air and caused my stomach to growl loudly.

A sound came from behind me just beyond the trees along the road. I held my breath standing perfectly still to listen. A rustling of foliage came from behind. Unable to shake the image of the man standing outside of the widow, my body trembled. I crooked my head around to look behind me and on to the brush by the side of the road.

Nothing moved.

Then I heard foot fall, and it was getting louder.

Run!

My legs wouldn't move, but my heart pounded like jackhammer.

Someone grabbed my arm. I screamed, tripping over my feet and falling to the ground.

"Why did you stop?" May looked down at me with a puzzled expression.

My hands locked into a fist and I wished I had a brown bag handy. Instead I counted down, slowing my air intake, until I could answer her. "I...I needed to rest," I pushed my body off the ground. "I'm okay now."

I couldn't tell her the truth, and I felt horrible about it. She had her secrets. I had mine, although in all fairness, her secrets were more of a game, she was playing with me.

I took hold of her little hand, and we ran back to the shack.

By the time we got back, Miss Mabel and Hunter were back to talking about breakfast. I missed the entire conversation.

Shoot!

I stomped my foot on the ground. Miss Mabel looked up at me. "There wasn't any mail today." I said quickly.

Hunter noticed my flushed face and looked somewhat concerned. May told him about my earthworm. They laughed.

"Well you's better get yourself somethin' to eat. I heard that rumblin' all the way from the road. Don't worry. It's worm-free." She laughed, handing me a plate. She leaned to kissed my cheek before she sat at the kitchen table. Everyone bowed their heads. I continued out the door to the porch swing to avoid the praying.

Looking out into the tree line, I revisited my plan to leave.

How long can I stay here? How long before the evil finds me? Or has he already found me? I'm going to put everyone in danger.

"But I don't want to leave," I said to myself.

I scooped up some food on the fork and shoved the scrambled eggs, cooked in the bacon grease and topped with cheese, into my mouth. I gathered up another bite. The grits and hot biscuit were just as delicious.

Visions of my mother standing before me came, shaking her bony finger at me and reciting a monologue. *Can you imagine how many calories and grams of fat you're consuming? Are you trying to embarrass me? You're trying to ensure Seth won't want to marry you. I can't be expected to take care of you the rest of your life, Jessica. You have obligations, and certain things are expected from you!*

I shook my head and snarled at the vision.

"What were you just thinking about?" Hunter asked as he walked through the screen door to sit next to me.

I didn't answer and gestured at my mouth full of food.

"At least you're enjoying the breakfast."

"It's very good," I answered, hoping nothing fell out of my mouth while I talked.

"I'm glad you like it. You know, when you came here, you were a bit underweight."

I swallowed hard. "So what you're saying is I'm fat?" I had noticed a few days back the jeans I had arrived in were not as loose.

Hunter might have been the one talking to me, but it was my mother's voice calling me fat.

He laughed. "Far from it. Didn't you eat where you came from?"

I didn't answer, putting the fork down to scoop up more food. I bit at the outside of my lip and stayed quiet.

What? Get a hold of yourself. So he called me fat. It's silly to cry about that.

"You're not going to talk about your past. That's fine. I'll find out eventually." He chuckled, looking out to the trees. "I know people." He clicked his tongue against the inside of his cheek, making me smile. "At least I can get you to smile." His charming, enticing smile made me wish he was the kind of guy who would steal a kiss.

The sudden rush of emotions rendered me a klutz, and I dropped a fork full of eggs on my lap.

Hunter pretended not to notice. "You know we get sixty inches of rainfall each year?" He changed the subject as I brushed the food off my shirt and back on the plate. "The Okefenokee Swamp is pretty big. It's the largest swamp in Northern America with over two hundred different types of birds."

"I bet May has names for all of them too," I said, surprised my words came out more naturally and not like a blundering fool.

He chuckled. "It's possible. She loves all of God's creatures, but she especially loves birds."

"I think they love her too."

"God created all the birds and all the animals. He created the world and all the stars in the sky. He created all things uniquely and for a purpose. Most people, though, wouldn't see the swamp as anything more than a mud pit." He looked over in my direction again.

The God talk made me a little uncomfortable, but I could relate to what most people thought about swamps. I know my mother would think that. "Exactly why I came here."

"So you did come here on purpose." He grinned.

"I've read about a lot of places," I said, scooping a big portion of grits into my big mouth.

What I hadn't read about was it being a magical swamp, hidden from the rest of the world. I had felt as though I had stepped back in time, like an episode of *The Twilight Zone*. I knew it wasn't really a magical swamp, but it was easier to pretend with May, and I was getting quite good at pretending.

"The really dark areas creep me out, but the garden is beautiful," I added. "Peaceful."

"Not so peaceful where you came from?" he asked.

"No, it wasn't," I answered and looked down at my plate.

"And where was that?"

"Oh, all over. This home, that home," I said, tracing my fork around an empty plate.

"Here. Let me take your plate," he said as he got up.

The sweetest, brightest smile I had ever seen was on his face and it was hypnotic. I stared into his eyes, which took on a turquoise hue. My stomach felt like it had a thousand buzzing beetles bouncing around inside and traveling into my ears. I heard nothing else as they swarmed. He inched closer. I couldn't look away. My breath went in and out faster. I could feel the pulsating blood, flowing through me.

"Jess!" I heard May's demanding tone and jerked my head away, breaking the trance.

"I'm out here," I whispered while viewing Hunter in my peripheral vison. He winked before taking my plate into the house.

Stupid, Jess. Really stupid. From now on, avoid eye contact.

I replayed over in my mind what he said and what I said like a tape recorder.

Did I give too much away? Why should I be worried he might not think I was an orphan? Silly. Of course an orphan would have had a miserable life being in and out of homes with different families. How miserable would that have been? I sighed.

I envied the orphan, wishing I were her.

Hunter, in an almost singing voice, called to May, "She's out on the porch!" Seconds later, May was on the porch, holding a book in her hand.

Hunter returned with a sketchbook. He sat down on the top step of the porch, leaning his back against the railing, facing me. Of course, I wouldn't be able to see what he was drawing. I wondered if that was his intention.

Joseph stormed out of the house. He shot an angry look in my direction before he brushed passed Hunter.

"Joseph, come on! We'll play the game later, I promise." Hunter called to him in a playful way, reaching out for his leg.

He kicked Hunter's hand off his leg. "Yeah, you said that last week." He kept walking until he disappeared into the trees.

Hunter sighed and shook his head as he flipped open his book. Josephine came out with Miss Mabel carrying bundles of bright-colored balls of yarn. Miss Mabel was teaching her to knit.

Josephine looked over at me with an approving grin, letting me know she didn't share her brother's attitude directed at me.

I sighed, opening the book to the last chapter I had read. May listened to me read as Miss Mabel and Josephine began to knit and Hunter sketched.

That had become our typical Saturday except for Hunter's new desire to stay with us. Normally, he was off the porch tossing a ball with Joseph or wrestling with him in the tall, yellow grass. It had become clear to me why Joseph stomped off. Hunter wasn't spending any time with him, and he blamed me for it.

Joseph's issues hadn't stopped me from enjoying these lazy Saturday afternoons. After all, before the swamp, I loathed Saturdays because I was forced to spend time with Seth in exchanged to keep my father alive. I wondered if my father could see me, if he knew I had found a piece of happiness. Or was it more likely there wasn't any sort of afterlife, and he lay rotting away in the fancy coffin buried beneath the earth?

Looking over at Hunter, I was glad for the events that led me there, even more so meeting a decent, attractive young man, whether or not he saw me as anything but a child. I continued to read with May's head resting in my lap for a few hours or so before she grabbed the book out of my hands and ran.

"Let's go explore," she said, looking at Hunter.

He flipped the front cover over his drawing. "I suppose."

May took off in a run.

I stood to chase her, but the smell of lunch stewed in the air.

Hunter shouted after her. "You should eat lunch first."

Wow. Is it really noon?

Stranger in the Clearing

May and I started out for our adventure after lunch. It was frequently just the two of us on these little escapades through the marsh. Hunter had come a few times, but it upset both Joseph and May. I knew why Joseph hated me and had hardly said more than two words to me since I'd arrived, but with May, it surprised me.

"May, how come you never want Hunter to come?"

She shrugged her shoulders.

Josephine never wanted to come either. She said walking around the swamp was a waste of time when she could be practicing her knitting. She was such a perfectionist, determined to complete at least one blanket to donate to the local orphanage. Time and again, I watched her unravel what she had done and throw the needles to the ground in frustration. She'd then pick them back up and start over. I admired that quality about her. She wouldn't give up.

"I think today we should look for unicorns," May teased with a wink, stepping down from the porch.

"Don't yous go too far in today, May," Miss Mabel said in her singsong voice. "Ya hear me?"

"Yes, Miss Mabel," she said before taking off in a run.

"Hey," I called after her, but she was already weaving in and out of the trees.

May and I ran fast against the peat moss, which felt similar to stepping on squishy sponges. The moss had absorbed the rain from the night before and was squirting out as our feet pounded hard on it. The little twigs covering the ground kicked up in the air and landed back softly on the earth behind May's feet. The trees were so dense in that part of the forest, just her getting a few steps ahead of me, made her disappear in the foliage.

May knew her way around the swamp, but I worried about the dangerous animals and reptiles living in the swamp. There were creatures that could eat up a little six-year-old in one bite. The cottonmouth snakes frequently made appearances on our little jaunts. Their greenish gray-and-black-striped skin easily camouflaged them in the trees and bushes. On my first trip into the swamp with May, I barely noticed a cottonmouth as it slithered past my feet. A few weeks ago as I leaned against a cottonwood tree, one came within inches from my face. Its body was curled up on top of a low branch, ready to strike out. Then something bizarre happened. The snake slowly unwound its body and dropped to the ground, where it scurried off into the bushes. I remembered thinking, *It must have found a better prey.*

My next encounter, I might not be so lucky.

May and I continued to wander deeper and deeper into the thickest part of the forest. The chirping sounds of birds were distant and hollow. Two black beetles flew overhead and landed on a tree stump a few feet in front of me. They circled each other before fluttering their wings to create a high-pitched resonance, grating the lining in my ear.

Staying behind May, I continued to follow her down the path. Vines, covered in a lush, dark-green moss, draped from tree to tree. The rain had made them heavy, so they hung close to the ground, blocking out most of the sun like a thick heavy blanket. The further in we went, the denser the vegetation, blocking out more of the sunlight. Only slender lines of light through the canopy, made it possible to see.

Why are we continuing to move forward in this creepy area?

I thought about those movies where I've yelled at the people, "Don't go in there!" The thought of enormous, hairy spiders dangling from a massive web came to mind.

Darn Seth for making me watch those types of movies with him.

"May," I called in a shaky voice. "Do you think we are going too far?"

May scampered ahead of me.

A new type of foliage and wild life I had not seen before stirred in the most mysterious part of the swamp yet. A thin layer of white fog floated close to the ground. I wondered if May knew where we were as she hopped from plant, to amphibian, to bugs, and then to birds very excitedly. I assumed the answer was no.

"May," I called louder.

I watched a blue heron land on a boulder. Determined to get May's attention, he squawked at her until she noticed him. She tippy-toed over to him while whispering something I couldn't make out. The bird stretched out his blue-gray wings, snapping his elongated, orange bill into the air.

"Watch out he doesn't bite you."

His neck, curved like a question mark. He turned to looked at me. His eyes were similar to a dartboard with the bull's-eye perfectly centered. The bird shook its neck and went back focusing on May.

"Sh." May motioned for me to come to her.

She placed one finger against her lips, squatting to eye level with the heron. She watched the bird with such stillness I could hardly believe it was May. I leaned against a tree, close enough to the bird to make her happy. I stared up through the tall trees, worried I couldn't see the color of the sky. The sharp smell of a lit match carried in the air and jolted my senses. A feeling of uneasiness crept through me followed by the urge to run. My eyes wandered thinking someone was watching us. The smell surrounded me, squeezing out the breathable air.

There I go again, thinking someone is watching us. Bring on the panic attack.

A gust of air spun around us, weaving in and out of the trees. Someone moaned in the distance, making the hair on my neck stiffen. The bird took off, flying inches above my head, in a flurry.

"Someone is coming," May snapped, standing to her feet.

Cicadas, which we heard mostly at night, began to buzz and clack.

"I think we should go back to the house." I took a few steps in the direction we had come from. "We've been out here a while, and it's getting dark."

May looked over at me and nodded in agreement.

We headed back the way we had come. We ran, jumping over decaying logs and thick foliage while we weaved in and out of the trees. Finally, ahead of May we saw a break in the trees. Although it didn't look like the passage we had come through, I was relieved to see the bright sunlight streaming through. May went first through the opening, between two oak trees. I followed.

The brightness of the sun, made it hard for my eyes to make out where I was. I turned away from the blinding light, blinking several times until I could make out May, standing petrified.

"What is it?"

She lifted her hand and pointed behind me. I looked, blocking May with my body.

In the middle of the field, surrounded by trees dripping with black moss, the sun's rays shone down on three figures. The yellow wheatgrass swayed around them in the hot breeze, sounding like paper being wadded into a ball. Slowly, the light faded from a blazing brightness to a gray. The breeze gusted, bending the long blades of grass close to the ground.

The swamp isn't dry. Am I imagining this? Am I dreaming?

Regardless, I focused my attention back on the strangers, starting with the one in the middle wearing a black hood, speaking to the man on his right, only they were too far away for me to hear what they were saying. He then turned his head to the man on his left, who rocked back and forth on his heels, just glaring at me. His long fire-red hair brushed against his shoulders. The cloaked man calmed him by placing his hand on his chest before all three trudged in our direction.

As they moved, the condition around us changed again. The air felt serene and inviting with the return of the light breeze blowing across the landscape. I smelled lilies. And it was unusual not to hear birds, insects, or other such creatures' living in the swamp. The only sound came from the wrestling of the dry grass.

Just your imagination.

May took my hand into hers, squeezing it hard as the men got closer. She tugged me back, but I couldn't tear my eyes off the man in the middle, who was about the same age as Hunter.

"Hello, May," the cloaked one called out.

So, he wasn't a stranger after all.

His voice echoed in my ears, and I wanted him to continue to speak. His tone was appealing and somewhat familiar.

I've felt this way before. Yes. Someone with no interest in me and thinks I'm a child. Who was it?

I really couldn't remember. Glancing back at May, I barely remembered who she was as I turned my focus back to the men. All I knew at that moment was I wanted to touch the cloaked man. I took a step forward. May stepped out in front of me, facing the men. She glared at the one in the middle until he shifted his eyes to her. May shut her eyes as though his glare could hurt her.

"Who's this beautiful woman friend of yours? You know it's rude not to introduce people. Surely they've taught you manners."

May did not reply.

The stranger stretched out his hand but stopped, wanting me to come to him. And I wanted desperately to see his face. I could only see the jet-black hair curved along his jaw.

May anticipated me, pushing her body against me, but I needed to go. The urge to move forward at any cost, including leaving May behind, grew stronger.

"Don't look into his eyes," she whispered, still blocking me from advancing. "Don't trust your feelings."

The stranger grinned as though he could hear her soft words, only he didn't remove his eyes off mine nor did I listen to May.

Mesmerized by spinning hues, I couldn't decide what color they were. Much like watching a spinning pinwheel, it was easy to get lost in the illusion.

May whispered again, pushing me back. "He's trying to control you. We should leave, now."

"It's okay. He's not going to harm us," I whispered.

The man huffed, moving closer.

May dug her heels firmly into the ground, not letting me go any farther. She crossed her arms over her chest.

The dark-haired one chuckled, and it echoed along the meadow. I focused on his face for any sign of familiarity.

Why I am I not afraid? I should be.

My curiosity was unhinged. If May wasn't standing like a statue in front of me, I would have sprinted forward.

I looked down at her, breaking the stare with the stranger. Blood rushed to my brain, and the ground stirred around me. I swallowed the uneasy mass back down, got down on my knees, and turned May's trembling body to face me. Her eyes wouldn't meet mine. Instead, she looked at the trees behind us.

The crunch of the grass beneath the stranger's feet stopped. From the corner of my eye, I saw his black shoes were only inches from us. Lifting my eyes, my heart pounded. The blood in my head rushed to my face, and the air felt thick with each breath. His black hair danced around his strong, angular jaw, and his eyes were deep brown with sharp auburn specks, which reflected like glitter. He was beautiful.

Just like Hunter.

He held me in a trance, from which I didn't want to escape from. His hand reached out to touch mine. His eyes stayed locked on mine as he brought my hand up to his lips, kissing the top so gently it felt more like the touch of the breeze.

My face burned, and I saw electricity in the air.

Please, don't faint in front of him. He'll think I'm a little girl too.

The outsider broke his gaze. A big smirk formed on his perfectly kissable lips as he released my hand. If it hadn't been for

May still holding on to me, I would have gone crashing down on the hard ground.

The man laughed. "Hunter, so good to see you after all these years."

"Is it?" I heard a cynical, winded tone reply. "You won't be saying that after I hurt you."

No. That can't be my Hunter. He'd never hurt anyone.

Sure enough, Hunter stepped out of the trees behind us. He was out of breath and gasping for air. He bent down, placing his hands on his knees. After a moment, he stood tall, taking a stance similar to what May had done. He shone, standing there surround by the grayness swallowing the daylight. With his jaw clinched and straight lips, something bad was about to happen.

The stranger walked backward toward the other two strangers, who paced back and forth like hungry lions in a cage. They were ready to fight—especially the redhead.

May appeared relieved by Hunter's presences and no longer shook against me. But his eyes pierced like tiny daggers through me, making me feel like a child who had done something wrong.

But why? I'm not a child. I'm not your little sister to be told what to do. How can he not see I'm an adult?

I wanted to scream out. Instead I sighed.

This guy doesn't see me as a child. He called me a beautiful woman, and I liked it.

Hunter wrinkled up his forehead and shook his head, briefly releasing the tension in his face.

"You could try." The man answered, breaking Hunter's stare.

Hunter marched past May and me, moving closer to the three figures. "Aren't you a little farther north than you should be?"

One corner of the stranger's lip curled up, and his eyebrows pushed together as though he were trying to read in a poorly lit room. "Really?" the stranger asked, as if something amusing had been said. He looked at me, then back to Hunter.

Hunter didn't reply, but narrowed his eyes on the stranger.

"We have every right to go where we please." The stranger held up his arms. "If you have a problem, you know who to take it up with."

"You know what I mean," Hunter pressed.

The redhead snickered and flipped his hair back with a quick whip of his neck. The other stranger looked down at the ground while wringing his hands in a frantic circle.

"Well, if you must know, we were retrieving a new family member. It's nice having family to support you. It's lovely so many are willing to join our cause. Lots of souls to recruit." He put his arm around the hooded boy. "Say hello to my friend, Charles." The stranger held up boy's face.

I couldn't see anything from where I was.

The stranger, changing his tone, twisted his head to look past Hunter. "And you are?"

Hunter moved to block his view of me. "She's no concern of yours. May, take her straight home," he said with no emotion.

She nodded, taking my hand.

"Wait," I said, looking down at May, feeling irritated.

"Please, Jess. Please," May whispered, stroking my hand and pleading with her eyes.

"So you speak for her as well?" the stranger asked. "You know you can't ha—"

"I think it's time you go back to where you came from," Hunter replied with his lips barely open, and his jaw extended. "Just leave."

The stranger smiled.

"Please, Jess." May whimpered again, tugging on my hand.

"Okay," I spat out, but I didn't move.

The two men stared at each other. Their body language seemed to be responding to a conversation that they weren't having. Something weird was going on.

May forcefully jerked on my hand.

Slowly walking across the grassy field, everything fell into slow motion. The crackling of the yellow grass breaking beneath my feet, the air on my face lifting the strands of my hair as if they were weightless, even the aromatic aroma of violets, lingered longer with each breath. It was delightful.

May and I stepped to the edge of the meadow, and everything was back to normal.

I smiled and took in a deep breath. "Did you feel that?" I whispered to May.

"Feel what? We need to go," she answered.

Well, whatever it was, I felt great.

"There's no need to be so impolite," the stranger said to Hunter and called out in my direction. "Well, it was nice to almost meet you." He winked. "Another time, perhaps?"

A snarl came from Hunter's lips. He looked ready to squeeze the life out of the stranger.

May pulled on me until we were out of the meadow completely and back into another forest of trees. As we moved farther away, the voices faded. I wanted to go back to listen, but May kept taking me farther and farther away from them.

Why am I being forced to leave? I didn't do anything. That guy didn't do anything. I don't get it.

Irritation gnawed at me the closer we got to the shack. I entertained the idea of meeting the stranger in secret. After all, I wasn't in any danger, and I didn't belong to anyone.

Not yet, anyway.

I'm Not a Little Girl

The time it took to get back to the shack seemed much longer than it should have. May walked unusually slow, but we finally reached the familiar area. As we approached, I heard Hunter's voice coming from the house.

How did he beat us back?

May stopped, bending down to tie her shoe.

Hunter's voice sounded angry, and he was arguing with Miss Mabel. The sharpness shocked me. They were both loud. The conversation was not only loud, but stern and serious as they talked over each other.

Not able to make out any actual words, I walked faster, passing May. "Why are they arguing?"

"Hey, I think I see something in the bushes." May pointed out.

"There is nothing there. We need to get inside. It's getting dark." I shook my head, willing to let her stay there if she didn't move.

I wanted to hear what was going on, but by the time I made it up the steps, they had stopped talking. May sprinted up onto the porch, being loud and obnoxious. "Race you to the kitchen. I'm winning," she called back to me.

No point now. They stopped talking the minute they knew we could hear them.

They didn't want me know who the stranger was or why Hunter appeared angered by him. May knew something too but pretended not to know.

And I have my secrets, which are way worse. What right do I have to be mad about it?

But I was.

Looking through the screen door, Miss Mabel swatted Hunter's arm. "Hush now. It will all work out." She leaned over to kiss him on the cheek.

Straddling the back of a kitchen chair, he rubbed his arm briskly back and forth where she struck him.

"Well I bet you three are pretty hungry." Miss Mable, with potholders in both hands, bent down, opening the oven door to pull out foil-wrapped plates. She placed each one on the table.

Hunter fixated on me as I entered the house. A look of sadness made me uncomfortable, but I didn't look away. He sighed, shifting his gaze back at Miss Mabel before he stood, placing his hands in his jean pockets and sulking out of the room. I sat down at the table. With so many questions in my head, I wondered if Miss Mabel would tell me the answers if I asked. An especially pressing question was what was wrong with Hunter, and why had he looked at me as though he pitied me?

I pushed around the food with my finger while May gobbled up her supper. Without saying anything, May got up, washed her dish, and disappeared out the back door.

May, silent? She hasn't been silent since the first day Miss Mabel introduced us.

Even though the pasta smelled good, I had no appetite. Instead, I twirled the noodles around the fork, thinking about the stranger.

Who is he? He called me a beautiful woman. How did he know what I wanted to hear? Is he still standing in the meadow now? Waiting for me to return?

A warm, tingling feeling fluttered up. The anger I had for being treated like a child faded. The desire to see the stranger again, stayed on my mind. Even though the others wouldn't approve, I'd find a way to make it happen.

May did say, "Don't trust your feelings." But she is only six! She knows nothing of a woman's heart.

I got up, scraped my plate into the dog bowl, washed, and placed it back in the dark brown cupboard. I needed to escape my thoughts—I needed a book.

The light of the day had dimmed, so I lit the kerosene lamp, hanging next to the back door, and grabbed a book from Miss Mabel's collection. I headed for the long swing on the front porch.

"Oh," I said, startled.

Hunter rocked in Miss Mabel's chair, his eyes staring out beyond the setting sun. I stood at the doorway, watching the line of sweat trickle down the side of his face. Even without the bright rays of lights beating down, it was going to be hot night.

The crickets and cicadas filled the air with their songs. The soft strum of the cricket's legs rubbing together along with the sharp rattling of the cicadas made a calming combination. The creaking of the rocking chair, back and forth, added to the orchestra's recital.

I turned to go back inside.

"Don't go," he said, still rocking back and forth, not moving his head.

The resonance in his voice compelled me to stay. I hung the lantern on the farthest hook from him and sat on the swing, curling one leg under the other with the book on my lap.

The music in the air softened, and my thoughts of the stranger changed to Hunter. His silhouette, even in the growing darkness, made me want to be closer. His long face and stern jaw didn't move. He seemed to be in deep thought. He arched his back, then brought his face into his hands resting his elbows on his knees. He stayed like that for several minutes.

Could the stranger really cause him this much grief?

I wanted to ask, but what would I ask? Everything that came to mind was in favor of the stranger. I wanted to defend someone I didn't even know. It was so illogical.

Hunter took a deep breath, stretching his arms up. He stood without a word, glancing over at me. The light of the lantern flickered across his face, as he forced a smile, sighed, and then walked out into the dark, moonless night. I watched him until he completely disappeared.

Go after him. The stranger is out there too.

My mind felt like a horse race with all my thoughts lined up behind a gate. They all kicked-up in their stalls, not wanting to be confined to such a small space. Then the race began, and they took off. The first one out of the gate was my mother as she clawed her way past everyone, followed by the life I'd left, snickering at my current situation. Gliding by was the stranger, dark and mysterious, until out of nowhere, it was Hunter ahead by a mile.

A silly childlike thought, described my mind perfectly.

Opening the book, I let the written word take me somewhere enchanting.

Hours had passed since Hunter had stepped off the porch. I closed the book and laid my head down on the seat. Before long, sleep took over.

I woke to a strange sound in the distance. I got up, rubbed my eyes, and walked into the trees, not thinking about the dangers of the swamp at night. I then found myself somewhere I had been before—the opening in the swamp where I had seen the three strangers. At least, I thought it was the same, but when I looked closer, it seemed different. The ground was covered in a stiff, dark-brown grass instead of the dry, yellow grass. My bare feet sank with each step, the indentions filling up with water.

A dark, masculine silhouette of a man sat on one end of a black, decaying log in the center of a clearing.

"Hunter?" I whispered.

A long chuckle followed my word as the figure gestured for me to come closer.

Like being in a fantasy, everything invited me to come. The cool air swirling around my body, the soothing sound of rustling leaves, and the sweet and luscious smell of flora touched all my senses.

Walking about halfway to the log, the atmosphere changed. A damp fog crept in from the south, but the air felt dry in my throat. A strong wind came up and shook the tree limbs, tossing them around as though a storm approached. The smell was no longer sweet. It was hot and bitter, burning my nostrils with every breath. I continued forward, but the steady ground no longer existed. It was like walking on Plexiglas covering over a deep well. Movement under the glass stopped me in my tracks to take a closer look. A hand reached up and struck the glass with such a force it wobbled beneath me. The force should have split the covering, but it didn't. Looking to the figure for an explanation, he stood and glided in my direction, barely touching the ground.

Or is he touching the ground at all? He's floating like a ghost. I should run.

In my heart and mind, I wanted to. I wanted to run back to the shack. I started moving toward the figure, but not of my own free will. Trying to resist, I fought to move in the opposite direction. Nothing was working.

Wake up, wake up. I'm dreaming. This isn't real. Wake up.

I heard a song which seemed to be coming from behind me.

Miss Mabel's voice rang out behind the thick-footed trees. Her melody grew louder, and I saw a white glow coming from behind the tree line. "Raise me up, Lord. Raise me up into Your light. I will cast out the devil from Your holy place. Raise me up, Lord. Raise me up," she sang.

Another hand with long, red fingernails reached up and clawed at the glass below my feet. It was the same color my mother use to wear—fire-red.

How can this be happening? Why am I not waking up?

The figure drifted closer, staring into my enlarged, frightened eyes. His eyes swirled, and I was hypnotized, paralyzed from resisting. A part of me, the part that believed the stranger in the clearing was the figure coming for me, wanted to be near him. If

I could just see his face clearly and know for sure, my imagination would stop playing tricks on me.

No, I'd just need to wake up.

Pinching the underside of my arm, I closed my eyes, hoping it would wake me, but as soon as I open my eyes, the dark figure was closer, gliding along the glass-like surface. I pinched several more times until a purple circle formed.

The figure's long, skeleton-like fingers with white fingernails, extended to me.

I couldn't breathe. I broke the eye contact again, allowing me to step backward, but then something below grabbed my foot. Looking down, the glass was gone, and the hand tugged me into the black nothingness. A burning sensation covered me as I screamed.

"Sh." I felt someone's hands on my face.

Confused, I flipped quickly on my back to look up. It was still dark, and the lantern no longer burned.

"Sorry," Hunter whispered.

"It was dream," I said. "Just a dream." I breathed in deeply. Hunter pulled at the hair around my face, looping his finger around the loose strands. My head rested on his thigh.

"Yep. Just a dream," he said.

"What time is it?"

"I'm not sure." He laughed nervously, tossing fragments of my hair around his finger. "But it must be pretty late."

There in the darkness, I couldn't see his face. The nervous panic, the clumsiness I felt around him, made me stay quiet and calm.

"Where did you go when you left earlier?" I stared up into the darkness where I assumed his face should be.

He let out a heavy sigh. "Uh…well, I can't be giving away all my secret hiding places."

"What happened in the swamp today? Who were those guys?"

"The dark-haired one who spoke to you, we don't quite see eye to eye on things. We were once friends long ago, but he let anger rule over him and chose a different path." Hunter swallowed hard. "Don't trust him. He's dangerous."

"I didn't feel in danger."

"He's not what he seems, Jess." he shot back at me. "I'm sorry, I shouldn't yell at you." He lifted me up in his arms. "It's late. You should be in bed."

"I can walk, you know," I said. "I'm not a little girl."

He bent down to release me, but my hold around his neck tightened. Hunter chuckled and carried me into the room. A faint light shimmered in the far corner of the kitchen, lighting up his face. I recklessly looked up at him.

"I know you're not a little girl," he said, letting out a soft puff of air.

The tingles started at my feet and worked their way up to my face. I felt the room spin around me. Nothing else existed as he laid me down in my squeaky bed. He knelt down beside it. "I'm sorry for being a bully earlier today. I didn't mean to." He paused for a moment, changing his tone to an older brother giving commands. "But really, it is for the best you stay clear of him."

I nodded even though I didn't agree. Hunter had his reasons, I suppose, but I knew evil quite well, probably better than he did.

But if Hunter wanted to me to stay clear because he wanted me for himself, I could agree to that.

"Well," he said, touching my hand. "Sleep well." He lingered a moment longer before he stood up and headed over to his bed. He stopped at May's bed to tuck her arms under the blanket and kissed her cheek.

"Good night," I called out in a whisper, wishing he'd stay and tell me another story to keep my mind occupied.

What if the dream comes back?

I yawned loudly, but not on purpose. My eyes closed easily from the emotional heaviness of the day.

Will Hunter ever see me differently than a little girl? Does he already? Is that the reason for the warning?

I also wondered if the stranger waited in the meadow for me.

Lovely Garden

After the event in the meadow, Hunter treated me differently. The little sister thing got worse—much worse. He rarely left the property. May no longer took me out into the swamp. I no longer got asked to get the mail, and every move I made was carefully watched. Thoughts of the stranger had begun to fade into distant memory. The good thing was the work kept us busy, and there was less time to think about him.

Time felt unimportant at the shack, except for when harvest time came. We worked hard to gather the produce before it rotted on the vines, on the trees, or in the soil. Miss Mabel's garden was tremendous and located in the middle of a large field behind the shack. On the west side of the shack, it stretched along the banks of the river, from north to south, like a long, slithering snake. Miss Mabel grew all kinds of vegetables like squash, carrots, cabbage, onions, potatoes, and tomatoes. She had fruit trees with peaches, apples, plums, lemons, and there were other trees not yet producing, so I wasn't sure what they were. If I were to guess, I would say the garden was as big as two baseball fields' back-to-back. Miss Mable had said because of the warm climate and rich soil, food grew all year long.

I had other ideas, like—the same ones May entertained about the garden being magical. Of course that wasn't a logical assumption, but it was one that made more sense, although what Miss Mabel said went along with Hunter's story about the Cherokee and their reason for not wanting to give up the land. The way the fresh water flooded over the banks and watered the garden was something to see. My mother had hired gardeners who used green hoses to water the plants around the grounds at the mansion. There weren't any hoses around Miss Mabel's garden. All she needed were people to plant the seeds, pull the weeds, and nature did the rest. Well, except at harvest.

We didn't see a lot of outsiders. The few people who knew of the shack would come out to buy food or barter for items we needed, like canned beans, cured animal meat, lamp oil, and other supplies.

One of our jobs was to collect the produce for the customers. Hunter, May, and I would run through the garden, picking produce fresh off the vine or digging it out of the dirt. It ended up being a race to see who could get their list filled first and grab the next list, if there were any left. The game, in the beginning, used to include Joseph, but as Hunter hovered over me more and more, Joseph stayed clear away. He also pulled Josephine to do the same. She looked sad sometimes, but Joseph had a way of making her feel guilty, if she didn't give in to his demands. An apologetic exchange had become a normal routine between the two of us. I apologized for being the cause and she for her brother's behavior toward me.

"Ready, set"—May sprinted—"go."

I ran after her, followed by Hunter, who pulled my shirt back so he could run ahead of me. I twirled in a circle, laughing, before finding my balance again and calling out "cheater."

He looked back and snickered.

The awkward moments, the fast-beating heart, and the fluttering faded as I became more accepting of our sibling type of relationship. It made me feel more at ease to be myself, instead of a lovesick puppy.

"What?" he asked innocently as he disappeared behind the fruit trees.

The garden was divided into four long rows and twenty sections. The row along the river was where the heaviest-drinking vegetables grew: celery, artichokes, tomatoes, and squash. The farthest row from the river, where the raised beds sat, was mostly herbs, garlic, and onions. Everything else grew in the middle.

I went in the opposite direction of May, who went for the herbs first. It didn't matter what we collected first, just to get our basket filled with the items on the list and back to the shack before the others. I rounded the corner to collect squash and carrots. May flew around the corner before I could make it to the next section, noticing her basket was almost full.

"How did you do that?" I asked, confused.

She reached down, pulled the squash off the vine, and tossed it into her basket. She winked at me, before taking off. May usually won. I guess it was all that energy she contained. It's too bad Miss Mabel couldn't put that in a bottle to sell. She'd make millions.

I sat on the damp, brown grass, watching the narrow, slow-flowing river push a twig along the rocky bottom. My eyes shifted to the trees beyond the river. The light struggled to penetrate the canopy there. My thoughts wandered, for the first time in weeks, to the stranger.

Is he still out there somewhere? Has he thought about me at all?

"Everything okay?" a voice asked.

When I looked up, all I saw was a dark shadow outline. My heart jumped and caused me to gasp. I shaded my eyes from the glare of the sun. It was just Hunter wearing a frown.

Hunter's voice almost sounded like the dark stranger's.

"I'm fine, but May already beat us. I didn't see any need to keep racing."

"Doesn't she always beat us?"

"Did you finish?" I asked, looking at his full basket.

"Yep." He offered his hand to pull me up. "Let's finish yours."

"No thanks," But he traded his basket for mine.

Really, I can do it alone. I've always done things on my own, and I don't need your help. I don't need anyone's help.

"So, Jess." He scratched his head. "Do you play an instrument?"

It was an easy enough question. But why was he asking? Did he find out something about my past? He had said he knew people.

"I've taken many years of piano lessons," I answered after my long pause.

"Do you enjoy it?"

"Yes."

"What do you like about it?"

"Well, I can go all over the world when I play." At the mention of the piano, I could hear the last tune I had played for my dad repeating in my head. A whirlwind of emotions flooded inside.

Would they kick me out if they knew my real past?

"Jess?" he asked.

Focus on another thought like the places the music has taken me.

"I've been to lots of places I've read about. I've imagined being all over Europe," I said, swallowing down the emotion and dabbing the corner of my eyes with my index finger without him seeing. "I've had high tea with the queen of England, and I've danced in the Trevi Fountain in Rome. The music is my escape from the real world and into fictional one that is just as lovely as the music." I spoke fast, and it chased my sorrow back into the vault of hidden memories.

Hunter was quiet.

I replayed the words over in my head, and they sounded ridiculous. I looked down at my basket. "Sounds silly saying it out loud."

"I don't think it sounds silly at all. You have a great imagination."

"I'm sure some of it comes from the books I've read too, so I won't take too much credit in the imagination department." I added another item into the basket Hunter held.

"I hope to hear you play someday. Have you been to any of the places you've dreamed about?"

"Only through the voice of the authors, although some authors are better than others at describing what they see." I paused. "But I do hope to see for myself someday."

My answer reminded me I hadn't planned to stay in the swamp. There were other places I wanted to go and experience. Keep on the move so neither Seth nor my mother could find me.

But I don't want to leave the only place that has ever felt like a real home—a real family.

It was a selfish thought because if they found me, no one would be safe. Seth would send his men in to destroy everything, especially if Miss Mabel refused to let them take me. I'd not only be responsible for my father's death, but for their deaths as well.

Hunter smiled, taking back his basket. "It's not quite the same, reading it in books. You really should see the world for yourself."

"So where have you been?"

"Oh, I've been to quite a few places." He chuckled, without giving details. "Have you ever composed a song? On the piano, I mean."

"No."

That had been something my mother pushed, but I rebelled simply to defy her. Even if I had wanted to, there hadn't been time between my home school lessons, arguments with my mother and Seth, not to mention the time I took care of my father.

"I bet you miss playing." He sighed, setting both baskets down to add another vegetable in my basket. "It's too bad we don't have a piano here."

I hadn't thought much about it. My old world and new world didn't have much in common. When I played, it was an escape out of my miserable life. I had no need for a made up enchanted world because I was living in one.

Checking over my list, I wanted to avoid any more questions about me. "That's the last items. We're done."

"Great, we can head back to the house."

"So do you play an instrument?" I asked, deflecting more questions about me.

"The river cane flute."

I gave him a puzzled look.

"It's like a flute. The Cherokee made the first one out of river cane. It grows wild here and resembles a bamboo stick."

"Is Cherokee Indian in your genealogy?" It would explain his reddish-brown tan he gets when he's been out in the sun all day.

"You could say that." He laughed. "I guess I talk about them a lot, don't I?"

"I…" Causally looking into his face, I forgot what I was going to say. I could feel my face getting hot.

Oh my gosh. Just look down and head for the house! Just go! No, no, no!

The feelings I was trying to suppress came back. I didn't want to be his sister. I wanted him to see me as a woman, not a silly love sick girl, which was exactly how I felt inside.

I swallowed hard. "I guess we'd better get back," I tore my eyes from his handsome face.

Hunter and I entered the shack moments later with our baskets.

Three ladies stood in front of us, two with welcoming grins on their faces, and the other looked me up and down with disapproval. She flirted with Hunter by batting her thick lashes.

May tugged at my shirt and mumbled something. I was too busy watching the young woman moving closer to Hunter.

"Good morning, Darling." She laced her arm around his. "It's been so long. Why haven't you been out to see me?"

"That's right. You haven't met our newest family member." Miss Mabel came behind the two women with a serving tray of snacks and tea cups. She set them down on the kitchen table.

I felt warm inside that she called me family.

Miss Mabel reached out for my hand, pulling me to her side. "Jessica, this is Miss Caroline, Miss Betsy, and the skinny, tall, redhead is Molly. She's pretty close to your age."

"Really?" Molly again looked me up and down until her eyes met mine. "You look much younger."

"Oh, you're just a dear thing." Miss Caroline bounced forward, pulling me into her round, soft body. Her cheek went against my chest.

I wiggled my hands free to return the hug, only I couldn't get my arms around her. Her hug was more than welcoming and showed me how big a heart she had.

If only Hunter would hug me close like this, I'd be able to tell how he feels.

I saw Hunter watching us with an approving smile. Molly noticed his smile too and whispered into his ear. Whatever she had said made her smile but had no effect on Hunter.

Could they be dating? She did call him darling.

Miss Betsy stood behind Miss Caroline and cleared her throat.

"Oh yes." Miss Caroline released my body, only to take my hands into hers. "Isn't she a pretty girl?"

"You're embarrassing her," Miss Betsy whispered while tugging her back.

"I just love your straight hair. No matter how much I try or how gray I get, curls, curls, curls. It's just not natural for a—"

"Jessica, you'll have to forgive Miss C." Miss Betsy reached to shake my hand. She bent down to my ear and whispered, "She's a little high-strung for a sixty-year-old. I'm hoping when she hits seventy, she'll finely act her age."

"I heard that." Miss Caroline folded her arms against her chest, and yet she didn't look mad at Miss Betsy's comment. "Don't forget, we are the same age, my dear and oldest friend."

"Yes, I am your oldest friend." She spun around, and her floppy straw hat covered in flowers flew off her head.

I caught it.

Her black hair barely moved along her long, thin face as she quickly snapped around to retrieve the hat. "Thanks." She took the hat and placed it back on her head.

Wow, she's fast for a sixty-year-old.

Miss Betsy paused with a puzzled look on her face and then laughed. "What on earth was I saying?"

Everyone in the room laughed.

Still laughing, Hunter interjected. "Hello, Miss C, Miss B," He set our baskets down, walking away from Molly, to hug the women. "It's been a while since last time I saw you both."

"Yes, I know, but we have some folks visiting tomorrow, some prospective parents, and we just wanted to make sure we make a good impression," Miss Caroline answered. "We know we will with Miss Mabel's special garden food." She smiled, looking at me. "Miss Mabel said you were an orphan."

"Yes ma'am." I looked down, feeling guilty for the lie.

"We hope to have four adoptions tomorrow," Miss Betsy added and clasped her hand together.

The bottom of Molly's yellow sundress, brushed across her boney knees while she strode next to Hunter again. I tried to ignore her.

"Well, that's just wonderful. Praise God," Miss Mabel added. "And I's glad wes can help. You's know, it's just about lunchtime, and I won't let yous leave until you've eaten and has some fresh baked peach pie."

"You don't have to ask me twice. I'm not afraid of more padding," Miss Caroline said, patting her stomach. "We'd love to, after we get all these goodies into the car."

Miss Mabel nodded, grabbed a handful of crocheted blankets, and followed the ladies out to the car. Hunter, Molly, May, and I also followed, carrying out boxes of produce.

Joseph and Josephine were already outside, loading other needed items into the van.

"Joseph, I can use your help this week." Miss Caroline touched his shoulder, but he shirked away, stomping to his usual retreat—into the swamp.

"I'll come," Josephine spoke out.

Miss Betsy nodded her head. "Well, Miss Mabel. You really do have a lovely garden." She changed the subject, turning to putting her arm around Josephine.

"It's just another gift from God, and I've been blessed to tend it," she answered with a wink in my direction.

It's something, all right. Strange and unusual, yes, but not a gift from God.

The Picnic

We all entered the shack. May went right for the kitchen and plopped her bottom on top of the table.

Molly leaned to Hunter's ear. "I found the most beautiful spot to have a picnic. How about we take our lunch there?" she asked, with her eyes meeting mine.

Why would I care? I thought, turning my eyes in May's direction, wondering if she heard what Molly said.

"That sounds nice," he said loudly.

"What sounds nice?" May asked him.

I couldn't help but chuckle when Molly winced.

"Molly found a nice picnic spot," Hunter repeated.

"I want to go this time!" May propelled herself off the table to Hunter.

"Of course you can, and Jess is coming, too." He put his arm around May's shoulders.

Molly's eyes narrowed. I wasn't scared of her because I knew if it came down to it, I could take the skeleton, but there was something in her scowl that chilled me to the bone.

She's just staking her claim and making sure I know what that is.

Seth had tried the jealousy thing with me. He'd talked about how other women wanted him and how upset they were when he told them his heart belonged to another. It hadn't stopped him from sleeping with them. Of course, he hadn't known I was the one strongly encouraging them to go after him.

But with Hunter, I felt very differently. "It's okay. I'm not much in the mood for a picnic." I faked a smile at Molly. If they were together, I had no right to intrude. "I'll keep Josephine company," I said, knowing Joseph wouldn't allow her to go even if she wanted to.

I was nothing more than a sister to Hunter. It didn't matter how I acted or what I said, things would probably stay the same between us.

There you go, Molly.

"Nope. You're not getting out of it," he said.

"No, really. I've—"

Hunter stood in front of me, not allowing me to decline the invitation. His eyes pleaded with me. "I'll drag you," he teased, looking deeper into my eyes.

My knees wobbled while the burning sensation traveled up my legs.

He only wants me to come so he can keep watch over me, nothing more.

"Fine," I spat. "How far are we going?" I turned my back on him, looking over at Molly.

"Not far," she answered, clearly irritated.

May and I gathered some food from Miss Mabel and placed it in a basket. We then headed out into the swamp. Molly hooked her arm around Hunter's arm as she led the way. May and I trailed behind.

"I don't think she likes me much," I said to May.

"Oh, she's just wants Hunter to herself. She doesn't want me here either. They've gone on lots of picnics, and never once have I been allowed to come." She smiled. "So I'm glad Hunter made you come so I could come too." She laced her arm into mine, like Molly did with Hunter.

We both laughed hard.

Hunter noticed how far back we were, making Molly stop until we caught up. "What are you two laughing about?" He smiled, grabbing my free hand.

I liked the touch of his strong hand surrounding mine, but I tried to pull it away. He only held it tighter. I shot him a look that apparently amused him, and he laughed.

"Just girl stuff." May giggled, watching him play tug-of-war with me.

Molly didn't like it. She changed the topic back to her.

"Remember the last picnic?" she babbled on about the many adventures she and Hunter have had. Mostly, she had the damsel-in-distress thing down to an art form. In every story, she was in some sort of peril, and Hunter came to save her.

How pathetic.

But I couldn't help but wonder if it really worked.

Molly stopped at a patch of green, long-bladed grass next to a stream. "Here we are," she sang.

The blue swamp irises reflected off the slow-moving water along the sides of stream. White water lilies floated on top, but were jammed together by the current underneath. The perfume of the flowers saturated the air.

May and I spread out the large blanket, we had brought, under an oak tree growing on the edge of the stream. Molly shook out her small blanket.

Hunter playfully, collapsed down in the middle of our blanket.

May jumped on him immediately. "Get off," she giggled, beating her little fist against his chest. "You're supposed to sit over there."

Molly cleared her throat loudly.

"There's plenty of room over here," Hunter replied.

"I'm just fine where I'm at," she sulked.

"I'll come and sit with you." May jumped up, leaving Hunter and me alone.

We ate lunch under the tree and listened to May talk about anything and everything. Molly put her hand up to her head, so similar to my mother when she faked a migraine. I felt a surge of anger toward Molly. But instead of acting on it, I pushed it back to the vault where I kept my darkest thoughts. I tried to close the door on the thoughts of pushing her head under the water, but it wouldn't budge.

I focused instead on the sounds coming from the stream. The flow of water created a smooth, steady sound with an occasional *plop*. I lay back, cupping my hands to hold my head, and looked up into the blue sky through the tree branches. A spider-web stretched between two of the branches, catching the light. In my peripheral vision, I watched Hunter scoot closer. My heart thumped loudly in my ears.

"What are you thinking about?" he asked, staring up into the sky.

My thoughts of drowning Molly were probably not good conversation, and I couldn't very well tell him my other thought of my heart jumping right out of my chest. So I went with a third thought.

"The sounds of the stream cascading down, flowing through the rocks and around the vegetation, the birds chirping high in the canopy, the wind softly blowing through the trees, the clicking and scraping of the branches—it's all like a mini-orchestra," I answered.

"So should we applaud?" he asked, trying to be funny.

"Maybe we should," I said in the same tone.

Hunter continued to ask me questions. Some I answered. Some I used to change the subject.

Glancing over at Molly, both hands rubbed at her temples. I almost felt sorry for her since May hadn't stopped chatting since we arrived.

Molly stood, brushing crumbs off her dress. "It's getting late."

"Yes, I think you're right, Molly." Hunter stood up and offered his hand to me.

I took it, and he pulled me up to him, so close I thought he would surely hear my quickened breath. Cautiously looking up at him, the sunlight bounced off his blue eyes and twinkled like when the sun hits the top the ocean waves. I gasped at their beauty.

"Hunter. Hunter," Molly said in a painful cry.

He turned slowly from me, still holding my hands.

"Hunter," she cried out again.

"Go," I said in a whisper, feeling out of breath.

May came right to my side and helped me pack up the remains of our picnic stuff.

A smug expression, intended just for me, gave her away. Molly pretended to have twisted her ankle. I didn't call her out on it as Hunter lifted her into his arms. Her arms went around his neck, resting her cheek against his chest.

I couldn't watch.

"May, I bet I can beat you back to the shack," I called.

May would never pass up a good challenge.

"See you back at the house," May called to both Hunter and Molly as she took off with me trailing behind.

We found Miss Betsy, Miss Caroline, and Miss Mabel sitting out on the porch.

"There you are," Miss Betsy called out. "Where are Molly and Hunter?"

"We're here." I heard Hunter's voice behind us.

I quickly turned around to see him standing there with Molly still in his arms. "Wow. I'm impressed," I bent over, exhausted from racing May.

"You're easily impressed," he replied, not breathing nearly as hard as I was.

"Molly? Now what happened?" Miss Caroline held out her arms as Hunter set the redhead on her feet.

"Oh, I just twisted my ankle. It's nothing serious. See, I can walk now," she said. "All better." She hugged Hunter. "You're my hero, as always." She kissed his cheek.

"Any time," he said, opening the car door for her. "See you in a few days."

"I can't wait," Molly said, before he closed the door.

I didn't wait for the car to vanish before going inside to fetch the book I had been reading. I went out back and sat on the cement step. Scraps curled up next to me. I stroked his soft, black fur. I didn't want to think about how Molly kissed Hunter's cheek or the way he said, "Any time." I didn't want to feel anything for him. It had been a lovely day, and the picnic was nice. I'm not sure Molly would have said the same. Everything in me wanted to push out these feelings.

There are no fairy tales, no princes, no love that lasts forever. I need to get my head together to start planning my future. Make the plans to leave here, and not come back. But if a prince does exist, could it be Hunter? Is he mine to have? No. Fairy tales do not exist.

Prince Charming Syndrome

"Everyone up," Hunter called from the back door.

I peeked out from my blankets, but no one jumped up at his command.

His eyes caught mine for a moment. "We have orders to fill." He looked away. "Ten minutes," he shouted, letting the screen door slam shut.

Did I do something wrong?

May whined, pulling off the covers.

We knew Miss Mabel wanted to plant a new vegetable. Someone had traded a bag of fresh produce for two big bags of corn kernels. Nothing seemed to thrill me more than being covered in dirt by the end of the day. Well, that wasn't entirely true. Feeling Hunter's hand wrapped around mine yesterday had given me a thrill. One I liked but didn't want to feel, since it would make leaving that much harder.

Everyone else followed May's lead, and soon, we were all dressed, fed, and bagging up the food we collected—all of us except Hunter.

"Where's Hunter?" May asked Miss Mabel.

"He's doing something else today," she answered. "You just worry about getting your own work done."

"Yes, Miss Mabel," she answered, shrugging her shoulders at me.

It was like May knew what I was thinking. Or maybe it was because I kept looking at the back door, waiting for him to enter so I could ask him why he looked away from me. It wasn't like I got in the way of him and his precious Molly. He was the one begging me to go on the picnic.

It's going to be a long day.

We worked all morning doing various chores along with pickling some of the vegetables that were overripe. Josephine baked pies while Joseph sat off in a corner by himself, slicing up the different kinds of fruit for her to use. Miss Mabel was in and out of the shack, washing clothes and the bed linens.

"Jessie," Miss Mabel called from outside.

I packed up the last bag for an order, folding the top down so the bugs couldn't get to it. I walked through the back door to see Miss Mabel standing at the front edge of the garden. She motioned for me to come to her. Hunter came walking down the center aisle of the garden, covered in dirt, and stood in front of Miss Mabel. He bent down to dust off his jeans, and dirt flew everywhere. I walked briskly over to them.

"You and Hunter are going to plant the corn," Miss Mabel said as she patted me on the back and walked to the house. "I's got so much to do today. Help me, Lord," she continued to pray aloud, her words fading into silence as she disappeared into the house.

Hunter and I stood there, silent for a moment. His eyes shifted everywhere except at me. He took out his water bottle and drank the last bit of water he had, letting the water dribble off his chin. He then wiped his chin and grabbed the two sacks of corn, using one hand over his shoulder like they were pillows. I didn't know how much they weighed, but they weren't pillows.

He chuckled at my astounded expression. "Come on. It's this way."

We walked through the middle of the garden. The aroma of apples, peaches, tomatoes, and all the other produce played with my nose. My stomach rumbled.

"Here." He tossed me an apple.

I took a bite, chewing slowly trying to soften the loud crunching sounds in the silence between us. He looked straight ahead, like I wasn't even there.

Maybe I did do something. Molly was not happy with me. This is getting way too complicated. Maybe I should fake a sprained ankle like

Molly. But if I did, I'd be no better than her. Stay focused on the next plan, which is figuring out when to leave.

My thoughts were beginning to get on my nerves. I knew the plan, but I was obligated to help these people who had been so kind to me. Once I thought my debt was paid and it was safe, I would get job, a place to live, and then travel. Maybe college but I didn't have to decide yet. I'd need money first.

But I don't want to leave.

"You okay, Jess?" Hunter asked.

"Oh yeah, just fine," I lied.

I wasn't any good at hiding how I felt. My mother had been able to read me like an open book. Thankfully, Seth wasn't as good, and it was easy to trick him. I had the feeling Hunter could see right through me, only he didn't press me when the topic got uncomfortable. He'd just let it alone. Could he see the fear on my face? I was more scared of Seth as each day passed. I knew the more he looked for me, the angrier and the more unpredictable he would become. I swallowed the dark secret inside.

"What's your favorite color?" Hunter asked out of blue, breaking the silence.

I gathered my thoughts back to the present.

Favorite color?

He nudged me at my long pause.

"I don't know. Blue, I guess."

"Why?"

Why does anyone have a favorite color?

I didn't know, but I needed to give him an answer. There's a saying the sky's the limit, meaning there is no limit, and the sky is blue."

Wow, and I came up with that in less than a minute.

"Huh. Wouldn't have guessed that one." He laughed.

"Okay, okay. So what's yours then?" I snickered.

"Hazel," he said immediately.

"And why?" I asked in the same manner.

He stopped to make eye contact.

I blushed, turning my eyes away from his to continue down the center path. He trailed behind.

Stop it. Don't read more into it.

"There's the field." Hunter came up next to me, pointing to newly plowed field about twenty yards ahead of us. It wasn't as big as the garden but was impressive all the same.

Who could have done all that work? Hunter and Joseph couldn't have done it alone.

I protected my eyes with my hands from the bright sun, scouting for signs of other workers but if they had been here, they hadn't left any evidence. It was easier not to think about how it got done, and even easier to assume the hired workers had already left.

"Wow! I'm impressed," I finally exclaimed.

"Race you." Hunter leaped out in front of me, running backward.

I couldn't help but laugh, chasing after him. He reminded me of May. The difference was I wasn't going to let him win, and since he was carrying the seeds, I would assuredly win. Of course, I was wrong. Not only did he keep in front, but he was way out in front.

Smack!

I didn't see the log.

A very small cry escaped my lips, and Hunter turned. He dropped the bags, darting to me, and caught me flying through the air. Our arms wrapped around each other in a full body hug, and we rolled in the soft, blond grass. Coming to a halt, he was on top, straddling my body. I wasn't hurt, except on the spot where the log came into contact with my shin. I was more surprised at how he caught me and how fast he was.

Hunter looked deep into my eyes.

Now don't get all swoopy. None of that silly love-sick girl stuff.

"Are you okay? Do you feel any pain?" he asked softly.

I felt something, but it wasn't pain. I shook my head, swallowing hard. My chest heaved as the air swooshed in and out.

Where is May when I need her to intrude?

He moved to my side, lying in the grass, propping up his head with his hand. He pulled back a strand of my hair and retrieved a piece of straw.

I jostled his light brown hair with my hand. Pieces of grass and yellow straw fell around us. "Well, at least we are both a mess," I teased, sitting up and tossing my hair around to get the grass out.

"That's okay by me," he said with a chuckle. "But if Miss Mabel finds we haven't planted the corn by dusk, we will also starve together."

I laughed, getting up to my feet first. I offered my hand to help him up and we walked over to the field side by side, my hand in his. Something had changed, and the damsel-in-distress thing had worked like a charm. Molly had it right all along. I liked being rescued, seeing the genuine concern on his face. With my hand securely in his, our two separate parts felt like one.

Dangerously, I was starting to buy into the Prince Charming syndrome.

And Then He Was Gone

It had been over two months since the incident in the clearing, and things followed the same pattern of planting, packing, and pickling. Hunter continued to probe me for more information and kept me engaged in conversations about me, from my favorite flowers to the best book I had read, and he listened intently. I had never talked so much in my entire life, and found out I loved having someone listen to me. But it got increasingly harder to leave out the parts of my life I was trying to hide.

"Jessie," Hunter whispered in my ear.

I gasped and sat up in bed. "What time is it?" I flipped over on my side, pulling the covers up to my eyes. "It's still dark."

"Sorry. Didn't mean to startle you, but I want to show you something," he continued to whisper. "I'll meet you outside." He stood up and walked out the back door.

I pushed off the covers and quickly changed into a T-shirt and jeans before meeting him. When I came out, he was sitting next to Scraps, scratching him behind the ear. Hunter looked up at me, reached his hand out for mine, taking it lightly into his. Lightning shot through my hand and traveled throughout my body as he stood up gazing at my flushed face.

A girl moment—I let myself enjoy it.

We walked through the garden with no conversation. I took in a deep breath of the dew and let it fill my nose. I loved the smell of a fresh, clean, new day. The sun leisurely rose with just a hint of light, tossing red and orange colors into the thin, wispy clouds lingering above. The ground held the dark shadows as I hung on Hunter's arm for support over the rocky ground. He led me to the edge of the established garden, looking over the cornfield. I hadn't been out there since we planted the corn two months ago. The cornstalks were taller than Hunter, and he was over six feet tall.

That's just not possible. May's right? It's a magical garden.

I stood there, not sure what to say.

There, more proof I slipped into a world that didn't exist in reality. How much longer could I go on pretending and making excuses for what I saw? I'm beginning to think God did exist, and this is His garden. How much longer would I deny His existence?

The thought scared me. If I accepted a god existed, I would also have to accept He allowed me to suffer—allowed my father to suffer. I tightened my grip on Hunter's arm.

No, I don't believe it. There is another reason.

The sun broke through the thick trees to the east, allowing streams of light to filter through each row. A light purple sky with hints of red and orange, faded into a clear blue morning.

Master Architect. Master Painter. I believe it or not. Make a choice, Jess.

"The corn will be ready in about ten, maybe fifteen days, and then we'll harvest," Hunter panned the field.

"It's the most beautiful thing I have ever seen." For the first time in my life, I felt proud of something I helped do.

"Well, I wouldn't say the most beautiful." He turned me to face him.

A light red glow appeared on his cheeks.

Is he blushing? Beautiful? Is he saying I'm beautiful? No. My mother is the beautiful one.

I felt a burning sensation in my chest and I found it hard to breathe. My heart and hands quivered.

Hunter pulled out a wrapped small box from his shirt pocket. On top of the wrapping was a rose carved out of wood. I had seen him working on something a few days before and had watched the long shavings fall to the ground.

"I wanted to give you this before I left. Happy birthday!" He smiled.

Birthday? How does he know my birth date?

"How did you—?"

Oh no! I've been found? Relax. If either my mother or Seth were here, they wouldn't keep their presences a secret.

"Open it." He placed the box in my hand, his hand lingering on mine.

I stared at the rose. Just the rose would have been the perfect gift, something he had made with his own two hands for me

"That's really not the present." He laughed. "Just something I whittled. Go on, open it."

The box was perfectly wrapped, so I carefully peeled back the paper without ripping it.

Did he just say, "Before I leave"? Where is he going, and why does he sound like he's not coming back?

It was silly to think he would never leave the house again, but he had never been gone for more than a day.

The box shook in my hands. "You're leaving?"

Hunter touched my chin and raised my face to meet his. "You'll have plenty of things to do to keep you busy without me pestering you." He moved his eyes off me to the tree line. His body stiffened. "Just make sure you don't get lost in the swamp." His jaw tightened.

I didn't say anything, holding the partially unwrapped present in my hands. I couldn't imagine even one day without him, seeing his smile or hearing him laugh. He was someone whom I had longed for my whole life, and if friendship was all there was, I wanted it. My emotions were trying to betray me. An ocean of tears swelled behind my eyes. I needed my mind to override them, to tell me once again how I didn't belong there and Hunter wasn't mine.

I tore into the rest of the paper, revealing a black, hinged box. I opened the box to find a heart-shaped golden locket with a cross on the outside covering.

"It's beautiful," I whispered, trying to stop the tears from flowing down my cheeks. "Is this a family heirloom?" I noticed the locket appeared worn along the edges where a vine of thorns surrounded the heart.

"Made by my great-great-grandfather for his daughter. It's been passed down from generation to generation."

I pulled the locket out of the box. "I can't take this." I wiped the tears from my cheeks.

"He gave it to her when he went off to war, to keep her safe. Open it."

I opened the locket. A tiny inscription was written inside.

Hunter recited the words, not looking at the locket. "Our Father, who art in heaven, hallowed be thy name. Thy kingdom come, Thy will be done in earth, as it is in heaven. Give us this day our daily bread. And forgive us our debts, as we forgive our debtors. And lead us not into temptation, but deliver us from evil. For Thine is the kingdom, and the power, and the glory, forever. Amen." Hunter lifted my head up to meet his eyes. "It's the Lord's Prayer." He took the locket out of my hands and placed it around my neck. "It will keep you safe," he continued.

"Are you going to war?"

Hunter chuckled. "I have another gift, only this one is from Miss Mabel. I did, however, bookmark a few things for you to read."

He pulled a book out of his pocket and placed it in my hands.

"The Holy Bible," I said, forming a half smile. Miss Mabel knew me too well, having Hunter give me a Bible.

Sadness settled on his words about leaving. Him giving me a family heirloom meant more than I wanted it to.

"Thank you." I paused. "When are you leaving? For how long?" I asked, holding down the emotions in my throat while I slid the locket along the chain.

He pulled me into a long hug. "I'm sorry. I didn't mean to worry you. It really isn't anything you should be worried about."

He still hadn't answered my questions. His tight grip gave me the impression his departure was soon and for a long time. "We'd better head back to the house. I bet I'm already in trouble for keeping you out here to myself."

I could have stayed there forever in his arms. Maybe he wished for the same, but then he moved his hands to my arms and rubbed them before taking my hand to lead me to the house.

He sighed when we reached the back door. "Ready for your next surprise?" He smiled gesturing for me to enter first.

As soon as I opened the door, I heard, "Surprise!" May, Josephine, and Miss Mabel shouted and sung "Happy Birthday."

But how did they find out? What else do they know about me?

The fear of someone unexpected in the room came back.

Scanning the room from top to bottom, I saw a white cake covered with candy roses, a handful of gifts, and happy faces beaming at me. A birthday party far from what my mother had planned—the birthday I never wanted to happen, and a gift of a ring I would have been forced to accept. I could almost feel Seth's anger in the air surrounding me.

Please don't let him find me.

"Don't just stand there, make a wish and blow out the candles, silly goose." May clapped excitedly.

What could I possibly wish for? Everything I need and want is right in this room. Why do I care if the place is haunted, magical, or whatever?

As I looked around at my unique family, my eyes stopped at Hunter, who lingered next to the back door. The light streamed in behind him. He looked angelic with the light filtering in, and his blue eyes sparkled. I felt the Bible in my hand and gripped it to my chest. Closing my eyes, I made my wish, and blew out the candles. I looked back at Hunter, but he was gone.

A few days passed, and still no Hunter.

I helped Miss Mabel stock the pantry, and she asked me if I started the book she had given me.

"No, not yet."

"Why are you so afraid to read it?"

"I'm not afraid to read it. I'm not afraid to read any book. They're just stories."

"I knows someone who was afraid." She reached, placing a bag of flour on the middle shelf. "Afraid of what God wants him to do."

I loved Miss Mabel's stories. Some were of her life experiences, but most were stories from the Bible. To me, they just were fairy tales.

"Now Jonah was an ordinary man. God tolds him to go tell the people about Him. Jonah knew the people had done wrong, and he don't think they's listen anyways. So insteads' of going wheres God told him, he took off in the opposite direction. Do yous know why Jonah tried to run away from God?" she asked.

I repeated her. "He didn't think it would do any good to talk to the people?"

"He don't want to hears God's plan. He's scared. He don't has the faith to believe God would make a way for him. So God puts him in the belly of a fish to think it over. We's don't has to be scared of God. If we listen closely, we's don't have to spend time in the darkness of a fish. Do you's understand what I's sayin'?"

"I'm not sure." I giggled, thinking about how her dialect came and went along with her train of thought.

"There's someone not of this world who lives in darkness. He wants our very soul, and he's the reigning king of liars. He feeds on our doubts and fears. He done that with Jonah at first until Jonah prayed and sang praises to the Lord almighty, liftin' away the fear. The fish spat out Jonah, and he wents to the town. The people turned away from sin and praised God." She stepped down from the stool to sit on top of it. "Nothin' much has changed in the world since time began. People do what theys want to do, what feels good, and not what they are supposed to do. They would rather believe in themselves, their control, than have faith in a creator. I think it takes more faith to believe we's was fish, sprouted feet, and walked on the land." She chuckled and shook her head. "You's got to have some sort of faith to believe you's here, don't you? Some of what go on here, can't seem normal, and yet yous continue to stay with us."

Her acknowledging the swamp was unusual, made me stop shelving the cans to wait for the explanation.

Her eyebrows went up as her serious expression had gone. She laughed. "What were we's just talking about?" She wiped the beads of sweat off her forehead.

"I think you were trying to get me to read my book." I grinned at her.

"That's all I'm tryin' to say. Whew! It's hot."

We both laughed. At least I knew I wasn't crazy to think the swamp was magical. "I'll get you some lemonade."

More days had passed, and still no Hunter. The rest of us kept busy with weeding, replanting, and tilling the soil in the garden. May spent her free time chatting at me, but it didn't fill the void I felt inside.

"Time for lunch," May called.

Everyone ate while we sat on the front porch. Josephine left and came back with a checkerboard, setting it up on the wood deck. Joseph immediately sat on the opposite side of her and made the first move. May hugged on her favorite doll, carrying it over to sit next to me on the long swing. Miss Mabel hummed as she started a new blanket. It was one of many she wanted to make before the coolness of the fall came back. Looking over at Hunter's usual spot, the empty space brought sadness.

Off in the distance, the sound of a storm approached. The dark blue clouds in the distance, flashed like crazy. Low rolling thunder, continue to get louder. A nice rain would be good for all the new little plants and for the seeds we had planted.

I ran my fingers over the soft cover of the black book with my name engraved on the bottom right corner. Holding the book in my hand, I couldn't help but be curious about its contents. I wasn't afraid to read it, like Miss Mabel had implied, but still I hesitated to open it. I didn't know much about religion or God. My mother wouldn't hear of it, even when it came up in my history lessons. She believed it was all a lie, and only weak-minded fools believed in it. Seth and his father were no different. Seth tried to explain the Big Bang Theory to me in detail, but I didn't care either way. If there was a God, He didn't care too much about me. However, for the most part, I agreed with Miss Mabel. It took a lot more faith to believe everything just sort of came together by chance. The other thing my mother said about religious people, wasn't at all true. Miss Mabel and Hunter were not weak fools who couldn't think for themselves. Actually, I believed the opposite after spending some time with them. They were confident and stronger than anyone I knew. So why was I hesitating to open the book they both wanted me to read—a read my father would have approved. I paused, staring at the cover. *It's just a* book, *and one my mother would despise me reading.*

An even better reason to read it.

Okay, Dad, stop pushing.

I took a deep breath and opened the book. I felt the air swish around me. The storm moved closer.

My pulse quickened when I noticed the letter from Hunter:

> Jessie, I have bookmarked scriptures and passages to help guide you along. Although the Bible can be read from beginning to end, I feel certain parts will give you a better understanding. Jess, I know you have felt all alone, and I know you have never felt someone truly love you, but there is One who loves you so much beyond what you can ever imagine. One more thing before you begin reading. Pray

for guidance and understanding. Think about this scripture from Matthew 7:7–8. "Ask, and it shall be given you; seek, and ye shall find; knock, and it shall be opened unto you: For every one that asketh receiveth; and he that seeketh findeth; and to him that knocketh it shall be opened."

With much love,
Hunter

I lingered on the signoff as I twirled the locket in my fingers. I could have lingered longer and thought about what it could have meant, but I didn't dare to let myself.

He might not come back.

I focused back on the letter. I had never prayed before, and I felt silly doing it. It didn't feel natural. I closed my eyes.

Dear God, please help me to understand why they want me to read this book. Amen.

My first assignment began in Romans. I read for hours, only taking breaks for a run to the outhouse. Finally, I was down to the last paragraph. "Now to Him that is of power to establish you according to my gospel, and the preaching of God's Son, according to the revelation of the mystery, which was kept secret since the world began, but now is made manifest, and by the scriptures of the prophets, according to the commandment of the everlasting God, made known to all nations for the obedience of faith: To God only wise, be glory through God's Son forever. Amen."

As I finished reading, I heard a pleasing sigh, but no one was there.

The raindrops fell, making little splashing plops as it hit the ground. Questions about what I read filled me, but I understood most of what it said. It flowed just like any other book I had read. I went inside shack. Everyone was sleeping, except for Miss Mabel, who sat at the kitchen table. She pulled two plates of food from the oven and set them down on the table.

"Come sit and eat some supper." She smiled. "Would yous like to pray?"

I was panicked, and the locket felt heavy against my chest. I pulled it out and read the inscription.

She smiled and said, "Amen."

"Do you has any questions 'bout what yous read?" she asked.

There was one and it seems important. "What is the mystery of God?"

"In Old Testament times, before God sent his only Son to earth, the only way peoples could be cleansed of their sin was to offer up sacrifices to God. I's imagine it wasn't easy. The Bible prophesized of a Savior whos would one day come as the ultimate sacrifice. By His death all sins whether it be past, present, or future, could be forgiven just by believin' in the name of God's Son and askin' Him to dwell in our soul. So yous see, the mystery is revealed when we ask the Son to dwell in us." She paused. "Did I answer your question?"

"God dwells inside us?"

"It's like a bottle floatin' in the ocean. The bottle is filled with living water, and it gets tossed around the waves. We's is the ocean and God is the water inside. No matter how big of a storm we's has to go through, He stays the same inside. Yous keep readin'. It will make sense. Don't expect to understand it all at once. His spirit starts out like a small light in the darkness of our soul, and as we grow in God, the light becomes brighter." She patted my hand as I took my last bite. "Well, you's better skedaddle off to bed now." She took my plate to the sink.

I kissed her cheek. "Goodnight."

So many things danced around my mind. The air felt hot and sticky, and I tasted the saltiness of my skin on my lips. I tossed off the sheets to head for the washroom.

After I wrapped my hair up in a knot, I cupped my hands, dipping them into a pitcher of water to wash the sweat off my face and the back of my neck. Patting off the droplets with a towel, I caught a glimpse of a dark hood moving behind me. I turned, but no one was there.

I raced back into bed, pulling the sheet over my head. I closed my eyes and tried not to think about what I had probably just imagined. I forced my thoughts on Hunter, trying to remember every detail of our last moment together. He thought I was beautiful, and in his note to me, he wrote, "With much love."

As I recalled his last words, a shadow of loneliness enclosed around me.

Well, Hello

It was like before, only I didn't remember falling into a dream.

Lying on my side on the bed, I felt his hands pulling back my hair, soothing me, comforting me. His nose touched the base of my neck, with his hot breath cascading down my back, making my pulse quicken. A thin layer of fabric separated our bodies. His firm legs spooned against mine as his hand moved from my hair to trace the contour of my side, down my shoulder, to my waist. Shivers of excitement and guilt filled me at the same time.

This isn't right. Push him away.

I should have pushed him away, but I didn't want to. He kissed the back of my neck, and it seared my skin. In shock, I opened my eyes. Hunter stood in front of me. In the dark, radiant light surrounded him, and his eyes burned. His lips pressed together tightly, and his jaw ground back and forth.

"What the?" I sat up and looked behind me. No one was there, just a wadded-up white sheet. I looked back to where Hunter stood. No one was there either. I lay back down with my heart pounding.

Just a dream.

My mind wouldn't let it go, nor would it let me sleep.

May moved around in the early morning light. "Good morning, May," I said, waking up everyone else. All eyes were on me. "Sorry," I said, jumping up to grab the water pails. "I'll fill the tub and while I make breakfast, you guys can get dressed."

No one argued with me as I ran back and forth with the buckets of water until the tub was half-full. Miss Mabel had already put the large pans of water on the stove, and they were bubbling over by the time I finished. I poured the hot water into the cold well water.

Joseph ran into the washroom, almost knocking me down. "I hope you can cook," he said before closing the door.

Ignoring his comment, I went to work in the kitchen. Miss Mabel joined me, but she let me do most of the work. I hummed tasting the food as I went along, so I'd know I was on the right track. Everyone, including Joseph, ate every last bite.

"It's not like French toast is hard to make." Joseph washed his plate, before storming out the back door.

"Don't listen to him. He's mad he couldn't go with Hunter. It was really good, Jessie, thank you," Josephine added.

"There's not much to be done today, Jessie," Miss Mabel said, looking at May. She shook her head disapprovingly. "Would you like to go exploring in the swamp today? I told May she can if you go with her."

I looked over at May. She forced a smile.

Shouldn't she be happy to take me out after all these weeks? May loves being in the swamp with all her little animal friends.

May turned her eyes to Miss Mabel. "But it's okay if you would rather read, or we could —" May said.

Miss Mabel cut her off midsentence with one look.

"No, I don't mind. My back is stiff from sitting too long yesterday. After that big breakfast, I think a nice, long walk is a good idea," I said to May.

I had other reasons for wanting to explore the swamp.

"Sees. I told ya," Miss Mabel said, putting her arm around May's shoulders and kissed the top of her blond head.

May smiled, although I could tell she didn't really want to go.

Miss Mable and Hunter had not been the only ones who wanted me to know who God was. May wanted me to believe as well. She said it would give me strength to fight against evil. I reasoned that was the reason she didn't want to go exploring. But I knew the real reason.

She is scared of the stranger.

I watched her squirm away from Miss Mable. She sucked in her bottom lip and stomped out the front door. I fiddled with the chain around my neck, thinking about Hunter and the stranger, before following May out the door, down the path, and through the trees.

Move on with the plan. Leave and never come back.

I quickly spun to look behind me, but no one was there.

There is no reason for you to stay now. All these people want to do is change you anyway, a voice, not my own was speaking to me.

The beat of my heart thumped against my eardrum. "May, did you say something?"

May's put her hands in her pockets. "It will be a nice day to be in the swamp," she answered. "Miss Mabel packed us some sandwiches for lunch."

Of course she wouldn't have said anything like that. It had to be Seth's voice in my memory or my mothers. Neither would want me to leave anywhere I was happy. Although, if I didn't leave, and Seth found me he'd do whatever it took to possess me. The more time I spent with my new family, the more I believed they would fight for me. Even if Hunter returned, he wouldn't be able to defeat Seth and his followers.

But if Hunter did come back, and I left, how would he find me? No. I need to stay busy and not think about it.

May and I continued to wander deeper into swamp. Seemed like every time we roamed, we were in another area we had not been in before. If I hadn't been a logical person, I would say it changed every time we stepped into the surrounding trees. If it wasn't for May, I'd never find my way back.

We walked most of the morning along the stream. May showed me where a family of toads lived, and she introduced me as though they could understand. I just played along. May liked sharing her knowledge as we continued on with our journey. "Did you know the name *Okefenokee* means 'land of the trembling earth'?" May said, balancing her steps across a decaying tree.

"I did not know that." I followed her lead, putting out my arms like an airplane for balance.

"The Cherokee gave it that name because of how the land constantly changes. I can walk by a huge, tall tree, and it will quiver." She jumped off the log, pointing to an opening where the sun was brighter.

I laughed.

Now she's talking about the Cherokee. I should look for the book both her and Hunter read. It's got to be in the little shack somewhere.

"Wow. Impressive information, May."

I heard her stomach growl. We both laughed and headed for a sunny patch filled with yellow flowers.

The sun hung high above us as we ate. The morning had been perfect with blue skies. We ate the sandwiches and drank the lemonade Miss Mabel packed for us. With full stomachs, we both fell on our backs and looked up. There drifted light, fluffy clouds. I thought about Hunter again, wishing he could have been there with us. The last picnic we all went on was just as nice. May had been lying between Hunter and me.

"New game," May had said, stretching her arms up behind her head. "We all look up at the clouds and describe what shape we see. Whoever calls out the best shape wins."

May made a game out of just about anything. Hunter and I would play along until she got bored and left to see what the twins were up to.

Hunter and I continued with the game.

"No way," I remembered saying trying hard not to laugh.

"It's a dragon. Look closer." He scooted next to me, his arm touching my side as he pointed up, tracing along the edges of the cloud. "There is the pointed-arrow tail, his snout, and his wings."

It had looked like a dragon after he pointed it out, but it was more fun not to agree with him. "Well, I still think it looks like a ship." My hand went around his wrist, using his hand to outline my ship. "There is the anchor, the bow, the stern, and the sail."

His hand took mine, his fingers closed in as he brought them both down to rest on top of his chest. "You win." He had sighed peacefully and looked over at me.

Luckily, May returned, interrupting us with a new game to play. Leave it to May to break up the awkward moments. I couldn't tell for sure if it had been on purpose or just May wanting all the attention.

With Hunter gone, she had me all to herself.

We finished up lunch. She stuffed the last orange wedge in her mouth and smiled.

I bet she misses him too.

May's focused changed to a bridge going across a creek to a thick set of moss-covered trees. I packed up our trash and stood up. May kept on staring as her body shivered. I scanned over the area again but saw nothing unusual.

"Come on," she said in a flat tone, snatching the handle on the basket. "Let's go across the bridge."

"I don't know. It looks pretty dark over there. Let's go in the opposite direction, where there's more sunlight."

But May headed to the bridge without a reply, and I followed.

She crossed over the old wooden bridge. Wet moss covered the walkway, so she placed one foot carefully over the other. She looked back at me before disappearing into the trees and vines.

"May," I called, following her steps over the bridge. May was nowhere in sight. "May," I called louder, realizing I had been there before. The clearing was the one I knew well, the one we had stumbled on before and once in my dreams.

The skies darken as I stood there. The tops of the trees blocked out the sky, hiding the sun, and the ground was no longer yellow blades of grass but dull and shadowed. The presence of something or someone approached.

My skin crawled.

This is not possible.

A familiar voice came from behind me, and I turned to face him. "Hello again," he said in a low, soft voice while his dark brown eyes caught mine.

The uneasy feeling swept past me, and I felt strangely comforted. "We haven't met, properly," he continued. "My name is Davior." He took my hand and brought it up to his face. His lips caressed on the top of my hand, sending shockwaves through my body.

"Davior? That's an interesting name," I said, feeling a tremble as my words came out.

"It's pronounced *Davior*, like *Savior*. My mother was quite the religious woman. I never quite measure up to her expectations." He then said, in almost a whisper, "Too bad the joke was on her."

"What do you mean?" I asked with the same tone.

He removed his lips from my hand. "I don't believe you've told me your name."

"Jessica." The feeling I had the first time we met resurfaced.

"So, Jessica, what brings you to Georgia?" he asked.

A weird, but wonderful feeling came over me. I felt like I was in a thick fog, and I couldn't see anything but the man in front of me, as if I had been looking for him and he for me. We were happy to finally be together. But there was something else in the fog—something I chose not to see. I began to tell him the story I told everyone else.

"No, no, no." He stopped me in a soft, gentle voice, shaking his head. His hands cradled my face to meet his eyes. They shone a soft golden color, not seeing the brown specks anymore. I felt mesmerized, like a baby staring at bright and colorful object. I heard a growl coming from the edge of the trees, and Davior looked away, smiling. I felt dizzy, my legs unstable. He caught me before I fell to the ground and then carried me over to a dead log. The log looked familiar.

How am I going to answer him? I can't tell him the truth!

I hung on to him for support and took shallow breaths.

"Better?" he asked, setting me down.

"Yes," I whispered, confused about what had happened.

"So, you were just about to tell me about yourself."

I had it in my mind to continue with the story I had started. But my tongue betrayed me. His arm went around my shoulders. I thought of the dream for a second, the one with the hooded monster in it.

Is he the monster?

"I would like to be your friend, Jessica, if you want me to be. I'm not here to judge you." His voice was so familiar, smooth, and easy to believe, like someone else I knew. "The world is full of people judging other people. The real truth is no one is perfect. Everyone has their own ideas about what is right or wrong. So who is right? How can we judge anyone? Shouldn't we just embrace who we are and have the things we want without feeling guilty, without judgment?"

I might not believe in God, but if there were no rules or morals, the world would fall into turmoil.

Davior frowned as if he had read my mind.

"You want to know the answer, Jessica?" He looked up as he talked loudly. "Religion! Religion is what causes wars, hate, jealously, anger, and death. Religion is what people fight about. God is just myth—a fairy tale. You have to get what you can out of this life because that's all we have. Here and now." He paused and moved his lips to my ear. "And to pay back those who have hurt us."

You know you want to tell him. I turned to look behind me, but no one was there.

Where is that voice coming from? It can't be mine, or can it? My mother's driven me mad.

Davior stared into my eyes.

The words rambled out of my mouth, one after another, and I lost my ability to filter what I had been hiding all these months. I told Davior everything, from my father's death, to my mother and her unrelenting need for power, and about Seth. I couldn't stop until it was all out, and even though I told the truth, I felt terrible he was the one I confided in.

"Even better than I thought," he whispered to himself, his hand tapping the side of his face. He sat there quiet, staring blankly forward, before addressing me again. "You did what you had to do. Any smart person would have done the same." He laughed. "I like this Seth person. Well, except for his obsession with you, of course," Davior said, turning to face me. "Tell me more, about Seth." I couldn't stop myself. It was like having the stomach flu and fighting the urge to puke, but not being able to hold it back. "So, he not only has a certain amount of power, he has followers willing to kill for him. Oh, I do like this one." He stood up, locking his hand together.

Suddenly, I felt uncomfortable. The log felt warm beneath me. I wanted to run.

He took my hands, pulling me in front of him. He smiled softly, touching my cheek with the back of his hand. It felt cool against my warm skin.

"You are an exceptionally attractive woman." He sighed, his eyes drawn to my lips. "Pity." He paused. "It looks as though our time is up, but I am delighted for our time together." He pointed at the edge of the meadow, where May stood next to the bridge. He wrapped his arms around my waist, holding me to his body with his lips at my ear. "Until next time," he whispered, kissing my cheek. He let go and walked in the opposite direction of the bridge.

I stared after him.

Why don't I want him to go? Why do I want to be with someone who scares me?

May didn't say anything on the way back. I felt guilty for not looking for her or even thinking about her while I sat there with him.

Where did she go? When did she notice I wasn't with her? How could I forget she was with me?

Tears swelled up in the corners of my eyes, and I felt nauseated as we headed back to the shack. I was glad she was okay and just upset with me.

I didn't talk much at dinner. Instead of sitting out on the porch with everyone, I heated up water and drew a bath. Laying in the warm water, I thought about every word I had told Davior.

Would he tell the others about me? That I was putting them in danger by staying here?

"How could I tell him everything? I'm so stupid," I said before dunking my head down under the water. I watched the air bubbles from my breath rise to the surface.

You better leave and leave now. Gasping at the strange voice in my head, I breathed in water, choking continuously until Josephine knocked at the door.

"Are you all right in there?" she asked.

"I'm fine," I choked out. "I should remember not to inhale while under water." I tried my best to sound normal. What could I tell her? "Oh, I'm just hearing voices in my head that aren't mine," I whispered so she couldn't hear me.

"Okay then," she said. "We're turning in, so make sure to put out the lantern when you're done."

"I will."

Maybe the strange voice was mine. My voice of reason was trying to be heard, over the voice of my heart to stay. But why had it sounded more like someone telling me what to think?

Or am I just going mental?

I finished my bath and crawled into bed. I stared out the window, wondering if I would see Davior again. The thought excited and terrified me at the same time.

To Dream or Not to Dream

The evening air felt the same as the night before, searing through the open doors and windows. Beads of sweat formed on my forehead and at the roots of my hair at the back of my neck. I wore a long, white, spaghetti-strapped cotton nightgown. It felt cool against my skin, but I was still hot. I looked around the room, wondering how they could sleep in such blistering heat, when I heard a scratching noise at the back door.

Scraps.

I got up, tossed some leftovers in a bowl, and opened the door. No dog. I turned back into the kitchen, setting the bowl back on the counter. A rustling sound came from the bushes not far from the back step. Curious, I exited the back door to investigate.

"Scraps, Scraps, come here, boy." I called.

Following the whimper moving away from me, I crossed the creek and went through the trees. Every step I took crackled and poked at my bare feet, which was odd, since the swamp wasn't dry. Above me, a fuzzy orange ring surrounded the blurred moon mid-sky with its light pouring down through the trees. A shadow of a man wearing a black, hooded leather jacket appeared. His long black hair blew around his shoulders as he looked up into the expansive universe.

I stopped.

Davior.

His eyes caught the last of the moonlight, disappearing in the clouds.

But then another light, a golden hue, illuminated around him and I could see his pleasing smile. "You are astonishing," he said, stepping forward. "I can understand why Seth doesn't want to let you go." He looked above. "I love the night, the dark shadows of mystery. It's my favorite part of the day. Some animals thrive in the night."

I then remembered why I was outside, unattended.

"Speaking of animals, did you see a black dog?" I asked, avoiding his eyes.

Davior raised his hand. A dog progressed through the brush, to sit next to his feet. "This one?" he asked.

The dog's hair appeared to be a deep black and badly matted. His eyes had a yellow, oozing slime in the corners. His lips rose, revealing his sharp, bloodstained teeth.

Davior moved to hold my hand up to his face. The dog stayed still but growled as Davior stroked my hand against his face.

I forgot about the dog.

"I'm sorry, but I couldn't wait to see you again," he confessed, waving the dog away. It scampered into the trees. "Please, forgive me for the hour." He kissed my hand.

"I wasn't sleeping." I caught his eyes.

"Of course you weren't. You were thinking about me," he said arrogantly.

I had, both scary thoughts and otherwise, but the scary thoughts were fading the longer he kept my gaze.

"Shall we?"

He held his arm out for me to take, which I did, and we walked through the moonlit trees.

"So was I right?" he pressed.

"Yes, but…" I hesitated.

"But?" he repeated with a hint of irritation.

"I'm a little afraid of you," I spat out quickly.

He laughed. "I'm not the one you should be afraid of." He grinned. "But that's not all of it. I feel like you are holding something back from me, Jessica. Something you want to tell me."

I went silent.

What is he talking about? I told him everything. Everything, except the light and how it led me here.

Somehow, I was able to leave that out.

He pulled me into his embrace and stared into my eyes. I suddenly felt another shiver run down my spine and out my feet. Davior's entire body felt cool against mine. My blood pulsed through my body, and I struggled to breathe. His lips were close to mine.

No, no, no, no. This isn't what I wanted. Not him.

My hand rose up against his chest, and I gently pushed.

Another low growl came out through the trees.

Davior's eyes burned amber as I pushed against him with more force. But his eyes weakened my effort. I couldn't escape his eyes. I was dizzy, and his hot breath on my face made it impossible to breath. His hands moved up my body to my face as he tilted my head up and exposed my neck. His lips moved to kiss the base of my throat. I swallowed hard, closing my eyes, not able to move.

All at once, everything went black.

The next thing I knew, I sat up, gasping for air as though I had been under water. I noticed I was back in the shack, on my bed.

How did I end up back here? Was it a dream? It couldn't have been.

Glancing around the room, no one was there, and all the furniture was gone, except for the bed I sat on. The pictures, the cross on the wall—everything had vanished. I ran to the back door. The garden wasn't just gone—the entire ground was a black pit.

This isn't right. It's just a dream.

I tried to stay calm, brushing off the grass clinging to my night clothes. It didn't stop the very real feeling that I was there, and it was all real. I reached for the Bible under my pillow, but it was gone, so I reached for the locket. Thankful it was still there hanging off my neck. I held it tight between my fingers.

Hunter said it would keep me safe.

I bravely went to the front porch. Davior was there, standing at the bottom of the steps with three others.

"Seth?" I whispered in shock.

My knees felt weak. Seth didn't look up, but I knew it was him. He reminded me of the stranger I had seen standing next to Davior when we first met. He kept his head down, staring at the ground. His body moved anxiously, and he murmured something over and over.

"How? What?" I didn't know what to ask. I stared, confused.

"Don't worry, my love," Davior said calmly as he put his arm around Seth. "I have great plans for him and for you. But you need to come with me, now."

"What are you talking about? What plans?" I shook my head, holding on to the screen door.

This isn't what I wanted. This isn't what I wanted.

My head spun, and I felt sick to my stomach.

He's dangerous.

I closed my eyes and thought about Hunter, as I held the locket tightly clutched in my hand. I remembered some of the words.

"Our Father, who is in heaven—"

"He doesn't care about you or for you, not like I do. He doesn't even really know you, Jessica. In his eyes, you're just like a sister, a little sister and someone to take care of," he said in a mocking tone, "and nothing more." He changed his tone again with a deep sigh, trying to sound sincere. "I see you for who you really are—a beautiful, strong-willed woman willing to go to any length to get what you want. I can help you get it."

I couldn't remember any more of the words inscribed in my locket.

Don't open your eyes.

I thought about opening the locket, but it was too dark in the shack to be able to read the words.

"You don't even know if he'll return for you. I personally think he's left you for good," Davior continued his speech. "You're just a child to him anyway. Like a little sister." He repeated.

Another stronger, deeper growl came from behind Davior, I opened my eyes. If it was his dog waiting for the command to attack me, I wanted to see it coming. I would fight as long as I could. The growl came again from the tall brush and Davior spun, facing it.

He doesn't even know who you are. Davior's voice sounded in my head and then he spoke out loud. "What if he knew you were here only to take advantage of him, telling your lies?" His tone changed as he spat out my own words like daggers to my heart. The things I told him, the things I couldn't help but tell him, were weapons against me. He held up my Bible in his hands. "The reason he wants you to read this is to change you, to make you more acceptable in his world. But, Jessica, don't be deceived. He is just as flawed, with indecent thoughts like everyone else. He's human with human envy and jealousy." He said *human* in a loud, booming voice.

No. No one here is trying to change me. They believe in something bigger than themselves, and they want me to feel it too, that's all.

I started thinking about the story of David in the lion's den. Although face-to-face with hungry lions, not one had eaten David. I pressed the locket against my chest with my hand over it. Davior went from a prince to a lion, and he was losing me fast. "Why would God, who loves His people, allow horrible and detestable things to happen? Think about it, Jessica. Think about what your mother tried to do to you. Think about all the bad things she did. Remember what she did to your father, what she took from you? You can seek out revenge for your father without guilt. I'll help you do it, Jessica," Davior said.

I swallowed hard, falling to the ground. The smell of iron caught my senses, making my eyes water. The surroundings changed around me, like being caught up in a twister, and then it stopped, leaving me on the floor of my old room. Waves crashed in the background while the voices of two people arguing grew louder.

"Remember, Jessica," I heard Davior's voice floating through the air.

Confused, I followed the arguing down the dark hallway. The people in the pictures, hanging along the wall, were moving. *That's not possible, I have to be dreaming.*

The photos watched and whispered, pointed and giggled, as I made my way down the long stretch of wooden floor. It creaked and moaned until I reached the end of the hall to the crack in the door of my parents' room. I peeked in to see my father packing.

"I've tried to understand, I've tried to love you, but you've only gotten worse. When I'm done, I'm packing Jessie's things up, and we are leaving. You don't love her. You've never loved her. This plan you have for her is completely insane, Evelyn. It's evil and I won't allow it."

"And where will you go, Samuel?" My mother laughed.

"I know of a place, somewhere she'll be safe, and you won't be able to get your hands on her," my father said, slamming the suitcase shut. He pulled it off the bed.

"No. You are wrong," my mother spoke in her smooth, calm voice. "Jessica will not be going anywhere."

A shadow passed the door, like before in my dreams. A lump formed in my throat, and I couldn't swallow.

Davior's voice filled the hall. "It wasn't a stranger, Jessica. Look and see for yourself."

I kept my eyes on the stranger, and he was right. "Seth's father?"

He crept behind my father. Holding a knife in his hand, he plunged the blade into his back.

I screamed, "Stop it! Stop it!" but no one heard me. I dropped to my knees, watching the blood pooling over the rug and reaching for me. The rug vanished into thin air, and I heard Davior's voice again.

"Do you see, Jessica?" Davior's voice hovered as the hall faded, and I was back on Miss Mabel's porch on my knees. Davior appeared at the bottom of the steps. "Don't you want revenge? If you stay here, the only resolution you'll get is to forgive them and let it go. Can you do that, Jessica? Can you just forgive them for what they did? Your father didn't deserve to suffer all those years, just lying there day after day with no purpose to his life." He paused. "And he did it all for you."

Davior is right. How can I just forgive them?

I just gaped at him with tears running down my face.

Is that what really happened or am I dreaming? Has Davior tricked me with some kind of dark magic?

"Come with me, and you can be a part of something amazing by my side. You don't have to become something else. You can be who you are. Great authority has been given to me, Jessica. I'm in charge of my own destiny. I can do things that will amaze you. We'll seek justice together." Davior offered his hand.

He lies. I heard Hunter's voice echoing stronger and louder in the depth of my mind.

I glared at Seth. His head still looking at the ground, seething. "What about Seth? What are your plans for him?"

"You know better than anyone that this was all your mother's doing. He was just a pawn like you. I'm sure we can come to some kind of arrangement we can all agree to."

I stood, taking two steps back into the house. It shook with tremendous jolts. It felt like an earthquake, and the ceiling fell down around me. The old wooden floorboards started flexing up and down, creating a thunderous clamoring. Every other plank wiggled loose and flew out the door. Through the open spaces below, hands reached up for me. I looked up, and Seth was staring right at me. His eyes were swollen and his fists were clenched. His breath came fast and furious, like a wild animal getting ready to attack.

I believe, I believe.

I closed my eyes, thinking about the Lord's Prayer again. The words came easier to me the second time, as I repeated it, clutching the locket with both hands. The room spun, swishing my hair against my face.

Suddenly, everything stopped.

My eyes flew open, and Miss Mabel's face smiled at me. I hugged her tightly.

"Must have been some dream you were having." She pulled me tighter to her, letting me hug her as long as I needed. "Breakfast is on the table. The rest of us will be out in the cornfield. It's time to harvest."

If it were a dream, had I really seen Seth's father try to kill my father? Had my mother planned it? I doubled over, wrapping my hands around my stomach. I wanted to throw up, but I swallowed it down.

I forced myself out of bed. My nightgown was covered in dirt, leaves, and grass.

Am I still in the dream? Oh please, no.

I got dressed and headed down to the cornfield, only to stand at the edge of the cornfield. It was an incredible sight. The stalks were taller than the house. I could hear everyone working out in the field, but I couldn't see anyone.

I heard Miss Mable and the two girls laughing. I heard another voice too.

Hunter is back.

I started to run, excited to see his face. I immediately stopped in my tracks.

He doesn't even know you. You are a liar, Davior's voice whispered into my mind over and over again.

I felt his presence, his spirit, near me even though I couldn't see him. A gust blew over the cornfield and moved to me. An eerie rustling sound swept over the ground. Light-yellow strands of grass tossed up in the air and encircled me.

I'm full of lies. Am I ready to tell everyone who I really am? How my mother was planning a life for me that I didn't want? How she treated my father? And they were all in danger.

I had to stop lying to myself. Miss Mabel had been right all along. I was afraid of God, and it was time to stop being afraid.

The wind stopped, and the grass fell down around me. I took slow steps backwards as I heard the voices in the cornfield getting louder.

You don't belong here. Davior's haunting whispers floated in the still air.

My chest felt like someone had grabbed it and was twisting it tighter and tighter until I couldn't breathe. I couldn't stay there, not as I was. I had something to do before they saw me again. I needed forgiveness from the only One who truly understood me.

Run, run, run! Davior's voice screamed.

I ran. My thoughts were not of revenge like Davior wanted. They were all about me and what I had done. I thought about the pages I read, in the black book that told me how to find peace. I wanted peace. I also needed to forgive and be forgiven. For so long I carried the burden, and I couldn't do it alone anymore. I had known who could give me peace and forgiveness, but it had been easier to deny it.

I'm done denying You. Please forgive me.

I ran in to the house, I grabbed my Bible, and went out the front door. I ran through the cypress trees and as far from the house as I could. Collapsing on the hard ground, I found myself in a field surrounded by oak trees covered in dark-green moss. The moss weighted down the tree limbs to the ground. Above, a bright-blue, cloudless sky looked down on me.

Davior's voice filled my head with doubts, making my head hurt and my eyes burn. I let the thoughts of hate and revenge consume me, before giving them all over to God. Every thought of forgiveness caused the voice to get angrier and louder. Tears flowed uncontrollably down my face. A blast of air swirled around me, lifting me off the ground. White-and-red flower petals blew all around, gently caressing my exposed skin. I could smell the sweet floral scent filling the air. All the pain eased out of me and into the swirling wind. As the air subsided, I landed gently on the ground.

God heard me.

But he wasn't the only one. The sky began to darken.

Out of the woods, Davior and three others advanced. I stood there with my feet planted firmly on the ground with one hand to my hip, the other held my Bible.

Davior laughed and smiled lovingly at me. "I love that you are so stubborn," he said, motioning the three to stay as he moved closer to me. "Why don't you just make it easy on yourself, Jessica, and come with me now? Someone might get hurt if I have to do things the not-so-pleasant way."

How'd he know my mother's words? Has he recruited her too?

I avoided his eyes.

He found me amusing. "I'm not the only one who can control you. It makes no difference to me how we do this."

I clutched the Bible with both hands.

He saw it and halted. "I know you love books, so I have a new book for you, one that won't judge you." He spoke softly. "My love."

I scoffed at his word choice.

He tried to catch my eyes as he held the book out to me.

I reached to take it, but he pulled it back to his side. "First things first, though. Toss that book over by the tree." Davior glared at the Bible.

I thought about it, tapping the book against my thigh, but I didn't toss it. I held my ground, letting his eyes meet mine. His eyes were similar to a thunderstorm. They flashed and twirled, but they didn't have the same power as before.

I smirked.

Davior's carefree temperament chipped away. The veins in his neck pulsed. But there was something else in Davior's eyes that didn't match up. The sad way he looked at me as I challenged him—like I had broke his heart.

"If it's the Bible you want, I'm sure I can get you one. Anything is better than whatever cult you joined."

He chuckled, then whispered, "Never again."

He waited for me to get rid of the book. It bothered him to be near it, so I tossed it to the tree. Davior's eyes softened, regaining control of himself. He once again extended his book to me.

Still looking in my eyes, I could see his frustration. Quickly, he reached out and grabbed my arm, hard. He was stronger and it hurt when he crushed me to his body. He put his cool hands on both cheeks, our foreheads and noses touching. He tried harder to gain control over me. I felt slightly dizzy from the pain in my arm and my constricted chest. His lips moved inches from mine with his sulfur breath on my face. I wiggled to free up one arm, to push him off, but I wasn't strong enough. He chuckled at my effort.

"So stubborn. You're mine," he whispered softly.

I closed my eyes and pressed my lips together, expecting to feel his lips on mine.

In a flash, his body was ripped from mine. My eyes opened. With a loud roar, Hunter lifted Davior into the air, throwing him across the field. Davior slammed against a tree and tumbled to the ground. Hunter, panting furiously, went after him again. The other three strangers with Davior ran at Hunter.

Davior screamed. "No! Stay where you are. This is between us." He stood up, brushing off the grass and straightening his jacket. "Seth," Davior called loudly.

Seth walked out of the trees and stood next to Davior, his head down as he approached them.

"Hunter, have you met Jessica's fiancé?" Davior asked, putting his arm around him.

I didn't like the way Seth snapped his head up at the sound of Hunter's name. His eyes were no longer blue, but a radiant yellowish-brown swirl. Seth grunted, shucking Davior's arm off, while he seethed at Hunter. The pulse in my throat moved into my head and pounded.

"Do you not know me, brother?" Hunter asked through his teeth.

Davior looked surprised.

Brother? Is that the connection? Why he feels so familiar, but so different?

Often I wished I had a sibling growing up. Sadness filled me for both of them to be so at odds with their own flesh and blood.

"Jessica has never accepted any proposal, so she is free of any claim he might think he has over her," Hunter said, staring back at Seth. "But as for your request that had nothing to do with your newest member, she has clearly made her decision."

"This isn't over, Hunter." Davior motioned for the two other men to come to him as they prepared to fight.

Seth smiled, still not releasing his glare at Hunter.

Six tall, slender figures appeared all around the edges of the field. I could only see their silhouettes, no faces, since they were standing in the shadows.

Davior laughed, looking around. "So that's how it's going to be? You're all going to gang up on me. I guess I shouldn't be surprised you'd take his side," he sang. "I'll be watching and waiting." He pointed his finger at me.

"She'll be well protected, I assure you," Hunter replied.

He leaned in whispering through his teeth. "This isn't over!" He turned to leave and screamed out to the silhouettes. "Do you hear me? This isn't over." A high-pitched sound came out of Davior's mouth. I covered my ears just before everything went dark.

Trail of Tears

I woke again from the twisted dreams—or not dreams. I wasn't sure. I heard a heartbeat in my ear while my cheek moved up and down with the rise and fall of someone's chest. The question was whose chest? Whoever it was held me tightly with one arm around my back and the other under my knees—as though someone had carried me. A warm cheek rested on top of my head.

I thought for a moment about my options. The last thing I remembered was Hunter attacking Davior, but who won? For all I knew, I could be still in the meadow. If I opened my eyes, Davior could use his mind tricks. I felt around for a weapon, something sharp, but my reach was limited without waking my capture. Realizing I had no choice, I opened my eyes slowly, noticing the wood railing of Miss Mabel's porch. I should have been relieved, but the dreams and not dreams had me confused. I was so done with the nightmares, I wanted to fight back.

Just get up and do it quick!

My eyes scouted out for a weapon just in case I needed one. The metal chair, next to the small table, would inflict some pain and get me far enough away. Even in a dream, if that's what I'm in, I would not go down without a fight. The person shifted just enough to loosen the hold under my knees, and enough for me to slide my legs off the lap and firmly onto the ground.

One, two, three.

I pushed off the swing, my knees bent as the swing moved backward. My bottom lifted from the swing, and I went for the chair. I felt pretty confident I'd make it, until an arm wrapped around my waist and pulled me back. The swing moved forward and knocked both of us to the ground. Keeping my focus, I crawled to the chair, got to my feet, grasped the top of chair, and flung it at the person after me. Whoever it was fell down the porch steps as I ran for the door.

Not so helpless after all.

"Jess…"

I stopped cold. The voice sent a wave of panic through me.

"Wow. She got you good." Joseph laughed, walking out the door, passing me, to go down the steps.

I turned slowly, swallowing hard, unable to utter a word.

"Would you like me to take her out for you?" Joseph sneered, offering his hand to help him up. "It would be my honor."

"I'm fine," Hunter said, taking his hand and getting to his feet. "It's my own fault." He looked at me.

Why should he apologize to me? I'm the one who should have made sure who I was swinging at.

Once again, my well-thought-out plan missed a step and hurt someone I cared about.

"Whatever," Joseph said. "Look, now that you're back, Miss Mabel said I could go…you know, but after chores. We got a lot of work to do. Where is the ax?"

The two exchanged conversation, but the voices were drowned out by my self-loathing.

Hunter came to me while Joseph headed out into the forest. "Hi," he said, slapping the dirt off his shirt, avoiding eye contact with me.

Tears flowed down my cheek. "I'm so sorry. I thought maybe… then, when you grabbed me, I panicked…then…"

His face lifted up. "Hey." He rose up his hand to wipe away the tears. "I'm totally fine. Not a scratch."

He was right, too. Nothing showed on him, except for the brown spots left on his clothes.

"I tried to put you into your own bed, but you have quite a firm grip. I sat out here to wait until you woke up, but after a while, I fell asleep."

My cheeks felt hot thinking about being in his arms, holding onto his firm, muscular frame, listening to the rhythm of his heart, and breathing in the very breath he exhaled. All, of course, things I didn't remember, but desperately wished I could.

"Time for breakfast," May hollered, pulling me out of my fantasy.

"It's morning? You mean another day?" I asked, smelling cooked ham and eggs, filtering out through the screen door.

"You've been asleep for a while." He stretched his arms behind him shuffling past me.

My stomach confirmed it by the pangs of hunger. "I guess so," I whispered to myself.

Does that mean this was all a dream? But if it was, when did Hunter get back from wherever he was? Is Davior Hunter's brother?

My stomach rumblings interrupted the echoes of questions as I followed Hunter through the door to the kitchen.

Hunter finished his breakfast and slipped out the back door. It wasn't until his fourth trip out I noticed he was carrying pails of water. "The tub is filled with fresh, clean water." His eyes seized mine and then quickly down to the floor.

Watching his feet shuffle to the back door, I said, "Thank you."

He glanced back at me, his lips parted, but instead of speaking, he let out a heavy sigh and nodded before leaving.

I tried not to think about what happened or about Davior as I sat in the bath water. Instead, I thought about the melody of the ivory keys. How I missed the sound of each stroke—the soft touch of each key pressing down to create a harmonious array of reverberation full of life. Music used to be my world, my world of escape, and for the first time in a long while, I needed that comfort. My thoughts strayed to Davior, seeing him all alone in the dark meadow. He looked sad, and it bothered me. He looked so much like Hunter.

My torn feelings made perfect sense now.

But it was Hunter I wanted, even if he didn't want me in the same way.

The water cooled, and I still hadn't washed the leaves out of my hair. I dipped my head below the water and scrubbed out the grime. Sitting up, I noticed the water was a rusty brown color with bits of leaves and grass floating on top. I dressed and opened the door to Joseph.

"Sorry. I—"

"Save it," he said hastily, with a bucket in his hands. "I'm the lucky one who gets to empty the tub twice today."

I reached for the bucket. "I can do it." I reached for the bucket.

He jerked it away. "Don't do me any favors."

"Don't worry about him," Hunter spoke from the table, standing from his chair. "It's good for him. Besides, we have our own work to do."

Quickly, I grabbed a comb, pulling all my hair to the side to make a braid. "Are we working together today?"

"Everyone is. We have lots to do before lunch." He paused before stretching out his hand. "Ready?"

I wanted to ask him so many questions, but my lips didn't move. I stared at his hand. A flash of Davior's hand reaching for mine crossed my mind. I flinched. Hunter curled his fingers into a fist and shoved it into his pocket.

Why did I hesitate? That might be the last time he offers.

As his face flushed, he looked away from me. "Okay. Well, everyone is out in the cornfield, so whenever you're ready." He walked out the door.

I bit down on the outside of my lip.

Go after him, dork! He wanted to hold my hand. Don't make it more than it is. Remember, he sees me as a sister—a younger sister.

Tired of hearing the conflict in my head, I walked down to the cornfield alone. When I got there, May and Josephine hugged me at the same time, nearly knocking me off balance.

"We were told not to say anything at breakfast, but I knew you wouldn't give in to him. I knew it." May laughed and clapped her hands.

Well, that was one question answered. It wasn't a dream.

Josephine squeezed my hand. "Miss Mabel and Hunter thought it was best to let you absorb what happened and not overwhelm you all at once."

I sighed. "So none of it was a dream? Davior, Seth, the fight—"

Josephine shook her head. "No, it wasn't a dream. None of it was. So tell me everything later, okay?."

"Sure," I said.

Miss Mabel approached us with Hunter following. "We's very happy yous still with us, Jessie." She hugged me.

"Not all of us," Joseph said from behind, passing all of us and going down the dirt path between the green stalks. "At least now I can go—"

"Never mind that boy. He's got his own problems. Anyhow, I knew yous would make the right choice." She glanced over at Hunter, who avoided her look, and back at me. "Well, ready to harvest, or would rest be best today? Yous been through quite a lot."

"No. I want to help," I answered, looking in the direction Joseph went so I wanted to make sure I'd go in the opposite direction.

Miss Mabel watched him kick up the dirt as he walked. "Now, don't go worryin''bout him. I think when yous become a teenager, yous just lose your mind. Aliens come down and takes over your body or somethin'." She hugged me again. "He'll come 'round. Don't yous worry."

Joseph turned around. His eyes glowed amber and I gasped. It wasn't Joseph's eyes I saw, but someone else's.

Seth. Since I wasn't dreaming, he now knows where I am. No one is safe and he wants to kill Hunter.

"What's the matter?" Hunter asked.

"It's nothing." I shook off the vision. "We should get to work."

Hunter folded his arms. "Miss Mabel, I think she should rest. She looks a little flushed."

"No. I've slept enough. I'd rather work," I argued.

Miss Mabel agreed with me and divided out the work to everyone. Hunter and I were last. "Hunter, yous and Jessie can start at the south end. Some of them husks is really high, so yous might has to put Jessie up on yous shoulders to get." She handed us both a large basket. "Fills them up, then come up to the house for lunch."

I have to get on his shoulders? Is she serious?

My father hoisted me up on his shoulders once. I remembered looking down, feeling petrified he would drop me. There had been nothing to grab if I lost my balance. I panicked. My father panicked too as I clawed at his head and he couldn't see. We both fell to the ground. The funny thing was I'm not afraid of heights. My climbing out onto a window ledge overlooking the Palos Verdes cliffs dispelled that theory. But when climbing out onto the ledge, I was in complete control over every step, and my hands knew where I could grab.

Hunter, not noticing I was panicking, grabbed my hand and virtually dragged me to our assigned location. Hunter secure grip on my hand relaxed me, a little. Occasionally, he would look over at me, his mouth opened like he was going to say something, and then he would turn his head before saying what was on his mind. I should have been extremely happy he was back. But my only thoughts were nervous ones about being hoisted up on his shoulders.

Finally at the section of the field we were assigned, we saw the ears of corn on top of the tall stalks. I could easily reach the corn if I were on his shoulders.

Or if I had a ladder.

I liked that idea better.

Hunter stared at me, trying to read my facial expression. "So which would you prefer? I can lift you up, or I can bend down." He bent down. "You can put your legs around my shoulders."

All that has happened, all that I've been through, and I'm scared of him dropping me. How silly.

I stalled, pacing behind him. He didn't budge, but glanced back at me with glittery eyes and a brilliant smile.

"Okay," I said, taking a deep breath. "Don't move."

I placed one leg on his shoulder and held the hand he offered to help me balance, then the other. He held both my hands tightly as he stood up. I let out a deep breath that I had been holding.

"Are you okay?" He laughed.

"Uh-huh." I locked my legs behind his back, still hunched over, tightly griping his hands.

"Ready to let go of my hands?" he asked.

Well, I knew the answer.

Duh. No.

"You know I'll catch you if you fall."

If he could catch me, like he had the day I tripped over the log, from yards away, he could catch me if I fell right in front of him.

"Okay," I said, closing my eyes. I let one hand go and then the other, keeping my balance as I straightened my back. Feeling secure, I opened my eyes. My lingering worries faded at the view, of the stream and trees in the distance, between the stalks.

Hunter's hand rested on one of my knees.

He is not going to let me fall, and even if I do fall, it's not like falling out a window of a three-story house.

Hunter bent down slowly to grab the basket. He hoisted it up briefly for me to remove the sharp shears inside. With them, I began to cut the ears off the stalks, dropping them into the basket.

The more I clipped, the less I thought about my position on his shoulders.

"So I guess you have quite a few questions for me." He broke the silence.

Of course I had lots of them, but most of them I wasn't going to ask while I was perched up on his shoulders. I wanted to see his face and read his expressions. I decided to ask simple questions while we worked.

"Is Davior your brother?"

He hesitated. "Yes."

"He seemed angry at you."

"He's angry for a lot of reasons. One being he's accused my parents of favoring me over him. They didn't favor me, I just didn't try to provoke them every chance I got. He saw it differently. "

I had more questions about my encounter with him, but I wanted the face-to-face conversation for that. "Where did you go when you left the shack?"

"I didn't go anywhere." He shook his head, making me drop the clippers to grab the sides of his face. "Oops. Sorry." Chuckling, he bent down, retrieved the shears, and stood tall, waiting until I released my grip to hand me the tool.

After regaining my balance, I continued snipping. "That doesn't make sense. If I wasn't dreaming—"

"I promise to explain later." He rubbed his hand against my knee.

"Okay," I said, feeling a little frustrated. "How did you know my real age?"

"Pastor James," he answered. "The pastor who comes out once a month to preach, the one you avoid like the plague."

I had avoided the pastor every time he came. Usually, I'd take whatever book I was reading and find somewhere out of ear shot so I didn't have to listen to his sermons. I'd join up after for lunch, so I knew who he was.

"I know who you mean." I felt a lump in my stomach.

Why did I ask that? Should I ask him how much more he knows? No more secrets, remember. This is another question to ask later, not on top of his shoulders.

The silence between us made me uncomfortable, and I wished May were there. I scrambled for something else to ask while he switched the full basket of corn for the empty one. Then I remembered I wanted to hear more of the story about the Native Americans. That was safe—neutral territory.

I continued to work. "You never finished the story about the Cherokee."

"Good call." He said, almost jolly. "Let's see. Where was I?" he teased.

"The Trail of Tears," I answered quickly.

He continued the story where he had left off, with the Cherokee being forced to relocate to territories in the west. The Cherokee Nation had been divided. Half wanted to stay and fight for their land while the rest wanted the peaceful solution to relocate. Hunter explained there had been many promises made to the Cherokee if they left peacefully. They would own land no one could take from them and could have their own government without interference.

"Those were empty promises," he said with disgust, describing the land as barren and dry. "Many died from not being able to survive."

"So what happened to those who stayed and fought?" I asked.

"The President ordered his troops to force them out by any means necessary."

"That's horrible."

"Many died in the battles, both the Cherokee and the soldiers. Those who survived were arrested and escorted to Oklahoma. Along the way, many more of us died."

"You mean your ancestors," I corrected. "You couldn't have been there."

Hunter became quiet.

I knew he didn't mean "us" to mean himself. That would be unreasonable.

"Yes, you're right." He said after a long pause said, "I mean my ancestors. Most of them died. On the Trail of Tears, four thousand to five thousand Cherokee lost their lives," he concluded.

He heard me sniffle, and he rubbed my leg. "It's a sad story." I tried to hide the sadness in my tone.

"There is another part of the story, one that is more folklore about what really happened on the Trail of Tears. Would you like to hear it?" he asked, as if he wasn't sure he should tell it.

My right hand tingled. "Is it happier?" I switched the clippers to my less dominate hand, not waiting to stop until our second basket was full.

"Yes, it is. I'm pretty sure you'll like it."

"All right then, but I'm warning you, no tears."

He chuckled and took a quick breath. "The story goes, God looked down and saw this great injustice, and He wept with them. His heart was burdened for those who fought so hard to keep their land. Seeing them chained and bound, hearing their cries to have mercy on them, He decided to save them. God put all the people under a deep sleep. The Cherokee were awakened by an angel, a great warrior. He told the people how God wept for them and heard their cries. He wanted to undo the injustice done to them by giving them another option. The people decided, each for themselves, then the angel left. The next day, those who had chosen to follow God appeared to die on the trail. God had put them into a deep sleep until the soldiers had gone. It is said God woke them and He would give them a chance to fight against the evil of this world in a great battle that wouldn't take place for centuries."

"So God made them immortal?"

"Yes, but it wasn't like the fountain of youth. They would still age, only at a slower rate. God designed it that way so the people could live normal lives and blend in with the rest of the world. Making them immortal was not a punishment but a reward, allowing them to experience all of God's wondrous creations, including marriage and families."

I wondered how that would work. "But wouldn't people around them begin to notice they didn't age the same?"

"There is a lot you can do to make it look like you're aging, but you're right. At some point, they would have to disappear or stage their own death."

"You sure have thought about this folklore a lot."

Hunter was once again silent.

I held a husk up to my nose, smelling the earthy, soil aroma, thinking about what Hunter was saying. "So they live among us?" I asked.

"Some, but God also built them a great fortress in the land they loved. A place kept secret and protected from even the worst evil. In the end, it would also be the place where they would all gather in the last days of man to prepare for battle. Until then, some are scattered around the world, some living normal lives and some devoted to God alone."

Wow, some fantastical story. That's probably why May thinks the garden is magical. That's just crazy. It's got to be just a fairytale story.

Hunter continued. "But there were some who would choose a different path. Most were angry about something else, but they also felt man didn't deserve our protection after what they did, so they choose to follow Lucifer. They too would fight in the last war. They would fight against mankind and God. They would fight against their own tribe, even their own families," Hunter concluded as I dropped one more husk into the basket.

The basket dropped out of Hunter's hand. "Ah, well, that basket is more than full. That means we are done for the day. Two baskets, right?" Hunter asked.

"Yep," I answered. "But why would they choose a different path when they just saw what God could do?" I asked, still thinking about the story. And what is the last w—"

Suddenly, without warning, Hunter lifted me off his shoulders, twisting by body around to face him. He brought me down slowly, my hair falling around my face and showering down on his. My hands rested on his shoulders. He held my gaze as my toes touched the ground. He leaned in closer, stroking back my loose hairs to cradle my face.

My heart burned. My pulse raced.

"Hey, are you guys—oops." We both turned to May. She blushed, spun her heels, and ran back up the path. "It's lunch time," she called, giggling. "Better not be late."

Hunter released his hands to grab the handles on both baskets. "Um, what was your question?" He went up the path with me following. "Oh right, you wanted to know why they would not choose to follow God. It's just like Adam and Eve. They were deceived by Lucifer. He convinced them his power was stronger. For some of his followers, just giving them authority, makes them feel important, especially if they felt undervalued before."

I remembered from my reading assignment, Eve thought she could become godlike if she ate the fruit from the forbidden tree. Of course, she ate it. It was about power, and she wasn't going down alone, which was why she gave it to Adam.

I thought about how Davior tried to convince me to follow him. "I guess I could see how wanting that kind of power could be temping," I said, thinking about my mother's obsession. "Although I wouldn't have cared about the power."

"But Lucifer uses our desires, our downfalls, our sins, and uses it for his benefit. For you, it wouldn't be power, but he could use other things." He spoke with tightness in his tone.

"What about the great war?"

"I think it's time you read Revelation, the last book in the Bible," he answered. "It's all in there."

We got to the back door.

I pulled him back before he entered the room and glared at him. "Later. You promised to tell me where you went."

"I promise."

Interrupted

We worked only half the day collecting produce. Hunter said Pastor James would be joining us for lunch. I couldn't help but wonder if it had to do with my encounter with Davior or the decision I made to follow God. It just seemed a little too coincidental and odd for the pastor to visit us on a Saturday, rather than on Sunday.

I liked Pastor James. After his sermons, I'd reappear for brunch and play a game with May, while the pastor and Hunter played chess. They acted more like brothers and were actually quite amusing to watch as each one accused the other of cheating. They were more entertaining than any television show. But I could tell it had been all in good fun as they laughed and teased each other. By the end of the game, Hunter would be the winner just about every time.

For once, I was looking forward to listening to the pastor's sermon.

Hunter opened the back screen door with his foot. "My lady."

I entered, shaking my head. "You're going to hurt yourself."

"They're no heavier than the buckets of water," he snickered, setting the baskets of corn on the table. "Want to play chest later?"

"May won't let me, besides, I don't know how to play."

"I can teach you."

"I think Pastor James looks forward to your game." We both looked around the empty shack.

Miss Mabel called from the front porch. "Food's out here. Come on and eat before its get cold."

May and the twins sat on the porch steps while Miss Mabel sat in her rocker. Pastor James watched us from the small table with the chess pieces already ready for play.

I couldn't stop wondering if Hunter would have kissed me in the corn field if May hadn't interrupted.

You've spent too much time here. It's time to leave. I froze at the sound of the voice, only I didn't turn to see if anyone was behind me. I swallowed hard. It was best to ignore it.

Just above the little house, a patch of crystal-blue sky hung. The sun felt warm on my skin, and a slight breeze blew over the roses, perfuming the air with their sweet fragrance.

Pastor James has his eyes on me. Hunter noticed, locking eyes with him. An entire conversation was exchanged between them without a word. Hunter casually slid his arm to my waist, guiding me to the large folding table laid out with country-fried chicken and all the trimmings. I liked the feeling of his arm brushing my back, sliding along the curve of my waist, and his fingers dangling just past my hip. Tiny little pins poked inside my cheeks, and a warm wave of giddiness became an embarrassing grin everyone would see. I quickly broke free of his touch to sit in my usual seat on the swing. Instead of taking his seat across from the pastor, he followed to sit next to me.

Pastor James stared at Hunter with a quizzical expression. The brotherly exchange made me think about Davior and the bad choices he had made. He could have been there with us, living a happy life and not in misery, separated from his brother. I felt so sorry for him. But at the same time, I was mad at him for trying to take me away.

He didn't want me. He wanted my soul.

I was still unsure of what was a dream and what was real. Had Davior really recruited Seth for his cult? Sure, Josephine said it was all real, but what did she mean? I wished Miss Mabel owned a television, because if Seth had disappeared, my mother would have broadcasted it all over the news. She'd make sure the world knew her puppet was missing.

Maybe, I could sneak a listen to the radio later. If he is missing, if Davior recruited him, it would be my fault. Remember how his eyes lit up when I told him about Seth?

After Pastor James ate, he began his short sermon. He talked about God's freedom for His people, the freedom to choose. It seemed a very relevant topic for my run in with Davior and the story about the Cherokee.

He read scriptures from Galatians as he went along. "We, as believers, are free from the old laws. People are so busy worrying about what everyone else is doing or not doing, we miss what God has called us to do." Pastor James pointed at the sky, reciting examples of real-life events going on around the world.

Some I could relate to. My mother wanted the same sort of power that my great-great-grandmother had as a ruler of a small England village in the early 1800s. To have that type of power was the most important thing to her. But that wasn't the only thing my mother focused on. She cared about what other people were doing or saying or having. Seth held similar views. He wanted what his father had. Actually, he wanted to become his father, taking all his influence, possessions, and the power he obtained through his work.

"God's Son healed a blind man on a holy day. All the people who knew him, knew he was blind from birth, and then suddenly, he could see. The people should have seen a miracle, but instead, the priests condemned the action. They said it was against the law to heal on the Sabbath. They then questioned whether or not the man had been truly blind. They did not want to accept the miracle performed in front of their eyes. They had missed the point entirely." Pastor James leaned on the railing, a bit out of breath. "So, in conclusion, don't worry about what everyone else is doing or not doing. Do not envy what others have, instead focus on what God has called you to do. Don't get caught up in rules man has created. Remember you have been set free by our Savior," Pastor James finished.

He looked over at me and winked. Then he caught Hunter's eyes. "Okay, okay." He laughed, softening the tension. "So, Jess, Miss Mabel tells me you've crossed over to our side. I'm glad you're not hiding anymore."

I stared at him for a moment. I wasn't sure what he meant. Davior's less frightful eyes stared back through the pastor's eyes, and it startled me.

They both have the same brown eyes, the same amber specks.

Hunter touched the locket around my neck, and I understood what he meant.

"Oh, yes. Well…" I squirmed, feeling uneasy by his question.

I had asked God to forgive me. I was no longer denying His existence, but I didn't know exactly what came next.

Unless I did it wrong.

He chucked softly. "It's okay. You don't have to know how to explain it. It's between you and God only. I still don't know all the answers, and I made the decision at eight years old, which was an eternity ago. When God touches us, He knows where we are in life, and that is where He starts. Don't expect too much from yourself or think there is some miraculous, instant change."

That was a relief.

"Just remember once you are forgiven, you are always forgiven." He paused. "Would you like to be baptized? I can do it in a shallow creek near by."

"I thought only babies got baptized."

"God's Son was baptized as an adult by his cousin John." He looked over at Hunter. "I thought you were going to have her read the Gospels."

Hunter smiled sheepishly. "It's been a busy few weeks."

"Well then, we'll finish this conversation later after you have read them," he said, smiling. He was so formal, as if he didn't want to step on any boundaries. He then relaxed crossing over to the small table. "You know, it's been months since I played a good game of chess."

"Bring it on." Hunter grinned, but before he got up, he kissed my cheek.

I blushed hearing Pastor James mutter "You lucky dog."

Don't get too excited. He kisses May's cheek too.

The rest of the afternoon consisted of the boys playing chess. All except for Joseph, who went off on his own again. Miss Mabel crocheted while humming something upbeat and rocking back and forth. The girls and I played. My eyes casually wandered to the porch on several occasions to watch Hunter. Each time, I noticed I wasn't the only one stealing a peek. I'd quickly turned so the upturned corners of my mouth didn't give away my feelings.

As twilight drew near, May curled up in my lap and listened to me read *Peter Rabbit*. Josephine picked up her latest crochet project and slumped down next to us. Miss Mabel had slipped inside to prepare supper while the two boys continued with their game.

"Checkmate?" Pastor James asked softly. May and I looked at him as he repeated. "Checkmate! I can't believe I beat you. Thanks, Jessie." He smiled.

I guess I wasn't the only one who noticed Hunter's focus wasn't on the game.

Embarrassed, I fumbled with the book, and it slipped out of my hands and onto the floor. Everyone on the porch looked at me, except Hunter. He looked down at the spine of the book.

Is he embarrassed too?

A logical reason for him watching me could be Davior. With May always wanting to head out deep in the swamp, he could have been watching us just to make sure we didn't break the rules. We were not supposed to go out there alone. With the possibility Seth was out there, I was relieved to know May couldn't go exploring either. Seth didn't like little kids.

Pastor James rose out of his chair, pulled Hunter into a hug, and then looked at his watch. "Oh my. I'd better get going."

Miss Mabel hollered from the kitchen. "Not before you eat, you don't."

"Really, Miss Mabel. I'm supposed to let the choir in the church for practice. I'm going to be a few minutes late as it is." He put the chess pieces in his bag. He hugged May and Josephine. "In answer to Joseph's question, tell him I'll be there at our regular meeting spot," he whispered to her. Then his eyes met Hunter's. "Maybe next time we'll have a real game." He playfully slugged his friend's shoulder.

"Enjoy your only victory while you can," he teased back.

Pastor James moved to me last. He observed Hunter while he pulled me into a hug. Hunter's brow went up.

"Thanks again for helping me win," Pastor James whispered into my ear.

Miss Mabel came out the door, handing him a bag. "Well, I's won't keep the choir waitin' a moment longer, so here ya go. Yous can eat it on the way."

"You're the best!" He hugged her and kissed her cheek.

"Now get," she said with a slight push on his shoulder.

He ran out with one last wave before getting in his truck. The baskets of corn were in the back, rattling back and forth as he went down the road.

After hours of reading several books, a cool breeze swept over the porch. The sunlight had dimmed, making it hard to see the words on the paper. "Time for bed," I said to May, closing the book.

After tucking May into bed, which she insisted on, I strolled back outside and stood at the edge of the porch. Looking up at the stars, there were so many sparling lights in the dark, moonless sky. The crickets strummed a soft and steady chirp, while the frogs in the distant bog made their own kinds of music. Together, the sounds blended into a harmonious concert, drowning out my fears of what lurked beyond my sight and what waited for me. The air carried a combination of woody, earthy smells as it blew over the trees before reaching my face to lifting the strands of my hair. I wanted to block out everything except for the peacefulness of the moment, although it was not an easy task with so much to think about, worry about, and be happy about. There were so many questions I wanted answers to.

But now would not be the time.

Hunter approached from behind, maneuvering his hands around my waist from both sides. He locked his fingers together just under my ribs to pull me into his faultless frame. His warm skin touched the coolness of my arm, sending my heart pounding, louder than the cicadas in July. I stayed perfectly still, afraid if I moved, he'd come to his senses and release his hold on me. His cheek rested against my hair as we both looked out into the night. Our bodies moved as one with each breath, and his heart thrashed with mine.

All the thoughts of Hunter caring about me like a sister were quickly dissolving.

I'm getting in too deep. Stick to the plan. What about Seth? What about Davior?

To add Hunter into the mix was so wrong. He didn't deserve to be caught up in my twisted life. He deserved better than me.

Hunter released his hands, to twirl me around. By lantern light, I stared up at him, ignoring the thoughts running through my head. I didn't care about anything else, as my body tingled all over, from the tips of my toes to the top of my head. His body trembled slightly, using the tips of his fingers to trace my cheekbone.

Closing my eyes, I delighted in the moment. "What are you thinking?" His voice was low as he moved close enough to touch his nose to mine.

"I need to remember to breathe," I whispered back with a dry laugh. "What are you thinking?" Swallowing down the lump in my throat, I opened my eyes to look at his.

"Uh," he said, his eyes burning through my soul. "I guess I asked for that." His eyes shifted to examine every part of my face. "I'm thinking I want to kiss you, but I don't know if I should," he paused. "This is all so new to me."

"It's new to me too." I timidly looked down at his checkered blue shirt.

My arms moved up his arms to circle around his neck. The movement felt natural, like I had done it so many times before, like he already belonged to me. As much as I tried to reason, as much as I wanted to resist, I was completely powerless under his charm. His satin lips brushed against my forehead and moved down my cheek, which felt hot. I closed my eyes, waiting, waiting for the kiss I wanted more than anything I could think of.

He stopped sharply and his body stiffened.

"What's wrong?" I asked, but I felt it too. Something intangible waited in the darkness.

My heart pounded differently, frightened, thinking it might be Davior and Seth. Hunter's body tensed again, and he shifted his jaw back and forth. He nodded his head a few times, glaring out past the porch.

His body relaxed as his head rested on top of mine once again. "I'd better get you to bed. We have plans to be up early tomorrow."

No, no, no.

The feeling of disappointment washed over me. Our very brief moment was over. "But I'm not tired."

"Jessica, please."

My mother insisted on calling me Jessica and nothing else, which was why I preferred Jess or Jessie. Hearing Hunter say my full name, I couldn't help but comply. I dropped my arms in a pout, walked into the shack, and changed for bed. Hunter stood at the door looking out until he heard me crawl into the squeaky bed.

He walked over and kneeled down at the bed. "Promise me you won't leave the house tonight and will go right to sleep. It's not safe for you to be out of this house right now."

I didn't say anything.

He kissed my forehead slowly, softly. "Sleep well." He pulled the sheet over me, tucking it in around me.

He walked over to Miss Mabel, putting both hands on the arms of the rocker, leaning into her ear. I couldn't hear a word he said. Hunter stood and walked out the front door. Miss Mabel followed.

I wasn't going to stay. I waited until the lantern light was far enough away for them not to see me following, before I left the house. Everything happening was because of me. If Seth were out there, it meant nothing good. No one would pay the consequence of me leaving him, even if it meant giving up my life.

I stumbled through the brush behind them into the black night.

See? You're making things worse for everyone, and now you're being sneaky. What if Seth was watching you with Hunter? And what would have happened if he saw him kiss you? I shut out the intrusive voice and continued to follow.

With no moon, and the light from the lantern hidden behind tree trunks, I relied on the swishing sound the branches made against each other when passed. It worked well until the voice repeated again and again with the same message, and I couldn't hear them anymore. *It's your fault.*

Lost, with mysterious trees looming overhead, my heart beat fast against my lungs, cutting down the flow of air. "Great. Just great." I spun around to go back the way I came. I spun around again. "Oh no." I felt a swoosh of air pass overhead and move forward into the brush in front of me. With nowhere else to go, I went ahead with my pulse thumping in my throat.

Finally, I heard a voice.

Peeking through a bush, I saw a greenish glow filling the familiar open meadow.

"We've made a deal. It's already done. He won't be letting her go easily, nor will I," I heard Davior's voice.

"Oh, and you are going to just let him have her?" Hunter spoke.

"One thing you know, my brother, is how my mind works. You tell me."

"At some point, he'll realize you've used him. What would stop him from killing you then?"

"We don't fall under the same rules you do. Besides, once he realizes the whole picture, Jessica will not be as important. However, a deal had to be made in order for him to come. The plan is already set in motion, and my only requirement is that I give you fair warning." He paused. "Consider yourself warned."

"She's protected here on this land."

"She's only protected if she stays inside that joke you call a house. You won't be able to keep her caged for long."

"I don't plan on keeping her caged. Apparently, that's your plan," Hunter spat. "And as long as she is with me, she'll be safe."

"Yeah, well, good luck with that. At least I'm not afraid to say how I f—"

"I'm still bound by honor and respect, unlike you, Davior. Do you even know what that means anymore, or have you let your mind get so twisted into evil you can't see past your own selfish desires? Have you forgotten where you came from?"

"Your time here is done, Davior," Miss Mabel added in her soft, loving voice.

Davior chuckled. "She will be miserable here. At some point, she'll miss the things she's become accustomed to, and she'll disappear. She'll leave here like she did her last home. It will be then I'll make her an offer she won't be able to refuse."

"Your little mind tricks are worthless on me, so just give it up. You don't know her as well as you like to think you do."

Davior's tone rose. "We won't be giving her up easily, Hunter. It wasn't a fair fight."

"I did everything you asked, and it's now over. She's clearly made her choice."

"Well, I see things differently. It's good I'm not bound to your rules of the game."

"Why her?" Hunter asked as the two, tall shadows paced in front of each other. "I'm sure you can find plenty of others to fill your—"

"Brother, why do you ask questions you already know the answer to?" Davior replied.

The tallest figure stopped, paused for a moment, then lunged at the other. Both fell to the ground, and they tumbled to where I stood, hitting the bush I cowered behind. I held my breath so they wouldn't hear me breathing hard. But they were too busy. One shadow threw the other off before landing on top of the other. I didn't know who to root for until Miss Mabel stepped in. She stood in front of the tallest shadow and put her arm on his shoulder before he lunged again.

"That's quite enough," Miss Mabel spoke, her hands stretching out between the two boys.

"She is not a trophy or some pawn to get what you want! You still act like a spoil child, always wanting your way." Hunter stated in a loud, booming voice.

"Hunter, I said that's enough," Miss Mabel said. "She is safe here with us. They cannot touch her anywhere within our border." She paused a moment. "There is another option to consider." She pulled Hunter's face close to hers and whispered something I couldn't hear.

Hunter stepped away from Davior.

"Yes, dear brother, she is safe, for now. But no matter where you take her," Davior said, "we'll find her, and she'll be ours forever." He grabbed his jacket and left through the other side of the clearing.

I realized I knew this area and my way back. But if I wanted to beat them to the shack, I had to hurry.

Davior is in alliance with Seth. This is not good. This is so not good. He won't give up easily or without a fight. He'll call out the entire police force and call in every favor from all his attorney friends and all those other "friends." I'm putting everyone I care about in danger. I'm so stupid.

At the shack, I ran up the front steps and tiptoed to my bed. I didn't have time to pull the covers over me as Miss Mabel and Hunter entered through the back door.

I lay very still.

Crap! I'm caught!

Hunter headed to me, and I closed my eyes tightly. His warm hand touched my cool cheek from the night air. I then felt the warmth of the blanket contouring over my body. Hunter sat on the edge of the mattress and placed his hand back on my face, already feeling warmer. I shifted slightly, leaning into his hand, pretending to be asleep. He bent over and kissed my cheek, holding his lips there for only a moment before he left for his own bed.

Besides the secret meeting and the still, small voice of reason echoing in the catacombs of my mind, telling me to leave, the day had proved to be amazing. Hunter vowed to protect me, to not let me out of his sight, but before that, before we were interrupted, he intended to kiss me.

Two Empty Pails

The morning light filtered into the room. I didn't hesitate getting out bed at the anticipation of the special trip Hunter had schemed. Making a run for the washroom, I grabbed my blue sundress with spaghetti straps and got dressed.

Ready to go, I noticed a round, floppy hat with blue flowers tossed on my bed.

Cute.

I placed the hat on my head. It reminded me of the hat Audrey Hepburn wore in *Breakfast at Tiffany's* as she was about to go to visit Sally Tomato, the mobster.

The secret meeting in the night hadn't changed the plans for the day. I watched Hunter and Josephine prepare breakfast while Miss Mabel and May packed lunches. Even Joseph seemed happy, whistling a tune as he stacked the wood next to the fireplace. I couldn't help but wonder if this little trip was putting the others in danger.

"Can I help?" I asked.

The old woman pointed, with the fork in her hand dripping with egg salad, to the bamboo basket in the corner next to the door. I grabbed the basket and began to pile in the items set out. Only a moment passed before I noticed his eyes on me. My cheeks turned hot, but I didn't glance up and kept packing. The voice I didn't want to hear whispered in my ear.

I told you this would happen, you silly girl. You should leave now. Save the people you love. You didn't help your father. "I am going crazy." I tapped the side of my head with the palm of my hand, stopping the male voice instantly.

Did I get out in time, or did my mother drive me mad?

"Did yous say somethin', dear?" Miss Mabel asked.

"Nothing important." I put the last item in the basket before moving it to the side, so I could wipe off the table.

"I'll take that." Hunter grabbed the towel from me.

"Hey, I wasn't done."

"I guess you'll have to come get it back." He twirled the cloth over his head.

I laughed at the challenge, letting everything else in my thoughts fade away as I went for the cloth.

"You two, out of my kitchen," Miss Mabel said, taking the towel out of Hunter's hand. "You!" She pointed at Hunter. "Go help Joseph." She sighed. "Kids today."

We finished eating breakfast. Miss Mabel handed out the gear for us to carry to our destination that was only a secret to me. Hunter led the way, carrying more than his fair share. I walked closely behind him with May chatting away, on my right. I didn't hear one word, watching Hunter scan the landscape around us. May didn't notice and kept talking.

We walked for at least a mile, crossing small streams, going through meadows, and rounding a few bogs until we came along a wide, swift flowing river. The water splashed over the stones along the banks.

There was no bridge, yet I asked, "We're crossing over it, right?"

My fear of rushing water welled up inside me. I stopped to watch everyone move closer to the water. Hunter ran ahead down to the bank, where an elongated wooden boat, bobbed up and down against a post. Everyone, except me, climbed into the boat as Hunter untied it. I stepped back, imagining myself slipping on the wet grass, splashing into the water, and drug facedown along the bottom of the river.

No thanks.

"Come on, Jess," May said.

Joseph wasn't amused. "Give me a break."

Hunter, with one foot in the boat and one on land, tried to keep the boat from sailing off without me. He held out his hand. "Trust me?"

I felt silly standing there, not able to move.

Joseph grunted. "Just leave her if she doesn't want to get in the boat. She can find her way back."

Hunter shook his head at Joseph but kept his eyes on me. Miss Mabel, however, smacked Joseph on the back of his head.

"Ouch." He stood and climbed out of the boat. "Fine. I'll help her." Joseph moved within inches from me. "Get in the boat."

He grabbed for my arm. I backed away before his hand touched me.

Hunter retied the boat to the post and sprinted to us.

"This is ridiculous." Joseph threw up his hands, walking away from the river. "I'll see you all later."

"I'm sorry," I said to Hunter, feeling bad Joseph walked off. "I don't know how to swim."

He hated me. He hated me the most when Hunter's attention was on me.

"I won't let anything happen to you." He stared after Joseph. "Besides," his hand covered mine. "There is no swimming required."

Lugging me behind him, he stepped into in the boat. "Trust me."

How pathetic.

I looked down at the water rushing around the boat. There were much worse ways to die. Seth's blood red eyes, pulsing at me while he strangled me was top on the list.

"If I fall out of the boat, you'll come after me, right?" I lifted my feet, which felt like heavy rocks, into the boat.

He laughed, stroking the top of my hand, before I plopped down on the hard wood plank stretching across the craft. "I'm insulted you feel you have to ask." He pushed the boat from the shore with one leg.

Okay, so it was a silly thing to ask, but it didn't change my death grip on the edge of the boat, noticing the white capped water bubbling up ahead. However, the river really wasn't so bad as we traveled along.

May pointed out and named each tree, bush, fish, bird, and just about everything else she saw. Hunter guided the boat while scanning the water ahead and the shoreline.

"Look." May laughed, pointing at two crocodiles. "What a bunch of lazy crocs."

They casually looked over. Not bothered by our presence, they continued to soak up the hot sun.

I pinched my nose. "Is that smell coming from them?"

"No. It's not them, though I don't guess theys smell like roses," Miss Mabel said. "It's the bog just over that ridge." She pointed north, the same direction the breeze came from. "The waters don't move much, so the ground rots, creatin' a gas. Keeps people away from that part of the swamp."

We continued to float down the river until Hunter pointed out a wooden dock ahead. Hunter steered the boat, lining it against the side of the matchstick platform. After a short walk from the dock, we entered a red-and-green colored meadow. Red, ripe strawberries covered most of the area.

May tugged on Miss Mabel's apron. "Let's eat first. I'm starving."

Miss Mabel spread out the big blanket along the ground. May grinned, showing me her red lips from devouring a juicy strawberry.

After taking my last bite of lunch, I let my body fall back onto the ground to look up at the sky. The aqua color speckled with white, fluffy clouds showed no signs of danger or darkness. I relaxed, soaking in the warmth of the sun just like the lazy crocs.

Hunter lay next to me. "So, what should we talk about?"

I shifted onto my elbow, catching a glimpse of Miss Mabel, May, and Josephine grabbing pails and heading away from us. I looked at Hunter, still gazing up at the cotton-ball clouds. The questions I had vaulted swam around in a giant vortex, bouncing off the walls of my skull.

Am I ready to hear the answers? Am I ready to accept the illogical?

I gulped, clearing a way for the words to come out. "So, you didn't leave?"

Hunter stayed silent.

"You promised," I reminded him.

"No, I didn't leave."

"How is that possible? You were gone for weeks."

"Before you came, I used to take May exploring into the swamp. I taught her everything she knows about it, from the time she was old enough to walk. She is very independent, as I'm sure you already know. After a while, I started letting her trail ahead of me, giving her some freedom. Of course, the whole time, my eyes never left her. I was always close enough to intervene if danger was near. Eventually, she caught on and knew I was there, but she continued to play the game. When you came along, she wanted to be the one to share with you, teach you, and show you what she loved most of all. She begged me not to tag along, and I agreed, but just as I had done before, I stayed in the shadows."

"Every time?" I asked.

If he had been there when I told Davior my life story, he already knew everything about me, yet they continue to let me stay.

"The swamp is a dangerous place, if you don't know what to look for. I've lived here long enough to spot danger or areas not meant for humans. Even May can wander in places she shouldn't," he said, answering my question. "The day you saw Davior, started out just like any other with May begging you to go exploring with her. I followed until I saw someone cloaked in a black coat also watching. When he noticed me, he went in the opposite direction of where you headed. I decided to follow him, but panicked when he disappeared. I ran back where I had last seen you, and then followed my instinct. Before I stepped through the clearing, I knew it was Davior. I also knew he was using his mind games on you by the way you looked at him." He turned on his side and met my gaze. "I wanted to kill him."

"Why would you want to kill your own brother?"

"You have to understand, Jess, Lucifer is very strong in this world. Not stronger than God, of course, but he has a way of finding our weakness and twisting it for his enjoyment. Davior chose that same deceitful way and he found something he could twist. He's not my brother in the same way he once was."

He could tell I didn't understand. Maybe he wished he had given me more time to read my Bible. He lay back, fixing his eyes on the clouds again.

"Seeing him there in the clearing, staring at you the way he was—I'd never experienced that type of emotion before. Davior was trying to take you away from…us." He shifted his eyes to the blanket, plucking at the strands of grass. "I couldn't allow that to happen. He knows what is going on inside my head. He knows what I'm thinking and feeling and I him."

"He can read thoughts?" I asked.

"Don't worry," he said at my surprised tone. "He can only read mine, but he can influence, or a better word, he can push thoughts and feelings into your head as though they are your own. We both can."

"So you were talking when I couldn't hear," I said, more of a thought to myself, but relieved he couldn't hear my thoughts.

"Something we were born with. I've heard it's common for twins to have a portion of the ability. My older brother can communicate with all of us in the same way, only we can't read his thoughts unless he allows us. That is only something Davior and I can do. It was fun when we were young—before things changed."

"Davior is your twin?"

"Yes."

Twins! Well that makes sense. That was the reason I felt attracted to him at first.

I could see it then in his jaw, body, and facial expressions.

"We were best friends long ago, shared just about everything. After…well at some point he started to resent me and my brothers because our parents gave us more responsibilities. If there was something to be done, my parents gave it to me instead of him, even though we were the same age."

"I'm so sorry." The brief feeling of sadness I'd had for Davior previously grew more.

"Anyway, of course he is attracted to you. I couldn't blame him for that." A crackle vibrated in his tone as he looked back at me. "You are quite a young woman. I'm sorry for not realizing it before. People's ages are subjective in my world."

What did he mean by subjective? Your age is your age, right?

He took my hand, brought it to his lips, and kissed the top of it. The little tingles moved all over my body, causing my heart to beat uncontrollably. I cleared my throat unintentionally.

"Oops. Sorry." He smiled before continuing. "He challenged me. In our culture, you have no choice to but to accept a challenge, whether you want to or not. Davior knows I believe in upholding our traditions and honor, so even though in my head I wanted to deny what he wanted, in the end he knew what I would have to say."

"What was he challenging you for?" I asked.

He stroked his thumb against the top of my hand. "You." The word fell out of his mouth and danced around inside my head. "The rules would be simple. You had to believe I was gone and Davior would get time alone with you. I'd be allowed to watch in the shadows to make sure you were safe, making sure he didn't cheat by pushing your thoughts. Miss Mabel thought it would be better if she kept watch, but I knew Davior. I knew he would try every trick he knew. At least I had the upper hand in knowing his thoughts." He paused. "But even more than that, I couldn't just leave you."

The tingling moved into my cheeks. I turned my face so he wouldn't notice.

"I have to admit it wasn't as easy as I thought it would be, seeing you and not able to be near you or talk to you. Of course, Davior knew. He played into the dark side of my soul I didn't know was there. Apparently, he didn't either at first, but he was all too thrilled about twisting it for his enjoyment when he found out. Anyway," he continued, "the time wouldn't begin right away, which was why he stayed away for a few of days. If I had pushed your thoughts, which I would never do, it would have worn off. Typically, it only lasts a day or so, but I've never done it to anyone. I've only done it with animals, only so they wouldn't hurt a human."

I thought about the snake in the swamp that almost had me for lunch.

"Davior accused me of using this power on you, so he claimed he needed time for my influence to fade. He called it a fair fight, but he knows nothing of the word. "I've never used it on any person," he stated again, squeezing my hand. "I'd never do that to you."

Turning my head, our eyes locked. "I remember how I felt. How he made me tell him things I didn't want anyone to know," I felt guilty I kept the secrets in the first place. "It was like an intruder inside my head telling me what to do."

Like the male voice I keep hearing.

I bit the outside of my lip and shook my head at my thought, but Hunter didn't notice and went on. "I think he prolonged it to torture me. His mind is warped. He's adopted a new set of moral values." He drifted away for a moment. "He got his time, and you refused him in the greatest way possible. I've never felt so relieved. But when I thought you were safe, sleeping in your bed, I didn't realize how much of you had gotten down into his soul. He was going to try again. When I finally got to you and saw you holding your ground, you really surprised me." Hunter pushed himself off

the ground to his feet. "I saw you down on your knees, praying."
He offered his hand, pulling me to him with tears in his eyes.
"Then to see you react to him the way you did was impressive
and very mature." Hunter's light-blue eyes twinkled at me as he
pulled a strand of hair from my bottom lip. "Of course, he knew
I was watching when he went in to kiss you. He knew I wasn't
going to allow it, provoking me to fight him," he said. "Although,
if you had made a different choice in the end, I—"

"Would have had to let me go," I whispered, "which is why
everyone seemed so happy after it happened."

Hunter put both hands on my face. "You and you alone make
choices for your life, and none of us can choose for you—not your
mother, and definitely not *Seth*." He spit out his name like poison.

Those last words worked in my mind, especially the mention
of my mother, who, to my knowledge, was thousands of miles
away. Hunter held me closer. All other thoughts and questions
faded back into the shadows.

"Of course, I'm happy about the path you did choose," he
said, speaking in a calm, low voice. "Some things in this life are
really bad. I'm sorry Davior unlocked your memory. You've gone
through so much in such a short period of time. You've carried
such a heavy burden. He needed to use whatever he could to
persuade you to follow the malevolent path of revenge, hate, and
power, all of which now consumes him."

"Like Pastor James was talking about yesterday," I added.

He chuckled. "You were listening."

"So it's done, then. He got his chance and lost," I said, knowing
the answer from being sneaky last night, but I was hoping to get
more information.

A heavy sigh escaped his lips. "No, there is more to it than that,
but he can't touch you now, like he could before. You can now see
him for who he really is. You are now one of God's children and
cannot lose salvation. However, Davior can still try to deceive
you, play on your fears, your sin, and even love."

"Love?"

"Yes. Love can be twisted and used as a gateway for evil, which is why you need to continue to read your Bible. It will help you be stronger mentally, making it harder for you to be temped. When you know God, evil ways are easier to spot. But unfortunately, things are never as black and white as we would like them to be. There is one other factor. They can physically hurt you or kill you, but I'll do what I need to do to keep you out of their reach."

But who's going to keep you safe?

It was my fault Davior found Seth. Although I'm sure he was an easy recruit, I wanted to know what he'd promised him. Seth wouldn't have joined unless it benefited his plans.

He'll come after everyone. Their deaths will be my fault.

My eyes shifted back and forth.

Hunter saw the panic on my face and frowned. "What's wrong?" "Seth. That's my fault. All the things I told Davior about him. He wouldn't have found him. He wouldn't be part of some cult. He was dangerous before—"

Hunter pulled me into his chest, stifling my shaking body, his hand stroking my hair. "It's not your fault, Jess. They would have found Seth without you."

I pushed my body away. "I don't understand. Found him for what purpose?"

"I know you don't understand, but it's nothing you could have prevented."

I turned my back to him. "You shouldn't say things that aren't true to comfort me." I knew it was my fault. Even though I couldn't stand Seth, I just was making things worse—a hundred times worse.

A demon-worshiping cult! Just great! I thought everyone was in danger before, and now, what have I unleashed?

"Jessica." His use of my full name took on another meaning. "I wouldn't lie to you. I don't think I could, even if I tried." He moved his hand gently down my arms until he found my hands. "Seth is, well, important for things to move forward for them.

They would have found him sooner or later, regardless of what you told them. The only thing you did was make it a little easier in their search." His lips met my ear as he whispered. "Please don't be mad at me. I don't think I can bear it."

"Now, you're talking about more than one person. You mean the cult he's in? I don't understand how or why if I hadn't talked about him," I answered in a low whisper, leaning into his chest.

His arms moved around me. I wasn't mad at him. I was mad at me.

Important? What does that mean?

A conversation began to fill the air around us. Three people surrounded us, looking at our two empty pails.

Warning

Joseph had not return after stomping off near the river.

"Should we go look for him?" I asked, thinking about Seth seething, just waiting to hurt anyone associated with me.

Miss Mabel washed off the strawberries over the sink. "Oh, he be back on his own. He just needs time to himself to gain proper perspective." She swished the strawberries around in a colander. "Better gets on these if theys are to be ready for the ladies to pick up." She dumped the clean strawberries into a plastic bowl. "Lots of pies to bake for the orphanage bake sale."

"Don't forget the crocheted blankets you made. I think Josephine is almost finished with hers," I added.

"Shes did finish." Miss Mabel handed me the bowl of clean fruit. "I has to say she done a wonderful job on it too."

Josephine pounded on the pie dough. "I only finished one, but next time, I'll have three. She divided the mixture, giving May a section to roll out.

"You'd has three done if yous wasn't a perfectionist." Miss Mabel winked at me. "There's only one perfect bein'. God in the flesh, amen."

We laughed as I took the bowl from her to take outside where Hunter waited at the small table.

"We've got more strawberries to slice." I placed the bowl in the middle of the table before sitting across from Hunter.

As we sliced the fruit into sections, I could smell the buttery dough of the first batch of pies, cooking in the coal oven.

"How much did you read last night?" Hunter asked.

"I read all of Matthew, Mark, Luke, and almost finished John."
I sliced another juicy strawberry. The liquid ran through my
already-sticky, red-tinted fingers, as I looked up at his scowling
face. "What?"

"That's a lot of reading in one night."

I shrugged before grabbing another piece of fruit. "I found it
interesting how similar the chapters were, but from a different
perspective. Really, I didn't realize how late it had gotten."

He reached for another strawberry. "That explains why you
keep yawning."

"I'm surprised you didn't notice." I teased.

He squirmed in his seat. "Just remember not to leave the front
porch without me."

May bounced through the swing door, letting it slam behind
her. "Ready for more?"

I took her bowl to empty into the one on the table.

"What's wrong?" May asked.

"Nothing," I said. "Here. You can take these." I handed her the
bowl with the sliced fruit.

"Okay then." She took the bowl inside.

"I'm sorry," he finally said. "I guess I'm mad at myself for
falling asleep before knowing you were safely in bed. It won't
happen again."

"I promise not to leave the porch without you. I don't want
to be responsible for you not getting enough sleep, but I wish
you wouldn't treat me like a child. You don't have to watch me
all the time." Although I loved how he wanted to protect me,
watching me all the time meant he'd probably see my not-so-
ladylike actions, like biting my nails. My mother said it was like
putting filth in my mouth. "So getting back to what we were
talking about, the chapters I read." I kept slicing.

"Yes." He cleared his throat. "They are all very similar and told
from different points of view to paint one beautiful picture of who
Jesus was." He plopped a sliced strawberry into the bowl, still not

looking in my direction. "Each disciple focused on one aspect of that picture. An example is how Matthew, writing primarily for the Jewish audience, focused on tying in old prophecies of a coming Messiah. Mark's account is a quick reflection on Jesus's miracles, while Luke, being a doctor, focused on Jesus's abilities to heal, bringing redemption for all people through ultimate sacrifice. Lastly, John focused on the deity of Christ. Each account is from the same period in history, but told just a little differently as it was revealed to them. Although all scripture is God inspired, He gifted each disciple to use their particular talent to reach many. Does that make sense?"

"Although I haven't finished John, what you're saying makes sense."

Hunter continued. "No two people who witness the same event will recall the same details, but will have the same general idea. Some people believe that means the Bible contradicts itself."

"I didn't think it contradicted, but what gifts does God give?"

"We have, as children of God, come together to use our abilities, our gifts, to accomplish His goals together. For example, Miss Mabel has many gifts. One is she is a great cook. She makes these pies so people will buy them, and the money goes to help the children. Now she doesn't like to be around all those people, so there are others who come get the pies and sell them. It's a team effort with one goal in mind. It's the same for all of us."

"When do you get a gift?" I asked, thinking I didn't have any gifts.

Hunter stopped slicing. "They come when you need them most"

"What is your gift?" I asked, but immediately felt stupid for asking.

The mind-reading thing between his brothers is pretty amazing, not to mention the ability to sway animals.

"I was saved for a purpose, but now...now I'm not so sure what that purpose is. It's possible...but then again..." he mumbled.

"Does it work in the opposite way? I mean for Lucifer and his followers. Do they come together with gifts to accomplish their goals?"

"Yes."

"So you said Seth is important. Is that what you mean? He possesses some sort of gift to benefit their side?"

"Yes."

My eyes lifted, noticing his frown. "That's bad, isn't it?"

"I don't know what it means. But we'll figure it out." He chuckled. "Davior isn't keeping to his boundary, so I keep reading bits of what's going on inside his head."

I thought about Seth's ability to persuade people. He didn't need to use special power to do it. I stared at the strawberry in my hand, biting the outside of my bottom lip.

Should I ask him how much he knows about me? Should I just assume he knows? Would it help him if he knew my secrets about Seth? About my mother?

Taking a deep breath, I decided it was time to ask. "How much, I mean from what you heard me tell Davior, do you know about my past?"

Hunter didn't answer. The acid in my stomach swished around. Looking across the table, Hunter wasn't in the chair. My eyes caught red eyes, beyond the trees, staring back.

"Hunter?" I whispered, as my heart thrashed against my ribs. *Seth?*

The eyes vanished.

Now, on top of the voice in my head, I'm seeing things that aren't really there.

"I'm here," Hunter said behind me, causing me to jolt in my seat. "I'm sorry. I didn't mean to startle you."

"It's okay. I just didn't realize you had left."

It was just my imagination. If it had been Seth, he would not have just been waiting out there. He would have come and taken me.

"And then I came up behind you," he finished for me. "Here. Let me take those. She's ready to assemble the next round of pies." He took the bowl, replacing it with more whole strawberries before going back inside.

He didn't hear my question. Maybe I should just assume he knows everything. Why do I need it verbalized? Besides, he's reading Davior's thoughts, so he'll know more than I do. Ask about Seth instead.

Hunter returned, sitting back in his chair.

"Why did Seth look the way he did? I mean with the red eyes. And, well, he acted differently, too."

"Seth believes you are his. He also believes by giving Davior what he wants, you will marry him willingly. He doesn't want to force you, but he will if it's necessary. He struck a bargain with Davior so now he's going through changes." Hunter shook his head. "Seth felt possessive of you before my brother got to him. Now it's amplified. Although at the moment, Seth is not in control, Davior is, but that won't last. I'm not sure Davior will be able to keep control over him much longer." He looked out into the field. "My brother has also given him other reasons to be even more possessive of you."

"And that would be?"

"He told Seth we have brainwashed you into staying with us. So he thinks you're a prisoner, and he's the only one who can save you." He let out a dry laugh. "He thinks you'll see him as your knight in shining armor, sweeping you off your feet, and you'll marry him on the spot."

Even with the sweet smell of the strawberries in the air, I smelled something foul lingering in his words, and I twisted my face in disgust. "Yeah, like that would ever happen," I spoke it loudly, just in case Seth was listening.

Hunter glanced at me with a pleasing grin before getting back to his work. "Davior is also doing all this for his own benefit as well. You know how he feels about you," Hunter said, picking up another strawberry, not looking up. "They don't keep to any rules, so once Davior gets what he wants out of Seth, he'll figure a way to get you for himself. He's unsure of many things, so I can't see clearly what he's thinking, but I know he doesn't plan to hand you over to Seth willingly."

I didn't speak. Minutes seemed to pass between us while I absorbed his words.

I'm nothing. Why does Davior want me?

Redness rose up on Hunter's cheeks, as he hesitated to continue. "There's one more reason Seth is agitated. Davior told Seth there is another man who is attempting to claim you. I think this, more than anything else, has caused Seth to be even more unstable. And now that we've met, he knows it's true."

"Oh," was all I could manage to say.

He knows it's true? Hunter wants to claim me? He wants me?

I felt short of breath as the blood raced throughout my limbs.

"So you can see why you need to be careful. You need to stay near the house or near me at all times. Neither of them can enter the house. It's protected."

I liked the "near me" part. I expected the voice to chime in, the one saying I was making it all up, reading into something that wasn't there, but it remained silent and still.

"Seth is going through a transition period for the next month, so we should be fine going off the property. Davior won't let him leave without supervision. It doesn't help his situation to bring him around you right now. It could ruin the work they have already done."

"Wait, what do you mean by transition period? Did Davior go through some strange ritual to be accepted into this cult? Is that how he learned to use black magic, and now Seth will be learning it as well?" If it were true, it would explain how he had played those illusions on me.

"You'll have to be ready to face him," he said, ignoring my question but prompting a more serious one. He sighed. "There will be much for you to do before then."

"Who? Seth? I have to face him?" I looked down at my red-stained hands. The memory of Seth's fingers around my neck flashed before me.

"You'll have to face him, Jess."

I shivered, letting the knife slide between my fingers. The knife hit the ground twice before it laid still. I could see a vision of Seth, standing in total darkness, his blood red eyes burning at me, waiting for the opportunity to take me captive. I imagined him bigger, much bigger and ready to attack anyone who stood in his way. His muscular arms would crush me against his body, squeezing the blood from my body like a packet of ketchup.

I stared at the finger bleeding from where the knife passed. It was interesting not to feel the stinging pain.

Hunter continued, not noticing. "You won't be alone. But we might have to give the impression you are alone with Seth in order to keep him from going out of control. We have to give him the chance to speak to you, for you to finally tell him."

I squeezed the cut, watching the blood run down my finger. "But why? I don't want to talk to him. My mother was forcing me marry him. I told him over and over I would never marry him of my own free will. I just wanted them to leave me alone, let me live my life. I only agreed to it to save my father, and when he died—"

"You're bleeding!" Hunter jumped up, taking the towel from his shoulder to wrap my finger.

"You don't understand. He's had people killed." The tears blurred my vision. "I'm so sorry I lied to everyone, even more sorry I didn't leave when I should have. I've put everyone here in danger."

Hunter pulled me into his arms, while keeping pressure on the cut. "Jess. Jess, please don't worry. There is nothing to be sorry for. You'll see, everything will work out."

"If you say so. Do I really have to face him?" I gathered myself together, wondering who would keep him safe.

"You'll be ready. Trust me. Even more, you can trust God." He pressed his lips against the top of my head. Removing the towel, he looked at the cut. "It's stop bleeding, but let me go get a bandage."

As he entered the shack, I heard Miss Mabel ask, "Have you two sliced the rest of those strawberries yet?"

"We are just about done," Hunter answered. Within minutes, he was back, wrapping the bandaged around my wound. "I'll finish slicing these."

I watched him. "What is this magic they are involved in? What can they do with it?"

"It's not magic," he said.

"I saw it. The way the sun darkened in the middle of the day, the way they glided across the ground like ghosts."

"It's not a cult either. Why don't you go wash up? We can manage the rest of the baking. It's time for you to know what we are dealing with, and the best way I know is for you read it yourself."

I shrugged, staring into his beautiful, soft face, letting go of all the worry. It wasn't that I didn't want to read, but I felt guilty not helping by getting lost in a book. Surely, wanting to pass up a reading time was a first for me. Although the Bible wasn't fairytales, I equated reading to an escape. An escape from a world I wanted to hide from. I was in a real-life fairy tale. I didn't need to escape, well, except for the whole Davior and Seth thing. If I could avoid them, everything would be perfect.

My thoughts drifted back to Hunter's face, especially his perfect pink lips.

In most fairytale romances, the two main characters would have kissed by now. Maybe I should just kiss him. Now there's an idea.

Thinking about how soft his lips felt, moving along my cheekbone, he would have kissed me if not for the interruption. I huffed as all those feelings rushed through my body like a raging river. The table was the only thing stopping me from carrying out the thought of taking the aggressive approach. My strongest desire—the only feeling I wanted to have was his lips against mine. I wondered, for a second, if the table could hold me.

I laughed loudly.

Hunter raised one eyebrow. I shook my head. After all, I was only human and a silly little girl.

"Go on, gets your Bible and start reading," he said, sounding a little like Miss Mabel.

A Vision of Things to Come

The darkness closed around me quickly. I squinted to read the words on the page. Suddenly, a light appeared above me, but instead of looking up to see who was providing the light, I continued to read.

I'm not sure how long I continued to read, but I read the last few paragraphs of Revelation out loud. "I am the Alpha and the Omega, the First and the Last, the Beginning and the End. Blessed are those who wash their robes, that they may have the right to the tree of life and may go through the gates into the city. Outside are the dogs, those who practice magic arts, the sexually immoral, the murderers, the idolaters and everyone who loves and practices falsehood. I, God's Son, have sent my angel to give you this testimony for the churches. I am the Root and the Offspring of David, and the bright Morning Star. The Spirit and the bride say, 'Come!' And let him who hears say, 'Come!' Whoever is thirsty, let him come, and whoever wishes, let him take the free gift of the water of life. I warn everyone who hears the words of the prophecy of this book: If anyone adds anything to them, God will add to him the plagues described in this book. And if anyone takes words away from this book of prophecy, God will take away from him his share in the tree of life and in the holy city, which are described in this book. He who testifies to these things says, 'Yes, I am coming soon.' Amen. Come, Lord. The grace of the Lord be with God's people. Amen."

I went back to the words "Outside are the dogs."

Seth was one of those dogs now. How many more were out there?

With little movement, I glanced over to the long, round hook holding the lantern glowing brightly. There was movement under me.

Hunter's arm rested across my stomach. His chest rose and fell softly against my back in a deep, peaceful sleep. I supposed he didn't trust me to keep my word and not leave the porch. A smiled formed along my lips, as I nestled down into his embrace. He tightened his hold as I swept my finger along his arm.

The pages I read swirled around inside my head. Some were questions, but mostly my thoughts were on a war. A bloody battle between God's army and Lucifer's army would be the one to end all wars. Only for that to happen, there were steps leading up to it. The steps sounded so much like what was happening around me. Mothers killing their children, children killing their parents, disease killing thousands of people, devastating natural disasters, famine, water shortages, Christians being murdered for their beliefs—a book written thousands of years ago was like reading the headlines of a newspaper.

I shivered.

Placing my cheek against Hunter's chest, the rhythm of his heart soothed me.

Why couldn't my world stay here just like this?

My thoughts were not alone. *You're putting everyone in danger, Jessica. You're being selfish.*

Shutting out the voice, I focused on being in Hunter's arms. I closed my eyes, remembering the moment we almost kissed. Whether I was going crazy or being played like a puppet, I had no desire to fight the intruder. I was happy with no other place I wanted to be. Finally, drifting off to sleep, I fell into white, fluffy clouds in a brilliant blue sky. But my dreams never stayed peaceful for long. The clouds turned black and covered up the sky.

Palm trees lined the city streets. The smell of hot black tar, burned in my chest making it hard to breathe. Coughing, I stood behind thousands of people in the intersection of Figueroa and Peco in front of the Los Angeles Convention Center.

Scouting the area for higher ground, I noticed a taco food truck parked in the lot across the intersection. I quickly made my way to it, climbing up the service ladder to the top.

The intense, orange-tinted sun peered through a brown haze of smoke, beaming down on a recently constructed stage, decorated in streamers, balloons, and banners in patriotic colors. Television cameras were everywhere, buzzing around the platform. With a clear view of the stage, I watched with anticipation on who would be address the crowd. Out of the corner of my eye, I caught sight of a little girl skipping her way out of the crowd. She was wearing a pretty silk blue dress with white ruffles on the bottom. Her curly blonde hair was tied with white ribbon.

Is it May? What is May doing here?

I climbed off the truck to make my way through the loud, chatty crowd, pushing when necessary. "Excuse me," I yelled over the noise, hearing the grunting and irritation. But I didn't care. I was getting closer to May. "May! May!" I screamed, but she didn't turn around.

The little girl hastened her pace as I called her name. She reached the end of the crowd, passing the Staples center and around a construction area with blue fencing. A park appeared out of nowhere. I stopped, watching her skip past the swings, to disappear into a thick line of purple bushes. If it was May, she was gone, away from the commotion of the crowd.

Should I go after her?

A loud noise sounded from above. A helicopter flying extremely low was over me. The air whirled, kicking up everything in its path. I covered my face, waiting for it to pass. The noise of the blades was replaced by the crowd cheering. I looked up. Everyone, but me, turned their attention to the stage.

The air changed as I made my way closer to the stage. It was stagnant and smelly, like the bog on the other side of the fast moving river, the one Miss Mabel said kept people from that part of the swamp. I passed one woman, who began to stare at me. Her mascara ran down her fake rosy cheeks, and her thick lipstick looked melted, dripping off her chin. A knot rose up in my throat as I turned away from her.

Finally I could see the stage, but I couldn't hear what was being said or make out who was standing in the center of it. Another person in the crowd began to stare at me like the woman had, only it was a middle-aged man. Black circles surrounded his eyes, receding into his face. He held out his arms, showing me his long, deep cuts from the elbows down to his hands. They looked like claw marks from an animal attack. The brilliant red blood oozed from his wounds.

I gasped.

Feeling nauseated, I spun away from him to be confronted with another person marred in some way. I couldn't breathe. They gathered around me, showing me their wounds, and talking at the same time so I couldn't understand them.

Suddenly, it went quiet. Someone else approached. I heard hard breathing, followed by footsteps that shook the ground. The faces of the crowd changed into melted, crayon faces. I panicked, not able to move in any direction. The person approaching stopped behind me. His hot breath smelled of rotten eggs, burning the back of my neck. I cried out in pain before falling to the ground. It sizzled on my skin, blistering my hands and searing through my jeans.

The crowd cheered.

I looked up. The sun blazed over me, scorching my eyes and face. I closed my eyes tightly.

Where is Hunter? He said he would never leave me.

I shielded my eyes, opening them slowly. I tried to call out, but no sound came. The crowd cheered louder with each attempt. The sweat flowed from my forehead, off my chin to sizzle on the tar road. I wiped my forehead with the back of my hand, but it didn't feel like sweat anymore. A thick, sticky substance smeared into my hair. I looked at my hand covered in blood—my blood. My head spun. I put both palms on the hot, sizzling ground, screaming, hoping it would wake me.

Just a dream. It's just a dream.

The person behind me shifted to stand in front of me, shading me from the bright glow. I couldn't make him out at first. The blistering skin peeling away from his face, made it difficult His blood-red eyes recoiled into his skull. When he spoke with authority over me, I knew for sure.

Seth raised his hands, motioning to the crowd. The little girl in the blue dress joined his side. Her face was also deformed. She laughed at my surprise, revealing her black tongue and missing teeth. Seth motioned again, making the crowd cheer. A tall man wearing a hooded black cloak handed Seth something shiny. He held it up for all to see.

They went crazy.

Seth grabbed a fistful of my hair, lifting me up, as I kicked and swung my arms. He held the small silver dagger to my throat. "I love you, Jessica," he whispered in my ear.

I screamed.

Hunter's voice floated in the air. "Jessie. Jessie. Wake up."

The cold blade ran across my throat.

<hr />

I pushed someone's hands off me, breathing hard, to run for the porch steps. Gripping the railing, I fought the urge to vomit.

He's out there.

Hunter leapt to my side, not letting me push him away. "Breathe, Jessie. Breathe."

I struggled to speak. "He tried to kill me."

The rain pounded on the roof over the porch. Flashes of light lit up the field as I glared out, wondering if he was out there. I struggled to stay still in Hunter's arms. "It's okay. It was just a dream," He stroked back my hair with one hand, holding me secure with the other.

"All those people wanted him to kill me. They wanted him to tear me apart." I knew it was a dream, but I also knew it was a warning. "You said they weren't involved in a cult."

Hunter didn't answer but continued to run his hand through my hair.

Think, Jessica.

Closing my eyes, I thought over everything the Bible taught me so far.

The faces in the dream, they all had a symbol on their forehead. The same symbol. The mark of the beast?

The other voice added. *You know he'll not only come after you but all of you. Everyone who stands in his way is already dead unless you leave now.*

The tears flowed uncontrollably, tasting like sulfur.

Regardless of who was behind the voice, it was right. I had to leave and soon. If it was Davior in my head, he would know what was coming.

Hunter put enough space between us to wipe my face. "Just a dream," he whispered again, stroking my cheek.

"Not a dream, a real vision of something coming," I shook.

"Was I there?"

"No."

"Well then you know for sure it couldn't have been real." He moved my chin to bring my face up to his. "I wasn't kidding when I said I wouldn't leave you." Hunter looked into my face and traced his finger along my jawbone.

I forgot the dream.

The light from the lantern burned dim, but I could see his face was filled with concern. My body relaxed against him. He cradled my face with his hand.

"Better?"

Can he see how much I needed him? I never needed anyone before. I never wanted to need anyone. How is it that it all changed so quickly?
I simply nodded and sighed heavily. "What time is it?"

"It's close to sunrise. You should get some sleep in your bed."

I clung to him. He wrapped both arms around my quivering body.

"No," I whispered, thinking of what I might dream about next or what might be waiting for me.

"Honey, you have to sleep," he softly whispered, touching his lips to my hair. The word *honey* sent a thrill throughout me.

"I'll leave a note for Miss Mabel to let us sleep in. She won't mind." Lifting me, I wrapped my arms around his neck, placing my cheek against his chest.

I can't leave, not now, not ever.

I clung to him tighter, before he set me down on the bed. He leaned in to kiss my forehead as he had done before. As soon as he turned to leave, the liquid swelled in my eyes. Of course, I was being silly again. His bed was only six feet away from mine. However, it felt like miles, and the dream felt more like inches.

My bed moved.

Hunter stood next to the bed. "I'm probably being a little overprotective and will get an earful later, but I think it's best if I stay close to you." He spoke softly.

I scooted to the other side of the matrices as he sat at the edge. "I was thinking the same thing." I whispered back.

He stacked the pillows, before lying down on top of the sheet, keeping a thin layer of material between us. Putting my head to his chest, he must have realized I was crying again. He wiped my tears again.

What he must think of me. I hate this new pathetic me. I should look him in the eyes, tell him that I'm just fine, and I can take care of myself.

The other voice couldn't resist. *You should walk out the door right now if you want to save them from destruction.*

Again, the voice was right, but I suddenly felt very sleepy, relaxed by the rise and fall of his chest.

"Jess?" he whispered, whirling a strand of hair in his finger.

"Yes?" I asked in a yawn, feeling safe to sleep.

"Never mind." He sighed and yawned himself. "No more dreams tonight."

"No more dreams," I echoed.

We woke up late, like Hunter had suggested. Everyone else was already up and out of the house by the time I stirred. Hunter hadn't moved.

He was still holding me as I popped my head up to see his face. "How long have you been awake?"

"Not long." He smiled at me, tucking a stay hair behind my ear. "How do you feel?"

"Hungry."

"That must have been some dream. You were really upset."

"It felt so real." Thinking about the hot breath on my neck, I reached back. Felt normal.

"What?" He sat up to look at the back of my neck.

"Just something in the dream burned my neck. I examined the palms of my hands which were also blister-free.

Hunter lifted up my hair, which caused me to giggle. He caressed the back of my neck with the tips of his fingers, sending delightful tingles all over.

He cleared his throat. "Looks and feels normal to me."

Does he really not know what he's doing to me?

I turned to face him with a half smile planted on my face.

"What?" He laughed. His eyes were almost sinister, sort of a different look for him.

"If you have to ask, then I shouldn't tell you." I went to get up, but he grabbed my hand to pull me back.

"Sorry." He laughed nervously. "You're not making things easy for me."

I never saw an example of real love, I mean other than my father. But all the feeling caught up inside me wanted out. We hadn't even kissed, and yet I knew I loved him. The real question was, did he love me? "And what does that mean, exactly?"

"I think it means we need to get dressed. The ladies from the orphanage will be here soon to pick up the pies. I'm sure you don't want them to see you in the clothes you wore yesterday, sitting here with me," Hunter teased.

Not the answer I wanted. I got dressed wanting to think more about love, but instead, I thought about the dream. Did it have anything to do with what I had just read? Hunter wanted me to read that particular chapter for a reason. Davior was not just in some devil cult.

Could he be the devil?

I laughed at my ridiculous thought. It wasn't like the devil walked around in plain sight.

Or does he?

Regardless of what the dream meant, it was a sign of things to come. I was sure of it. What I wasn't sure of was what Hunter meant by me not making thing easy for him. If he cared about me in a boy-girl way, then why couldn't he just tell me how he felt? Was there a reason we couldn't be together?

Molly came to mind.

All Dressed Up

It was just before noon when I exited the washroom, ready for our visitors. Hunter jumped in after. As I waited for him, I continued on with my reading.

I opened my Bible to the first chapter—Genesis, the creation of it all. I knew about Adam and Eve, well, the basic story anyway. I couldn't understand how they could be tempted into believing the serpent. They had paradise, God walking with them, and they wanted more. Eve wanted the power. That wouldn't have been my trigger. Power over others had never sounded appealing to me. My mother, on the other hand, had been exactly like Eve in that way. She had wanted more than anything to have status, control, and any man she could get it from. She'd twist them into doing what she had wanted. My father had often hesitated at her nonsense requests or demands, but gave in eventually—except for the last request she'd ever make from him. It was clear which path Seth would have chosen. He would have chopped the entire tree down. I couldn't blame him completely for the way he had been brought up, since ultimately, it was my mother's devious plan from the beginning.

If Davior is the devil—no he can't be Hunter is his brother. Demons? They are demons.

The blood left my face, and I felt light-headed. Hunter was back at my side, dropping the towel he was using to dry his hair. "You're so pale." He put his hands on my face. "Are you dizzy?"

I nodded. I also felt sick, but I didn't share.

"Don't get up," he ordered, moving into the kitchen to pull out a plate from of the oven. "You probably need to eat." He smiled gently. "You didn't eat much last night."

"Have they turned into demons? Davior and Seth?"

He tried to feed me, scooping the dry eggs onto the fork, but I grabbed the fork.

"I can do that," I said.

He smirked. "You didn't seem to mind last night."

"Oh. Well, I was sort of in a trance, so that doesn't count. You haven't answered my question."

He made me take a bite, but the food tasted dry. "Better?" he asked before leaping up.

I nodded. "Okay, so now—"

We both heard cars coming down the path. Hunter went over to the screen door combing his fingers through his long, wet hair, tying it back with a rubber band. He then sat on Miss Mabel's rocking chair to pull his boots on. "Company time," he said with a heavy sigh. "They brought lunch, so don't worry about breakfast." He got up from the chair to take my plate.

"I'm okay now," I said, glad I didn't have to finish the plate of food.

"Be good," he whispered in my ear, his lips slightly touching it. He inhaled a long, steady breath.

"You still didn't answer my question, and I don't know what you mean about being good."

In a superior tone, he answered, "I know." He set the plate in the sink before dragging me out the door behind him.

Two cars pulled up along the side of the shack. I knew both.

I was surprised to see Pastor James pull up in his red, beat-up pickup. He wasn't due out until next month, and he had never brought anyone with him. Another man stepped out of the truck. He was over six feet tall, slim, with the same blue eyes as Hunter's. His long, blonde hair, with white streaks, was fastened back with brown twine. Hunter talked about an older brother, and they looked alike. It was possible they were related.

The other vehicle was the van Miss Caroline drove. Miss Betsy sat in the front seat. Molly slid open the side door just as the ladies got out of the car.

Miss Caroline immediately whisked me up into an embrace, giving Hunter no choice but to let go of my hand. "Oh, it's so good to see you!" Miss Caroline sang.

My eyes stayed on the new person with Pastor James. "It hasn't been that long," I stated before Miss Betsy grabbed me next.

They both seemed happier than usual to see me.

"You look very pretty today," Miss Betsy sang as she hugged me, looking over at Hunter, who shrugged his shoulders.

Hunter took back my hand, but his eyes were also on the person with Pastor James. Molly stumbled on the bottom of her dress, making a commotion. She looked up sharply in confusion, since Hunter didn't jump to her aid. I was amazed at how quickly she recovered her balance.

It felt awkward the way Molly pretended not to notice Hunter holding my hand. "Hello, Jessica," she said dryly. "I hope you are well."

"I'm good. Thanks." I tried to sound friendly. After all, I didn't dislike her, not really.

I did have thoughts of drowning her when she was mean to May. Maybe I do dislike her.

The crease in her forehead deepened as it pained her to even speak to me. Her eyes narrowed, sending me the nonverbal message, she wasn't going to give him up without a fight. Hunter's body tensed, catching Molly's expression. I tightened my grip on his hand, hoping he would understand my gesture not to say anything.

Molly's countenance swiftly changed when she realized he was watching her. "Hello, Hunter," she said in a melancholy tone.

She watched his hand let go of mine to move around my waist. He gently pulled me closer to his side.

That wasn't what I meant by my hand squeeze.

"Hello, Molly. It's nice to see you." His tone wasn't rude, but it wasn't friendly either.

She looked away from his glare, but her skin turned red like a bad sunburn. I couldn't tell if it was because she was embarrassed or really mad.

I grimaced at him so he knew I disapproved of his cool tone, but he didn't waver. Instead he leaned to my ear, but no words came out.

"We have something for you, Jessica." Miss Betsy interrupted.

Miss Caroline grabbed my arm, once again pulling me from Hunter. She took out a garment bag from the van, tossing it into my arms before she grabbed out two more.

"Hunter, shoo. You have other things to take care of." She motioned him away from us as she hurried me into the house.

Hunter tried to follow.

Miss Betsy stopped him. "She'll be safe with us. Go."

How would they know to keep me safe? I'd be the one keeping them safe. Another reminder everyone around me knew more than I did. Why haven't I asked more questions? Why didn't I press Hunter to answer more questions?

More people Seth will kill if you don't leave. "Shut up," I whispered to the voice, shaking my head.

Miss Caroline didn't hear me as she tugged me into the shack. Looking over my shoulder at Hunter, Pastor James, along with the other man, moved alongside him. They joined Miss Mabel and strolled into the swamp. An achy feeling came over me. He wasn't supposed to leave me.

"Lunch first, then the makeovers." Miss Betsy held a picnic basket. She pulled out little sack lunches.

"What about the guys and Miss Mabel?" I asked. "Should I get them?"

"No, no. They have already been taken care of, my dear. No worries." Miss Caroline flashed me a big-toothed smile, handing me a paper bag.

I went straight for the swing, hoping I could see Hunter out near the tree line. No such luck. May followed behind me, sitting next to me in the swing. Molly and Josephine came out next and sat on the steps.

"I didn't see Joseph when we pulled up," Molly said to Josephine.

"No. He's been, well, gone for a few days," she answered.

"Where did he go?" Molly pursued.

"Where he usually goes." Josephine looked over at me, while Molly grinned. She liked knowing the secrets being kept from me. "Still pouting, I'm sure. I just hope he stays there until he's ready to apologize."

May spoke to me with her mouth full. "I've wanted to ask you something, but I'm not sure how to ask."

"You can ask me anything, May. You should know that by now," I said.

She shrugged her shoulders. "You and Hunter have been spending a lot of time together."

Molly stopped talking to Josephine.

"Well, do you love him? Are you guys going to get married?" She asked.

Both Molly and Josephine turned for the answer. I felt a hot flow of blood rush to my cheeks.

There is so much more going on than just the little world here. I'm still not even sure how Hunter feels. I should leave and never come back.

I might have told her I loved him if it were just us. With Molly leering at me, waiting to hear my answer, I didn't want to reply. May put her small hand in my lap. "I'm glad. He's been alone for a long time."

I didn't have to answer to make Molly furious. Her eyes met mine with the same look as before.

"Okay. Are we ready?" Miss Caroline sang, motioning for us to go inside the shack.

We filed into the room. Molly sulked, lingering behind. It tore at me to see her so sad.

Miss Betsy giggled, shutting the door and pulling the curtains. "I have something for all the girls. And we can't have anyone peeking." Molly stood in a corner, not really participating.

Miss C grabbed the three garment bags, laying two on a bed and hanging the other on top of the bathroom door frame. She slowly unzipped the bag and gasped.

I giggled at her over-the-top expression.

The turquoise dress with white roses and thick eyelet lace around the hem was for Josephine. Her eyes sparkled. "You made this for me?" Josephine managed to utter softly.

Miss C nodded.

Josephine giggled, hugging the woman, including Molly.

Molly beamed. "You're welcome." Evidently, the hostility just shot my way. "You'll look very pretty in it." Molly showed her the big bag filled with all kinds of hair trimmings and makeup. "We have shoes and ribbons to match."

My mother had been the queen of pretty dresses and frilly things—all the things I never cared for. I really didn't want them dressing me up like some poor girl who needed to feel pretty. I had closets full of dresses. Some I never wore, mostly because my mother bought them from designers for an insane amount of money—enough to feed an entire city for months. Yet I knew these ladies didn't have much. They had made these dresses with their own hands. I should be grateful, not just for me, but for May and Josephine.

The next dress pulled out of the garment bag was frilly, pink, and beautiful. It screamed May. A white sleeveless jacket, with embroidered flowers, draped over the shoulders. Of course, she completely loved it, running around the room to squeeze everyone.

"I saved yours for last, Jessica." Miss C unzipped it very slowly, taking the dress out of the bag.

I stared at it for a moment. My dress was made from a silk-like, thin material and not frilly or lacey like the others. The white embroidered roses along the bottom were of such fine, intricate detail, I knew it had to have taken a great amount of time to do. I was touched someone would do something like that for me.

"I didn't think you were into the girly, lacey things like the other two. You can wear this just about anytime, anywhere," Miss B said, smiling. "Do you like it?"

"I, I love it. It's beautiful," I answered, holding back the tears.

"Okay. Now everyone needs to put them on to make sure they all fit, and then I still have another surprise," Miss B said. "Jessica, you can use the washroom to change if it makes you more comfortable."

That's what I did. I took off the clothes I was wearing, neatly folding them before slipping on the dress. It was light, flowing, and felt soft against my skin. I stepped out of the bathroom, and everyone but Molly clapped their hands in excitement.

"Didn't I tell you?" Miss C said to Miss B.

"Yes, yes, but we definitely need to do something with her hair," Miss B said with a little bit of concern.

The girls looked just beautiful in their dresses. Even Josephine twirled around. She was so different when Joseph wasn't near her.

Molly jumped up. "I'll do May and Josephine's hair," she said, digging through the bag she had brought.

"Perfect." Miss C grabbed out the makeup, while Miss B undid the wild messed under the scrunchie. "Jessica, you'll need to stay still unless you want Betsy yanking out your hair." She winked over at her, while Miss B playfully stuck out her tongue.

I sat uneasy in the kitchen chair as they fussed over me.

The ladies talked to each other as if I wasn't there. I focused my thoughts on the girls enjoying all the pampering.

"You know, I didn't think you could do it, but you did," one of the ladies said to the other.

The chatter had been so loud and for so long I couldn't tell who was speaking to whom. I heard Molly giggle with the girls from time to time, so I was glad she was enjoying herself. However, I wished she'd drop the daggers glances at me.

"Of course she's beautiful. God gets the credit for the foundation to work with. I just polished it up."

Miss Betsy motioned for me to stand up. "Give us a twirl." Both ladies were clapping their hands, joined by May and Josephine. The girls looked like china dolls. They were gorgeous. *Why though? We don't go anywhere. Why get us all dressed up?* From the dimness in the room, I assumed the sun had fallen behind the trees surrounding the property. A knock at the door, sent the ladies into a panic. "One moment please," one of them called.

Molly made her way to the door and was about to open it. Miss Betsy shook her finger at her. Molly turned from the door to go inside the kitchen.

Miss Caroline hurried me out the back door. "It's okay, dear." She took me to the side of the house, stopping to admire her work. "Ah, Cinderella!" she exclaimed, before placing me in front of the red maple tree. "Now stay here. Don't move."

I felt silly standing there alone. But it wasn't a second later when Hunter stormed around the corner of the porch. He frantically scanned the area, until I came into view. His smile brought a warm tingle to my cheeks.

Embarrassed, I skimmed the ground, taking a shy step toward him. I felt so impractical all dressed up with a thick covering of make-up smeared over my face. My hair, up in a loose bun, had a few stray curls dangling down. We were close enough to touch. I glanced up then quickly down, looking at the jute sandals on my feet. He touched my face, lifting up my chin.

He chuckled. "You are radiant."

"I feel silly," I added, fidgeting with the dress.

"You were a good sport to let them dress you up." He encircled his arm around my waist. "I'm sure it wasn't easy."

"I would have broken their hearts if I had refused. I didn't want that on my conscience." His embrace washed away any awkward embarrassment.

"I'm glad you let them, although you are beautiful in whatever you wear, and your hair is just as lovely after a good night's sleep."

He twirled a finger around one of the curls dangling along my face.

Someone cleared their throat, letting us know we were no longer alone. Hunter turned around to the group watching us. Miss C and Miss B were absolutely giddy. Miss Mabel, with an approving smile, came alongside them as did the man I had not yet met. He stood there without any visible emotion.

Hunter placed one arm around my waist and led me to him. "Jessica, this is John Fox."

"Hello," I said.

John gracefully nodded.

Hunter stared into the man's eyes. "He would like to talk to you for a few minutes."

The look caused my nerves to go into overdrive.

"It's okay," Hunter whispered. "You're actually safer with John than anyone else, including me. He just wants to ask you few questions."

Questions? See, I told you it's time to leave. The voice was angry, speaking louder than before. I was sure everyone else heard it, but if they had, they pretended not to. I did think of Davior and his abilities.

Could he be in my head? Pushing my thoughts like Hunter said?

"Let's go for a walk, Jessica," John took my elbow gently, leading me into the woods.

"Tell me, Jessica, how did you find your way here?" His voice was deep but soft.

I thought about everything at once. Not just all I had experienced since my arrival, but the progression of my entire life that brought me to the swamp. I told John the whole story, starting with my father. I went on about my mother striking deals with me so I could keep my father alive, followed by the last deal and the reason I left—the arranged marriage to Seth.

I hesitated when it came to the light, though. Unsure if that was real or not, I still ran the risk of ending up in a mental institution. But I told him anyway, in great details. I mentioned the encounters with Davior, then the dreams as we walked among the deep-green trees.

John listened carefully before responding. "A light led you to a postcard of the area, then the same light appeared again when you were on the road?" He stopped walking.

"No. I had already wandered into the forest and gotten lost. I was ready to give up but then the light returned and I followed it."

"Was your father, your natural father?"

That is a strange question to ask me? But I never doubted he was, or would my mother have kept that from me too?

"Of course he was. If it hadn't been for the attack, he would have taken me away a long time ago, a special place where she couldn't touch me," I said, remembering the scene Davior had shone me.

John paused for a moment, glaring into my eyes. The nervous feeling subsided as his face softened. We continued our walk, until we were back in the meadow in front of the shack. "Thank you, Jessica. I have enjoyed talking with you, and I appreciate your honesty."

Hunter, carrying a garment bag, sprinted to us.

"Jessica, can I have a moment with my son?" John asked.

Hunter's father? How is that possible?

John couldn't have been more than ten years older than Hunter.

I nodded, walking over to May standing on the front steps. Everyone, except me, chattered in excitement on the porch. I focus on the two men in conversation. Hunter's face didn't look too happy as he kept glancing over at me.

You still have time to leave. No one would notice. He knows you're putting his son in danger.

"Be quiet," I said, and everyone looked at me. "Sorry, I...I didn't mean for you to be quiet. I was talking to myself."

"Look, they're coming back. I hope we can go," Josephine said.

Everyone stepped off the porch, leaving me to trail behind. "Go where?" I asked, as they gathered around the two men.

John put his hand on Hunter's shoulder. "You know what needs to be done. Don't make the situation worse."

"Yes, sir. I know."

"James, time to go," John called out. "I'll see everyone tonight." They all cheered. He smiled big and winked at me. "My wife will be delighted to meet you."

Miss Caroline and Miss Betsy high-fived each other while Josephine jumped up and down.

Pastor James hugged Hunter then me. "See you tonight."

Hunter nodded.

The ladies went for their car. "Have fun tonight," Miss Caroline sang while Miss Betsy tried to hush her.

Molly walked over to us limping. Her feeble attempt to draw Hunter's attention away from me, wasn't working. I had to give her credit. It had worked before. Molly stared in disbelief at Hunter's scowl. With all the disapproving glares she shot my way, I wondered how many times she plotted my demise. Really, I shouldn't blame her. Instead I should pray she'll get over him to find her own happiness.

As our visitors left, the five of us waved as the cars drove off. Molly watched out the side window, bewildered.

My heart hurt for her. "She's sure not happy with me. I feel sorry for her."

"That's my fault, and I'm sorry," Hunter said through his tight lips. "She knows I've never had those types of feelings for her. She shouldn't be taking it out on you." He sighed and faced me. "I don't like the way she was looking at you."

"It's hard to resist your charm. It's not entirely her fault either."

He gave me a troubled smile, but changed his tone. "So, are you up for a little party?"

I swished the dressed from side to side. "Ah, was that what this was all about?" I pointed to the garment bag slung over his shoulder. "I guess it's your turn to get prettied up?"

"Why are you so suspicious?" he asked.

I laughed. "Suspicious would mean I have some sort of clue to what's going on or where we're going. I've got nothing!" I added. "Good," he chimed.

Enchanted Ball

Hunter led me back to the house.

"Now it's my turn." He stepped into the washroom for a few minutes, then back out wearing a white button-up dress shirt and black slacks.

Stunned, I inhaled at the way his blue eyes stood out against the black jacket he swung onto his shoulder. He did a quick spin, putting male models around the world to shame.

"You are breathtaking," I managed to say as the words seemed to linger in the air.

Could it even be possible that someone like him could be in love with me?

Once again, the gatherings of all my insecurity were coming to order, sitting around the table of self-doubt. The head of the table, the one telling me to leave, slumped in the chair with nothing to say.

Hunter's hand reached out for mine. His pulse raced through his wrists. "No. You're the one who's breathtaking." He beheld my eyes for a short moment, blushed, and looked elsewhere. "Ready?" he asked, clearing his voice.

"Yes," I said, trying to breathe normally. "Where are the others?"

"Oh, they left as soon as we came in for me to change. It's just us."

I tilted my head. "So we're not going far? I'm really confused now."

Hunter smiled, leading me out the back screen door. We didn't walk far before I saw a white horse, with white beads laced in its mane. The harness was attached to an old buggy with four large wooden wheels.

It was official. Cinderella was going to the ball with Prince Charming.

And he is very charming.

Soft rays of light faded, revealing the stars twinkling above. In the air, a fragrance of roses and lavender made everything even more perfect. The horse led the buggy across the lazy creek to follow the snakelike bend heading south. We stayed close to the creek but in front of the tree line. I watched the stars get brighter and clearer. The dark shadows of the swamp, that haunted me in my dreams, felt welcoming and peaceful. Little lights danced around us, but I knew for sure they were fireflies, not my father's spirit.

Is it possible I'm in another dream? A sweet and romantic dream that I'd be happy to never wake from?

Afraid to speak, I glanced over at Hunter. He nervously scanned the area around us. Trying to be inconspicuous, I slowly slid my body closer to his. He relax a little, but he didn't stop patrolling the area as we entered into the forest of trees.

The carriage stopped after a short time.

I looked around for a building but saw nothing other than more swamp. The party couldn't be in the middle of the marsh, the place Miss Mabel said people were kept out of by the smell. Whiffing at the air, the smell of sour, decaying odor was replaced with the perfume of flowers. However, it was odd not to hear the music or people talking. He said we were going to a party, but all I heard was the natural sounds of the cicadas'.

Hunter helped me down from the seat only to whisk me up in his arms. He looked at my shoes. The ground appeared gooey, but he knew where to step without losing a shoe. He carried me through a set of moss-drawn trees.

"Close your eyes," Hunter whispered.

I did without question as he continued forward. I felt a tingling, similar to when a hand or foot goes numb, except it felt lovely all over my body. The sensation didn't last long, but after I heard music and laughter.

"Okay. Open them." He set me down on the hard path.

A beautiful Southern colonial-style house with white roman pillars all lit up by more than lantern lights. Solar lights lit up the cobblestone path that led to the grand house.

I felt Hunter eyes on me.

He's looking for a reaction. Did he not think I would be impressed?

On one side of the house was a huge glass atrium filled with people.

"It's stunning. Why out here in the middle of the swamp? This kind of house belongs in Newport, off the seaside cliffs, not the middle of a swamp."

"My dad designed and built it with help from others. But it's more like a compound with a fancy exterior. At any one time, it can house around fifty people. But there is more to it than just what you see," he answered.

"Really? But why out here? Who stays here?"

"I'll answer all your questions. I promise." He held both my hands. "But if I don't get you inside, someone might send a search party." He chuckled, his eyes no longer scanning for danger. "You're safe here. I want you to have fun tonight. Don't worry about anything." He reached out to touch my cheek.

My legs wobbled.

My handsome prince glanced up at the house. He nodded, taking my hand. "They're ready for us. Let's go before I get in trouble."

Hunter led me down the path, up the porch stairs, and in through the grand entrance. We proceeded to the atrium, which looked more like a palace ballroom. Crystal chandeliers hung from the gold-lined mirror squares under the glass ceiling. It curved all the way to the ground. Everything in the room sparkled, from the prism centerpieces to the gem-laced tablecloths.

I could only reason I was dreaming.

My mother's intoxicated laugh played in my head. I squeezed Hunter's hand for reassurance, it wasn't a dream. Conversations carried on all over the room, creating a soft buzz. Someone played a piano soft and low. *It's cocktail hour, my dear.* I imagined my mother swaying with a drink in her hand. *A little drink might do you some good.* My memory felt so real. I turned my back, with the mindset to run, letting go of Hunter's hand.

He took back my hand. "There's no need to be nervous, Jessie. They've all come here to meet you."

We continued further into the room. "Why? Why do they want to meet me?" I whispered.

Hunter didn't have time to reply as people began introducing themselves and talking to me like they'd known me forever. There was a lot of, "Nice to meet you," and, "I've heard so much about you." It all blurred together until I caught the eye of a slender, tall, greyish-blonde haired woman, elegantly making her way through the crowd.

Hunter's mother?

But she seemed so young, just like John, to have grown sons. My mother would hate her.

The woman glided across the marble dance floor. Although she appeared happy with my attendance, it didn't calm my mental strain.

What will she think of me?

I felt so underdressed next to her.

Hunter followed my eyes and smiled. The pianist started another low melody, as the crowd went back to mini conversations around the room.

"Hello, Mother," Hunter sang, still not releasing my hand but swung his other arm to hug her.

A few ladies lingered around me.

"Love your dress."

"He is quite the catch," another whispered, before rejoining the party.

Hunter's mother waited until they left before she spoke. "It's been awhile, son." Her hand stroked his face.

"I know. I'm sorry."

"I hear it's for good reason, so I forgive you." She kissed his cheek and leaned to Hunter's ear. "You should speak to Joseph, if he hasn't left already. Your father and I have tried to talk to him, but he's still quite upset."

"Later."

"I know you don't mean to, son, but you can't drop everyone else in your life. He looks up to you and you're pushing him away. You need to keep a balance," she whispered. "Also, your father has good reasons for his suspicions. Don't push it. Give him time."

Even though it wasn't meant for me to hear, I knew she meant me.

"I know," he mumbled.

Even she knows you're trouble. Poor Joseph, he might seek other friendships. Ones he can count on. Find your moment to sneak away before they throw you out. Cross over the cobblestone path. They won't follow you. I shook my head, taking a few steps away from Hunter, to peek out through the glass walls and past the lights lining the path. I expected to see red, glowing eyes beyond the trees but saw nothing.

Shut up!

"Mother," Hunter pulled me away from the window. "This is my Jessica." He announced it proudly, which made my cheeks feel hot.

"Jessica, this is Annabel, my mother."

"I'm honored to meet you," I curtsied.

After all, she looked royalty.

Hunter snickered at my gesture, but his mother gave him a scowl. Mortified, I quickly straightened my posture to offer my hand instead.

She took it with both her hands. They were warm and soft, like the look in her eyes. "No, child. It's my honor." Her eyes left me for second. "We will have another time to chat and get to know one another. Enjoy the party." She left us to join John in the middle of the ballroom.

The music stopped. More instruments were brought up to the stage, while a short man, in a blue tuxedo, stood at the microphone. "We'd like to start the evening off with a slow dance," he said, turning to the band with his hands positioned high in the air. Down his hands went, and the music began to play.

John and Annabel didn't move at first. John looked just as handsome as she was beautiful. They looked at each other with a love I envied. John walked to the center of the dance floor, twirling his bride in her white sparkling dress, before securely locking her to his body. They kissed softly before they waltzed across the dance floor. Her eyes never left him as they kept in step with each other around the room. They danced brilliantly, leaving everyone breathless, with their hearts pounding and their faces flushed. As the music faded, John lifted Annabel into the air before slowly setting her feet down. She laughed, wrapping her arms around his neck.

The audience clapped loudly.

Another song began, only at a much faster tempo. The man on the stage flung his arms around, trying to keep up. He looked like a bird flapping his wings, ready to take flight.

Someone took my hand, tugging me slightly.

"May I?" his father asked.

Hunter nodded as he took his mother's hand.

Nervously, I let John lead me to the dance floor. He whirled me around, having perfect control over my movements, making it appear I knew how to dance—even though I didn't. It was exhilarating. I smiled so much my face hurt. If John disliked me or didn't trust me, it didn't show. Others' joined the dance floor.

Hunter did more talking than dancing with his mother. It must have been about something funny because they kept laughing.

The music tempo changed again, back to the softer, calmer melody. John twirled me out of his arms and across the floor. I thought I was going to fall until Hunter caught me. His arms went around my waist, pulling me close to his body. Reaching my arms up to his neck, I intertwined my hands, laying my cheek against his chest. We swayed slowly, our hearts beating to the same rhythm. His hand was wide on the small of my back, sending brilliant shivers throughout my body. I liked this kind of dancing. Nothing else existed around me, and my thoughts were silent—all of them. His protective arms around me appeared too good to be true. I still wondered if it was all dream. I closed my eyes, listening to the sound of his heartbeat. Another fast tune followed, but Hunter didn't change his sway as everyone danced around us.

"Excuse me," someone interrupted.

We both looked up. It was Pastor James.

He cleared his throat. "May I?"

"Of course," Hunter offered my hand with a half-smile.

We both caught a glimpse of Joseph standing in the corner of the room. I non-verbally urged Hunter to talk to him. I really hoped they could work out their issues.

Pastor James wasn't as good of a dancer, but he was a great storyteller. At least it kept me from watching Hunter and Joseph.

"It was our first time hunting without adults. Neither Hunter nor I enjoyed the whole hunting thing, but it was a part of our culture to go out at a certain age to bring back your first kill. If we didn't, the older boys would have teased us to no end. Although, it wasn't the threat of teasing that bothered us, but the disgrace our family would face. The elders would have punished us in some way that was not pleasant. So there was a lot pressure not to come back empty-handed.

"We had been out most of the day, and still neither of us had caught anything. We saw rabbits, squirrels, and some deer, but we couldn't point the arrow to shoot a living thing. We came to an old log in an area we had played in before. There were always snakes living inside the decaying hollow. If we brought back a snake that would be good enough for the elders. We looked inside, hoping to find one curled up, but instead, we found two raccoons. They weren't moving. At first, we thought they were sleeping, but after making some loud noises and shaking the log, we realized they were dead. We didn't look at them closely, when we used two long sticks to put them in our cloth sacks before tying the bags closed. We were just so relieved we didn't have to kill anything.

"We walked to the elders, who were starting to get worried about how long we had been gone, and plopped our bags proudly at their feet. It was something to get a raccoon. Most boys went for the easy catch, like rabbits, squirrels, or even large swamp rats, but raccoons—they were fighters. The elders knew how we both felt about hunting, so they beamed. They were so proud, especially John. He was one proud father." He paused. "Oh yeah, by the way, I'm Hunter's older brother. I'm sure he hasn't told you yet." He glanced over at Hunter. "He knows you know now." He smiled.

"I only knew of Davior, but I'm not surprised." I paused. "Okay. Continue the story."

"Oh yeah. Well, the elders opened my bag first, grabbed the skin of the animal, and plopped it down on wide tree stump. They did the same with Hunter's bag. If we had looked closer, we would have noticed they weren't raccoons exactly," James said.

"What were they?"

"Hats. Raccoon hats." He laughed.

I laughed loudly too. Hunter stopped talking with Joseph to head in our direction.

"Wait, that's not the best part. The hats were ours."

We both laughed loudly, and tears filled my eyes. Others turned to look at us, but it just made me laugh harder until Hunter joined us.

James continued while laughing. "We must have left them there a while ago, and then forgot about them. Probably an animal drug them inside the log for warmth."

"Ha-ha. Okay, brother. You've had your dance." Hunter faked a chuckle.

Slower music played as Hunter claimed me. "So now I'm completely embarrassed," he mumbled, wrapping one arm around my waist, while the other held my hand to his chest.

"Really? Your own hats?"

"I was young. James should be more embarrassed since he's older." He looked at James with a smirk.

I assumed they were sharing a mind-to-mind conversation, remembering Hunter told me his older brother could communicate through thoughts. I had never heard of such a thing. The twin thing, I had heard of, but I didn't think twins could actually read specific thoughts. Maybe I had misunderstood.

I leaned my body to his. "Well, I think it's an adorable story, and I haven't laughed this hard since...never "Well, in that case, I'm sure you'll hear all kinds of adorable things about me. Besides, I like hearing you laugh, even if it's at my expense." He twirled me around to one of the faster parts of the song, bringing my body back to his.

"Did you speak to Joseph?"

"He's not being reasonable," he snapped. "I don't want to think about him tonight." His nose touched my ear, followed by a grunt.

"My turn." A tall boy, with reddish-brown hair and freckles stood before us.

Hunter gave him my hand. "Paul, Jessica. Jessica, Paul."

"Charmed." He lifted my hand and kissed it.

Hunter raised his eyebrow at him.

The boy paid no attention to him. "Shall we, my lady?"

I must have danced with half a dozen men before falling back into the comfort of Hunter's arms. I couldn't help but wonder if we were being kept apart on purpose.

"I need some air," I managed to say, completely out of breath. "Let's step out to the courtyard," Hunter suggested nervously. I caught Molly, talking to Hunter's mother, watching us leave the room. She looked sad and angry, trying to catch Hunter's attention, but it was no use. She was invisible to him.

Out in the courtyard on the east side of the house, Hunter sat me down on a marble bench. "I'll be right back. Don't wander off. Stay right where you are," he said with more concern in his voice. He scanned, the area, before heading back inside.

My eyes adjusted to the outside lights before I was able to see the tall, purple, pink, and white wildflowers all around the polished stone court. Angel statues made of marble were scattered among the flower gardens. A path curved along the back side of house, lined with cylinder-shaped fire pits burning to light the way. I took a long, cleansing breath. The air smelled fresh, like after a rainstorm on a summer's day. Alone in the majesty of it all, I felt completely safe.

Hunter returned carrying a cup in each hand. His eyes purposely avoid contact with mine, as he handed me a cup.

"Thanks." I took a sip, wrapping both hands around the cup to keep me from fidgeting.

He sat next to me, setting down his cup, to place both his hands in his lap, looking even more uneasy than before.

"How are you feeling now?" he asked.

"Better. I've never done so much dancing before." I smiled in his direction, but his eyes were turned down, looking at his shoes.

It was the first time I had ever danced because I wanted to. At the parties my mother had, I was forced to dance with old, smelly men. Once, Seth tried to dance with me, but I intentionally kept stepping on his feet—over and over again. Eventually, he had decided it wasn't worth having swollen feet and never asked me again.

We sat for the longest time, listening to the music change from slow to fast, from fast to slow. I could tell he was thinking about something, perhaps something John might have said to him or maybe his conversation with Joseph.

I swallowed the last drop of liquid in my cup.

Suddenly, Hunter was on his feet, taking me into his arms. My cup fell to ground, bouncing a few times before settling. The instrumentalists' played soft, slow, and lovely. He held me like he had when we danced. He swayed slowly, holding one hand against his chest, the other on the small of my back. He pulled me away slightly. Our eyes locked into each other. I felt a rush of blood on my face, stinging my cheeks. His eyes flashed over every inch of it, as his right hand touched my face. Our chests pounded together, almost at the same tempo, echoing in my ears. I no longer heard any other sounds. I closed my eyes, hoping this would be it, my first real kiss.

He moved in closer, brushing his lips against each one of my eyes, proceeding slowly across my cheek. As his lips came close to my ear, a low sigh escaped. "No matter what happens now, I want you to know I care about you deeply."

He swept his lips up to kiss my forehead, then snapped his head away. My heart sunk. The forehead kiss was a universal kiss of friendship, not love. I opened my eyes, afraid he was going to stop—afraid he was coming to his senses.

His face squinted out into the night with a look of confusion. *He's too good for you. You know that.* The voice returned, but it was right.

My eyes wandered off Hunter's face. A wave of disappointment washed over me, consuming me like a tidal wave of emotions.

I'm not right for him. I bring trouble for them all. I know it, his family knows it, and now he knows it.

I grounded my teeth, clutched my hands, trying to control the onset of tears.

Hunter lifted my chin.

One moment, I was on the highest mountaintop, looking at endless possibilities. The next at the bottom of a ravine, so deep there was no light.

I turned my back to him, not wanting him to see my tears to feel sorry for me. "I'm not good enough for you. I should leave before anyone gets hurt." My voiced choked.

Finally, you've come to your senses. I heard the voice and squeezed my eyes shut.

I didn't ask you. Get out of my head.

Hunter yanked my hand, spinning me back around. He pressed his lips to mine. My body relaxed into his. His kiss, although hard at first, turned soft and gentle over and over again. I returned the kiss, not able to tell his lips apart from mine as they fused together. A thousand little shocks rang throughout my body, as I melted into him.

The moment wasn't quite perfect as the voice boomed in my head. *You're putting everyone in danger.* I pressed harder against his lips, defying the voice growing louder until I noticed the music had stopped and we were being watched. Someone in the shadows cleared his throat, pulling us apart. Hunter dropped his arms to his sides, turning quickly with a smirk on his face.

John stood in the shadows. "Jessica, would you mind playing something for us?" It sounded more like a command than a request.

My erratically beating heart said no, but I nodded at his request.

"Lovely," John glaring at Hunter. "I'd like a few words with you in my office, now."

"Yes, sir," Hunter answered, letting John disappear along the path around the back of the house. "I'm sorry. I shouldn't have done that, but it has nothing to do with you not being good enough. No one is in danger here, except you. And as long as I live—"

I grabbed his shirt, pulling him to me. There was no reason for him to be apologetic. I kissed him, lacing my hands around his neck, feeling his arms embrace me again. The voice kept trying to squeeze back in, but it was no use. It let out a cry, piercing, but manageable. Then it was gone.

His nose touched mine. "I think they are all waiting for you to play." He smiled, breathing hard.

I dropped my hands down to my side, like he had done earlier. "I'm sorry your father doesn't approve."

"It's complicated. I won't be long. I really want to hear you play." He took both my hands.

"Don't rush. I'm really not very good. I'd rather you didn't hear."

He chuckled. "I doubt that." Hunter leaned to my ear. "Play something special for me?" he whispered, sending another wave of sensations tickling the back of my head.

How could I not? I was his in every sense of the word. He could have asked me anything at that very moment, and I would have done it. Well, almost anything.

"Okay, but first, I want to know what's going on with you and your dad," I demanded.

"They're waiting on us," he said, but I didn't budge. "I told you, it's complicated, and that's all I can tell you. I want to tell you more, but I can't. Not yet, anyway."

We saw someone else watching us in the shadow of the garden.

"Molly?" I whispered, looking at the tall, thin shadow staring in our direction.

"Can we go inside now?" he asked.

I nodded hesitantly.

It's about Molly.

We walked into the room just as the announcer spoke my name. Hunter squeezed my hand and then released me to find his father. I walked forward, keeping my eyes focused on the floor. It would not be a good time to fall flat on my face. I wondered if Molly saw us kissing. I bet she would enjoy watching me fall to the ground. I know I would have if the shoe was on the other foot.

The man leading the band helped me up the steps to the piano. The keys were bright ivory and shined up at me. I felt like it was talking to me, saying, *Hello, friend.* It had been a long time. I had missed the touch and the sounds they made. There was unfamiliar sheet music in front of me, so at the risk of fumbling over notes, I decided to play one I knew by heart.

Without speaking, I struck the keys. I drifted into my imagination, picturing John and Annabel's dancing. Getting lost in the melody, they faded out of the vision, leaving me to continue. At first I was alone, like I had been before when I played. Although it was peaceful, I didn't want to be alone anymore. Hunter appeared, in a white suit, presenting me with a rose from Miss Mabel's garden. He took my hand, dancing me under the white blossoms of the cherry trees. With our eyes locked together, he twirled me around until we both fell to the soft ground. He touched my face, softly, tenderly, kissing me. An explosion of white petals fell from the sky, covering us. Another kiss came, lasting longer, with more passion than before.

And then the music was over, along with my imagination.

Tears streamed down my face, but not from sadness. Emotions that were old, emotions that were new, and emotions that were beyond words, flowed through me. I didn't hear applause until I looked up and saw just about everyone had tears in their eye, even Molly. She quickly wiped them away when she noticed me looking at her.

Standing, they applauded.

The announcer jumped up on stage. "Brilliant. Just brilliant." He clapped. "Promise me, you'll play for us again soon?"

I nodded, making my way off the stage.

Hunter was already back and at the edge of the stage, offering his hand to help me down. "You are amazing. I can't believe you said you weren't any good." He choked back the tears in his throat. "You know lying is a sin, right?" He wiped my tears and swung me into his embrace as the band went into full swing.

"Maybe you're bias."

"You told me when you play, you imagine you're somewhere else. Where were you this time?"

"With you," I whispered as we swayed.

"Why were you crying?" He sounded a little concerned.

"I guess I'm not very good at showing my emotions. I was happy." I giggled from embarrassment.

"So you weren't thinking about what you told me earlier?"

"What?" I asked, really not remembering anything before the kiss.

"That silly talk about you not being good enough, putting everyone in danger," he said.

"Oh, no," I answered, even though I still thought it.

Unfortunately for him, I'd rather be selfish at the moment.

"Good," he said. "Because if you did leave, I would go after you, and then my whole family would be involved, and—"

He made me laugh. "Okay, okay. I get the point." Then I had no choice but to stay.

The sound of teeth grinding behind a door, filled my head, but it wasn't me. I looked at Hunter, but it wasn't coming from him, either. I looked to my right, just as Molly headed in our direction with her nose turned upward.

"May I?" she cooed, not taking her cold eyes off me.

Hunter held me tighter, not at all being courteous.

"Of course." I handed him over, similar to how he had all night to various takers.

It was a strange feeling, his eyes on my back as I walked away. Once I reached the edge of the dance floor, I observed Molly drawing him closer for my benefit. But Hunter kept locking his frame at arm's length. She kept on, so I thought about stepping out into the courtyard again. As I went to leave, another man swept me out to the dance floor. Hunter tried to watch me, but Molly was doing her best to keep his attention on her. He had a look of pain in his eyes, and was in need of rescue. She, on the other hand, chatted away, laughing at her own words.

"I'm Jordan, by the way. I feel sorry for Hunter. Molly lives in her own little world, you know." My dance partner finally spoke, sparking my interest.

"What do you mean by her own little world?" I looked at Jordan.

"Oh, you didn't know? Interesting." He stopped speaking.

"You might be surprised at how much I don't know." My observation went back to Hunter and his partner.

His gazed locked with mine.

"Oh, don't worry. You'll know everything soon enough. At least, I think John will get over his protectiveness. You being here is a sign, besides, you don't look—"

"What about Molly?"

I already got the impression his father didn't approve. It only confirmed he feared the danger I was putting his son in, but with Molly, I was dying to find out the connection.

"Oh, sorry," he said. "Well, in our culture, usually our parents pick out our future mates."

Oh no. Why he didn't tell me that when he knew what I was going through? How could he not tell me? I may not know the Bible, but I knew about arranged marriages.

Jordan watched me drag my top teeth along my bottom teeth. He then looked to Hunter, shrugging his shoulders.

I focused on Jordan. "Go ahead, continue."

"His parents picked out Molly, but Hunter knew all along she wasn't the girl for him. After many years, they realized forcing people to love one another is the same as God forcing us to love Him. God wanted us to choose Him, so in that respect, Hunter was free to choose a girl he loved. It's been a long time, Jess. We've joked he would be like the apostle Paul who believed it was better to not marry to serve God wholly. Of course, that wasn't really funny. Paul had a great ministry. It just didn't seem right for Hunter." He looked apologetic for spilling the secret.

From the corner of my eye, I could see Hunter trying to wiggle away from Molly.

"I assume Molly felt differently," I said.

"Pretty obvious, isn't it?" He laughed. "Seriously, she's worse now. At least before, there was a chance for her. Annabel's been trying to talk sense into her. At least now, she realizes the truth, but it doesn't mean she'll give up easily."

"What truth?"

"I think our dance is over." Jordan smiled, taking my hand and kissing the top. Hunter snatched my hand.

They looked at each other for a moment. Jordan's forehead wrinkled up before he whispered something in his ear. Hunter nodded before he left.

"I'm sorry." He sighed. "I should have told you sooner. I really thought after she saw me with you, she'd understand. I really didn't think she'd take it out on you. I'm sure apologizing a lot tonight. Are you angry with me?" he asked, his lips pressed to my hair.

I wasn't really mad, just disappointed he didn't trust me. If he doesn't trust me...

I kept Seth from him for long time, and he found out on his own. Really, he should have been mad at me. He wasn't, so why should I have expected him to trust me?

"No," I huffed. "But you could have told me." I snuggled into his embrace.

He didn't say another word, just held me close, melting away my insecurities. That was enough. I hoped there wouldn't be any more interruptions. Nothing could have been more perfect except for the displeasing glances John continued to fire in our direction. Hunter would loosen his grip, only to pull me tight again when John turned his back. We were like two beings clinging to each other like it was the last moment of our lives, neither wanting to part from the other.

May shouted from across the room, tapping her foot. "Good night." She giggled.

It was funny how everyone from our small little house was there, in the same room, and yet I never really noticed them. If it hadn't been for Molly's stares, and Joseph sulking, I wouldn't have known they were even there. In fact, if it hadn't been for the interruptions, the only person who would have existed would be Hunter, my handsome, protective prince, who took me to the ball and slipped on the glass slipper, which fit perfectly. And the best part was I didn't turn into a pumpkin at midnight.

All was well and good, at least for the time being.

Lights Out

May continued to stare in our direction, from the double doors, tapping her small, black, shiny shoe against the floor.

Hunter continued to sway to a rhythm of our own. "My mother has suggested we stay here tonight."

Watching May yawn made me yawn. I didn't want the night to end. I didn't want to leave his arms, but it had been a long day.

"Shall we?" he stopped dancing.

I yawned again, thinking there had been more than fifty people at the party. "Is everyone staying?"

"The compound goes back for miles. There are other houses on the reservation, although this house is the biggest."

"Reservation?" I asked, fighting to keep my eyes open.

"Questions tomorrow." He smiled and kissed my hand.

May waited for us to reach her at the entrance, where she took my other hand. She didn't look nearly as sleepy as I felt.

Hunter led us up a golden staircase. Large painted portraits of people lined the wall. I recognized some, but I must have been so tired my eyes were playing tricks on me. I could have sworn I saw one of Hunter as a young boy in a black-and-white photo. It must have been an ancestor, who resembled him, standing in front of small stone hut. We climbed up the steps to the second floor. There were at least three more floors above us. The house seemed even bigger than it looked from outside.

May and I followed him into a hallway of rooms. He pushed opened one of the doors. "May, this room is for you."

May went inside. "Wow. I knew all along I shouldn't have stayed away from that smelly old bog. I would have been here a long time ago." She played with the switch on the wall, turning on and off the light.

"Let's just say it's not easy to find," Hunter said, still holding the doorknob.

"Thank you, Hunter." She jumped into his arms to hug him. He hugged her back, lifting her slightly off the floor.

"Don't thank me. Thank Annabel, but in the morning, of course. She decorated it just for you. She also filled the closet over there with clothes and other items you might need," he said.

Us staying wasn't a last-minute thing? Why?

He started to leave.

Noticing I wasn't following, he stopped to reach for my hand. "Your room is next door." He smiled sheepishly.

May gleamed. "My own room? Really?"

She was so excited I thought she'd burst. My thoughts of being in a room by myself didn't give me comfort. I had enough of being alone in my old, rotten life. I hesitated, as he led me down the hall, walking very slowly.

Paintings of wild horses in yellow meadows hung on the walls. I stopped at one I recognized. One was of the tiny shack with the lazy river on one side, and the towering trees around it. The roses, surrounding the porch, were missing. My hand touched where the roses would have been.

"My mother painted that before Miss Mabel moved into it. She is the one who added the roses. She said it reminded her of someone." Hunter opened another door across from the painting. "This is your room."

"Thanks." I lingered on the painting before turning around.

"The rooms are all connected by an inner door, so if you want privacy, make sure to lock it." He entered the room, and I followed, noticing my small pack on the bed. "My mother stocked your room as well with clothes and other items, but I grabbed the bag from the shack just in case you'd rather wear what Miss Mabel gave you. My mother tends to go overboard." He shifted his eyes everywhere, fidgeting with his hands. "I'm...I'm just on the other side of May. This place is the safest place I know, so don't go having one of those crazy dreams of yours and end up outside." He smiled, trying to break the tension.

Please don't leave.

"I'll try," I finally managed to say in a low, mumbling voice.

A smile crossed over his face but quickly faded. "Sleep well." With his hands in his pockets, he leaned to kiss my cheek. He turned, walked out, and shut the door behind him.

I quickly opened the door to May's room. Her smile filled the room. "Can I come in?" I asked.

"Sure." She beamed. "Isn't this just the greatest?"

She was acting a little more like her age as she climbed up onto the bed to jump up and down. She fell down, fluffing the pillow under her head. "I could never do that on those small beds without falling straight to the floor." She giggled.

"So you've never been here before?" I asked. "You've never wandered into this part of the swamp?"

She yawned big. "I was told to stay away from this area. Besides, it smelled horrible. If I had come close, everyone would have known I disobeyed." She yawned again. "Annabel said I can come over as much as I want. Molly told me they have a pool and Joseph said they have a big screen they watch movies on? I don't even know what a movie is." She laughed. "But it sounds great."

The two people who hated me most in one place...that's just great. Maybe they'll plan my death together.

"Depends on the movie, I guess," I shook off the worry to laugh at her excitement. I playfully sniffed at the air. Her room smelled like fresh cut flowers. "Doesn't smell bad now."

"Nope, it sure doesn't. I think the smell is just to keep people away. It's a secret place."

She was funny to watch, squishing the soft feather pillow around her cheeks. She really wanted to tell me all kinds of other things she had learned, but her eyes were disappearing behind her heavy eyelids. "I love you, Jess," she said with one last yawn.

I leaned over to kiss her cheek before covering her up. "I love you too. Good night, May," I whispered into her ear.

I wondered why she had been kept from being there. Joseph knew. Josephine also knew, remembering she told Molly she knew where he was. So why not May? Just another question I'd add to the growing list. I stood to leave when I saw Hunter open his adjoining door to May's room. He nodded before crawling into his own bed.

I shut my door to dress for bed. I found a soft cotton nightgown and slipped it over my head. It flowed down to my feet. I re-opened the connecting door slowly, peeking to see if Hunter still faced in my direction, but with his light off, it was too dark to tell. The open doors gave me a little comfort. I inched into the giant, feathery bed. It was big enough for all three of us to sleep on. I lay on my back. Unable to close my eyes, I stare at the ceiling with questions running through my mind.

Will Seth try to kill me? Is Molly the reason John wants Hunter to "not make the situation worse," or is he talking about Seth, Davior, and the danger I brought with me? After all, Davior is John's son too. Davior is John and Annabel's son. Why didn't that click with me until just now? How sad that must make them.

No longer at the brink of sleep, I thought about the piano downstairs. There had been many nights I argued with my mother, and couldn't sleep after, so I'd walk to my father's room to play my fingers along his arm. I remembered every tune each white-and-black key made. Playing helped to unravel the knotted-up thoughts in my mind. My mother would have heard if I played on the actual piano. But I wasn't in my mother's house. The ballroom was located on the opposite side of the bedrooms, three floors down. Far enough away, so I wouldn't disturb anyone. Hunter had said I was safe in the house.

I thought about it for some time, before making up my mind. I tiptoed down the staircase, across the entryway, and into the atrium. I shut the big oak doors and all the other doors so the sound wouldn't escape throughout the house. The moon glowed enough for me to see my way around the room. I noticed a round light-dimmer switch on the back wall, next to the piano and slowly turned it. A light for just the stage beamed down on the piano. I walked along the piano, caressing its long body with one finger. It was an absolutely stunning instrument, like everything else I had seen. I sat on the soft bench, feeling like it was made just for me. My hands gently glided over the keys, not making a sound at first.

I took a deep breath and began to play.

My fingers traveled along the white-and-black keys softly. Letting the melody decide which notes would come next as it guided my fingers. I allowed my imagination to go anywhere it wanted. I might have been playing terribly with no real plan, no notes to follow, but I didn't care. I was on a rollercoaster ride for one.

The melody, in my head, played soft and lovely, taking me to beautiful places I had read about, places I wanted to go someday. I strayed to thinking about what heaven might look like. I pictured a tall, white, embossed entrance gate, and a path made of gold bricks leading me to Hunter. He waited for me holding a red rose.

The music flowed from my fingertips. In my fantasy world, people gathered all around me, laughing. There was no sadness anywhere, only peace. I felt calm, safe, and loved. But my world began to betray me, as the music changed to something ugly. I thought about the other place, the Bible described as eternal fire. The dream, with the twisted faces, haunted me as the people showed me their deep gashes. Then they danced around me, with flames leaping into the sky, chanting—*Kill her Kill them all!*

My memory of dream went further with visions of May, Josephine, and Miss Mabel, being prodded into the lake of fire.

My soul burned as I fought against the nightmare I created. The tune changed. My mother stepped into the vision to stand next to the piano, drumming her long, bony fingers, with her perfectly manicured nails against the rim. I couldn't stop from playing. I had to finish. It was the only way to make it all go away. Tears flowed down my cheeks.

I am safe, happy, and I have more than I could have ever imagined.

I thought about the fairy tale stories, of the princes battling the evil witches and dragons, my father had read to me.

Hunter is that prince. He would stand between me and the darkness. He wouldn't let the evil take me.

My fingers slowed, still playing only softer, until my heart beat normal again, before completely stopping. I rubbed the tears off my face. All the characters I had read about in the Bible had some sort of battle, something they needed to rise above so God could use them. Although I had suffered in my life, something worse was coming.

I shut the fallboard over the keys, then reached over for the light switch.

"Lights out," I mumbled, laying my head on top of my crisscrossed arms.

A New World

I tried to remember if I had made it upstairs on my own or if someone found me curled up next to the piano and brought me to my room, because that's where I woke up. I went to window next to the bed, pulling back the heavy drapery to allow the sunlight into the room. Living at the shack for so long without a clock, I got used to telling the time of day and it was at least mid-morning. I peeked in May's room, and she was already gone, so then I tiptoed to Hunter's connecting door, which was cracked open, and he was gone as well.

I went back to my room, wondering if I should dress first or slip on the robe before heading down the staircase. I peeked out the door to the hallway where the bathroom was located. A note, written by May, was taped on the door. *The towels are in the closet.* And she signed it with a smiley face. I chuckled, then looked through the array of clothes, Hunter's mother had picked out for me. I hoped it would make a good impression on her if I wore the clothes she selected. However, it wasn't a great sacrifice on my part, as I struggled to pick just one.

I entered the bathroom, walking onto the cherry wood floor to cabinets that matched. I grabbed a towel out, noticing the crown molding along the ceiling. Shutting the cabinet, I turned to the bathtub. "Running hot water!" I gasped with excitement, turning the brass knob. I looked up to see it also had a shower head. "Yay!"

Letting the hot water run for a minute, filling the room with steam, I looked at the Victorian photos against the dark green wall. Hunter's mother really had a taste for style.

I adjusted the temperature of the water, before stepping into the tub. It had been a long time since I had enjoyed the calming feeling of warm water pounding on my back.

My hands were beginning to wrinkle, so I finished washing, dried off, and let out a squeal when I saw the hair dryer. I hadn't realized how much I missed having the basics.

After, I took my time going down the staircase. I heard voices as they floated up. The nerves in my stomach flip-flopped, and my hands went clammy.

What should I expect, John and his disapproving looks?

At the bottom of the stairs, I continued to follow the low rumblings of conversation until I stood at the threshold of an average-sized kitchen. It was much smaller than my mother's. Instead of one room, it opened to a dining area with a long rectangular table big enough for twenty or more people. I had expected to see servants, but if they had any, I didn't see them

Hunter's parents shuffled around the kitchen, preparing breakfast while May, along with a few men I had met at the party, sat at the table.

Hunter saw me first and rushed to my side.

"Who said chivalry is dead? I bet he pulls her chair out too," someone teased.

"Where are Miss Mabel, Josephine, and Joseph?" I asked, sitting in the chair Hunter pulled out for me, followed by laugher. "Thank you," I said, over their expressed amusement.

I knew why Joseph wouldn't have stayed.

"My pleasure," he whispered in my ear, touching his cheek to mine.

I blushed, noticing everyone's eyes were on us.

May giggled. "Josephine wanted to stay, but Joseph made her leave, so Miss Mabel thought it was best to go with them. Boy was he mad."

"Oh."

Annabel set a basket of hot muffins on the center of the table, followed by waffles, pancakes, fried potatoes, and a variety of omelets. "I didn't know what everyone likes, so I made pretty much everything," Annabel smiled. "Would you like coffee?" She asked me as John set orange juice on the table.

"I'm okay with orange juice, for now. Thank you."

Hunter poured me a glass.

"Hunter, would you say the blessing, please?" his father asked, sitting down at the head of the table.

He nodded, setting the pitcher down to reach out his hands. Everyone took a hand, making a complete circle.

"Heavenly Father, thank You for this beautiful day You have given us. Thank You for friends and family You have continued to bless. Thank you, Father, for bringing Jessica into my life, and I pray for Your guidance along with patience and understanding." He paused for a moment, squeezing my hand. "And thank You for providing this wonderful feast to nourish our bodies for Your glory. I thank You in your Son's holy name. Amen."

Even though we had been a little family at Miss Mabel's, breakfast felt so much like a real family, with a mom and a dad, stories being shared, and everyone having a great time. Although since most of the stories revolved around Hunter, I assumed it was for my benefit.

I wondered, again, if it was possible I had been dreaming. Maybe when Seth had tried to strangle me just before my father's death, I actually went unconscious and was in a coma like my dad. In dreams, anything was possible. However, even with the impending doom lurking over me, I'd choose this world over my own and stay in a coma, forever. Could it have been my dad was in a dream? If he was, were they happy and the reason he never woke? I decided if he had dreamed, they would have been happy. It made me feel better. My eyes moved to John, who seemed much more relaxed and jovial than the day before. There weren't any disapproving stares across the breakfast table aimed at Hunter.

I rose to help Annabel gather the dirty plates. "Thank you. That was wonderful."

"No, dear. You're our guest." She smiled, placing her hand on my shoulder before taking the plates from my hand.

"Hunter, I need to speak with you and Jessica in the study," his father said softly.

A collaboration of snickers filled the room before John stared them down.

"Yes, sir," Hunter replied. "This way." He took my hand. "Don't be mad." He turned to face me, stopping in the hallway.

"Why would I be mad?" I had no idea what he was talking about, unless it was about Molly, which I had already forgiven him. If anyone should be mad, it would be him at me. Molly wasn't nearly as dangerous as Seth.

"Well I...I heard you play last night."

"I'm sorry. I didn't mean to wake anyone. I thought it was far enough away."

"No, you didn't wake me. I watched you do a lot of tossing back and forth before you finally got up. At first, I thought you were having one of those dreams of yours. When you left the room, I followed," Hunter said nervously.

"I didn't wake you? Did anyone else hear me?"

He shook his head. I felt relieved. "I couldn't sleep. Playing the piano helps to calm my mind."

"You were pretty out of it after." He chuckled. "I'm pretty sure the drool is still there."

"Oh." I was horrified.

"I'm kidding." He smirked. "So what happened? You were playing beautifully, something very serene, then it changed."

"Into a nightmare." I added, staring blankly at the rose-colored wall behind him.

"I wouldn't say that," he said. "It was still amazing, the notes you were able to create. I could see you in a tranquil world with sunshine all around. Suddenly, the dark black clouds covered up the sun before my eyes leaving you lost in it."

"When the music changed, I thought about the nightmare I had on the porch. The one with visions of marred people, wanting Seth to kill me. You remember, I hit you with chair thinking I was still in the dream."

Hunter smirked. "You barely touched me, but go on."

I left out the part about May, Josephine, and Miss Mabel being thrown into the fire. "As I fought to come out of it, my mother appeared. It just felt so real. I think it's a warning." I talked as if I strayed back into the dream.

"You play with such emotion. I didn't want you to know I was there. I fought not to go to your side when you were clearly upset. I knew those weren't happy tears." The corners of his lips turned down slightly. "So you're not mad?"

I thought about it for a few moments before I answered just for my own amusement. "You did tell me you weren't going to leave me, so I guess I deserve what I get when wandering off." I placed my hand on his face but quickly pulled it back when I saw John coming round the corner.

Hunter leaned to my ear. "I guess that's true, but really, it is okay for you to be alone in this house. You're safe from harm." He smiled widely. "That doesn't mean I want you to be without me."

And with that, we followed John into the office.

His office reminded me of my father's, with the large cherry desk and books lining the walls from top to bottom. An oversized chair, sat next to a bay window, overlooking a courtyard with an in-ground pool. Behind the oak desk, I noticed an old chest identical to the one my father had, down to the same kind of gold key stuck in the lock.

That's strange.

"Hunter tells me you are quite the reader, Jessica," he said, catching me eyeballing all the books perched several feet above us.

"I love to read. I used to read at least four to five hours a day. I suppose I got that from my father. He read to me a lot when I was young. When he couldn't anymore, I read to him. Have you read all these books?"

John sat at his desk chair. "Yes. So has Hunter. This is actually his collection."

Another thing we had in common, more personal than just the arranged-marriage thing.

"You are free to come in here anytime you like and help yourself to any of the books. I'm sure Hunter would agree," John said. "So, we must get down to business. First of all, Jessica," he said softly with adoration in his voice. "We need to consider your safety. Obviously you will need more protection than living at Miss Mabel's can provide, so Annabel and I would like for you to consider staying here with us."

Does John mean me alone? Will Hunter go back to Miss Mabel's? Is this the conclusion his obligation?

The annoying voice tried to squeeze its way through the door without success.

"Just me?" I managed to ask. "Isn't everyone at the shack in danger? Seth will hurt anyone who—"

Both John and Hunter chuckled.

"You don't need to worry about them," Hunter answered.

"He'll be coming after you too," I said softly, feeling my emotions burning in my chest.

Hunter looked at me firmly. "I already told you I'm not leaving you, I meant it."

"May will be staying here as well. I'm not sure we could keep her away if we sent her home." John chuckled. "You're free to stay in the room you're in, or you may pick another. There are many rooms in this house to choose from. At the moment, most of them are empty." He looked at Hunter. "Maybe a room on another floor."

Hunter fidgeted, looking embarrassed.

John didn't approve of me for his son, or at least I saw it that way. But he was letting Hunter stay at their home and not make him go to the shack.

"So, Jessie," John asked. "What do you think?"

I glanced at Hunter, but he was no help. His face was downcast, with a reddish tint on his cheeks. I thought about everyone's safety. If they said I was safer by staying, then everyone was safer. I also thought about the party, the close dances, and the kiss. Just the thought sent another pleasing tingle down to my toes. I was all for more parties.

They want me here so they can keep their son safe. That is a good enough reason to stay.

I nodded my head.

"Good," John cheered. "Now that we've got that settled, we have another matter to consider." John cleared his throat to get his son's attention.

Hunter looked up rather sheepishly at his father.

"You know my feelings, Hunter. However, your mother sees things, differently. You know I'm not going to argue with her, so…" John cleared his throat again, which looked painful.

Was that John's way of giving us his blessing? Although, he did say he felt differently than his wife. At least she was on my side.

"There are some rules you both must follow for spending time together."

"Dad!"

"Son!" He raised his eyebrows. Hunter got quiet. "As I was saying with regards to spending time together, you need to have a chaperone at all times." Hunter shifted uncomfortably in his chair. "May has already volunteered. She's assured me you both have been pretty well behaved." His eyes never left his son's face. "There is a complication. Seth isn't going to take this well, and he's not going to let her go without a fight. Soon, he will have gone through the transformation period."

There's that word again. He's not a butterfly.

"He'll filter back into his life, if he hasn't already. He's very strong, with powerful connections. James has come across Davior several times in the last few weeks. He knew you were bringing her here. They'll be looking for any opportunity to get her off the property." John reached across the desk for my hand. "Jessica, you're safe here, but no wandering off into the swamp past the cobblestone path. Think of it as an invisible wall surrounding the entire property. Davior, nor any of his kind, can cross over it. I'd suggest you stay far from it. I've already talked to May about it." John turned to Hunter. "Most of the families staying on the property have left on assignments. Since the compound is in need of repairs, I'll be putting the family to work. Jessica can help your mother here, while you, your brothers, and I will do the repairs."

What does he mean by invisible wall? Was that the tingling I felt when Hunter carried me through it?

Hunter ran his fingers through his hair. "I can help around the house as well. Work the gardens—"

"No," John's stern look hadn't changed. "It's best you're not around each other all the time. We'll start on the properties closest to the house so we're not far. I want Davior to think he's got a window to get closer to the house. Maybe we can track Seth's plans better."

Without realizing, I had chewed off all my fingernails on one hand. Not only was there some magical wall of protection around that place, but Hunter was going to be kept away from me. I wanted to leave the room before he revealed any other absurd ideas.

A weird tingling feeling wouldn't stop Seth from entering. No one is safe from Seth. This is beyond common sense.

I went over all the weird things while John kept talking to Hunter about the work needing to be done.

I thought the garden at Miss Mabel's was weird, but at least I could wrap my mind around special soil, allowing the crops to grow faster. An invisible wall? And what was Seth turning into? Davior was part of it and he didn't look any different.

Flashes of the way Seth looked in the dream sent a chill down my spine.

"Jessica, you look very pale. Are you all right?" John asked me.

"I'm fine." I shook my head. "What were you saying?"

John stood up, walked over to the front of his desk, and leaned on the corner, looking at me alone. "Back to staying on the property, Davior has been appointed Seth's steward. There are many things uncertain right now, and Davior will use everything he can to get you off the grounds. He's made a deal with his... boss." John paused. "If you ever need to question something you think or feel, please feel free to talk to me about it. Hopefully, your stay is only for a short while, unless you choose to stay longer, of course. I don't want you to feel like a prisoner here."

I nodded, not at all feeling sad by his request. I did think of Miss Mabel needing our help. "What about the garden and harvest time?"

"We've got some folks who will be stopping by to help Miss Mabel with the daily work. You danced with a few of men last night. At this time, you are free to visit her as long as Hunter or James is with you. You'll have to be cautious, and no wandering about," John said, still looking sternly at me.

"Why wasn't May allowed to come here before now?" I asked.

"The little house was meant to bring up children who were left as orphans on the compound. We wanted them to develop a strong understanding of what it meant to work hard and help others. Miss Mabel, an orphan herself, is the one who started it all when she was just a young girl. Of course, now, there is no reason to continue it since May is here." John turned to Hunter before I could ask any more questions. "Hunter, there is one more thing I would like to talk to you about, alone. Please excuse us for a moment, Jessica. I see May is by the pool waiting for you. There is a swimsuit up in your room."

"Thank you." I sighed heavily, following his gaze to see May leap into the water.

Hunter stood to walk me out of the room. He encouraged me to go, as John shut the door.

Lingering at the closed door, I couldn't hear anything through the thick cherry wood. I gave up and walked up the staircase to my room. A light-blue, one-piece swimsuit lay on the bed next to a cover-up.

After dressing, I went down to the sparkling pool. May was already having the time of her life splashing around.

"Jess, come on. Get in," she called.

The crystal-clear water splashed up against the marble blue titles along the sides of the pool, causing the water to shimmer.

"Are you coming in, or do I have to come get you? It's not deep." She stood up.

Although I wasn't frightened, I was relieved to see the pool wasn't deep, for her sake. I sat on the edge of the pool, dangling my feet in the water.

She made her way to me. "Are you scared?"

"I might have been, if I couldn't touch the bottom. I never learned how to swim." I playfully kicked water at her.

I had been scared the day at the river, but it had more to do about being pulled under by the current. The memory of the seas current, dragging me out from the shore, still gave me chills.

May splashed back. Soon, we were in a full water fight with water flying in all directions. I jumped in as we continued to pound each other with water. Laughing hard, I inhaled water up my nose making me cough uncontrollably. She stopped so I could catch my breath. Another splash came up from behind me. Hunter came to my defense, pulverizing May with water. Of course, she loved it.

I rejoined the fight taking May's side. We both splashed him until he waved his hands above his head to surrender.

Soon after, the entire family was in the pool.

"Volleyball," Annabel called. "Girls against boys." She tossed the ball to John as he jumped in.

"You've been dying to say that, Mom," someone said.

"Yes, well, it's nice not to be the only female for once." Annabel fastened her grey blonde hair into a bun with a scrunchie.

"Jordan," John chimed in. "You play with the girls."

Another brother. I should have guessed.

"I'm already here," Hunter called back, standing next to me.

"I don't want anyone hurt." John pointed at Hunter. "You, on this side."

"Fine." He pouted, kissing my cheek before he moved.

Annabel set up the net and jumped in.

I wasn't sure how to play. I had seen people play on the beach below the mansion but never actually played.

Jordan stood next to me. "When the ball comes to you, send it straight up, so I can spike it over the net."

"I'll try," I said, unsure of my ability.

"Zero to zero." Annabel hit the ball.

John returned the ball. Of course it would head right for me. I held my breath, closed my eyes, and then on contact, I pushed the ball straight up.

Jordan stepped in and spiked it down on James. James hit the ball, but it went out of bounds.

"Yeah!" Jordan called out and hugged me.

Hunter twitched, and I was pretty sure it wasn't because we got a point.

The game continued just like that. Jordan and I were the score makers for our team. We won the first game. John had James switch places with Jordan. James told me to keep doing what I was doing. When the ball came to me, I pushed it up in the air. James smacked it hard downward on the other side of the net. James hugged me at the win, lifting me out of the water. Hunter grinded his teeth through his fake smile at his brothers' attempts to annoy him.

Somewhere between the numerous games, we stopped to eat lunch, poolside. I sat next to May, listening to her talk up a storm to Jordan. She enjoyed having someone new to talk to, and he enjoyed her nonstop chatter. He'd try to interject, in-between her breaths, but it wasn't easy. He'd just laugh, letting her continue on.

The last game we played, the boys won as they showed no mercy.

We all laughed as my team went under the net to congratulate the other team. Hunter grabbed me before one of his brothers did, hugging me tightly. I giggled as he set my feet back on the bottom of the pool. I felt that same rush of feelings, the one that begged to be kissed.

Someone cleared their throat, making us look in the same direction. James tossed towels at us. Hunter caught them before they hit the water.

"So what did your father want to talk to you about?" I asked, drying off.

"Oh, it was nothing. We talked about Joseph's behavior. He also wanted to know if you knew about Molly. I told him Jordan already spilled those beans. Molly was acting pretty strange last night. Both he and my mother are concerned about her. It's pretty obvious she is very upset."

"Obviously," I echoed.

"John's afraid she might try to get back at you somehow, so he's told everyone it would be in her best interest not to come here for a while. Besides, Miss Caroline and Miss Betsy have a lot of work to do, so that should keep her busy as well."

We walked into the house and up the stairs.

"I'm not an infant. I can handle her if she does come. I don't think she should be kept away. It's clear she has a relationship with your family," I said, thinking about her thin frame.

"I don't want you to deal with her. My family and I will keep a close eye on her. She won't be able to get close to you, just in case she snaps. It's amazing what some people will do in the name of love, or in her case, obsession."

"Molly has shot me some daggers. Good thing looks can't kill." Still, I understood the pain she must have felt. "I do feel sorry for her." My tone changed. "I mean, if my parents had brought you to me, and you didn't want me." I couldn't believe I said that out loud.

"Well, that wouldn't have happened," he said, sarcastically.

Did he mean there was no way his parents would have matched us up, or did he mean that he wouldn't have wanted me?

"You know what I mean," he said. I looked over at his face, hoping more clarification would surface.

He said nothing more as we continued to walk. Something else occupied his thoughts, but I hesitated to ask him about it. Actually I had so many other questions I wanted to ask.

Why does his mother and father look so young? Everyone keeps talking about Hunter being alone for so long, but he's not that old, is he? Even if I asked, would he tell me? Could he tell me? He's been good at skirting around questions, so I guess if he didn't want to answer, he'd come up with something else. So why not ask?

"How old are you really?"

"Here we are." Hunter leaned against the frame of my door and folded his arms against his chest.

"So...you're not going to tell me? I thought you were going to start answering my questions?" I moved closer to him.

He smirked, tilting his head sideways. "Does it matter?"

"No. I guess not."

"You know things are different here. You've asked me questions, but really you knew the answers. I thought it would be easier to discover some things for yourself."

The weird stuff wasn't feeling as weird as it had at first. He could have said they were aliens from another planet and I don't think I would have flinched.

I'm becoming one of them.

After a moment of uneasy silence, I passed him to enter my room.

He caught my arm, pulling me to him. "Oh, so I see how it is."
My heart skipped a beat as his arms circled my waist. The pool water streaked down my legs, sending a wave of shivers.

"You're cold," Hunter said, wrapping his damp towel around my shoulders.

"I should change." I twisted away from him.

I was done with him being evasive. I wanted answers, concrete answers to at least one of my questions. Hunter's hand reached for mine, not letting me get away. "Remember how I told you about the Cherokee, about the Trail of Tears?" he stroked my hand.

"Yes," I answered, confused.

"The legend about what happened after, and what God had done for them?" he said a little more seriously, bringing his eyes up to meet mine.

I thought about it for moment. The Cherokee were forced off their land, where many died on the journey to the new settlements. The legend, which I had liked, had been about how God saved the people to fight against Lucifer in the battle between good and evil.

He's out of his mind if he thinks I believe he was one of them.
I shook my head.

"I was twelve when the soldiers came," he said. "Playing a game with my brothers in a field, close to here."

"You don't look Native American to me. If you don't want to tell me…"

Are you kidding me?

I thought I would be okay with whatever he told me, but that was insane. I'd believe a fountain-of-youth story easier than dead Indians. I tried to go into my room, but Hunter refused to let go of my hand.

"My grandfather fell in love with a missionary, and they were married. My mother is only half Cherokee. My father is full-blooded, but he took on the fairer skin and hair color, which is why I look more like a white man." He chuckled.

I remembered he said they were immortal but they could marry and have families of their own and they aged, but slower.

"Jess," Hunter said sternly, "I still remember feeling, like I wanted to die, before God took mercy on us." He paused. "God gave us this gift of life to be able to help mankind and to offset the plans Lucifer has for this world."

"So if you're all part of this and you lived so long ago, how do you live in the world without people knowing? A wife would know if her husband wasn't aging normally, wouldn't she?"

Okay, I'll play along even though he has to playing with me. It couldn't be true.

"James, for example, will appear to grow older in the church. When the time comes when he can't fake it anymore, he will have to leave. It's pretty easy to fake aging with some hair color and make-up. Jordan has recently left his mission work and will be staying here until his next calling.

We hold on to knowing in the end, Lucifer will be defeated. But until that time, we'll continue to recruit, and help people, leading them away from the darkness to the light until the final battle."

"The same battle as in Revelation? Come on," I said, but I was starting to believe him. It would sure make sense of everything. The demons, the protected land, the magic garden—the pieces of the puzzle were coming together.

The voice came back, knocking the door down with one big push. *See? He's lying to you. It's time to leave this place, Jessica. Continue with the plan to leave here. There is a wonderful life outside of this new prison full of deceivers.*

I put my hands up to my ears to block out the voice, although it didn't do any good. I only made Hunter frown. I needed time, alone. My head felt like exploding. A thousand thoughts colliding into each other made my knees weak.

I clung to the door. "You've given me a lot to think about, but I need to take a shower before this chlorine leaves a permanent smell in my hair." My mind was trying to put together all the puzzle pieces I'd been collecting since the day I arrived in the swamp. I couldn't do that with him staring at me.

"I'm sorry." He hugged me close. "I was a little insensitive to just blurt that out. John warned me this would be hard for you to understand."

The voice in my head wouldn't shut up. "I…I don't know what to think. I spun from him to enter my room. "Just give me some time to sort it out."

Hunter looked crushed as I shut the door.

I sat on the edge of the chair, next to the vanity, trying to recall all of the story in more detail. It didn't help ease my mind, but the voice quieted.

May, already changed, skipped in from her room. I could see Hunter's connecting door on the other side of May's, was shut. "What's wrong?"

"Nothing. I'm fine, just a little worn out. It's been a busy couple of days and I haven't slept well."

"Oh, but I slept wonderfully. Better than I ever have." She climbed up on the bed. "Maybe you'll sleep better tonight."

"I hope so. You really like it here, don't you, May?"

"I do, and everyone is so nice. I especially like Miss Annabel. She let me braid her hair. It was so soft." She laid her head down on my pillow. "Jordan is a goofball, but I like him."

The pit in my stomach felt like a giant hole. If Hunter was telling me the truth, and deep down, I knew he was, they would all outlive me. I guess that wasn't so bad. I wondered if May would also outlive me. Was she also part of all of it, too? I wouldn't ask her. She might not know.

A soft knock came from my bedroom door. "Jessica?" Annabel asked. "May I come in?"

"Yes, of course." I stood from the chair.

"May, would you excuse us for a moment?" Annabel asked.

"Sure. I'll get ready for dinner." She bounced into her room, shutting the door behind her.

Hunter's mother sat on the edge of the bed. "Sit, please." She patted the spot next to her. "It seems my son has shared our story with you."

I nodded, sitting on the edge of the bed. "It's not that I thought he'd lie to me, but it's pretty out there. Reminds me of the stories my father told me about a society of furry little creatures who can speak."

"It's a hard story to swallow. I'm sure you have some questions. Hunter thought you might feel better talking to me about it. But if you would rather be alone to your thoughts, I understand."

Does it really matter? When my lifetime is up, Hunter will still have to continue with his life. It seems, from that perspective, I get the better end of the deal, unless there is a way, but how could there be? I'm not Cherokee, although if the war between God and Lucifer is close, maybe I won't die.

I liked that thought better.

"I knew something was different at the shack. I pretended it was part of May's imaginary world."

She patted my knee. "But it wasn't her imagination."

"There's so much to take in at once. Being here has been really nice. I feel like a part of real family for the first time in my life." I paused, realizing most of the stuff in the Bible seemed unreal, but I believed it to be truth. "Maybe I'm just making it more difficult than it is and I should accept…no, it's still a weird concept to accept." I chucked.

Annabel laughed. "Seeing an angel standing before you is pretty weird too."

I smiled. "I need time to process it all, but I'll be okay."

She squeezed my hand and stood to leave.

"I do have a question though. How long do you think it will be before the war begins? The one between God and Lucifer?"

She hesitated. "Honestly, we don't know for sure. Most of the signs are there, but we've thought that once before."

"Who?"

"A man in Germany. He had potential to be the antichrist. At first, he was debonair. The people loved him. But then, he got to power hungry, too self-absorbed, and the people could see he was evil. No, the one who will start it, the people will love him, and he will rule all nations. There will be a time of false peace and prosperity with this ruler. He will gain their trust. He will make people believe his rules are for the good of mankind, slowly taking away their freedoms. He will start in the most powerful nation before gaining control over the world. It will only be God's true followers who will see him for what he really is." She sighed.

"By control over the world, you mean the United Nations?"

The wheels in my head started to turn, like two gears fitting tightly together.

"That's what we think," she answered. "Of course, this is all man's interpretation of Scripture, so take it as such. We need to keep focused on the present and our individual calling until then." She paused. "Anything else you want to talk about?"

"No. I think I'll turn in."

"I can have Hunter bring up your dinner if you would like."

"I'm still full from lunch." I rubbed my stomach.

Annabel hugged me and kissed my cheek. She was quickly becoming the mother I had always dreamed of. "Good night, Jessica."

"Night, and thank you," I said quickly.

"My door is always open if you need to talk woman to woman." She smiled as she shut the door.

As soon as the door was closed, I lay back on the bed. What she said about the Antichrist described Seth perfectly—not only what he had done, but his future goals.

Do they think he's the Antichrist? Is that the transformation he is going through? Oh my gosh, this isn't good.

I curled up into a ball in the middle of the bed.

Somehow, I ended up here, on a reservation with Cherokee Indians who fight demons, and since there are no coincidences, what reason would God have to send me here? Why me? What makes me so special?

I grabbed the pillow and fluffed it under my head. My eyes grew heavy as I thought about my new world and what gift God would give me to battle with.

He sent me here for a reason. But what?

A House Full of Boys

The weeks flew by in a wink of an eye. I spent some of my time getting accustomed to the house and grounds. Annabel took me and May from room to room, letting us pick out pieces we liked for our own rooms. She wanted us to make them our own. Annabel pulled out an array of paints for us to choose from. The three of us painted. Annabel, the gifted artist, painted a mural of a farm with horses along a white fence for May. I found country cottage pictures, of white houses covered in flowering vines, surrounded by a matching picket fence, tucked away in another room. They were too pretty to be stored, so I hung them in my room. Annabel surprised me by creating a mural to match.

Besides decorating, I used some of my free time to read while the men were out working. I wanted to read the entire Bible from start to finish, so I picked up where I left off in Psalms. So far, it had been my favorite. I loved poetry anyway, but that poet knew me. Every struggle was my struggle. My very favorite in Psalm 18:16–19. I'd repeat it over and over while looking in the mirror. "He reached down from on high and took hold of me; He drew me out of deep waters. He rescued me from my powerful enemy, from my foes, who were too strong for me. They confronted me in the day of my disaster, but the Lord was my support. He brought me out into a spacious place; He rescued me because He delighted in me."

The more I read, the closer I felt to God, but it didn't stop me from missing Hunter. Some days the men were gone until sunset. When I asked what they had been doing, Hunter's only reply was that they had been working on the property. I knew John and

Annabel were keeping Hunter and me from spending too much time together. But he was always back by dinnertime, leaving us a few hours together to walk the grounds before bed.

We talked about various things, past and present. We kept the topic off Davior, Seth, or anything unpleasant. May trailed behind or in front of us, in her own world, until she would begin to complain about how late we were keeping her up. It was then, followed by an uncomfortable good night under May's watch, we knew our time together was up. The only kisses Hunter gave me rested on my cheek or on the top of my head.

Although I was living in a strange world, it was more normal than my life before. Everyone who came and went appeared to be regular people. Nothing was shocking or unusual about them. I could easily forget the whole weird story to live a normal life.

I wouldn't have worried at all, if it hadn't been for the following week. Annabel explained they were traveling farther from house, which was why I saw less and less of Hunter. When I asked where, she just answered, "Oh, here and there."

I just prayed they would be safe until the next time I saw them.

May stomped into my room. "You're not dressed!" she scowled, until she saw the look on my face and softened her tone. "Why do you look so sad?"

"I haven't seen Hunter all week." I gave her a big hug, mostly because I needed it.

She looked at me with a big smile. "Well, you'd better get dressed. We are having a bonfire tonight! Doesn't that sound like so much fun?" She twirled around. "Hunter will be there." She giggled. "They'll all be there."

I smiled at her excitement and at my own. "Okay. I will."

And with that, she pulled on me until I got up, and pushed me into the bathroom.

Family events had kept Hunter and me apart even more. I was excited I would get to see him after not seeing him all week, but I would have much rather taken our quiet walk in one of the gardens. Maybe I would get kissed again. It seemed so long ago—more of a distant memory.

A bonfire with everyone around didn't sound all that great to me.

If he loves you, he would fight for you, instead of letting his family run his life. You don't have a chance against them. "Leave me alone," I said out loud. "I'm not leaving. You should give up."

Instead of a shower, I filled the deep, long tub with warm water, adding a splash of strawberry bubble bath. The bubbles overflowed the tub as I slipped into it. I was tired. It was my fault for staying up so late again, overanalyzing John's motives and everything else. I drifted into a trance, nothing particular, just soft music playing in my head, and a vision of a swan or two swimming in a pond. Concentrating on the music kept the voice from barging in.

Knock! Knock! Knock!

I jumped up at the sound, slipping in the ceramic tub to bump my head on its edge. I made some kind of painful sound, and the door flew open. Thankfully, the tub was slippery enough, that I slid back down under the bubbles.

"Oh, Jess, I'm so sorry. I didn't mean to...you've just been in here so long. You didn't sleep well..." Hunter was in a panic, looking over my head where my hand clung. He found the bump with his hand.

"Ouch." I squirmed.

He bent down like he was going to lift me up.

"Uh...that's probably not a good idea. I'm not wearing a bathing suit under all these bubbles." He looked confused at first but quickly caught on, blushed, and turned his back to me.

"Oh right! I'll go get Annabel."

"No! I'm fine. Hand me a towel, please," I ordered.

I was less embarrassed with him there than the thought of his mother carrying me, naked.

He protested. "I really think you should—"

"Hunter, please?"

He handed me the towel, behind his back. I stood up slowly, feeling a little dizzy, but not from the bump. I wrapped the large towel around me.

"Okay. I'm decent," I said, wrapping a smaller towel around my hair.

"I don't think I can agree with you." His smile was quite sinister.

"What?" I sounded irritated.

"You are anything but decent." He swept me up and carried me back to my room.

"Ha-ha."

He laid me down on the bed and removed the towel on my head, allowing my wet hair to spill out over the pillow so he could examine my injury, which I knew was minor. He sighed. "Did you know on average, three hundred people a year drown in bathtubs?"

"Are you kidding me? That's not very many, considering how big the population is," I answered with a small smile.

"Yes, I know, but I don't know what I would do if I lost you because you fell asleep in the tub." He couldn't suppress his laugh.

"It would be so much better for another reason," I said sarcastically. *Like demons annihilating my existence or Molly strangling me.*

"That's not funny."

May entered the room. "You're still not ready?" she huffed, taking Hunter by the arm to push him out the door. She shut and locked the door before giving me the evil eye. Well, at least she tried to look serious.

"I slipped in the tub and hit my head. Hunter ran in, but I was completely covered in bubbles, I swear." I showed her the bump to confirm my story.

"Well, all right," she said. "Now get dressed!" she ordered.

"Yes, ma'am," I said, watching her walk to her door, placing one hand on her hip and the other on the doorknob.

"Ten minutes, and I'll be back." She shut the door.

I was done in less time and bounced into her room wearing a yellow summer dress, with daisy buttons around the neck. I hated the clothes my mother had bought for me, but Annabel's taste in clothes was like she knew me perfectly.

I twirled for May.

"I love it." She glowed. "Let's go."

She pulled me downstairs into the game room with soft, white couches around a glass coffee table. Annabel came over to me quickly. "Oh, Jessica, let me see your head."

"I'm fine, really." I mouthed a sarcastic *Thanks* in Hunter's direction as Annabel searched my head for the bump.

I shrieked when she touched it.

"Go get some ice," she called to him. "It's not bad, but we should try to bring down the swelling."

Hunter was back in a second with some ice wrapped in a damp towel. I reached for it, but he wouldn't let me have it. He led me over to the soft chair, forcing me to sit. He slid in behind me, holding the towel to my head very gently. I relaxed against him, feeling his chest rise and fall along with my breaths.

A flat screen hung on the wall like a picture frame above the stone fireplace. It was on a news channel, and all the men, except for Hunter, were glued to it.

"What's going on?" I asked.

The television clicked off as May pulled out a board game from the cabinet under the table.

"Hey, May, whatcha got there?" James looked at the box. "Monopoly? I haven't played that in years. I'm in."

Jordan sat on the floor next to the table. "That means I'd better play too since James cheats." Jordan went to sit at the table. "I'll be the banker."

"Oh yeah, I'm the one who cheats," James called back.

"That's right." Jordan smiled. "At least you can admit it."

They sounded like little boys as they exchanged witty banter.

"I should help Annabel in the kitchen." I stood, but Hunter pulled me back down putting the ice wrapped towel back on my bump.

John smiled at me. "I'm sure she would love the help."

I went to get up again. Hunter didn't try to stop me with John staring in his direction.

"You and I have a chess game to finish, son." He winked at me.

I didn't look back as I left the room, even though I felt multiple eyes on my back.

As if she already knew I was coming, Annabel said, "Jessica, would you mind chopping up those veggies over there?"

At the kitchen island, there were already two tall chairs and a prep station ready for workers.

"Sure," I said, sitting in a chair. "So, what's this bonfire thing for tonight? May is so excited."

"Oh, it's just our away of keeping in contact with our friends to share information or happy tidings. With some of the families traveling, it can get quite lonesome here. With the chapel in the process of a remodel, we haven't seen those who live near here since the ball," she said, as if I knew about a chapel.

"Ouch." I sliced my finger, my fault for getting distracted.

"Here." Annabel handed me a napkin before rifling through a small drawer. "I always have these on hand." She pulled out a Band-Aid.

She took the napkin from me and wrapped my barely bleeding finger. "All better," she said.

We heard May laughing and accusing someone of cheating. We looked at each other and laughed.

"It's so nice to have girls in the house." She touched my arm. "It's been just me with these boys for so long. Molly, Josephine and some of the other girls come to visit, but it's not the same. I love my boys, but sometimes I wished I would have had a little girl." She went to the cabinet and pulled out a skillet. "I've been meaning to ask, if you like the clothes I picked out? I really don't know what is in fashion these days for girls. I ordered them online, so if you don't like them—"

"I love them. I wondered how you could have picked such beautiful and practical clothes. They are exactly things I would have picked out, if I had been allowed to buy my own clothes." I felt rather ashamed I hadn't thanked her. "Thank you so much. I should have told you before now."

Annabel turned to me, carrying the skillet. "You've had a lot to think about these last few weeks. Please don't worry about offending me." She put the pan below the cutting board, while I scraped the vegetables into it with the back of the knife.

"You are such a cheater!" We heard James yell out from the other room followed by laugher.

I chuckled. "So what's next?" She pulled up a chair next to me, placing a new cutting board in front of me while she used the one already set out. She pulled out small pieces of dough from a bowl, rolled them into a ball, and flattened them with a tiny rolling pin. Taking a small scoop of a meat mixture from another bowl, she placed it in the center of the dough. She folded then pressed the dough around the meat to seal it inside. I followed her lead and soon the first batch was ready to go on a greased cookie sheet and into the oven.

We continued to make more when Davior popped into my head. When I had first met him, he thought his name was a joke. *That might not be a good topic. It's got to hurt knowing her son is fighting on the wrong side.*

"So, Jess, what's your mother like?" she said first.

Talk about a hurtful topic.

She put her hand over mine, noticing I shifted in my seat a few times. "John has told me some things, but he's much more into the mechanics of things and less into the emotions. You don't have to talk about, her if you don't want to."

She was reaching out to me, yet I was shutting her out. At least it felt like I was. "No. It's okay. I just didn't know what you already knew." I tried to play off my initial reaction.

I told her about my life from my earliest memory and worked my way up through the years. It was harder talking about my father. I almost felt his presences around me—which wasn't logical. Annabel listened carefully, jotting down notes in her mind. I left out my recovered memory about what I saw that night of my father's attack, the one Davior dug out from the vault.

Annabel and I finished stuffing the little, round dumplings.

"It's hard to believe a mother can be so cruel." She said. "Let's get these last ones in the oven." She grabbed two trays, and I grabbed two, and we walked over to the oven.

"I have forgiven her," I added, sliding my trays onto the rack. "What she did is in the past."

Annabel put one arm around me, giving me a squeeze. "That's very mature of you." she said, proudly, which gave me a different kind of feeling—a true mother's love. "Please don't hesitate to treat me as a mother. You know, someone to talk to and confide in. We can do each other's hair," she teased with a silly look, making us laughed. She kissed my forehead. "Would you like to tell May and the boys' dinner will be ready in ten minutes?"

"Can I ask you one question first?"

"You can ask me anything, Jess." She kept her arm around my shoulders.

"Davior," I looked at her face. Her expression didn't change, so I continued. "He said something when I first met him, something about you having a sense of humor or something."

"He's always hated his name." She shook her head. "I thought it was quite original."

"Why would that be comical?"

"It's not." She went over to the sink to wash the heads of lettuce sitting out on counter. "One day, my mother was reading from the Bible. It was the story about King David. After all these years, I'm not sure why I heard it or even where in the story the two are close together. Anyway, I heard the name Davior. It was David and Savior jumbled together. From then on, I said if I had any male children, one of them would be Davior."

The correlation of Davior thinking his name was some sort of joke wasn't obvious to me, but I was trying to figure it out on my own.

Annabel noticed my eyebrows drawn together.

"Because of the path he has chosen, he finds it funny. David was a man after God's own heart and, well, you know who the Savior is."

"Oh," I said. It made sense.

"I still have the hope he'll change his allegiance. I don't believe the light he once had inside is gone completely."

"I'm so sorry." I just stood there.

"All right now. No gloomy face, okay? Go." She smiled, pointing toward the game room.

"Okay." I forced a smile.

I thought about how Annabel must have felt to have lost her son, as I went into the hall then entered the room where everyone else were playing games.

May saw me and fanned her money. "I won! I won!" She jumped up and hugged me.

The two brothers winked at me. "Of course you won. You're the smart one," James said.

The attention then went to the two men playing chess at the small table next to the fireplace. They didn't look up at all the commotion. Jordan whispered in my ear. I nodded. I walked over behind Hunter to kiss him softly on the cheek. Hunter, surprised, made a quick chess move before he looked up and smiled.

"Checkmate!" John yelled loudly.

James and Jordan roared.

I stood back for a second, enjoying the way my lips felt on his skin. Hunter whisked me up quickly, not minding every eye focused on him.

"So I guess you're not mad at me for barging in on your bath."

I shook my head. "Embarrassed is more accurate." The words escaped my lips.

We both noticed everyone had left the room, and we were alone for the first time in weeks. Hunter placed his hand on my face, tracing one finger from the top of my eyelid down to the bottom of my neck. He kissed me softly, releasing my face to circle around my back, holding me closer. My hands moved along his chest and around his neck. My heart raged for more of his sweet breath and the touch of his skin against mine. I pulled back to catch my breath, mostly to look out for prying eyes.

"Sorry," he said, only his smile didn't look sorry. "We should join the others."

I couldn't help but giggle at how much he looked like a child who had just got away with something.

Jordan yelled from the kitchen. "Hey, we're waiting for you two!"

Hunter sighed. "I'm glad to be forgiven yet again."

"For now," I teased in a whisper. "I guess I don't have to worry about drowning in bathtubs either."

The Bonfire

After dinner, the family sat around the game room talking and laughing. Hunter told some childhood stories about his brothers since they had embarrassed him earlier. We talked until dark swept into the room. May hovered at the window to point out the first star of the night.

John and James left our conversation earlier to prepare for the evening event.

"See! It's time! It's time!" May jumped up and down.

"Okay, okay. Calm down. We're going." Jordan laughed as she took his hand and pulled him out of the room.

Annabel, Hunter, and I followed. We were in another courtyard set away from the house, one I didn't recall running into on my strolls around the grounds.

The fire was already in full blaze when we arrived, with flames reaching out for the dark-gray sky. The fire pit was at least twenty feet wide with wooden benches horseshoed around it, enough for two hundred or more. Off to the side of the campfire sat a table with large sticks, marshmallows, chocolate, and graham crackers, along with other snacks in front of a small, white building. May noticed the treats right away.

Hunter kissed my hand before he disappeared with his brothers.

May was overexcited, clapping her hands at everything. I imagined steam shooting out her ears. The more I watched May there on the compound, the more I understood why she had been kept at the shack. Although she was still young, May was well grounded and quite mature. I knew what it meant to grow up quickly. I might have been twenty physically, but I had turned into an adult the moment my father faded into his own world, forcing me to be the responsible adult. My mother had known nothing of responsibility.

The air felt like early fall. Warm during the daytime but it quickly cooled once the sun set. I gave up trying to gauge time and just let the season speak to me. I was glad for the cool air because the fire blazed, putting out some massive heat. I sat on the bench farthest from the flames. May stood closer with a stick in her hand. I watched her catch the marshmallow on fire and whirl it in the air. She finally blew it out, leaving the marshmallow charcoaled.

As May ate her burnt marshmallow, I stared into the raging fire.

Tornado-like flames of red, orange, and blue shot up wisps of smoke into the night sky. The bonfire came to life as a strange melody began to play in my head. I hummed along with the leaping blazes of light, falling into a trance. For a moment, I imagined myself dancing in the fire, but no harm was coming to me. I couldn't feel the searing heat. It was just a soft, warm touch as each flare shot me up higher into the sky, twirled me, and then cradled me back to the red, glowing embers where it all began.

Someone grab my arm, and it all stopped.

"S'more?" May offered.

"What?" I laughed, shaking myself out of the daydream.

"Do you want one? It's a toasted marshmallow and chocolate sandwich. I made this one for you," she said. "I didn't burn this one."

"Thanks, May." I took a bite. It was very gooey, but good and very sweet.

"What were you just doing?" she asked.

I hugged her. "Oh, I suppose I'm just letting my imagination run away with me, again."

The flames were inviting me to join them.

"Well, you looked ghostly." She giggled.

Our guests began to arrive. Both May and I noticed Miss Mabel entering the courtyard and jumped up to greet her.

"Well, don't yous two look just lovely." She beamed.

I wanted to tell her I still wanted to help her, but she read my face before I could say a word.

"Yous needin' to be heres, where yous safe. Don't go wanderin' off. Yous hears me?" She kissed my head. "We all has a purpose in life. Mine's been lookin' after young'uns, to teach them morals, hard work, and God's ways. My time's ending, and soon, very soon, I'll receive my reward in heaven," Miss Mabel said in her singsong voice. "So yous do as yous told, young lady. Keep yourself out of harm's way".

"Yes, Miss Mabel."

"Mabel," John called.

"Excuse me, ladies, I's bein' summons." She winked before leaving us.

I heard a commotion coming from the small, white shed to the left of the fire. Hunter and Miss Caroline were arguing. I knew it was wrong, but I moved closer to eavesdrop. Miss Betsy saw me and hurried in my direction.

"Hello, dear." She hugged me. "Come sit with me," she said, placing her hand around my shoulders. "Are you enjoying your time here?"

"Yes. Annabel is taking very good care of us," I answered, trying to look behind.

"Oh, she is just a doll." Miss Betsy continued, "She plans the best parties and even better weddings."

At the bonfire, all the wooden seats were taken except for a few in front. I sat down next to Miss Betsy, who held on to my hand. Miss Caroline soon followed, sitting next to her friend. She looked flushed, as she smiled over at me. She then whispered something into Miss Betsy's ear.

I couldn't see where Hunter or his brothers had disappeared to, but there was a female shadow on the other side of the flames, staring at me. No one else seemed to notice the slender framed woman as she moved around the pit.

It was Molly. Her eyes reflected the red, hot flames, burning through me.

Maybe we should talk woman to woman. I could tell her I'm sorry things didn't work out for her.

I stood, keeping my eyes on Molly, but Miss Betsy gently sat me back down. "That's not a good idea, dear," she whispered into my ear.

Molly watched me as she stepped into the shadows, but not out of my sight. Her eyes drifted away from me to Hunter, finally appearing with his brothers by his side. His eyes narrowed at her.

I stood again, but Miss Betsy pulled me down. "Just wait, dear." She patted me on the leg.

I grunted as John stepped out in front of the large crowd.

Hunter walked out with his brothers. They stopped at John's side to hug him before sitting with the crowd.

Hunter headed directly to me. He sat down, not meeting my eyes. His feet tapped the ground, shifting in his seat. I reach over to touch his hand. He laced his fingers in mine, pulling my hand up to his lips, keeping a firm eye on his dad who stood before the crowd.

"Welcome, friends. Thank you for being with us on this very special night." John paused. "God has truly blessed us all. He has taken us from the deepest and darkest hour to raise us up with His own hands, chosen to fight with Him in that final hour to defeat the evil of this world. Praise be to God," John cheered.

Everyone said amen.

Hunter rocked on his heels.

"We have been honored to walk among the weak, to share with them the hope that is only in the risen Savior. You have allowed God to use you to snatch the souls of people from the very darkness and bring them into the light. So when the day comes when they depart this world, they will stand before the gates of heaven instead of being fed to the hounds of hell." He continued on with his pep talk, and the people clapped and cheered. "Our enemy is on the move. We need to be more watchful than ever. The time is near, my friends. Our time is coming to show God what we are made of. It's time our faith be tested in ways unimaginable, and we need to stay firm." He stared out into the darkness. "Even in our darkest hour, God knows our pain, and He wants to comfort us. We need to lean on Him and not let the evil sweep us away." He paused for a moment with a long sigh, continuing to stare into the darkness. "Praise be to God forever."

Everyone echoed, "Praise God."

"Now, friends, let us rejoice tonight, for God has blessed us once again," John said, although he didn't sound very excited—more of a sound of defeat.

I could feel the pulse in Hunter's wrists quicken. His eyes stayed focused on John.

"Let me first tell you a story about a young man. He was our great grandfather of long ago," John said, sitting in the chair in front of the fire, his hands up in the air.

I was already at the edge of my seat, ready for his next words to pour out.

"A young man wandered along a river, his heart filled with love for a girl in his village. All the other young men had tried to get her attention, but she showed no interest in any of them. He wandered for hours, thinking of how he could stand out in the crowd of suitors. How could he make her see he was her one true love? He wasn't tall like some of the other boys, who could reach up high for the best fruit on the trees and leave baskets of treats at her feet. He wasn't strong, so he couldn't hunt the buffalo to offer to her parents. He wasn't even the most handsome or sought after as some of the other boys. He had nothing special to compete against them. He got down on one knee and prayed to God. He asked God to send him a sign, a thought, something to help him win the girl he loved with all his heart. Just then, an object hit him hard on his knee, sending a strange sensation throughout his body. He didn't remember kneeling in the stream." John paused and reached down. "He looked at a long stick, and a vision of music flooded his mind. God had given him the answer. With God's direction, he hollowed out the stick with a hot stone and dug out five holes, all the time recalling the image God had placed in his head. Once he was done, he blew into the stick. The most beautiful music came out.

"The young man was out in the woods for hours. He listened to his heart as he composed a song just for her. That night, he played her song outside of her hut, and she fell in love with him. That song became their song and would follow them into the afterlife, binding them eternally," John concluded and stood up.

Everyone had tears in their eye, including me.

I glanced over at Hunter, holding a thin stick in his hand. John's hand reached out to Hunter. He stood, faced the crowd, held the wooden flute to his mouth, and began to play.

With each breath, a haunting old sound filled the air, floating into the sky. As each note escaped out the holes of the instrument, I let them flow into my soul. I closed my eyes, imagining us dancing together. Hunter's soul and mine floated together like no other feeling I could describe. All at once, it was just us in our own little world of magic.

The music stopped.

No one made a sound. Hunter's eyes were on me, and tears swelled in my eyes. He took my hand and pulled me to him.

"No..." We both heard a small voice stepping out from the shadow. "No, no, no..." Molly continued getting louder with each one.

No, no, no. You stupid girl. The intruder's voice in my head drowned her out. His screaming stabbed against my eardrum.

"Go away," I screamed back, not caring if everyone thought I was losing my mind.

Maybe I was crazy.

You know you aren't good enough for him. Leave now. Run. Run.

"No," I cried and fell to my knees.

Molly was no longer anyone's concern as I tucked my shaking body into a ball, covering my ears. It wasn't muffling the high pitch.

"Jessie, what's wrong?" Hunter dropped next to me with his arms around me.

My temples pounded beneath the tips of my fingers. I pressed hard, hoping it would help. Nothing helped, as the voice wouldn't let up. "The voice in my head," My teeth bared down against each other. "It's awful."

Hunter shouted. "Davior!"

"What?" I asked, through my clinched teeth. "James!" Hunter hollered.

"Yes, I'm on it. Hang in there, Jessie," James said before running off into the trees past Molly, who just stared at me with a look of enjoyment across her face.

Then, just as quickly as it came, the voice was gone. My hands dropped from my head to go around Hunter.

He hugged me, tightly, stroking my hair. "Is the voice gone?"

"Yes," I answered with tears in my voice. "I'm sorry I didn't tell you. I wasn't sure it was him. I mean, I knew it wasn't me, but—"

"You couldn't have known. He was making you think it could have been your own thoughts. I should have seen what he was doing. He's been in and out of my head, but I've been... distracted," he soothed. "James ran him off. He won't be trying that again, now that you know it wasn't your voice."

"That's good." I rubbed the spot between my eyes.

Looking over his shoulder, Molly had gone.

The commotion hadn't stopped the eyes of our guests from watching us. They were all too quiet—waiting for something to happen.

Hunter noticed too. "Just in case, next time you hear strange voices, I want to be the first to know." He whispered.

I nodded my head against his strong chest.

He spoke softly, getting down on one knee. "So, where were we?"

Hunter reached into his pocket and pulled out a beaded ring, covered with tiny turquoise gemstones. "Jessica, the song I played was for you, your song, like the song the young man played for his love. I love you, and I will love you all the days of my life." He held the ring out, his hand shook while he slipped it on my finger. "Will you marry me?"

My world went silent, the crackling fire, the crowd, the birds, the wind—all held their breath, awaiting my answer. Overwhelmed, I stared at the gemstones, along the dark-brown leather strap. Everything was happening so fast. I looked into Hunter's nervous face, and I couldn't help but smile. He looked so much like a little boy, waiting for my answer.

Why am I hesitating? I love him. I love him more than my own life.

My emotions got the best of me as I lunged for him in a long kiss, knocking him off balance.

A loud, painful cry ripped us away from each other.

"Molly?" I said under my breath.

"I told them she shouldn't be here tonight," he said, not caring about the sorrowful cry in the darkness, guiding my face back to meet his. "Was that a yes?" he asked in a nervous chuckle.

"Yes," I said softly. "I love you."

John jumped up and put his arms around both of us. "Annabel and I are pleased at this union. You both have our blessing," John said, looking at Annabel.

"Finally," someone called out, and the crowd cheered.

He said "our" blessing, but he really meant Annabel's blessing. John turned to us so only we could see his serious face. "It's your decision to set the date, but there are certain things that must be done first. You are to be married, unless—"

Hunter cleared his voice, and John got the meaning and changed the topic.

John whispered, "We'll talk more, later. I must go find Molly. I'll take your brothers with me. You stay here and play for our guests."

"Yes, sir," he said, still looking at me.

"I would love to hear you play more, although not my song."

He nodded. "I'll only play that one for you from now on." His lips brushed against mine before he began to play.

The evening continued on as if nothing bad had happened. After Hunter played a few more melodies, people began to socialize. There were plenty of snacks and s'mores. I warned May of an unpleasant stomachache to follow if she didn't slow down. She just gave me a big, chocolate-toothed smile. Hunter stayed by my side, sneaking in soft kisses and tight embraces where he could.

Miss Mabel caught us at one of those moments. "I's so happy for yous both." She hugged us. "God brought yous to us, and now we's knows why. Everything else will work out. If yous trust the good Lord, He will sees you through."

"Are you leaving?" I asked.

"Yep. Best to get back, before gettin' too late. Josephine wanted to come, but yous know Joseph. Don't want to leave her alone with him for too long, she may just punch him out. Night, loves."

After Miss Mabel left, Hunter pulled me from the crowd, through the house, to a garden far from the celebration.

My head was spinning.

I'm engaged. And not to just someone, but someone I want, someone I love more than I could ever have imagine. My mother was right about one thing, I did want to marry.

"We need to talk." He sounded serious. "Just listen to me first, please. First of all, I didn't want to propose to you this way. It's just part of our traditions, and I didn't want to take it away from my family. By traditions, I shouldn't have kissed you before now."

Oh no. What's this about?

He read my worried expression.

"No." He smiled. "I warned you to let me finish, my love," he said softly. "I want to marry you. I would marry you right this moment if I could. But there are certain matters out of my control, which means our engagement might be longer than we both want. But at least this way, my parents won't be hard-pressed to keep us apart."

I know he wants me, that's enough for now. I'll wait as long as I have to.

I nodded, taking a deep breath.

"There is one other thing you should know before you agree to marry me." He took my hands in his to place them on his chest. His heart was pounding fiercely. "When God saved us and blessed us with this life, He also gave us all the glories of the life He created. As you already know, I'll age, but much slower than you will. The older I get, the less I age."

Unless the war comes first.

"The elders in our faith have tried to decipher codes from scrolls God left us. The one man who knew how to read them vanished years ago. He took some of the scrolls and hid them, so we only have fragments. In the scrolls, there are prophecies made about our people. One of them is about the last days of earth as we know it. In the last days, our women will no longer be able to bear our children. The sign of this would be the last child born would have special gifts. One was he or she would be able to communicate with animals. We believe it's May. No woman in our tribe has given birth in more than six years." He paused, looking at me sadly.

I smiled, "You can communicate with animals?"

"No, I can't actually speak to them. May can have actual dialogue with them, and they with her."

That explained the crane, although I never actually heard her speak to it in her soft whispering voice. "You said gifts. What are the others?"

"Uh…" A funny look came over his face. "Um…the child would be able to change the hearts of men who have turned to the darkness, bringing them back to the light. The child would also have healing powers. We take these things for what they are, humans trying to understand the mind of God. The facts are she does communicate with animals and women have stopped having children, it seems to fit."

"Wow. Our May. I knew she was special."

Hunter appeared frustrated. "Jess, by marrying me, you'll never be able to…I mean, we won't be able to have children together." He swallowed hard.

I sat there for a moment. In all the times I had dreamed of my future and what I wanted it to be, I had never considered children. *Uh, that's sort of weird for a woman to not think about having children, isn't it?*

"It doesn't matter to me. As long as I have God and you, I'm complete." My hands reached out for his face. It felt hot, but began to cool at my touch.

"You don't seem too sad about it," he said.

I noticed even though he was relieved by my reply, he seemed almost sad.

"Does it bother you? I mean not to have children?" I asked.

"Yes. I think to have a child is one of the greatest gifts God gave to his people." He looked very dreamy. "God has blessed me with you, and I have no right to ask for more." He pulled me to him. "So you really do want to marry me?"

I wrapped my arms around his neck. "Unless you have something more to toss at me to try to scare me away…"

"Oh, well, just the end-of-the-world stuff. You seem to be adjusting well to that already."

"That works for me too, because then I don't die before you." I paused, seeing his expression change. "I know God is in control, and everything will work out in the end. I'm actually luckier than the other humans," I said halfheartedly and smiled.

Hunter looked at me funny. "And why is that?"

"For one thing, I get to live here, where they can't go. Since I know you all age slowly, you don't have to stage your deaths. When I go, I'll have you all around me."

"I guess that's a different way to look at it." His face turned sad again. "Only you are very young, my sweet girl, and there is no need to talk about death."

"Sorry. You're right." I nuzzled against his chest. "We should focus on the time we have together and let God handle the rest."

"Well, we still have to be watchful and obedient. God does handle every situation, and if we listen close enough, he'll guide us through it. Just because he knows the decisions we make and the situations we put ourselves in, doesn't mean he wants us to take that route. Always remember that," he said little more seriously.

"So don't purposely seek out dangerous situations. Got it."

"Exactly!" He kissed me softly, letting it linger.

Jordan came around the corner. "Hunter, um…sorry." Hunter looked up at him. "I need to talk to you." He winked at me. "Sorry, Jess."

I nodded. "Go. I'll find May."

James came around the corner followed by John.

Hunter took my hand. "I'll meet you in the study in five minutes."

"No. I can find my way back, really," I said.

"Yes. Take her back to where the guests are, to Annabel," John agreed with Hunter.

Hunter led me back to the party. "I thought you said I was safe here? Why can't I—"

"Something has changed, Jess, and until I know what's going on, stay near my mother."

I pouted.

"Please, Jess. Don't fight me on this. Promise me."

"Okay," I agreed.

Annabel saw us and walked across the courtyard.

"I'll be back soon." He kissed my cheek and ran toward the office.

"Do you know what's going on?" Annabel asked.

"Molly?" I guessed.

"I'm not sure. She was pretty upset. Come on, dear. Let's have a cup of tea." She led me into the house. "Miss Caroline will take care of our guests."

She led me to a room with vaulted ceilings made of glass, and angled like the side of a triangle. There were flowers and plants everywhere.

"Is this a greenroom?" I noticed on the back wall, where we entered, had a shelf with books, stretching from one end to the other.

She laughed, opening the elegant white French doors to a veranda that spilled out of the room. "It does look like one, doesn't it?"

I sat in one of the white wicker chairs clumped around the room. The smell of the flowers perfumed the air. The room smelled like Annabel. Right away, it was my favorite room.

She left for a moment, returning with a tea set. She sat on the chair next to me, setting the tea on the coffee table. She fluffed a pillow with yellow daisies on it, then tucked it behind her back. "This is my room. John has his study, and this one is mine. Do you like it?" she asked.

"It's beyond words. I can't believe I missed seeing this room all these months." I sipped the tea.

"Then it's yours, too. Feel free anytime. After all, you will be my daughter-in-law soon enough." She smiled. "It seems like everything is moving so fast. I know." She sighed. "It happened the same way for me, only I was nineteen, practically a child, and scared out of my mind, but then I saw John standing in front of me. We were married two months after we met, and I thank God every day for this life."

"There's something else I have been wondering." I wasn't sure how to ask it.

She poured more tea into her cup. "Like I said before, you can ask me anything, Jessie."

"Well, everyone has said how happy they are for Hunter and he's been alone for so long. What about James and Jordan? I haven't met a wife."

"Jordan's wife died over six years ago. She died in childbirth. We lost the baby as well. There was nothing the doctors could do."

"Oh, I'm sorry."

"It was hard on him, but she's with the Lord, and they'll be reunited soon enough."

She paused. "James was married, oh, seventy years or so. You lose track when you've been around as long as we have." She laughed. "His wife had a rare tumor when she was young. To save her life, they had to remove her ovaries, so they weren't able to have children of their own. They both loved children and spent a lot of time at the shack with Miss Mabel. She died in her sleep at the age of ninety."

Maybe Hunter and I could live there too.

But then I remembered there would be no more children. I felt sad for Miss Mabel living in the shack without children to raise.

Annabel continued. "Recently, he started thinking about remarrying, but I think he changed his mind."

I wondered if it had to do with me. I remembered how he sort of flirted with me until Hunter just about attacked him.

Annabel placed her hand on my knee. "How are you feeling?"

"Happy?" I answered in a question. Honestly, my feelings at the moment were twisted into a knot, worried about what was going on in John's office. "I'm not sure," I said. "Like you said, everything is moving pretty fast."

"You two have been flirting with each other since the day you met." She laughed.

"I guess that's true, at least on my part." I thought about the way John had looked at the bonfire. He didn't act happy about the announcement, prompting me to ask another question. "But

I didn't think John wanted..." I paused, thinking I shouldn't say anything.

"We have a lot of old traditions, which is why Hunter has been kept busy. John was hoping to put off the engagement as long as he could." She leaned back in her chair. "Even with keeping you both apart for most of the day, with a chaperone following you both around at night, it was clear to me you belong to each other. I didn't see a reason to delay the engagement any longer. My husband means well. He wants what's best for both of you and there is a matter not quite cleared up. John wanted to tie up those loose ends before giving his approval."

Molly. He wanted to give her time to accept it.

Annabel poured another splash of hot water into her cup and mine. "So, should we include your mother in the planning?" Annabel asked straightforwardly.

Wedding. Mother. Was she not listening when I told her how evil she was?

The thought echoed in my mind, taking the two words together to leave a bad taste in my mouth.

What would she think of me marrying Hunter? She would be impressed by the fine paintings and lavish details of this house. Would she think I was marrying better than she had planned and give me her blessings? No, she wouldn't. My mother wants the power and Seth is close to obtaining it.

"I don't think that would be a good idea," I finally answered, staring at the fine features in the terracotta floor. "Anyway, I thought regular people couldn't come here?"

"We can have the wedding off the property. We have connections with most of the churches near here."

"I appreciate the offer, but I don't think that's such a good idea."

"She wouldn't be able to hurt you. I wouldn't allow it. No one would allow it. She should be there, at least for the wedding. No matter what, she is your mother, the woman who carried you in her womb for nine months." She placed her hand back on my knee. "Pray about it, Jess, please."

"Okay." I sulked down in my seat. "I'll pray about it."

Dear God, Please say no.

She patted my knee and got up, carrying the tray. "Oh, by the way, the boys are not allowed in here, so if you need a place to think or just get a moment to yourself, just shut the door." She winked. "Shall we go tell our guests good night? It's getting late."

Annabel had given me even more to think about. I almost felt guilty not wanting my mother to be part of my life at all. I might have forgiven her for those things I knew had happened, but what if she had planned my father's attack? I didn't know how I would react face to face. Could I forgive something so horrible?

God forgave all of David's sins and he had a man killed.

David was a good example of how far God's forgiveness would stretch. Although I hadn't sinned like him, I was forgiven and had no right not to forgive.

Easier said than done. Shouldn't my wedding day be about me for a change, not her?

If she was a part of the wedding, she'd complain about everything, making it all about her and what she wanted. I sat there for a long moment in the soft chair, staring out at the shadows in the garden, allowing her negativity fester inside.

"Jess," someone whispered.

Looking around the room, there was no one, just a low breeze coming through the open door to the enclosed outdoor garden. I wiped my tears before wandering to the open doors to gaze at the night sky. The stars beamed down.

Hunter's arms went around my waist, drawing me into his warm body. He whispered close to my ear, sending chills down my spine, "You are going to get me in so much trouble for coming in here," he said in an uneasy tone.

I found it funny he didn't fear demons, Seth, or even my mother, but being caught in his mother's sacred room, terrified him.

I leaned into him, letting him support my body, still looking up at the sky. His head moved down to rest his cheek to mine. It felt nice, soft, and cool against my chapped skin. "Is everything all right?" he asked, stroking his cheek against mine.

"Your mom thinks I should invite my mother to help with the wedding plans." I turned to nuzzle into his embrace. His cheek rested on top of my hair.

"She can't hurt you anymore. She has no power over any of us. But it's totally up to you. I'm not sure I agree with the timing, but you do need to face her, Jess."

It surprised me to hear him say that. Confused, I looked up into his beautiful face. "But then she'll know I'm alive. She'll be in our lives. She's a horrible, terrible person. She will make everyone miserable. I don't know what will come out of her mouth. She's..." I blurted out, pulling away from him to gather control. In a softer tone, "I said I forgave her, but maybe I really haven't."

"Seth already knows where you are." Hunter reminded me.

"That's true," I said, wondering if he would share his newfound friends with her, too.

"Just because you forgive someone doesn't mean it doesn't still hurt. You need to confront her about..." He paused. "I'm sorry. I know you don't want to talk about it."

She's evil, and I don't ever want to see her again.

He drew me to him. "You're worrying too much, honey. Let's not talk about it anymore tonight. Okay?" he pleaded, working his fingers into mine. "Besides, it's my job to take care of you, now. I don't want my future bride to worry about one single thing." He kissed away my tears, coming closer to my lips.

We heard someone clear their throat. It sounded like one of his brothers.

Hunter huffed. "First, can we please leave before she catches me in here?"

I chuckled as we left the room. Mission accomplished. Hunter didn't get caught.

Everyone had left by the time we returned to the bonfire, reduced to smoldering embers. James and Jordan were putting out the fire. They acted like little kids in the middle of the street on a hot summer day, dumping water on each other instead of the fire. John, carrying a bigger bucket, snuck behind the two, drenching them. Both boys looked at each other. The boys picked up John, carrying him down the path. We followed them as they got to the pool. Still holding John, they jump into the water.

We roared in laughter.

The three in the pool looked at each other before smiling at Hunter.

"Oh no." He backed away, but they were already climbing out of the pool.

"I thought you weren't afraid to take the plunge, little brother," James teased.

"Ha-ha." He darted out of his reach, only to be caught by John. They all grabbed a piece of him and jumped into the pool.

May, Annabel, and I laughed at the silly boys. "Come, ladies. Let's retire for the evening." Annabel put her arm around both of us.

Both May and I yawned. It had been one busy, crazy, unexpected day. I glanced back at my fiancé, who in turn was watching me. I felt a little sad leaving him for night, but once we were married— my heart thumped wildly.

I wouldn't have to.

As I was getting ready for bed, I thought about the song Hunter wrote for me. He had already given me so much, but what had I given him in return? In my head, parts of a melody of my own creation played when I felt stressed. Every time I played the rough notes, Hunter was there, calming me right down.

That's it, I'll compose something for him! Something to compliment the song he wrote.

Of course, if I left my room, he'd follow me, so I'd need a plan and an accomplice.

Talk to Annabel in the morning. She'll know what to do.

I heard a soft knock at the door. I opened it slowly.

"I just wanted to say good night." Hunter touched my hand, curling his fingers into mine, bringing my hand up to his lips. "Sleep well." He kissed it softly.

I was less, tender, thrusting my arms around his wet body. I didn't care. How much I wanted to fall asleep, listening to his heartbeat, to taking my mind off of everything bad.

He rubbed his hands along my arms. "Annabel wanted me to mention again, inviting your mother is up to you. Don't let that keep you from sleeping."

As our foreheads touched, we noticed May watching from her room.

Hunter kissed me quickly. "I love you."

"I love you," I giggled as May shooed Hunter to his room.

"I'm so tired!" she exclaimed, shutting my door. "Can I sleep with you tonight?" she asked.

"I thought you liked your own room."

"I do, but—"

She didn't have to explain. Molly's painful cry echoed in all our minds.

"Sure. Climb in. Which side do you want?" I asked.

"This one okay?" She took the side closer to Hunter's room.

Of course she would. I wasn't the only who felt safer just being near him.

"Perfect. Good night, May."

"Night, Jess. Love you." She yawned.

I meant to say it back, but she was already snoring. I guess it was a good thing we had all slept in the same room for such a long time. Her snoring had become comforting.

My New Secret

May stayed asleep, curled up with a pillow in her arms, while I snuck out of bed.

The night still held on to the dark, shadowy world but would soon give way to the light of a new day. I slipped on my robe and slippers, listening to the birds' soft and cheerful song coming from the open window. Annabel mentioned she was always up before the rooster's crow, so I hoped to catch her alone as I went quietly down the staircase into the kitchen. She was the only one who could help me pull off my secret—my big surprise.

"My, you're up bright and early." Annabel folded up the newspaper, placing it in a basket on the long table. "Would you like some coffee?"

"Yes please," I answered. "Is anyone else up yet?" I looked around for signs of tall, masculine figures.

"No. Just us."

"There is something I would like to do, but I'm not sure how. I thought maybe you could help me."

Her eyes lit up as she set the coffee in front of me.

I continued as she sat next to me. "I want to try to compose a song. I've never done it before, so I don't know if it will be any good, but I want to try. The problem is how can I work on it without Hunter knowing?" I sipped the hot beverage.

"We have a small piano in a storage room. No one would know if we rolled it into my room," Annabel suggested.

"But wouldn't someone suspect something if they heard the music?"

"No, dear. Those doors are solid oak and are built specially to keep sound from escaping. You will have to make sure you lock all the doors and windows when you play. Even though Hunter knows he is not supposed to be in my room, if he knows you're in there, I'm not sure he'll keep to the rules." She winked, letting me know she knew he broke the rule once, already. "Anyway, we can cover the front of the piano with plants and flowers, so if anyone glanced in there by chance with the doors open, no one would know it was there. I'll take care of the arrangements. You can start tomorrow if you wish."

"What about Hunter not letting me out of his sight?" I asked.

"I'll take care of that, too. For the daytime hours, I have a list of projects for John I've put off." She paused in thought. "For the evening hours, you'll need some alone time, maybe a book to read on those nights when you can't sleep." She winked.

"Thanks." I got up to hug her. I didn't like the idea of keeping him away, but I couldn't very well compose with him around, either.

We both heard a loud commotion, coming from the staircase. A stampede was heading in our direction.

Hunter entered the kitchen, breathing hard. "Oh there you are." He whisked me up, kissing my cheek. "You're up early." He tried to disguise the worry in his tone.

"Girl talk," Annabel said. "Hunter, I need to talk to you after breakfast for just a few minutes."

"Am I in trouble?" he asked, with a quizzical look in my direction.

"Not yet."

"Good girl." Annabel laughed.

At breakfast the talk centered on the night before. May devoured pancakes, while talking to Annabel about how many s'mores she ate. James and Jordan teased their younger brother while John read the paper.

"I told you he wouldn't pass out," Jordan argued with James.

"He was this close," he said, making his fingers form sort of a pinch.

"Nah. He did better than we did." Jordan sat next to Hunter, nudging his shoulder.

"That's right," Hunter joined in. "James, you passed out. How did I forget that?" They both looked at James.

Jordan laughed. "It was almost a century ago."

"Yeah, well, you try being the first one to have to do that." James's cheeks turned a rosy color.

"That had to be very hard to do," I offered, "especially in front of a crowd."

Jordan began to clear off the plates. "No. Hunter is the only one who had to do it in front of the tribe. We did it with only our family present."

"Oh." I thought for a moment. "Why only Hunter?"

Hunter pushed back his chair to look at me. "Their soon-to-be wives knew nothing of our real life. James and Jordan lived in the world. They found love there, but could never tell their wives about this place or our history. Our family traveled to where they were living to meet the ladies and carry out our traditions. So they only played their song for the family, but in tradition, it is supposed to be in front of the entire tribe."

"We had to play in front of their family members, too. My mother-in-law just about attacked me after I played," James interrupted.

We laughed. I understood. The music was so alluring.

"But how is it that I am allowed to know? Don't get me wrong, I am completely happy about it, but why am I so different?"

John folded his paper, joining the conversation, "Jessica, no one, not since we have been immortal, has ever just stumbled onto this land. At first, we were worried you were part of some scheme of Davior's to get inside our borders. After you faced him and turned to God, it was clear you weren't. God sent you to us, to my son. But we don't know why. It's the reason I've asked Hunter to wait on setting a date."

"We?" I asked.

John stood from the table. "The elders of the tribe."

My dad was planning to take me somewhere, somewhere my mother could never find me. Could it have been here? Was that the reason I could enter their walls into their secret world?

I thought about the painting of the chief in my father's office and the identical crosses hanging above the mantel in the shack. *If my dad was one of them, could that mean...*

I stayed quiet until May pulled on my shirt. "Will you come in the pool with me? Please!"

I held her face in my hands. "How can I refuse you?" I hopped up, leaving Hunter staring at his father.

"Oh, wait. With all this intense conversation, I almost forget. Today is Sunday, is it not?" Annabel questioned. "James?"

"Yes, it is. Sorry, May. After lunch?" James offered to her. She nodded in agreement. "We reopen the church today." He looked over at me. "That's what we've been working on. We finally finished on Friday."

"How much time do I have before we leave?" I asked, looking down at my robe and slippers.

Hunter jumped up. "We've got thirty minutes to be in the sanctuary."

Everyone scattered to get dressed. Hunter, May, and I jogged up the stairs.

"So where is this church?" I asked.

"You've only seen a fraction of the grounds, my love." He smiled. "Twenty-five minutes and counting." He kissed my cheek then head for his room to dress.

Staring into the closet, I had many dresses to choose from. A light pink dress caught my eye. Normally, I would stay clear of anything pink, since my mother crammed pink into everything I owned because it was Seth's favorite color. But Annabel knew my likes better than my own mother. I snatched out the sparkly dress and the pink and white heels to match. I had never been in a church before, except for one time, but it had more of funeral home feel than a church.

I hope this is okay to wear.

The dress went over my head. As I tried to zip up the back, the zipper got stuck midway. Since I was running out of time, I sat at the vanity to fix my hair. I didn't wear it up often, but it would be much quicker. In the top drawer, there were all kinds of ribbons, combs, scrunchies, clips, bobby pins, and other hair accessories. I piled my hair up, fastening it with a handful of bobby pins. Lastly, I added a wire comb adorned with white flowers and pink sparkles before admiring my work.

My mother's face flashed in the reflection. I gasped, turning around, but she wasn't there. Looking back at the mirror, it was just me.

Seth was right about one thing, I did look a lot like her.

I went over to May's room to ask her to help me with the zipper, but she had already left.

I heard a knock. "Ready?" Hunter asked through the door.

"Um...yes, but..." I paused. "May left, and I can't seem to zip my dress all the way."

"Can I help?" I looked in the mirror to see how much was revealed.

Past the bra strap. I guess it's okay.

"Jess?" he called again.

"Come in," I said. "I guess it's fine."

I turned around, with my back to him, before he entered. His hands touched the back of my neck. Gently skimming my skin, his fingertips went up and down my back, sending chills along my spine.

"Please," I whispered, not really wanting him to stop.

His fingers fumbled for the zipper, slowly but deliberately touch my skin, until the dress was zipped closed. He pressed his lips to the base of my neck, lingering there for a moment.

"Are you trying to drive me out of my skin just before going to church?" I huffed, placing my hand on my heart before I faced him.

"Sorry. I couldn't help myself." He smiled, slightly blushing. "You are very hard to resist and beautiful, as usual."

"And you are very handsome." I straightened his tie, staring into his blue eyes.

The room faded around us as I pressed my lips to his. Our moment was interrupted by someone's catcall from the hall.

He blushed. "Ready?" He held out his arm.

We walked down the stairs and out the back door. We walked for about ten minutes along the cobblestone path before reaching a white church. The building was another large structure, only adorned with stained glass windows on all sides. There were familiar faces walking up the steps, once again congratulating us as we entered through the thick timber doors.

Instantly, I tried to sit in the back of the church, but James ushered us to the front of the church with the rest of the family.

Soon the music started. "Amazing Grace" was the first song. I knew the first verse but had to follow along in the song book Hunter held up for me. Song after song touched my soul in some way, like it was meant for me at that exact moment in my life. I tried not to cry, feeling the powerful emotions, one right after another, flowing through me as I sang praises to God.

After the music, John took center stage. "Good morning." He addressed the congregation.

"Good morning." Everyone echoed.

"It's a beautiful day God has created for us. Amen." John prayed then opened his Bible and began his sermon on John the Baptist.

"Christ was baptized by an ordinary man...an imperfect man. Why? So we can follow His example." John summarized his preaching.

The entire time I had the suspicion his topic was directed to me. James asked me about being baptized, and I had yet to follow through. I knew it was time to make my decision.

"James, can you take Jess back to the house? I need to talk to Dad for a minute."

"My lady." James offered his arm.

I raised my eyebrows.

Hunter kissed my cheek. "I'll be just behind you."

James and I started our walk back.

"James, how is it that you are here and not at your church?" I asked.

"Oh well, it was time to move on anyway," he said.

"Why? Miss Mabel told me you hadn't been there very long. I doubt they noticed you weren't aging yet."

"I'm needed here right now. Dad said I can preach here from time to time, if I want to."

"That's good." I thought about the sermon as we walked. "How does the whole baptism thing go?"

"First, you make a public affirmation in front of the congregation. After that, you follow through in believer's baptism."

"What is a public affirmation?"

"You are just letting others know you are a fellow believer in Christ. We then take a short walk over to the stream behind the church and submerge you under the water." He laughed, "Are you all right? You look a little pale."

"You hold them under rushing water?"

"Dunked is more like it. Jess, no one would let you drown."

"I know. It's just..." I tried to think of an excuse for my fear, but I couldn't think of one. "I think I...I'd like to be baptized," I said quickly, like pulling off a Band-Aid.

"Of course you can. I can let my dad—"

"Would you do it?"

James looked at me, surprised but happy. "I'd be honored, if that's what you want."

I nodded.

"I'm supposed to lead the service in a few weeks, unless you want to do it sooner."

"No. A few weeks is good. Just let me know for sure which Sunday so I can prepare."

"Okay," he chuckled.

"Don't tell Hunter though," I added.

James looked at me, stunned.

"I want to surprise him."

"That's a nice surprise. He'll be very happy," James led me into the house, where May stood in front of us with her swimsuit already on.

"You're going to turn into a fish," I teased.

"After lunch, May," James said with a fatherly voice.

She huffed and walked in the direction of the kitchen. We followed to help Annabel prepare lunch.

After we ate, we played in the pool and relaxed on the chaise lounges for the rest of the afternoon. Annabel came over and started asking me questions about wedding details, while the guys discussed which character in the Bible had suffered the most. It was funny watching them huddled at one end of the pool, arguing.

May jumped into our conversation, adding she wanted to be included in the planning. I still couldn't grasp the fact I was going to be married. If I was lost in one of my musical daydreams, I'd be able to stay there forever. Every silly little girl's dream landed just where I was. The stories of kings and queens, the princes, the princesses, the dark evil outside the gates, were real after all—not just fairytales my father told me. I was glad my plans were not the ones God had planned for me. His plan was better, bigger, and more beautiful than the one I had planned.

A week dashed by.

James and Jordan spent the mornings helping out with some missionary churches up the Florida coast. They were always back by midafternoon to play a game or have deep conversations with John, neither I nor May were privileged to hear.

Hunter was not left out of those meetings. So, I used that time to work on my song project, but it wasn't coming together like I had hoped. Feeling rushed, I'd stare at the blank note paper until it was time to leave without Hunter becoming suspicious.

The following week, Annabel kept her word, by sending Hunter several times to Miss Mabel's and to the orphanage where Miss C and Miss B worked. Although he was never gone for very long, it was enough to get a few notes written. A few times, I had snuck into the parlor, late at night when the melody called, but Hunter always managed to follow me. The reason I knew, I found him on several occasions asleep, hiding behind a potted tree next to the doors. I didn't wake him so I wouldn't have to explain what I was doing, but I began to see the dark circles around his eyes from the lack of sleep. Not only that, but Hunter seemed much more anxious in the evening hours than during the day. I remembered how Davior had said the best part of the day was the night.

Demons come out at night.

The real truth was they were always around.

A few more Sundays had gone.

I heard James going over his sermon notes in the game room. Passing the room, he looked up from his notes and winked— the day had arrived. I nodded and continued on to the kitchen, thinking about the rushing water. I took some deep, casual breaths to calm my nerves. I didn't want to let on to my secret.

We ate together before heading for church. Along the way, new faces joined our walk, and I was introduced as Hunter's fiancée. I loved hearing "the future Mrs. Fox."

We got to the church and sat in our normal spots. James got up and began after the music. I didn't hear the sermon at all. I did, however, watch every move James made across the stage.

The moment had arrived. James asked if anyone would like to come forward to join the fellowship. Everyone looked around in sort of an amused sort of way. Of course they all were believers, all baptized, so why would he ask such a question? He looked right at me as I stared back, feeling like a deer caught in the headlights. I couldn't move. He kept his eyes on me until everyone was looking at me, which made the situation worse. I finally went forward with my head down.

"Jessica, do you know Christ as your personal Savior?" James asked.

"Yes."

"Will you follow Christ and be baptized by submersion?"

I hesitated. Hunter slipped his hand into mine, giving me comfort. "Yes," I said confidently.

"Amen," James called out, and the congregation repeated.

"Let's sing 'Praise Be to the Lord' as we walk out to the river."

Everyone exited out of the church behind us, singing as loudly as they could. At the river, the water flowed gently. There was no reason for me to hesitate. I kicked off my shoes, putting one toe in and shivered. The water was ice cold.

James, already in the river with his teeth chattering, held out his hand for me.

No, I can't go through with it. I can't step out there. It's too cold. Yeah, that's it.

I made excuses while James turned into a Popsicle, his lips matching the color of the sky.

"It's not that bad," James said with his whole body trembling.

Hunter jumped in, and his teeth began chattering too. "I'll freeze with you." He held out his hand "The water is barely moving." He knew the other reason I hesitated.

With no more excuses left, I stepped into the water. James held me securely by the waist, telling me to plug my nose when he leans me into the water. Hunter jumped next to me, holding my free hand.

I'm safer than anyone could be, safer than I deserve.

"I baptize you, Jessica, my sister, in the name of the Father, the Son, and the Holy Spirit, dead to sin and risen to a new life in Christ."

The three of us wore blue lips and shivered uncontrollably.

James dismissed the congregation in one quick word.

"The pool is nice and warm." Hunter smiled.

The three of us took off in a run to the house. James was the first to jump in, followed by me and Hunter. It felt so nice and warmed up my body quickly. I pulled off the wet dress to reveal my swimsuit underneath. James had swim trunks on under his slacks. We both looked at Hunter, still wearing his dress shirt and tan slacks.

"Oh, so this was planned." He smiled, pulling me to him.

James splashed at him. "Sorry, bro, she swore me to secrecy."

I faced Hunter. "I'm sorry, but I wanted to surprise you."

"I'm very proud of you." He pushed back the wet hair covering my face to kiss me.

"All right, all right. Break it up." Jordan jumped in, clothes and all, splashing next to us.

We all roared with laughter.

Molly Returns

I wasn't making much progress on my piece of music. I complained to Annabel as we weeded one of the gardens.

"How about I arrange a girls-only party in the garden room? Hunter will know you're with me and May. You can spend as much time as you want." She pulled out a clump of weeds and tossed it into bucket.

"That might help, as long as he doesn't hide behind the potted tree and wait for me to leave."

"He does that?"

"Yep," I said, wiping my forehead with the back of the gardening gloves I wore. "Every time."

"I'll have John make the rounds and send him to bed if he's in the hallway. When do you want to do it?"

"Tonight too soon?" I asked. "With them being gone all day at Miss Mabel's, he'll be pretty tired already. Maybe once John sends him up, he'll just go to sleep."

"Sure. I'll mention it after dinner." She smacked her gloves together, making the soil fall to the ground.

"Thanks, Annabel."

"We'll need to start getting dinner ready pretty soon." She looked over the rest of her clothes, covered in dirt. "I think I'll clean up first."

We both laughed.

After Annabel's delicious dinner, she announced to the men about our party with the expressed statement to not wait up. Hunter didn't like the idea, but he wasn't going to protest. I

kissed him before following May and Annabel into the parlor.
"So what's it going to be tonight, May?" Annabel asked.

"Checkers." She set the box down on the round table. "Jordan taught me how to play yesterday, and I need to practice so I can beat him."

"Sounds like a good reason to me." Annabel laughed.

I sat at the small piano with my clean sheet of paper and sharpened pencil. I had composed a few notes but none written in any sort of pattern. My focus needed to be putting all the notes together.

May and Annabel stayed in the room playing games while I composed. Their playing didn't distract me in the least, once I got going. In fact, I almost forgot they were there. I'd play a few notes, write them down, then scribble more notes, before striking the keys. Hours had passed before I realized I was alone. I arched my back, stretching my arms before I went back to work. Music told a story. If I couldn't tell our story in just the right melody, I would give up the silly notion I could compose.

Hesitating to play what I had so far, I took a final deep breath. The melody started out in confusion as I was lost in the woods. It was cold, gloomy, and I didn't know which way to go. The tune went softer, as I saw the light streaming down. It circled around me, lifting me into the air—

Bang! Bang! Bang!

I jumped out of my seat.

Bang! Bang! Bang!

It was coming from one of the windows. With my heart racing, I cautiously walked over to it.

Molly.

Her face was swollen, with dark circles surrounding her eyes. "You have to come. Something has happened. You have to come," Her tone was frantic.

"What? What's happened?"

"You have to come. You have to. He's going to kill him," she said again.

"Wait." I pushed open the glass. "Now, what's going on?"

"If you don't come now, he'll kill him. You know he will. You know him better than anyone," she repeated.

Seth?

"Okay. Let me go get help."

"There's no time! No, no. He'll kill him. Don't you understand me? You need to come now," she said, grabbing my shirt through the open window, her fist twisting my clothes.

"Who is he going to kill?"

"Hunter. Seth is going to kill him." She paused, looking angry at my delayed reaction. "Well, fine, if you won't help him, I will. She let me go. "I'm not going to let Seth kill him. At least I'm willing to fight for his life."

"What? Molly," I called, climbing out the window.

Darkness surrounded me. The shadows of the night disappeared by the cloud covered moonlight. Not one star shone as I chased after Molly, catching only glimpses of her red garment flowing behind her. Once we passed over the cobblestone path, she vanished.

Oh no, I ran through the barrier!

But I didn't stop. I had to find Molly.

Out of breath, I stopped to look around the forest. The ground felt soggy, and my bare feet sank down into it. A light appeared and filled the area. At first it frightened me, but then I saw the moon peeking through thick clouds.

Molly appeared through the trees, calm and with a smirk on her face. "I guess you're not as smart as everyone thinks you are."

"Molly? What's going on? Where is Hunter?" I shook my head hoping I was just dreaming.

"Seth is going to kill him." She pretended to be scared, then laughed. "Stupid girl, if I knew it was going to be this easy, I would have done it way sooner before he proposed."

"So where is Hunter?"

"Oh, I'm sure he's sleeping in his bed. That's what you wanted, right? Of course, he's secretly dreaming of me, not you."

"So this is a joke?"

"No, it's not." Her eyes blazed. "Ever since you came here, you have made everything very difficult for me. Hunter is mine! I'm not letting you come in here and take him from me. That song belonged to me, not you!"

She moved inches from me, lashing her hand to strike my cheek. The blood dripped down my cheek, and the sorrow I felt for her broken heart faded into pain.

She paced. "Hunter looked at me in a way he never had before." Tears filled her eyes and ran down her cheeks. "He was furious with me for how I was treating *you!*" She twisted her hands together. "So I ran. I ran until my feet bled."

I looked down at her feet. They were bare and bloodstained.

"I fell to my knees, and I cursed God for allowing this to happen. He's not a fair or just God!" She raised her hands up, and her tone changed.

She continued to talk with her back to me. Squatting down, I picked up a thick tree branch, and hid it behind my back. I wasn't going to go down easy if her plan was to kill me.

"I knew I had to take matters into my own hands. It was the only way," she said under her breath, as if she were talking to herself. "I knew they were looking for you. We all knew. The best part was I didn't have to go far to find them." She chuckled. "Apparently, they have spies everywhere."

I wondered if Molly had met Seth. They were a perfect match being two-faced and all.

She stopped. Whatever it was in her head, made her angrier as she moved closer. I swung at her with the branch. As it connected, the force knocked her into the thick black mud.

Molly looked up in disbelief, wiping her bleeding cheek. "Who do you think you are? You already have a man. Why would you come and take mine? I wanted to like you, Jessica. I really did." She laughed. "But that time has passed." She got up.

I stood ready with my stick for another round. But a figure moved out of the trees. I was praying it was Hunter and his brothers coming to my rescue.

Well, I had one thing right.

Davior walked out from the darkness just as the clouds cleared. He stood in the moonlight with his eyes fixed on me. He briefly glanced at Molly, covered in mud with her cheek bleeding. He smirked at me. I was positioned like a baseball player standing at home plate ready to bat. "I'm impressed." He crossed his arms against his chest.

Molly got up. "Okay. So I got her here. Remember, you promised me I can go back to my life without anyone knowing I helped you," she demanded.

"Go," he said, not allowing his eye contact with me to be broken.

I stared right back, still holding my stick. Davior noticed the deep scratch on my face, and his mouth turned down.

Molly yelled. "You said she wouldn't be able to return. I have your word."

Davior laughed loudly, and it echoed through the trees. He turned his fierce eyes on her. "I said go!" Davior pointed in her direction. "Before you can't."

Molly stumbled backward before she found her footing, then vanished.

Davior turned back to me, regaining his smooth demeanor. "It's been so long since we last spoke, Jessica. I've missed you."

Someone came up behind me, forcibly taking the stick from my hand.

Davior's hand came up to caress my stinging cheek. The bleeding stopped. "She doesn't like you very much. I'm sorry I had to use her. She was upset when I found her in our part of the woods, ready to sell her soul to the devil to get you out of the picture. I've been trying to get to you since the day Hunter ripped me away from your beautiful face." He grabbed my hand to bring it up to his lips and noticed the ring I wore.

"Ah. My great-grandmother's. So you agreed." He dropped my hand, looking betrayed.

"What do you want from me?" I demanded.

"It's not about me anymore," he said softly. "I have a higher purpose for you."

"Seth?"

"Yes. He's quite angry with you. He believes you belong to him, and he's not letting you go. He would rather see you dead, but now—now he wants to see Hunter dead as well."

"But he can't die."

"Oh, did he tell you that?" He sounded amused.

"Well, no, but I thought he was immortal."

"We don't die from age, but we can be killed, I assure you," he said. "It's just too bad though. My brother and I might not agree, but I hate to think he's going to be killed over you."

"Why? Why doesn't he just kill me? Why Hunter?" I asked with tears forming.

"Really, it's the only way. About now, Hunter knows you are missing. I can see he's desperately searching the house and blaming himself for not keeping a better watch over you. Very careless of him, I might add. It was like he wanted me to take you away. He knew I was near, watching, waiting."

I knew who Davior served, someone higher than Seth, and I knew he was a liar, but what he saw through Hunter's thoughts I knew to be true.

"So how is it you can read his thoughts? Doesn't it work both ways? He'll know where you're taking me."

"He's too angry to unfocused to notice me in his head. He's been very unfocused lately. We'll be long gone before he gains control." He smirked. "Oh, my poor mother. He's destroying the house she so carefully decorated." He chuckled. "And Molly, too bad she's a terrible actress. No one believes her."

"Why kill Hunter? I'll go willingly," I said. "I'll do whatever you want."

"Because he will look for you day and night. He'll try to kill Seth first, but we'll be ready," he said with a confidence that terrified me. "It's not about Hunter or any of my family, really. This is all about what Seth wants, so he'll serve my master. However, I know my entire family will do whatever Hunter wants. He's always been the favorite. Right now, he wants you, and they will rally to his side like they always have," he said in a very careless way. "A battle is unavoidable at this stage. You should have come willingly before you got my family involved. Honestly, I tried, Jessica. If you would have just listened to my instructions, to the little voice inside your head, it could have been avoided."

"It wasn't so little."

"And yet you still didn't listen." He wiggled his finger at me. "Oh well. What's done is done."

Davior was playing on my guilt. I tried to remember he didn't care at all about his family.

"Where is Seth?" I asked.

"He's been busy. Lots of people to meet, but I'm sure it won't be long, before you're reunited." Davior offered his hand. "I have more than adequate accommodations for you until then."

"What if I don't want to go?"

Davior raised his hand, and two men came into the clearing. "I'd prefer you go the easy way. I don't want to see you get hurt any more than you have been." He reached out to stroke my cheek again.

I flinched away.

He offered his hand again, as his three companions waited. *What choice do I have?*

I prayed for God to keep Hunter safe as Davior led me out of the forest and into the unknown darkness before me.

Into the Dark of Darkest Places

I never enjoyed scary movies, mostly because I lived in one. My mind had not required a movie to create dark images, since they had already existed in my world. The scratching at the windows, wrestling in the trees, creaky doors opening, and my favorite—footsteps in the shadows getting closer. When I lived in the mansion by the sea, I remember the countless people walking along the sandy shores of the beach, looking up at me. I was a pale, thin girl staring motionless at them. How many of them thought of me as a phantom trapped in the immense, pallid house on the hill?

Seth, on the other hand, loved horror films. On weekends, he spent the majority of his time at my mother's house. The time was supposed to be used to connect with me and persuade me to accept the fate I had no choice in. He'd watch the vampire-slasher-killer-type movies, trying to pry whatever novel I was reading out of my hands. I'd look up and be nauseated from seeing all the blood or, worse, someone being slashed to pieces. To top it off, Seth would proceed to explain how unreal it all really was, giving his own play-by-play of how it should have been done. I didn't know what was worse, the details he used, or the pleasure he had from watching me turn white as a ghost.

At least in those days, the days before I left, I knew what to expect, how to act, how to hide, but there was so much more on the line and nowhere to hide. Neither one of us were the same people. I belonged to a life of good, forgiveness, and love. Seth belonged in the world of evil, hate, and all-consuming power.

Davior tightened his grip on my hand. I had a feeling we were somewhere in the middle of both worlds.

With the ramblings only in my mind, I walked in silence as others joined us in our walk. Two men walked in front of us, then one to my right and one to the left of Davior, plus two more came up behind. I was completely surrounded. Davior wasn't taking any chances as he continued to hold my hand tightly and occasionally ran his index finger across the top. I wanted to pull it from him and run, but I was no match for all of them.

"Would you like to know why John wants you to wait?" He was practically gloating about having information I would obviously want.

"I don't trust the words you say, so you can keep it to yourself," I snapped.

"Jessica, I have no intention of lying to you." His voice softened, sounding more like Hunter's voice when he spoke in a normal tone.

The way he acted toward Molly, after he noticed the mark she left on my cheek would have been similar to Hunter's reaction. Except I don't think Hunter could threaten to kill anyone.

Maybe he can be saved from this fate. Maybe he still has some good left inside his soul.

The forest floor felt soft under my feet with tiny granules sinking in between my toes like sand—very different from the swamp. The moon hovered directly above us, full and bright with ribbons of light pushing through to the thin path between the trees. The shadows moved around us silently, peeking out through the tall cypress leaves. No rustling, no animals crying, no birds chirping and, even stranger, no crickets or beetles buzzed. Except for my footsteps touching the ground beneath me, a dead silence filled the air.

As we continued down the path, I noticed the corridor ahead disappeared into a set of dim, bulky trees and bushes.

On closer approach, the trees and bushes looked more like an impassable wall.

"You'll need to wear this." Davior held out a long coat. "It's going to get very hot, my dear. This will keep your skin from getting scorched."

As much as I didn't want to cooperate I reluctantly plunged my arms through the sleeves and zipped it up. He also threw down black boots for my bare feet.

Davior, taking the first step into the bushes, reached for my arm to escort me through the wall. I felt despair as we left the light of the moon into an unknown world of blackness. It surrounded me like a dark cloth. I held out my hand to my nose, and I couldn't see it. Tightness constricted my chest from rising and falling due to the hot and thick air sticking to my throat.

There is nothing here. I'm walking through a void with not even the sound of my feet against the ground.

I gripped Davior's hand.

"I'm here," he whispered in my ear. "You're safe as long as you stay close to me."

I winced at his words and the touch of his lips on my ear. Holding on to him with both hands, I was forced to trust him. The only person I felt safe with was worlds away.

Oh, why did I not listen to him? How many times did he remind me not to leave the cobblestone boundary without him? How many times did he tell me to be watchful? I should have known Molly's plan. I should have known she would try to trick me. I've put him and his family in danger. I know he'll come after me, but at what cost? And it would be my fault once again.

Through the complete darkness, a red, glowing light appeared, growing larger as we got closer. An outline of a tall mountain began to take shape. The light wasn't a light, but an entrance into another unknown. I heard faint moaning as we got closer.

We entered into the red glow.

"Ah. Home at last." Davior took a deep breath.

The air smelled of thick sulfur, with clouds of smoke sparking like lighting above us. I choked with each breath. A red tint shadowed over everything including the gray clouds of smoke billowing into the air. Tall, pointed mounds of dirt stuck up from the ground, and some dangled down from the cavern walls like icicles. Fire roared all around me, and I tasted the salty sweat of my skin on my lips.

There were people, with thick collars around their necks, attached to chains. They were all thin and looked malnourished, with bruises and scrapes all over their bodies. The chains were covered with thistles and thorns digging into their skin every time they attempted to move. A group came closer, while Davior spoke another language to the men who had accompanied us on the journey. Not understanding what he was saying, I watched the group of people until I realized they weren't people, not all of them. The larger figures were nonhuman, with horns and twisted faces, pushing and pulling the lines of people behind them. One of the creatures looked up as he passed and hissed. His three long, sharp limbs reached out for me.

I jumped back behind Davior, who raised one hand. The creature went back to his work, pulling on the chain. "Sorry, Jessica. He thought you were one of them." He pointed to the people chained together. "They are being taken past the gate."

At first, they looked like regular people, until one of them turned its head to face me. It had more than one face.

I gasped. "What are they?" I asked, frightened, still behind Davior.

"Those are the two-faced liars. The people who lived in your world, the ones who claimed to be God's followers, but in secret, they lived sinful and lustful lives. They only served themselves. Isn't there a saying? There is a special place in hell for those kinds of people?" Davior laughed.

I had heard it, but I didn't find it amusing.

"They do serve their purpose though," he said.

I thought of Molly and what she had done. "Am I in hell?" I asked with a hard swallow.

"Now, now, Jessica. You have to be dead to get in there. Think of this as more of an outside gate or processing area where souls are collected and sorted. It's also for those of us who are living and serving our master until our time comes to live above ground."

"So then at the compound, was I outside the gates of heaven?" I asked.

He laughed loudly. "Not quite."

"I'm glad you find me entertaining," I tried to hold back the fear brewing inside.

I watched all the warped, pained faces working and suffering. Some were high above, working on thin ledges. One fell, taking a chain of others with him into the pit below, but there were plenty of others scattered throughout the cavern. Moaning and cries mingled with the crackling of the fire.

What a horrible, horrible place.

Sweat dripped into my eyes, which were already burning from the sulfur. I tried to wipe the ash off my skin, but it only smeared into a black mess.

"I'm sorry. I'm not being a very good host." He sounded upset with himself. "Come this way."

I followed Davior to a narrow bridge between two sheer cliffs with a lava lake flowing far below. It moved rapidly striking the sides of the cliff, sending lava splashing straight up into the air. The canyon went on for miles and miles.

I swallowed hard, pushing some of the ash accumulating in my mouth down into my throat. I stayed close to Davior. We got to the other side of the bridge before I noticed it was the only bridge within my sight crossing over the ravine to a big house held up by stilts with nothing else around it.

One way in. One way out. I'm trapped! Trapped in a mansion at the gates of hell.

Davior led me up the steep steps, and he stopped.

"Make yourself at home here. Seth designed this house for you, to make your stay comfortable. I add a few touches of my own, ones I hope will please you." His eyes lingered on my frozen reaction before he continued. Davior opened the door to a grand room with a high ceiling and a golden staircase.

I took off the coat and boots as he went over to a window and pulled back the curtain. "Even the view is for you."

"I don't plan to stay here long." I rigidly walked over to the open window in shock. Outside was a country garden of roses and tulips, not fire and ash. I could even smell their soothing fragrances. "You're using mind games on me, that's not what's out there."

He ignored me and continued with the tour. "The kitchen is fully stocked. Seth said you would prefer to cook your own meals, but if you would like, we have someone who can cook for you." He walked over to the entrance of the kitchen and leaned against the wall. "I've also been known to be an excellent cook." He grinned.

I looked away. The panic brewed deep inside.

How am I going to get out of here?

Davior went to the open door, taking the handle with his back to me. "No one can enter through the blackness, especially any of my family, without me knowing about it. You cannot leave here unless you are escorted out by Seth or myself. So please, Jessica, don't cause any further harm to yourself by trying to leave here. Whether you believe me or not, I don't want you harmed." His voice softened. "It will be awhile before Seth joins you, so try to make yourself comfortable." He paused. "I'll be coming by daily so you won't be alone. So if there is something you want, something I can bring—"

"My freedom?" The tears fell off my chin as I ran the locket along the chain.

His back stiffened, but he didn't face me. "I'll be back soon. Try to rest now. It's been a long journey. Good night, Jessica." He walked through the door and shut it.

I ran to the door and reopened it. Davior was gone. In disbelief, I walked out onto a front porch with a hanging swing. Out into the yard, a white bunny hopped across the green, thick-bladed grass and disappeared into the purple lilac bushes on the outskirts of the yard. I stepped out cautiously onto the grass, feeling the suppleness seep between my toes. I took another step, cautiously wondering what would happen next. Nothing happened. No arms punched through the turf to grab me. No black, swampy, snake thing slithered around my feet. I was slightly impressed with Seth's attention to detail, or Davior's, in their make-believe world to keep me calm. I continued to step forward, moving faster each time until I was running. I ran fast until I could no longer breathe and had to stop. Bending over, trying to catch my breath, I scanned behind me to see how far I had gone. The house was only a few yards back.

A sensation rose up inside, causing my heart to beat hard against my chest with a stabbing pain, and it journeyed throughout my skeleton. The burning traveled into my heart, constricting its rhythm and making it hard to breathe.

How am I going to get out of here?

My heart and soul were breaking. I dropped to my knees and did the only thing I could do. I prayed. "Dear Lord, thank you for the many blessings You have given to me. Please keep Hunter and his family safe. Please give me the wisdom and knowledge of how to escape."

I prayed the same prayer many times a day for weeks, or what I thought were weeks. Time at the entrance to hell felt like it stood still with no way of telling the days apart. There was no night, no moon, no stars, only the bright sunny fake sky created just for me. So I slept when I was tired, ate when I felt hungry, and tolerated Davior's company. Even though I lived in the dark of darkest places imaginable, Davior kept the sun shining.

Comfort came in the one thing they couldn't ever take from me— my relationship with God. And prayer connected me with

Him in a new way. It was His strength I leaned on to get me through the valley I couldn't escape from.

I began to notice Davior only came after I prayed or would leave right before I began to pray. If it bothered him, was there still a chance he could change?

If there is anything left of Hunter's brother, would prayer help him? Was he my way out?

Although I had said basically the same prayer over and over for what seemed like weeks, Psalm 3 came into my head, just as Davior entered into the house, followed by one of his servants. He walked over to the pantry, sounding out items for the small man to write down. "Any requests?" He asked me.

My eyes boldly matched his. "O Lord, how many are my foes! How many rise up against me!"

Davior ground his teeth as I continued.

"Many are saying of me, 'God will not deliver him.' But You are a shield around me, O Lord. You bestow glory on me and lift up my head. To the Lord I cry aloud, and He answers me from His holy hill."

The servant dropped the clipboard and put his hands over his ears.

I kept on. "I lie down and sleep. I wake again because the Lord sustains me. I will not fear the tens of thousands drawn up against me on every side. Arise, O Lord! Deliver me, O my God! Strike all my enemies on the jaw, break the teeth of the wicked. From the Lord comes deliverance. May Your blessing be on your people, amen."

Davior shook his head and kicked at his servant. "Get up." He locked eyes with me. "Last chance. Do you have any special requests?"

I shook my head, and he left.

God would use me for his purpose. I dropped to my knees and prayed to be ready when the time came. If it wasn't Davior, then I needed another plan.

The house holding me prisoner was beautiful enough to be on the cover of *Better Homes and Gardens*. The inside decor spoke more of my mother's taste than my own. It made sense Seth would have mixed the two. My dream home would be more along the lines of a simple cottage covered in flowery vines and honeysuckles. One of my favorite cottages I had seen in a magazine was Anne Hathaway's family cottage. Annabel had told me Shakespeare married Anne and wrote some of his sonnets on the very porch of that cottage. I closed my eyes and pictured the cottage. Tunes began to fill my head—Hunter's song.

Davior said if I wanted something, just ask.

Davior came a few days later from my prayer outburst. I asked him for a piano, and soon enough, one was placed on a platform overlooking another fake view of a garden. I decided to play random music when Davior was around, songs I knew by heart. When he left, I'd worked on finishing my song for Hunter. Unfortunately, I wasn't alone often but got really good at faking being asleep so he'd leave.

Davior's visits became even more frequent. He brought me books and scores of music just about every day. I had been working on my song when the front door creaked open.

As I was quickly stashing my notes behind the music books, Davior meandered into the main living space. "I thought you might like this." He held out a book by one of my favorite authors.

I shut the fallboard over the keys and took it from his hands. "Just because you've been nice to me doesn't change anything. You can bring as many flowers and plants in here as you like. You can change the scenery a hundred times to please me, but it won't change you're forcing me to live here."

"You're not giving me much of chance to make you happy, Jessica." His voice was sincere.

"Keeping me a prisoner is not a good way of going about it." I thumbed through the book, glancing up at the anger building on his face.

Only it wasn't me making him angry.

Hunter and James are close by!

Without another word, he spun on his heels and hurried out of house as though someone was calling him. He returned moments later, a look of confusion on his face, carrying a tray of food. "I'll be back later." He set the tray down and left in a hurry.

If it was Hunter and his family, if they were close enough to read Davior's thoughts, they were in danger. Seth would kill them all.

Instead of going back to the piano right away, I fell on my knees and prayed for them.

After a while, I sat back down in front of the piano. If anything happened to me, Hunter needed to hear it or, at the very least, see the notes written for him. I didn't know how, but somehow, I'd get the message to him. I was willing to do anything in my power to keep him safe and alive, and if that meant a show, a pretense, to make them think I'd change sides, so be it.

God is always in control.

I didn't know the reason or the outcome, but a plan was forming. It wouldn't be easy, and I didn't know if I could pull it off, but I also didn't believe it was my own plan.

Seth's Rise to Power

He didn't just walk right in. Davior came in first.

"Seth is outside and would like for you to join him on the porch." He stared off in the distance past me.

Taking in a deep breath, I walked to the door with my plan clearly in my head.

Lord, give me the strength to be convincing.

Davior grabbed my shoulder, leaning into my ear. His cool cheek brushed mine, and I shivered. "Do not anger him any more than he already is."

Shaking his grip off me, I walked out onto the porch, not sure what I was going to find. I kept seeing those hot, red eyes staring at me from the bottom of Miss Mabel's porch the night Davior made me remember my father's attack.

Seth stared out at the fake world. From behind, he appeared larger than I remembered. His shoulders were wider, his body was stout, and he almost touched the rafters with the top of his head. His breathing was hard and fast, like an animal panting.

"Seth," I whispered.

He didn't move, but took in a deep breath. He was absorbing my presence, letting it soothe him. One time, I slapped him across the face for trying to kiss me. He wanted to hurt me for it, but instead he gained control using the same breathing method, which meant only one thing: he was mad enough to kill me on the spot and he knew it.

After a long pause, his fists unclenched. "I've been worried since you left." Seth spoke in a deep, raspy voice. "Your mother is absolutely beside herself." He paused, still with his back to me. "I looked everywhere. I investigated every location you had pinned on those maps in your father's office. My father helped with all his connections, until he died a few months back."

I took some satisfaction in knowing that.

I wonder if he's around here in the pit of hell where he belongs.

"I'm sorry," I said, although didn't mean it.

Shame on me, I shouldn't want revenge. Besides, I don't know for sure if he tried to kill my father.

"No matter. Now it's all mine." He shook his head. "No. It's all ours," he corrected, finally turning to me.

I shivered at the sound of "ours." I'd never be his, although if I wanted the plan to work, I had to play along. I'd have to play nice—really nice. I swallowed hard.

Seth's appearance had changed. He looked older, tired, and worn-down. His eyes were black and sunken into his face, much like the slaves that followed Davior around.

And the people in the dreams wanting Seth to kill me.

I touched my locket and swallowed down my fear, hoping I still had womanly powers over him.

"Don't be afraid of me, Jess." He walked toward me. "I'm still undergoing changes, and I look, well, different here than I do up top. It's only underground I appear this way. It's a small price to pay for all that has been given to me."

"What has been given to you, exactly?"

"You, for one."

"That doesn't explain why you look the way you do."

"No." He laughed. "I've been given immortality. I've denounced God and now worship the real king of this world. You'll see, Jess, they can do the same for you."

I would never denounce God!

"You never believed in all that God crap anyway. Lucifer is the real king, and he can grant you whatever you seek. His only requirement is you join him," Seth said with excitement, not thinking for one moment I might not agree.

"You're a demon," I stated, not at all surprised, but the fact he was immortal sank deep into my fears.

"Such an ugly word. I prefer the devil's associate." He took a few steps closer to me. "Don't be scared."

"I'm not scared," I said, fighting the chill in my tone.

"I'm still the same." He looked at my hand.

Before I knew it, my head was lying against the porch deck with broken wood around me. I could taste iron in my mouth.

Davior jumped out in front of me, furious with him. "Seth!" He held out one arm against his chest, holding him back from me.

Seth was going to kill me. Forget the plan. I could see my death in his eyes. His body seethed, growing larger, busting through the roof of the porch, breaking anything and everything in his reach. His face swelled up, and the purple veins in his neck protruded as the red blood pumped through them.

Oh no, he's no match for anyone. He'll kill everyone I love. Oh Dear God, please let me at least warn them. Get me out so I can warn them all.

"What is that on her finger?" Seth's scream stabbed at my eardrum.

"We already talked about this, Seth. Remember?" He spoke to him as though he were a child having a tantrum. "She cannot take it off as of yet. It's not her fault. Remember who did this to her. It's not her doing."

I was grateful not to be dead, but he was turning Seth's anger against Hunter. I couldn't let that happen. I picked myself up and ran past Davior, jumping up to throwing my arms around Seth's neck, pressing my lips to his. I didn't know if it would work or if he would kill me on the spot, but it was worth the risk. And in my reasoning, I knew Seth well, and if he was still in there somewhere, he wouldn't refuse me.

Seth's kiss felt the opposite of what I felt with Hunter. It turned and wrenched my stomach as he pulled me closer, pressing even harder onto my burning lips. He began to relax as my feet touched back down, and I put my hand on his face as he released me.

Showtime!

"I'm so happy to see you," I said, fighting the urge to vomit. The tears should have given me away, but he didn't seem to notice. I pulled at the ring, but it wasn't coming off.

Seth smiled wide revealing his black teeth. I couldn't help but wince.

"I know. I'm sorry," he said. "But really, I am quite handsome up top," he said again, touching my cheek with the large scar.

He looked over at Davior.

"Molly, sir. She was quite upset with Jessica."

Seth stroked my cheek. "I hope you killed her."

Davior spoke calmly. "No. I wasn't to harm her, remember? If it hadn't been for her, Jessica would still be in that prison."

Davior left out that he wanted to kill her.

Seth grunted. "But her mouth is bleeding too," he said, looking at the swollen lip he had just created by smacking me across the porch.

"She tripped." Davior's answer was accepted.

Making Seth angry was bad. I'd have to avoid doing anything to provoke it, only I had forgotten about the ring. My beautiful gemstone ring reminded me of what waited for me if I made it out alive.

Lord, give me strength.

We walked toward the entrance into the house. I tried to tug off the ring again, but it wouldn't come off.

Davior noticed and whispered, "It will stay on your finger until you accept another's proposal or if Hunter dies. I think death is more likely. Think of the ring as a binding contract. Once the contract is broken, it no longer applies, and it will disappear forever. Seth already knows this, but his emotional state is a bit unstable at the moment. I tried to keep him away longer, but he wouldn't hear of it." Davior handed me a pair of white gloves to wear. "He could forget again."

I grabbed the gloves from his hands. "Why don't you look like him?"

"Let's just say I work here, but they don't own my soul. I'm already immortal with my own set of abilities, and because I'm not much of a fighter, there is no need to take on the ugliness of a demon."

Maybe the light inside hasn't gone out completely.

I wanted to believe he could come back to his family. I wanted it more for Annabel than anyone else. She loved all four of her sons.

"It must be hard for you to take orders from him," I said sarcastically, slipping the gloves over my hands. I paused for moment trying to read his thoughts, for once. "Thanks for the gloves," I forced past my lips.

"I see what you're doing." Davior smiled slyly, placing his hands in his pockets. "You're a pretty good little actress, aren't you? Well I can be quite the actor as well."

"I don't know what you're talking about," I said dryly, joining Seth already inside the house.

I needed out. I was feeling confident my plan was going to work. At least the first step seemed achievable. Seth was my "get out of jail free" card.

Seth stood by the piano, looking at the scrap pieces of paper with my composition notes.

Crap. I forgot to hide them.

"Did you write something?" He smiled.

"Yes," I whispered, thinking quickly on how I could use it to further my plan of escape.

"I don't remember you writing your own music. Would you play it for me?" He sat on the bench and patted the seat next to him.

I couldn't play for him. An idea raced through my mind. I grabbed the papers, trying to look playful. "Well, I've had a lot of alone time here. However, this song is special, and don't you think it should be revealed at one of my mother's gatherings? You know, with all of your friends and associates. She always wanted me to compose, and now I have."

"Oh. Did you write it for me?" He grinned from ear to ear, and I intentionally looked away from the rotting teeth. "Sorry," he said, noticing my look of disgust.

It bothered him to look the way he did, which could be used to my benefit as well.

"I guess you just have to wait and see." I forced a smile and changed my tone. "How is Mother?"

"She's strong as usual. Everything has gone according to her plan as far as everyone else is concerned. Now that I have you back..." He looked down at his watch.

"Sir, you should be leaving soon." Davior stepped between Seth and me.

"Is there somewhere you need to be other than here?" I asked, looking past Davior, batting my eyelashes at Seth.

"I was only to stay a few minutes. I wasn't even supposed to see you yet, but I had to. Jess, I've missed you so much." He pushed Davior aside to hug me.

I whispered desperately. "Please, don't leave me here. I don't want to be alone, not here." I hugged him, burying my head in his chest. *This was it. Was I convincing enough?*

"Davior said I shouldn't. Don't you like it here?" He stroked my hair.

"It's nice, but I don't like being here all alone. If I would be in your way, I could go visit my mother. It's been such a long time."

The idea was floating in his mind. He was struggling with the reasons and the consequences Davior gave him not to take me out of this place.

I needed to seal the deal.

I locked into his eyes and then turned sharply away. "I want to kiss you, but I have to admit it's sort of difficult." I offered to kiss him willingly.

It was the deal he couldn't pass up. "Davior," he called, releasing his grip. "Jessica is coming with me."

My heart soared.

"Seth, we talked about it. It's not wise to—"

I shot Davior a look of victory.

"She's coming. You will be coming as well. She'll need a companion when I am working," Seth ordered again.

"Yes, sir," Davior said through his teeth, looking right at me.

I looked away quickly from his stare with a thin smile on my lips. Like John mentioned, Davior would lose his control over him, making Seth the master. I had control over the master—at least at the moment.

Seth beamed. "You'd better pack some clothes. We have to leave in ten minutes."

I beamed back before racing up the stairs to the room I slept in to grab some clothes. Soon I'd be in the real world again. The first step of the plan was complete.

"I know what you're doing." Davior came in with a blue bag. "It's very becoming on you, liar."

"I don't know what you're talking about." I shoved a few tolerable, clothing items into a bag.

"He still can't come close to you with me around." He tapped his head with his index finger. "And if he tries, he'll be dead before he can even lay eyes on you. Just keep that in mind."

"I still don't know what you're talking about. Please take this down. I'm ready," I ordered, handing him my bag.

"Yes, my lady." He moved to stand right next to me, brushing his arm against mine. His thin, nervous smile gave me hope.

As long as I could manipulate Seth, there was no problem. Even the monster within him gave in to my attempt to persuade him. Davior had no choice but to follow his orders. That was very, very good for my plan to work.

Seth opened the door, and fire leaped up into sulfuric air while the soot danced around. Seth wrapped me in the coat I came in and carried me out to a helicopter waiting, just outside the entrance gate. Davior followed close behind.

Next, we landed in an airfield, where we boarded a small plane. Once it landed, we got on another helicopter, which then landed on the roof of a building. Several men in black suits hurried us into a glass elevator.

No one spoke.

Seth turned to me, and his appearance took my breath away. Seth was physically attractive before, but the changes made him even more so. Seth grabbed my hand as we stepped out of the elevator. Cameras flashed all around me, and the men in suits stepped out in front to shield me.

One called out, aiming the camera in my direction. "Is this the fiancée we've all heard about?"

"When is the wedding date?" another called.

Seth kept on until we reached the back of a stage. I thought about the nightmare in front of the Los Angeles Convention Center.

My body trembled.

"Davior, there are two chairs reserved in the front row." Seth squeezed my hand so hard, he cracked a knuckle. "Wish me luck."

I grunted under my breath, rubbing my hand. "What's going on?"

"A lot of things have happened since you've been gone. Today is a big moment for me. All that time I spent with my father and working in his offices, well, part of that dream has finally come true, Jess. I'm so glad to have you with me today. It wouldn't have been the same without you here." He kissed my cheek, almost knocking me down. He motioned for Davior to take me.

"What's going on?" I whispered to Davior.

"You'll see." He smiled, taking my hand in his, but I quickly jerked it back.

He laughed and led me to the front of the stadium. Red-and-blue streamers blew in the light wind. There were thousands of people gathered behind our chairs. I couldn't tell where we were as I looked around for landmarks, but I was relieved to know it wasn't the Convention Center. Davior motioned for me to sit.

A man came out from behind the curtain. "Welcome, Californians!" he announced and the people cheered. "I know you are all here to congratulate the youngest governor in the history of California, so, without further delay, Seth Mackenzie Worthington the Third."

The crowd cheered so loudly making me put a finger in each ear.

How can these people be so blind? A governor was the first step in his plans. I bet my mother is overjoyed.

Glancing around the front of the stage for any signs of her since this was her big moment just as much as it was his, I didn't see my mother.

I caught Seth's eyes on me as he took the stage. "Thank you. Thank you so much for all of your support. I couldn't have made it this far if it hadn't been for the support of my friends and family."

The crowd cheered louder.

Worrying about growing old and Hunter outliving me had become a minor concern. The war between God and Lucifer was coming. Seth would be governor and then a senator if he was still on the same course he had always talked about.

Would it be the United Nations next? Of course, would it matter now? Would I ever see Hunter again? Even if I did, Seth would kill him. No, I needed to warn them to leave me behind, maybe then he'd leave them alone.

Rubbing the ring beneath the glove, I wondered where my prince was and if he knew I had gotten out.

Seth continued to talk to his supporters. He talked about things he was planning to change and other political topics. He actually believed what he was saying, as the teleprompter kept in step with his speech. Everything he said sparked the crowd, gaining their trust and confidence. I guessed Davior had written his speech for him, because he mentioned God a few times, for good measure. After a while, my eyes were beginning to gloss over. Davior, amused, nudged me a few times to keep me awake.

Coming to a close, Seth wrapped up all the promises and lies. "And before I leave you today, there is one more person I would like to thank, my future mother-in-law, Evelyn."

Although I knew she'd be there, I gasped at the sight of her walking onto the platform. I wished Annabel, the person who treated me more like a daughter than my own mother, was sitting next to me.

Seth whispered in her ear, and she looked right at me with a smile that chilled me, the one saying, *You've ruined my moment.*

Seth walked to the edge of the platform, reaching for my gloved hand. If it hadn't been for Davior, I would have blown it right there. I would have run, the media would have slowed me down, Davior would have caught me, and I'd be back in Hell. Instead, Davior led me up to Seth. As soon as Seth took my hand, Davior grunted and took off through the crowd, pushing people out of his way.

Is Hunter's here?

"And this is my beautiful fiancée, Jessica, for those of you who have not been introduced." He played it off like I had been always by his side.

The crowd cheered and cameras went off.

I thought about Hunter's feelings as I stood next to Seth taking his hand. My pretense wasn't over until I was completely free. I had to believe if Hunter saw me, he'd know it was all an act, even though my ring was covered by a glove. I prayed Hunter had a plan of his own, and somehow, some way, we'd meet somewhere in the middle where I could tell him and no one got hurt.

Seth wrapped his arm around my waist, and I fought the urge to push him away. Cameras flashed like crazy. Suddenly, my body felt hot all over, and I wanted to throw up. My legs tingled, and my hands shook before everything around me went black.

The Diversion

I woke in familiar surroundings, but there was no comfort in that. I was back in my original prison.

I lay in the parlor on my mother's brown leather couch.

"Oh goodness. My poor darling." My mother's voice echoed from another room.

We weren't alone, or else her performance of a concerned mother wouldn't be live on stage. I could hear Davior explaining the lie about me being kidnapped and brainwashed.

Why hadn't Seth told her where I was before now?

I couldn't tell for sure if she was buying it or not, but I'd know soon enough. Davior entered the room moments later, carrying a tray of food. "You need to eat something." He set it down in front of me on the clear glass table.

"I'm fine," I snapped.

"You need to drink, too. I think you're dehydrated, and that's why you passed out." Davior looked over his shoulder like someone had said something to him, but no one was there. An agitated expression was all over his face.

"Is something wrong?" I asked, wearing a smirk across my face.

"No. Eat!" he said, annoyed at my question or at something else.

"Fine." I grabbed a finger sandwich and stuffed it into my mouth.

I was already starting to feel my old self creeping back into my body. I detested everything around me, from the sight of the fancy furniture, to the familiar smell of my mother's perfume, and most of all, the clicking of her steps as she paced in the kitchen.

"After you eat, you need to go upstairs and get dressed. Seth's reception is tonight, and he has requested you play the song he thinks is for him in front of everyone. You have four dresses you may choose from, and I've already laid them out in your room." He stood up and left the room.

My mother came in next. "Jessica, you look absolutely horrible! How did you get that scar on your cheek?" She sounded more annoyed than concerned. "That's what happens when you run away from home."

I didn't run away. I am not a child.

I kept quiet. She didn't believe Davior's story either. I'd rather her believe the truth that it was all me. There was no reason for her to be mad at Hunter and his family.

"Well, you look dreadful. Maybe we can cover the scar with some makeup. I'll get someone over here now." She tapped her foot, whiling dialing. "We don't have much time to talk now, but we'll converse later." She scowled at me. "Go up to your room and get dressed. I'll be up in a minute. Susan, yes, I need you here in five minutes," she said to the person on the other end of the phone, dismissing me with her free hand.

I felt like I had never left at all, and despair filled me. No second step, no part two of the plan was forming. Instead, a blanket of doubt and emptiness surrounded me with every step up the staircase to my familiar cell. To end up in this house and in the same situation, should I have even left?

Yes, of course.

Regardless, I found a love that surpassed all understanding, a love that would be with me always and I would never turn away because I was always His—the love I felt for God and He felt for me. No one could ever take that away from me, no matter what they forced me to do.

I clung to my locket, and prayed for His guidance. Whatever God wanted to happen, I would embrace it.

We entered the reception arena, which was bigger than I had anticipated, with every news station, magazine reporter, and newspaper outlet covering the event. Seth moved me from one section of people to another, keeping me close by his side. He introduced me as his fiancée to everyone who approached us.

Seth had never actually asked me to marry him, and I was grateful I could still feel my beaded engagement ring beneath the white lace gloves. My eyes swelled with liquid, and I felt hollow inside. With no new plan sprouting and with so many people there, I would never be able to escape without being noticed.

Seth appeared to be very charming and intelligent in his new position, moving from room to room very smoothly with eager faces to meet him. Everyone around him was a fool, in my opinion, not able to see his sudden burst of anger or rolling eyes when someone would talk about contributing to the poor or elderly.

I'm the only one who can see him for what he really is.

Most of the guests were not overly interested in me, so I stepped behind Seth trying to stay in his shadow. I was back to being invisible, which had been the way I liked it.

Someone somewhere clinked a glass. It was time for Seth to make a speech, and we were rushed to another outside area with a platform.

Davior slithered to my side as Seth took center stage. "Nice party isn't it?" he cooed.

"Yes, it is," I said obligatorily.

"Jessica, please don't continue to be mad at me." He turned me to look into his eyes, and I felt faint.

"Don't do that!" I shouted, shaking myself out of it.

"Sorry. I wasn't trying to." He swallowed hard. "Jessica," he pleaded with me. "Just be careful, please."

"Why?" I asked softly, not wanting anyone to overhear. Davior looked at me, puzzled.

"I know what's going on here. Why bother with me? I'm not going to support him, ever." I continued to whisper.

"You should know the answer. Seth is willing to do whatever it takes to keep you with him, including joining our family and our cause." Davior whispered into my ear. "There could be another option for you. You could join me, and I will keep you safe from any harm. I can keep you free of Seth." His breath was warm. "I know you care for me."

I bit down on my teeth, resisting the urge to punch him.

How dare he act like he's looking after me, that he cares about me, when all along he has been the one who has put me in this situation to begin with.

I turned away from him, but he pulled me back, looking at me differently, not with the same glare as before, just inches from my face.

"Jessica, darling," Seth called loudly from across the room. Everyone's eyes were on me and Davior.

Davior quickly jumped back, releasing his watch.

"Would you mind playing for us?" Seth asked me softly.

I walked down the aisle to step up onto the stage. I sat on the piano bench. Since my hands were blocked from everyone's view, I took off the gloves to stroke my ring. "I love you."

As I began to play, the notes flowed together perfectly. The music I composed for Hunter was actually a duet. I took the soft, haunting melody of the river cane flute and intertwined it in the notes I wrote. I prayed if Hunter could hear it, he would know. He would always know my heart belonged to him forever, no matter what happened.

As I played, I reminisced on all my memories of him, from the first time I saw him standing in the dark shadow in the shack, to the first time he smiled at me. I laughed inside at the memory of him jumping over the porch railing to hand me a rose and the time we argued about the shapes in the clouds, laying in the meadow. My heart raced, remembering how he lifted me off his shoulders in the cornfield, just to stare into my eyes and the time his arms wrapped around me as we gazed up into the night sky. My last memory, the one I'd hold onto for eternity, would be the night he played my song and asked me to marry him.

The music stopped. Tears streamed down uncontrollably as I rested my hands in my lap. I was glad my mother had asked for waterproof makeup, or I would have looked like the women in my dark dream, the ones with the melted faces.

Seth clapped loudly and unexpectedly pulled me off the bench into a hug. I hid my hands as the gloves still lay on top of the piano. He kissed me hard, breaking open the cut on my lip.

The guest applauded.

Musicians stepped up to the stage, and music began to play. I quickly snatched the gloves, before Seth carried me down to the dance floor. Clumsily, he danced me around like I was a rag doll. It was nothing like the soft sway of dancing with Hunter or the precise steps with John. I was thankful when the guests cut in. Davior didn't like the other men dancing with me, but Seth attended to other concerns and had called Davior to him.

Something else was going on, and they both disappeared behind the stage.

Is this my chance? If I don't act now while I'm free from their sight, when will I get the chance again?

I had no clear answer, as an old man swept his arm around my waist and began to dance. He smelled of Old Spice and vodka. His steps were clumsy, and he kept stepping on top of my feet. I was glad when another stepped in to take his place.

"You look beautiful tonight." I knew that voice. I pulled away to look at his face.

"James! Oh, James!" I hugged him, and tears began to fall. He pulled me back.

"Careful. You don't want to draw attention." He wiped my tears. My joy turned into panic. "He'll kill you. You, you shouldn't be here. It's not safe. He turns into this, monster. You need to tell everyone in the family. Go, I'll distract him so you can get far away before he knows you're here."

"Yes. I know. Really? Okay," James said like he was talking to someone else. "I'll tell her."

"Who are you talking to?"

"Hunter said to tell you to stop worrying. You're the one we're here to save. We know what Seth's capable of. Really, Hunter? We don't have much time for this." James argued with himself.

"He can hear me?" I asked, feeling excited and alive for the first time in a long time.

"I'm allowing him to read my thoughts, but it's rather annoying. Yes, yes, you love her. Can we get her out yet?" He paused for a moment.

I closed my eyes and imagined Hunter saying he loved me and standing right there next to me. It was so hard not to be giddy, clinging to James like a life preserve.

"I guess you'll have to endure my dancing for a little while longer."

"Where is he?" I whispered, my eyes scanning the crowd.

"You remember Hunter telling you about how he and Davior can read each other's thoughts?" he said.

I nodded.

"So you can understand he has to stay farther away from where Davior is, or else he'll know we're here." He paused, listening to the voice in his head. "Hunter is just close enough to distract Davior, to get him far enough away to get you out of here."

"So how it is that you can hear him?"

"Being the oldest, I can tune into all of my brothers, but I can also choose to tune them out. My gift. Davior can detect me if he's really close, but he can only read my mind if I allow him to." James sounded anxious. "I've been testing the perimeters for weeks now."

"So that's why I would see Davior's facial expression get angry and he would leave." I laughed thinking I was right.

He nodded but then frowned. He looked at my face. "I saw how you got this." He touched my bleeding lip from the hard kiss Seth had planted on me. "But how'd you get this?" He touched the scar the makeup couldn't hide. He rolled his eyes. "It's a scratch. I just asked her."

I hesitated to answer.

How can I blame her? I don't want them to go after her. She has a fate worse than death waiting for her when her time does come.

I looked up at James. He had those same soft, caring eyes that belonged to my love. "It was Molly," I answered.

"I know," he said to Hunter. "We'll deal with her later, bro. Focus or else he'll know." James shook his head.

"I shouldn't have told you," I said. "I'm sorry."

"You don't have anything to apologize for, Jess. Hunter wanted me to tell you that, but I'll second it." He smiled.

Someone tapped on his shoulder.

Oh no, don't let go.

I held James tighter to me. He laughed. "It's just Jordan."

"May I?"

James handed me over reluctantly. I didn't want to let James go either. In some small way, Hunter was there with him.

"Well, young lady, you have made things very interesting since the day you met my brother." He twirled me around the dance floor.

"I'm sorry." I looked down at his sneakers poking out from the slacks.

"No, no, no." He lifted my head up. "I love it. I haven't seen this much excitement in years."

"Oh, well, that's my world, filled with drama. You should meet my mother while you're here," I teased.

"Oh, I already did. I danced with her just a few minutes ago. She's quite fascinating. Evil, but fascinating."

James was back, tapping him on the shoulder.

"Hey, I didn't get much time—"

"It's time," James said, with a long, black jacket in his hand. Both men escorted me into the non-dancing crowd. James slipped the jacket on me, pulled the hood over my head, and zipped me up. I saw across from me someone dressed just like me.

She looked up and smiled. It was Annabel wearing a wig. I knew immediately what they were doing. She was a decoy.

"But what if she gets hurt? She doesn't look anything like me. I can't let anyone get hurt because of me. It's my fault all this happened. If Seth finds out it's not me, he'll change into a demon and kill her." I shook my head as I unzipped the jacket and tried to shimmy it off.

James stopped me to look into my eyes. "Annabel will be perfectly safe with John. He'll keep her busy dancing. With Davior and Seth occupied and the rest intoxicated, no one will notice until we've left. It's just a diversion to get you far enough away."

I was still shaking my head, almost hysterical.

"Look, Jessie, if you don't follow our plan, my brother will not go along either. He will crash this party. We are family, and we stick together, so either we do this quietly, or it will be open war in front of all these people, who could also get hurt," James said sternly.

I understood exactly what I must do—follow their plan.

To Kill or Not to Kill

Jordan, James, and I walked quietly out of the crowd. Not one person looked in our direction as Annabel stepped out onto the dance floor. I took one final look back before exiting the hall.

Seth stood off stage, holding a scotch bottle at his side, while flirting with a brunette. She would keep him busy for a while. However, Davior was nowhere in sight. James would know if Davior knew something, so there was no need for me to worry about that as we stepped out of the building.

It was a beautiful California evening as the coastal breeze blew the smog off to the east. The sky gleamed a brilliant purple, red, and yellow, as the sun set behind the ocean. Waves crashed against the cliffs, echoing through the canyon.

James opened the door to a blue Infiniti parked just outside the reception hall. We climbed into the backseat while Jordan stepped into the driver's seat.

"Safety first." Jordan grabbed his seat belt and fastened it.

James did the same and looked to see I hadn't. "Yes, I know," he said under his breath and reached over to fasten mine. "Let's get out of here."

I took off the gloves. "I could have done that." I opened the window to toss them out.

"Someone messed with my mirrors." Jordan adjusted them before turning on the radio. "Life is a Highway" blared on the radio. "Cool," he said before he pressed the gas pedal to the floor. "Hang on."

Moments later, a phone rang. James dug into his pocket to pull out a cell phone. He-handed it to me.

"Hello?" I said, looking strangely at James.

"Jess!" Hunter's voice brought another onset of tears.

"I'm so sorry. I should have known better. I shouldn't have followed her," I rambled on until he stopped me.

"No, honey, it's not your fault. You're in good hands now. Don't worry please," he pleaded with me.

"I miss you," I said, pulling myself together.

"I miss you so much," he said back. "I wanted to come get you myself, but..." He paused.

"I know. I'm glad you didn't." I continued trying to sound brave. "Davior is going after you, isn't he?"

"I can handle Davior. Don't worry so much," he said calmly.

"Davior was using me so they could get Seth to do what they wanted. But he wants to kill you and he can turn—"

"Jess?" he said softly.

I took a deep breath. "Yes."

"I know all of Davior's plans, so let my family and I take care of this. There's more than you know, and I promise to tell you later. Right now, you should get some rest. Okay?" he said, trying to calm me.

"I love you," I whispered.

"I know." He paused again. "I love you too."

The phone went dead.

"What happened?" I looked at James for an answer.

"Cell phones are great, but the hills cut off the connection. Hunter's fine. He said you should try to sleep. You look like you haven't slept in days." James pulled off his jacket and folded it for a pillow.

"I can't remember the last night I slept well. Please don't take offense, but your driving is making me nauseated." I smiled, looking at Jordan in the rearview mirror.

Jordan looked back. "Hey, I've been given strict orders to get you home ASAP, and since we can't fly..."

"Just make sure we get there in one piece," James said.

"I'm an excellent driver. See? No hands." Jordan laughed.

"Hunter's going to drown you," James snorted.

Jordan jeered. "Bring it on, bro. I'm up for it."

I enjoyed the little spat between them. I felt like I was home already, and Hunter was just in the next room. I laid my head on the jacket and quickly fell asleep.

The hot sun on my arm woke me. I was disorientated at first as I yawned and stretched, looking out the window. "Where are we?" I asked, rubbing the sleep out of my eyes.

"Alabama." Jordan looked back. "We're close now. Just a few more hours."

My stomach growled loudly.

He laughed. "We'll stop at the next station. We need to fill up the gas tank anyway."

I looked over at James sleeping peacefully.

"That whole mind thing takes a lot out of him. Hunter and I agreed he needed at least a few hours of sleep, although he should wake up now."

"No. Don't wake him yet. Wait until we stop."

He nodded.

Jordan slowed down closer to the speed limit as we approached a town. I stared out the window, amazed at how fast time had flown by. The trees didn't have any leaves on them, so I assumed it was late fall, maybe early winter. It hadn't felt overly cold in California, but that could have just been one of those summerlike days that happen in the concrete city even in the dead of winter.

I couldn't wait to be home with my new family, back to planning a wedding, my wedding. The words Davior had said about knowing the reason John wanted us to wait dangled in my mind. I should have let him tell me.

The car stopped.

"James," Jordan called loudly, slamming his door shut.

James's eyes popped open wide, and he gasped. "Jess, you okay?" He looked around to see Jordan helping me out. "Yes. She's right here," he answered. I assumed it was Hunter he was speaking to. "Sorry. Jordan just scared me to death. Nothing unusual."

Jordan handed me some money.

"What do you want to eat?" he asked James.

"I'll go in with her. I need some aspirin." James rubbed the spot between his eyes with his fingers.

"It's like a hangover," Jordan laughed intentionally loud.

James nodded. "I'm fine. Let's go in."

The cashier, who couldn't have been more than fifteen, stared at me from behind the counter.

James laughed. "Seems like you've got him in awe."

"He's just wondering which one of you beat me up."

"Not funny, Jess." He paused for moment, looking rather curious.

"What?" I asked.

"Hunter didn't respond." He looked at my concerned face. "I'm sure he just moved out of my range. We're traveling in opposite directions until we get you to the Georgia border. He knows we're close. It just took me off-guard for him not to comment on some guy checking you out." He chuckled.

"You heard him in the car just a few minutes ago, right?"

"Actually, no. I was trying to respond before he asked. But now that I think about it, he hasn't said anything since I feel asleep. Everything is fine, Jess. Don't worry," James said, trying to lighten my worry, but he couldn't hide it on his face.

He took out the cell phone, but we were out of service range.

Isn't that just the way it always is?

"Do your headaches block, what's the word, transmission?" I asked.

"I don't know," James said, looking at Jordan, who walked in on the conversation.

Jordan looked serious, but that quickly turned to excitement.

"We need to get her out of here and fast," James said.

I wasn't sure I understood, but I hustled out the door.

Jordan threw money at the cashier. "Keep the change, and have a nice day."

We got into the car. Jordan peeled out from the driveway back onto the highway.

"Okay. What just happened?" I asked.

"There's going to be a fight after all. I knew I could count on him." Jordan howled like a wolf.

"Jordan!" James scolded his brother before answering me. "Jess, if I can't hear Hunter, he can't hear me, and the phone is not working. He warned us if he lost contact for any reason, he was coming for you." James was still rubbing his head.

I opened the aspirin bottle and handed him two tablets, remembering Davior was following him.

"But if Davior is behind him, shouldn't we be able to reach the grounds before him even if Hunter catches up to us?" I didn't see the urgency.

"If Hunter changed course and got close enough to Davior, he would have known we had you and where we were going. We can hope he's out in the middle of nowhere with no phone connection or else."

"Or else what?" I asked.

"It's not just Davior and Seth we'll have to deal with."

"Oh." I sulked into the back seat.

"Come on and get us," Jordan hollered out the window in excitement as another song he liked played. "I need a radio in my room." He beat the steering wheel to the rhythm.

"I'll put it on my list." James shook his head.

We drove along the snakelike road for miles. I tried not to look out the window at the blurred trees, which made me a bit queasy.

Then suddenly—"Jordan, stop!" James called out.

Jordan began to apply pressure to the brakes, but it was too late, and we smashed into a fat tree trunk lying across the road. Fortunately, we didn't hit as hard as we could have if Jordan hadn't slammed on the brakes, causing the car to spin and hit on the side of the car.

My head hit the passenger side window. James scrambled out of the car and pulled me out.

"Jess, are you okay?" James touched the small cut on my forehead.

"I think my hands softened the blow. My wrists are sore, but I'll live." I tried to stand, but I wobbled from the spinning.

"She okay. It's just a scratch," he said to Jordan

Jordan smiled. "The log was placed here." He paced the tree-lined road. "Come out come out, wherever you are."

The air was still and quiet. The sky, bright with sunlight, began to darken, just like before in the meadow.

"Come on, you coward," Jordan called. "I can smell your stench, so I know you're there."

The tops of the trees swayed like someone or something moved through them in our direction. The sky had changed into a gray mist, as a thick fog rolled in around us.

Seth stomped out of the trees first in his demon form. His face burned a bright red with blue veins bulging along his neck. His teeth were jagged, covered in black soot. "Trying to steal her from me again?" Seth asked in a deep, wheezing voice.

"Seth, let me handle this." Davior walked to stand in front of Seth.

"My brothers! You don't have to be involved in any of this. Why fight over this girl? Is she worth dying for?" Davior spoke calmly, looking at me. "Just hand her over, and we'll be gone."

"James, did you hear someone call us brothers? I don't see a brother standing before me." Jordan danced around, looking right at Davior. "I see a worm, a little worm who follows his master's orders. Guess you're no longer the big shot, huh? Why don't you go back to the hot, stinky hole you crawled out of? You're no brother of mine."

"It's not about her," James called out. "It's about you trying to control your new pet. You don't have to do this. It's not too late to change—"

Davior sneered. "Why should I change? Why do you care so much about humans? They were the ones who ripped us from our lives and left us to die. I have no desire to change for them."

James shook his head. "They aren't the enemy, Davior. The one you work for is the enemy. That's not your only reason, either."

Davior's jaw shifted back and forth. "We want the girl."

"Yeah?" Jordan added. "Well, you can't have her."

"Then I guess you've made your decision." Davior broadcasted. "You leave me no choice but to have you terminated."

"You can try. Bring it on, little worm." Jordan sneered at him, pacing in front of him.

"I think I'm going to enjoy this more than I anticipated." Davior expressed his amusement as he lifted his arms.

Ten creatures stepped out of the trees. They were bigger and scarier than Seth. He at least resembled a human. These were monsters. They gnashed their razor teeth at Jordan, then James.

Oh no. How can they fight against monsters?

James bent down to me. "I have to join Jordan. When the fight starts, run." He pointed in the direction we had come from. He shook my frozen body. "Jess, are you all right?"

"They're monsters. How are you going to fight against monsters?" I breathed hard, watching Davior strut in front of the large, red beasts, with horns, towering over him.

"Jess, I know you're scared and it understandable, but we have fought them before. If Davior's here, Hunter can't be far behind." He stood up to join Jordan. "Oh, and Jess," James called out over the low growls. "You are part of our family, which makes you important to all of us. Don't listen to his lies."

But they are outmatched! How could I not be worried?

The disfigured demons circled around them, not really paying any attention to me.

"No," I screamed, but no one heard me.

Just as I was about to get up and run to Davior to stop the fight, another person swung from the trees into the middle with them. It was John.

John will reason with his son. Davior won't fight his own dad, would he?

"Son, do you really want to fight all of us? Your family?" John asked calmly.

"You're not giving me a choice, old man." Davior joined his deformed army. "You shouldn't have been involved in this." He glanced in my direction.

John snapped his fingers, getting Davior's full attention. "Jessica is part of our family, you know what that mean. I know you're still in there, Davior. I can feel the conflict inside you. You still can—"

"I can what, come back home? Travel to the missions? Save the humans? Not live up to your expectations? As appealing as this all sounds, I think I'll pass," Davior said.

"So be it." John waved his hand.

More men swung in on vines, leaping into the middle of the circle, outnumbering the demons. Seth, continuing to grow bigger, stepped up next to Davior with excitement in his eyes. He was ready to kill.

Even with more men, they were still outmatched against the hefty, monstrous demons. Two of the monsters, with bloodstained, sharp, spiral horns, circled around the men, while another batch, with pointed, spear-like tails, growled and scuffed their feet at the men. Both the men and the demons hunched into attack mode, staring at their competitors until Davior took the first step into the circle.

The fighting began. Seth started for the men, but Davior held him back.

Run, James told you to run.

However, I stayed frozen, watching the men fight off the demons.

John kicked one squarely in the chest, knocking him on his back as another came forward. He pulled a knife from his back pocket, slicing at its ankle. The creature fell. James was able to knock one down by sweeping his legs in front of it. Another tribe member tossed him a spear, and he stabbed the twisted horned creature into the chest. Meanwhile, Jordan perched himself on the back of a beast, putting his arm around its neck. It stomped around trying to get him off while crushing the smaller monsters, coming out of the forest, under its feet.

Each man had their own style of fighting. They knew what they were doing.

Davior stood back from the fight. Then I noticed Seth was no longer standing beside him, focused on the fight.

Run, you fool.

I got up and ran as fast as my legs would go in the direction James said—away from the fight and in the direction we had come from. I ran on the road, hoping to see a car coming for me.

But he'll kill Hunter. Seth is too big, too strong, too angry. He'll kill us both.

"Where do you think you're going?" Seth yelled in an unpleasant tone, filled with rage vibrating in his throat.

The cement shook harder the closer he got to me. My only hope was to weave in and out of the trees to slow him down. At least I'd have a chance, maybe not much of one, since he could crunch the smaller trees under his feet. I needed to go deeper where the older, larger trees were, which meant straying further from the road. Seth was getting closer, so I made my way deeper into the forest. My arms and legs scraped against the thick brush, going deeper and deeper, but it was worth it. The ground below me didn't quiver and I couldn't hear him panting. My plan must have worked, only I couldn't see the road at all.

I stopped to catch my breath, my head bent down to my knees. That's when I heard the hum of a car's tires on the road.

Hunter!

But I couldn't tell what direction it was coming from. I climbed up a tree, high enough to see where the road was. I didn't see the car, but I saw the road, and that was enough.

Leaping down from the tree, I ran as fast as I could go toward the road, tripping over the bushes and fallen trees. I ran right onto the road, but there was no car, except the one smashed against a log.

No, it can't be. I'm right back where I started.

Breathing heavily, my chest tightened, and it burned to breathe. The tribe continued to fight as more creatures came out of the forest. There were three demons lying motionless, until they vanished into smoke. Some of the men were hurt, with gashes on their legs and blood on their mouths and face, yet none had fallen.

"Please, Lord, let none of them die." I gasped for air.

The ground shook under my feet and I felt his breath on my back. I had nowhere to go.

His teeth grinded, "How could you?" Seth's voice boomed. "I loved you! I could have given you anything, and this is how you repay me? I'd rather you be dead than with anyone else." Seth slid his feet against the cement, savoring his moment to strike me down.

This is no time to give up. Everyone is fighting for me. I need to fight too.

My eyes scanned the ground for a weapon. I spotted a broken wooden post, on the side of the road, laying a few feet from me. It was sharp on one end.

I darted for it, taking it firmly into both hands. "I'm not going back with you!" I waved the post back and forth in front of me.

He laughed, moving in closer.

Lunging with my weapon, I jabbed his chest, but it didn't pierce him. I stepped away ready to strike him again.

No, that's not the way it should go. He can't win.

Amused, Seth reached for the post, twisting it out of my hands. He toyed with it for a moment, swinging it back and forth to jab at me. He chuckled, stepping closer as I continued to step back.

I winced, thinking he was going to kill me, but instead he crumbled the weapon into dust to plead with me. "There is still a chance for us, Jessie. No one else needs to get hurt." Seth looked over at the group in combat, drawing my eyes there.

Even more demons joined the fight. The men were growing weary. Jordan, who never seemed too tired, wiped the sweat from his forehead before bearing down a spear into another monster.

Something else in the road caught my attention, something shiny and sharp.

A spear?

Seth's manner began to calm, and he was changing, shrinking, and looking more like a real person again and not the monster who fed on anger and rage.

"Marry me, Jessie." He paused, reaching his hand for mine. "And I'll spare your friends. I'll even spare *him*," he said, not wanting to say Hunter's name.

I looked to the battle, watching another demon fall and billow into smoke. It would be better for Seth to kill me than to give up. All those men were ready to give their lives to save me. Hunter would give his life to save me. The time to fight back had come, and if that meant Seth killing me, so be it.

I'll die wearing his ring to heaven. A bond never broken.

I narrowed my eyes on Seth. "No," I said under my breath at first. My eyes glared into his, flashing him my ring. "No! I will never marry you! I'd rather be dead than marry you!"

I watched his face instantly change back into the hideous monster. I ran for the object in the road. I was almost there when I felt him grab at my arm. He didn't have a firm grip, allowing me to fight my way out of his hold, although my struggle sent me tumbling hard on the black, rocky asphalt.

My gouged skin burned, but I needed to get up to get the metal pointed object. It was the only chance I had to fight back, and it was only inches from the tips of my fingers. As I reached for it, Seth's foot came down on my arm.

I screamed in pain.

Seth released his foot to grab me by the neck. I didn't care anymore. The pain had taken over. I wanted to die.

"Let her go." I heard a familiar booming voice. "Now!"

Seth's smile widened, before he turned around with his hands still on my neck. I felt like a rag doll, limp and motionless in his grip. He laughed, dropping me to the ground.

I gasped for air, pushing my body up with one arm. The other, burned like fire and wouldn't move.

"So we meet again," Seth said, staring at Hunter, as he began to pace. "This is a domestic issue between me and my fiancée."

"That's where you're mistaken, Seth. She has never accepted your proposal." Hunter eyes connected with mine. "However she has accepted mine."

I pleaded with him in my head not to fight.

I want him to kill me. I want this to be over.

Tears ran down Hunter's cheeks as his chest heaved in and out. His shirt appeared to get tighter. No, his body was growing, and his shirt ripped. Hunter fumed at Seth. "Jessica is mine."

He's almost as tall as Seth. I'm hallucinating, I must be.

Seth grabbed a handful of my hair, lifting me off the ground. I cried, still watching Hunter's anger change him.

"Well then, I guess it's too bad neither of you will live to fulfill your vows." Seth chuckled.

Hunter lunged for Seth, dropping me to land on my busted-up arm. My breath left me for a second. I couldn't allow the pulsing pain to stop me. I dug deep into my soul, into my strength.

If I could just get to that sharp metal object.

John, James, Jordan, and other members of the tribe continued to fight. They were stronger and doing well as I watched another two demons fly into the air to fall to the ground. Seconds later, they were puffs of smoke. Davior yelled out in another language, bringing out more demons. I couldn't tell if he noticed Hunter and Seth circling each other like in a wrestling match.

Seth, back in full demon mode, yelled. "I've been looking forward to this moment. I'm going to crush you."

Hunter, almost as big as Seth, leered. "You don't scare me. But just so you know, I will always protect her from you and your kind."

"Jessica is mine!" Seth yelled, sending vibrations through the air.

Hunter laughed at him, flashing his smile at me. The pain vanished for a second as his love filled me like a drug.

Seth charged for Hunter, knocking him across the road. Hunter landed hard, but bounced up quickly. "Is that all you've got?"

Seth went over to the car and lifted it up over his head. His breathing was fast and furious. With one loud grunt, he flung the car in Hunter's direction. I tried to warn him, but nothing came out. The car flew through the air, twisting and turning, missing Hunter by inches. He then yelled. "Incoming."

The car landed on its side kicking up sparks, tearing into road. As it headed for the other fight, the men along with Davior heard Hunter and scattered. The demons didn't and half were killed instantly.

"Well, that worked out well for you, didn't it, Seth?" Hunter mocked.

Seth grunted loudly in frustration, lunging for Hunter again, only, Hunter was ready for him. He flipped Seth, wrapping his arm around his neck, in a headlock. Seth choked while digging his black nails into Hunters arms. Hunter raised Seth into the air to slam him on the road.

The gravel split.

Seth shook it off, brushing off the little bits of asphalt on his clothes as Hunter came for him, again. Seth swung his arm around, knocking Hunter to the ground. The monster stood over him, punching his face several times.

"Get up, please get up." I sobbed.

Hunter rolled out from under the demon. He stood, but his legs wobbled.

I have to help him.

I went to touch my locket for strength, but it was gone. With no time to look for it, I went for the spear. My adrenaline kicked into high gear, feeling a surge of energy flow through me as I dragged my body along the ground. With my eyes on the fight, I reached my fingertips to touch the metal object.

Seth gloated. "You didn't have a chance to win against me."

"You haven't won." Hunter wiped the blood dripping from his nose.

Seth punched him again, and he stumbled back. "Well then, fight back. Don't tell me you're giving up? I barely touched you."

Seth slammed both hands against Hunter's chest, sending him in the air clear across through some trees.

Hunter moved slowly.

"It's now or never," I said to myself, seeing my only opportunity to fight back with Seth's eyes on Hunter.

"Oh, come on," Seth said. "I barely pushed you." He laughed, watching Hunter struggle to stand.

I forced my legs up, gathering all the strength I had inside to move. All the pain I felt all those years, visions of my mother, visions of Seth's father and what he had done to mine, the life taken from me, and him trying to kill Hunter.

"Once you're dead, she'll be in my bed."

That was enough. A power moved through me as I let out a loud, deep grunt of my own.

Seth turned.

I stabbed the metal into his right shoulder instead of his heart, although the metal went all the way through his body.

He screamed, grabbing the weapon to pull it out, as I backed away from him. He grunted, snapping the spear handle to the ground. "It's too bad, Jess," he said in a dark, raspy voice, absorbing the pain he felt. "Maybe I'll just kill you." He came for me.

I couldn't outrun him, so there was no point in trying. He reached with one hand, putting his fingers to my throat and lifting me so only my toes dangled against the ground.

I heard a growl, and once again I landed on the ground.

As painful as it was, I sat up to watch Hunter knock Seth into several large, thick trees. Seth tried to get up, but Hunter punched him back down. "You will not hurt her again." He picked him up again, lifting Seth high above his head. He yelled and threw him again across to the other side of the trees. "I'm going to tear you apart." Hunter had lost control.

I heard Davior say something to his remaining army. They surrounded Seth to protect him, as Hunter was going for him again.

Hunter laughed. "You're not going to stop me, Davior."

My eyes lids grew heavy, but I fought not to close them. I watched Hunter grab a horned demon to throw him over his shoulder. He was going through them to get to Seth.

"Hunter!" I heard John call several times, getting louder each time.

My eyes began to close as I laid my head against the asphalt.

John got to my side, still yelling Hunter's name. "Paul, get my car."

My head throbbed like never before and I wished he'd stop yelling.

"Jess. Jess, can you hear me?" I heard another voice, one frantic and desperate.

I tried to open my eyes, but they felt so heavy. I tasted the thick iron in my mouth and coughed. Pain shot through me as someone lifted my arm. I felt a burning sensation, followed by a cool liquid poured over my wounds. I tried to sit up, but I couldn't.

"Don't move please, honey," Hunter pleaded with me, cradling me in his arms.

"Okay. That should help and stop the bleeding." John said.

I whimpered.

"I know it hurts." I could hear the tears in my love's voice. He stroked my face with the back of his hand.

"When we get you home, we'll give you something for the pain," John tried to encourage me. "James, call Mike and tell him what's happened. We'll be home in less than an hour."

Hunter carried me into a car, and I rested in his lap. The pain was terrible, but not as terrible as it would have been to never be in his arms again.

"You're going to be just fine," Hunter said in a worried tone, resting his lips on my hair. "Focus on something other than the pain." He paused for moment then started to hum.

The lullaby was my song. I closed my eyes and imagined myself at the piano, wearing a long, white gown flowing over the bench. The intricate, small sequins around the bottom glistened. My hair was twisted up into a bun, with loose curls dangling along the sides of my face and down my back. I wore my locket along with diamond earrings that glistened off the keys.

My fingers glided along the notes of the song I wrote for him. Drifting into my dream world we danced in a white gazebo with white flowers everywhere. He twirled me around with his gaze only on me. Then he pulled me in a tight embrace, tracing my lips with his finger. My heart, filled with love, beat along with the melody. His lips were inches from mine.

Everything was soft and lovely as the pain faded into splendor.

New Beginnings

I started off my life in despair.

From the time of birth until the time I ran away, I had hated everything and everyone, except my father. I had felt like God delivered me to the wrong family, or maybe I was switched at birth. Then, my real family would find me, taking me back where I belonged.

Finally, it happened.

I awoke from a very deep sleep, feeling groggy and a bit unsure if I had really experienced all the events in the last year. I almost expected to wake up in my old room, hearing my mother chastising me for something. My eyes scanned the room to catch the wildflower garden mural Annabel had painted just for me. A big sigh of relief triggered movement next to me.

"Good afternoon." He swept his lips against my ear, sending wonderful sensations throughout my body.

My heart pounded, turning face to face. He carefully kissed my chapped lips, his eyes never moving from mine. The tingles of excitement and passion rose out of the horrible, dark place I had been in for so long. He kissed me softly again, taking deeper breaths, trying to control himself. But I had no intention on controlling myself. I needed him, pressing my lips harder against his. A sharp pain from my lip registered in my brain, but I didn't care as I pressed even harder. My hand moved to his face.

He pulled back slightly with a brilliant smile on his face. "Careful," he said, touching my lip.

I ignored his request and went to raise my arms to go around his neck, well—one hand went around the back of his neck. The other was covered in a thick plaster and didn't move so easily.

I only need one.

"It's been so long. I don't care. I've missed you so much." My hand tugged his face closer to me. His heart thrashed against my chest as his kisses moved all over my face and down my neck.

He pulled me closer before he stopped. "No, Jess," he said, breathing hard. He got up from the edge of the bed.

"Sorry," I said, a little frustrated, but I really didn't mean it, and he knew it.

He propped a pillow up against the backboard and sat against it, letting me rest my cheek against his chest. "Nothing to be sorry for my love, except your lip is bleeding again." He casually leaned over to grab a tissue from a box on the nightstand next to the bed.

I took in a heavy sigh sitting up, causing static to appear. "Maybe that's not such a good idea." I laid my cheek back against his chest. "How long was I gone?"

"Two months." He sighed. "I thought I was going to go crazy, but all that is past us now, and you're safe again." He stroked my cheek with the back of his index finger.

Everything came back, starting with Molly tricking me and ending with Seth trying to kill Hunter.

"Was anyone hurt?"

He answered calmly. "A few scratches. Besides you, everyone's fine."

"I'm so sorry. If I hadn't followed Molly—" I tried to sit up again. My eyes filled with water, but Hunter held me to his chest.

"Don't get worked up again. It's not your fault. Molly fooled all of us. We should have kept a better watch over you." He held me tighter to him.

I raised my head. He leaned down to kiss my tears. I stared into his eyes with the same passion that had flooded me before.

The feeling consumed me, as I reached my hand to comb through his hair, kissing him again. He returned the same passionate kiss, rolling his body on top of me.

"She's awake! She's awake!" I heard someone say.

Hunter sat up quickly, trying to breathe again. His face was flushed, his hair frazzled, and he looked like he was wearing bright red lipstick.

I sat up next to him, dabbing my bloody lip. I didn't feel as dizzy as before. "You might want to look in the mirror."

He ran into the bathroom before everyone was standing over me. Miss Caroline, Miss Betsy, and Miss Mabel were the first to enter, followed by Josephine, Jordan, James, John, Annabel, and May, who jumped on the bed, throwing her arms around me to give me a giant kiss. There was one other person who entered whom I had not met yet, and there was no sign of Joseph.

"How are you feeling?" John asked first.

"Good," I answered. "So how long do I have to wear this?"

John looked at the person I didn't recognize.

"Hi, Jessie. We haven't met formally, but I'm Mike."

"Mike is one of our doctors," John added. "He travels a lot, to and from the mission fields, so he's not always here."

"The thing is, Jessie, I've never seen this sort of thing before." Mike hadn't even finished, and I was thinking bad thoughts. "See. An injury, like the one you have, can normally take a while to be fully healed, but your bones...well..." Mike hesitated.

Oh no. They won't heal. Something is wrong.

Hunter saw I was thinking something bad, so he jumped in. "You're healing much faster than a regular person would."

John added. "Sorry. Yes, Jessie, you are healing very quickly, and we should be able to take the cast off in about three weeks or so."

Mike stared at me, so dumbfounded he couldn't seem to say anything more.

"She's looking a little flushed." Hunter moved everyone out of the room. "She needs rest." He looked back and winked at me.

I lay back down on the pillow. I was thinking the same as they were.

Why me?

"We'll talk later," John said to Hunter, before walking to the door. "Door stays open." He winked at Hunter.

"Yes, sir." He smiled back.

They all left, and it was just us again.

"You're going to get me in big trouble." He sat back in his spot, and I laid my head back on his chest.

"I'm not the only one to blame," I said.

"Which brings us to another topic." He twirled a strand of my hair around his finger. "I think we should set a date. My mother is getting anxious."

I sat up to face him. "I thought your dad wanted us to wait?"

"He's okay with us setting a date, just not too soon."

"What month are we in?" I asked.

"It's September."

"It seemed so much later."

"So, what do you think?" He reached out to stroke my hair.

"I don't' know." I wondered if I should mention a date earlier than my twenty-first birthday and see what his reaction was.

"What do you think about June?" he asked.

"No. Not June," I said, thinking about my birthday and the wedding plans originally planned for me.

"Sorry. I forgot about your mother's original plan. Then how about July?"

"It seems so far away."

"There are lots of things we need to do before then, my love." He paused. "It will be here before you know it."

"July it is," I said, giving in, but my mind was on other thoughts.

Hunter pulled me to his face and kissed me gently on the cheek. I looked up into his face, wanting to kiss him like I had before we were interrupted.

Hunter turned his head. "Let's let your lips heal. They've been beaten up enough."

"Fine!" I pouted, laying my head down on his chest and yawning.

We didn't talk anymore as pain medicine took over and I fell asleep.

When I woke, Hunter wasn't next to me anymore. I sat up quickly in a panic.

"I'm here," he said, getting up from the chair in the room.

"You left me," I accused.

"No. I've been here the whole time. You thought I was overprotective before." Hunter smiled.

"But." I was referring to him being next to me, and he knew it.

"You know why." He blushed.

"Oh. I guess you're right," I said, sounding frustrated as I sat up.

Hunter leaned down to kiss my forehead. "I'll get you something to eat."

"I'm not hungry." I looked at the cast. "Someone must have guesses on why I'm healing fast."

"Your father isn't who you thought he was. We think he might be…" Hunter paused.

"What?" I sat up. "You think he was what?"

"One of us," he quickly added. "But we don't know for sure. We planned to visit the grave before you were taken, but then—"

"I know," I said in shock.

"We're not directly related," he said quickly, smiling again.

"What? How do you know that if you don't know—"

"The day you cut your finger in the kitchen, John sent the cloth for Mike to test. That's why John didn't want me, well, to get too close to you before we knew. Of course, by that time, it was too late anyway." He chuckled.

"I guess you wouldn't have chuckled if we were related," I said, my mind trying to work out what he was telling me. "You think my father was…like you?"

"It's possible."

I didn't just randomly stumble here, I belonged here.

"There is something else you should know, too," Hunter said rather hesitantly. "We can't seem to trace your mother's heritage either."

"Oh, but you don't think—"

"We don't know anything. It's just that in tracking your father's background, we found out your mother's background is just as covered up. It could be because of the political influences your mother's parents were involved in, but we can only guess. Honestly, it doesn't really matter, but John would like to know for sure who they really are."

"I'd like to know for sure too," I said, thinking of what it all could mean.

Have I started to age slowly too? Would I be like him?

"Doesn't matter, Jess. You are with me now, and your past is your past. I know what you're thinking." He smiled. "But it doesn't matter to me if you age slower or you age like everyone else. I love you for you, and nothing would change that. We'll be married in July, and I already have ideas for our honeymoon."

"Oh really?" I asked, taking my mind away from the topic at hand.

"Yep," he said, standing up. "You need to eat something before I give you another pain pill. I'll be right back."

"No. You can't go without telling me where," I said as he got to the door.

"I guess you'll just have to just wait and see," he called, walking into the hall and down the stairs.

There were so many thoughts running through my mind, so many possibilities. They were all amazing and happy thoughts. The words my father spoke to me so many years ago flooded my mind as he seemed to be speaking to me.

There are magical places that exist in this world, places that the master architect created to balance good and evil in this world. The time will come when you will leave this house and go into another life that awaits you—a life you deserve, a life with a greater purpose.

"Now it's time to find out exactly what you meant, Dad." I yawned, fighting the overpowering urge to rest again.

I wondered about the journals in the old wooden chest—the one just like in John's office.

Could the papers inside contain the answers everyone is searching for? I hope Hunter is ready for our next adventure.

Epilogue

Seth sat back in his fine black leather chair. Scotch on the rocks, his new drink of choice, was an empty glass in his hand. He shook the ice around and around until the ice began to spin fast, gliding around the rim of the glass. He slammed the glass bottom on the oak desk. He reached over for the bottle of scotch, finding it was also empty. Frustrated, he threw the bottle, on the desk, sending millions of tiny pieces of glass flying across the room.

One larger piece slid in front of the picture frame Seth kept on his desk. Jessica's photo stared at him, her eyes piercing through as he recalled the screams flowing from her mouth.

"I couldn't control myself," he whispered to her, touching the face of the picture to stroke her cheek. "I didn't mean..."

The vision of her dying and his tight grip on her throat seemed too much for him to take. After all, he loved her and never meant to hurt her.

He reached again for the scotch, forgetting he shattered the bottle all around the room. He grunted, reaching down into the bottom drawer where he hid his liquor from prying eyes.

The rain pounded at the double-paned bulletproof glass behind him.

He heard something else but chose to ignore it. No one besides him ever worked past ten. He glanced at the clock, which read 2:15 a.m. Seth found it humorous, the thought of a thief sneaking in. Actually, he would have enjoyed killing someone he cared nothing about, someone on whom he could take out all his frustration and anger. Maybe it would help. The thought began to fester as he stared at the door, forgetting the scotch sitting in the drawer waiting for him.

The door opened. A smile crept over Seth's face.

"It's just you." Seth pulled another bottle out of the drawer, unscrewed the cap, and poured the scotch into the glass.

"Sorry," Davior said slowly. "Sir?"

Seth spun his chair around to look out into the dreary night, swishing the ice around the glass.

"Sir?" Davior asked, but Seth remained silent.

"Seth?"

"Did I...did I kill her?" Seth knew it in his mind, but he needed to hear it.

"No, she's not..."

Seth quickly spun around in his chair, staring Davior in the eyes. "What? What did you say?" He leaned across the table.

"Jessica is not dead but is recovering at a faster rate than a normal human," Davior said with some amusement in his own tone.

Seth fell back in his chair in shock. He picked up the photo and stared at her portrait once again. That time, the picture did not move or scowl at him. He poured himself another round and downed it quickly.

"There is something going on, something to do with Jessica, but I'm not able to figure it out yet. She did throw a spear through your shoulder. Even if she hadn't been injured, I'm shocked at the power she had."

"Forget about her," Seth said in a low mumble, setting the picture back down on the desk.

"Seth, what are you saying?" Davior asked.

"I'm saying we have a lot of work to do, and I suggest we move forward." He saw Davior's strange expression but continued. "There is still a matter of finding me a wife. That should be the next order of business. We'll find someone smart and savvy to our way of thinking. Don't you think that's a better plan, Davior?" he asked.

"Seth, are you sure? There are other options we haven't considered. I still have other sources inside the compound."

"Let her be happy, at least for a little while. Let him know what it means to have her love, and then, when the time comes, when the final battle begins, I'll be ready." Seth's eyes filled with rage. "Hunter is mine!"